THE LOST ORDER

STEVE BERRY

THORNDIKE PRESS
A part of Gale, Cengage Learning

GALE
CENGAGE Learning®

Farmington Hills, Mich • San Francisco • New York • Waterville, Maine
Meriden, Conn • Mason, Ohio • Chicago

GALE
CENGAGE Learning

LIBRARY OF CONGRESS CATALOGING-IN-PUBLICATION DATA

Names: Berry, Steve, 1955- author.
Title: The Lost Order / by Steve Berry.
Description: Large print edition. | Waterville, Maine : Thorndike Press, a part of Gale, Cengage Learning, 2017. | Series: Thorndike Press large print core
Identifiers: LCCN 2017002646 | ISBN 9781410497567 (hardcover) | ISBN 1410497569 (hardcover)
Subjects: LCSH: Malone, Cotton (Fictitious character)—Fiction. | Large type books. | Political fiction. | BISAC: FICTION / Espionage. | GSAFD: Suspense fiction. | Spy stories.
Classification: LCC PS3602.E764 L67 2017b | DDC 813/.6—dc23
LC record available at https://lccn.loc.gov/2017002646

Published in 2017 by arrangement with St. Martin's Press, LLC

*For the staff and financial supporters
of the Smithsonian Libraries*

ACKNOWLEDGMENTS

For the third time, my sincere thanks to John Sargent, head of Macmillan; Sally Richardson, who captains St. Martin's; and my publisher at Minotaur, Andrew Martin. Also, a huge debt of gratitude continues for Hector DeJean in Publicity; Jeff Dodes and everyone in Marketing and Sales, especially Paul Hochman. In addition, there is Jen Enderlin, the sage of all things paperback; David Rotstein, who produced the cover; Steven Seighman for the interior design work; and Mary Beth Roche and her innovative folks in Audio.

A bow to Simon Lipskar, my agent and good friend, and to my editor, Kelley Ragland, who's a joy to work with. Finally, my thanks to Elizabeth Lacks, Kelley's assistant, who is wonderful.

Now for a few extra mentions: Meryl Moss and her extraordinary publicity team (especially Deb Zipf and JeriAnn Geller); Jessica Johns and Esther Garver, who continue to keep Steve Berry Enterprises running; Rich-

7

ard Stamm, the curator of the Smithsonian Castle, who showed me the secret spots, fielded countless questions, and helped proof the manuscript; Nancy Gwinn, the director of the Smithsonian Libraries, for giving me the benefit of her careful eye; William Baxter of the Smithsonian Libraries for an excellent tour of the National Museum of American History; Jerry Conlon, who provided a similar education about the National Museum of Natural History; and Tina Muracco of the Smithsonian Libraries for organizing and participating in an enlightening day across Washington, DC, which included: Tom Wickham, the parliamentarian for the House of Representatives; Matthew Wasniewski, the House historian; Kenneth Kato, the associate House historian; Brian Reisinger, formerly of Senator Lamar Alexander's office; and Representative Marsha Blackburn, who arranged with her staff a fantastic tour of the Capitol. My sincere thanks to all of you.

As always, my wife, Elizabeth, was there every step of the way, offering nothing but encouragement (and a little butt kicking, when necessary).

This novel brings the Smithsonian Institution front and center in Cotton's world, something I've wanted to do for some time. I currently have the honor of serving on the Smithsonian Libraries Advisory Board. There are 21 libraries, one located inside every

Smithsonian museum and research facility across the country (and another in Panama). Each is tucked away, out of the limelight, away from the crowds, but without question these libraries are the intellectual heart of any Smithsonian facility.

Collectively, the Smithsonian Libraries form one of the world's greatest repositories of knowledge, used annually by millions of people. The Smithsonian Libraries are currently headed by Nancy Gwinn, who oversees a staff of 130. Together, they help fulfill James Smithson's desire *to found at Washington an establishment, under the name of the Smithsonian Institution, for the increase and diffusion of knowledge among men.*

But it takes a lot to keep these libraries functioning.

For fiscal year 2016 the total was right at $17 million.

Congress funds roughly 70% of that annual budget. The other 30% comes from various external (nontaxpayer) sources. One of those is corporate and individual contributions. Most are small, others modest, a few large. But combined (for fiscal year 2016) they represent $1.5 million, without which the Smithsonian Libraries might not remain open, free, and available to all.

So this book is for the staff and those countless supporters.

If men were angels, no government
would be necessary.
— JAMES MADISON

[But] if you make yourselves sheep,
the wolves will eat you.
— BENJAMIN FRANKLIN

PROLOGUE

Washington, DC
January 24, 1865
2:45 P.M.

He spotted sudden alarm on his host's face. An unusual sight given Joseph Henry's somber reputation as one of America's leading scientists, not to mention the man's prestigious title.

Secretary of the Smithsonian Institution.

He was sitting in Henry's chilly office on a comfortable leather couch, their business nearly concluded. He'd made the appointment weeks earlier, and it was supposed to have occurred yesterday, but he'd been delayed. Understandable, as a civil war raged just across the river in Virginia, though the conflict seemed to be in its waning days. Everything had changed since Gettysburg. Over 250,000 Confederate soldiers lay dead. Another 250,000 languished in Federal prisoner-of-war camps, and 125,000 more were crippled and wounded. Where before a

Southern victory had seemed possible, it appeared now that the high tide of the Confederacy had finally run out.

"Did you hear that?" Henry asked.

Actually, he had.

A sharp, crackling sound from overhead.

The office sat on the second floor, behind a great rose window, between two of the building's trademark towers.

"Could simply be ice sliding from the roof," he said to Henry.

The day was bitterly cold. The Potomac barely flowed, littered with dense ice that had all but halted river traffic and delayed his arrival. Entering the northern capital had not been easy. Forts ringed the Federal district. Troops were encamped everywhere. Security had grown tight. Access in and out came with questions and restrictions. Luckily he possessed the necessary credentials to come and go, which was why he'd been chosen for this mission.

The noise came again.

Then, again.

"It could be ice," Henry said. "But it's not."

His host rose and rushed to the office door. He followed him out into a cavernous two-tiered lecture hall where dense clouds of smoke billowed against the ceiling.

"The house is on fire," Henry yelled. "Sound the alarm."

The secretary hurried off down the stairs to

the ground floor. Beyond the windows, past the ceiling oculus, the natural light that normally flooded the interior had turned dark and gloomy. Smoke had swallowed the exterior and was beginning to claim the inside. He heard heavy footfalls, doors opening and closing, and shouts. Men flooded into the auditorium, then fled down to the ground floor.

He ran up one of the aisles toward the adjacent picture gallery, where plaster from the ceiling rained down, exposing flames that were already busy consuming the attic and roof. A few of the canvases had caught fire. As a painter, the sight sickened him. The blaze seemed extra intense here, which might indicate its point of origin. He purged the artist from his brain and started thinking like an intelligence operative, analyzing his options and reaching conclusions.

Black smoke gathered in thick clouds.

Breathing was becoming difficult.

He'd traveled from Richmond on secret orders from President Jefferson Davis himself. The fact that he was acquainted with Joseph Henry and familiar with the Smithsonian had made him the ideal choice. A secret peace conference was already scheduled for two weeks hence at Hampton Roads. Lincoln planned to attend, as would Vice President of the Confederacy Alexander Stephens, who'd been trying for two years to end the war. Jeff

15

Davis hated his second in command, considering the impish Georgian weak and treasonous. But Stephens harbored high hopes that an honorable end could be negotiated.

He raised an arm and used the sleeve of his wool coat as a filter to breathe. On the far side of the lecture hall, past another doorway, flames ravaged the apparatus room, its collection of rare scientific instruments soon to be no more. He knew the interior walls both here and across on the other side of the lecture hall did not attach to the ceiling, the idea being that they could be removed and the auditorium eliminated, converting the entire second floor into more exhibit space. That convenience, though, now aided the fire, which spread overhead unimpeded.

"The building is gone," a man screamed, running through the auditorium hauling a box to safety. "Everyone must leave."

That assessment might be right, so he should hurry. The purpose of his visit remained inside Henry's office, lying on the desk. It had to be protected. Flames had yet to find their way there, but it would be a matter of only moments before that happened. People rushed about, some toting paintings, others books and records, a few cradling specimens apparently deemed too precious to leave behind. The building had stood since 1846 when Congress finally decided what to do with the $500,000 left in a will by an obscure British chemist named James Smithson, his directive from the grave as to how to spend the money somewhat puzzling.

To found at Washington an establishment, under the name of the Smithsonian Institution, for the increase and diffusion of knowledge among men.

Even odder was the fact that Smithson had never once visited the United States, yet he left his entire fortune to its government.

It had taken years for Congress to act.

Some thought the *establishment* should be only a great library, others a mere museum, a few pushed for a self-financed lecture series, while another group wanted to publish only respected treatises. Southern congressional representatives were wholly skeptical, thinking the proposed entity would become some sort of forum for antislavery advocates. They'd resisted doing anything, wanting simply to give the money back. Eventually, cooler heads prevailed and an *establishment* was chartered that called for a library, museum, art gallery, and lecture hall, as well as a building of *liberal scale* to accommodate it all. The resulting Romanesque edifice, in the style of the 12th century, with long wings, tall towers, arches, and a slate roof had become unique to the country — its shape and red sandstone exterior like a monastery. Which had been intentional, creating a startling contrast with the Greek Revival architecture that dominated the rest of the capital city. Joseph Henry hated the finished product, calling it *a fantastic and almost useless building. A sad mistake.* But many had started referring to it by another name.

The Castle.

Now it was burning.

He raced back to Henry's office to find it occupied. Another man had gained entrance and, at first, he thought him part of the staff. Then he noticed the dark-blue uniform with a trim greatcoat, the insignia of a Union army captain on both shoulders. The man turned and, without a moment's hesitation, reached for his sidearm.

Earlier, he'd thought someone had been following him. His plan had been to get in and out of the Castle unnoticed. But things did not always go according to plan.

He heard a shot and a bullet splintered the jamb, but he'd already dived from the doorway. He'd also noticed that the revolver was one of the new ones with a double action that automatically cocked and released the hammer, turning the cylinder.

Expensive and rare.

He landed in the corridor and reached for his own double-action revolver, tucked into a holster beneath his coat. He'd hoped to avoid violence, but now there seemed to be no choice. He rose and prepared to take down the man in Henry's office. Twenty-five feet above him fire raced across the ceiling in a blackened path, the entire auditorium nearly engulfed in smoke. Chunks of burning wood rained down both here and inside Henry's office. The captain ran out, the gun in one hand and what he'd brought for Joseph Henry in the other.

"Give this to the secretary," Jefferson Davis had instructed, handing him a brass skeleton key. *"And retrieve your journal."*

He'd seen the volume lying on Henry's desk, but the captain now held it along with the key. That this stranger knew exactly what to retrieve was disturbing.

So he tackled the captain to the floor.

Together they rolled toward the podium that faced the semicircular rows of seats. The captain broke away and sprang to his feet, but a yank on both ankles staggered him back on his heels, arms flailing in the air, the uniformed body toppling hard to the wood floor with a thump.

Which caused the man's grip on everything he held to release.

He grabbed the key and the journal.

"Thank you kindly," he said to the dazed captain.

He stood and kicked the gun off into the smoke. He was about to make an exit when the captain regained his senses and rolled up on all fours, ready to pounce.

19

"Why must you?" he muttered to the officer.

Then he planted the toe of his boot to the
underside of the captain's chin, sending the
man back to the floor unconscious.

"Now please stay there."

He hustled for the stairs and descended to
ground level. Thankfully, the fire seemed
confined to the upper floors, with only minor
smoke below. He noticed that pails of water
spaced throughout the Great Hall — surely a
precaution for just this emergency — sat
frozen, useless to stave off the growing
conflagration. Even if they hadn't been ice,
the fire was simply too big to fight with
buckets.

He heard a crash and realized that more of
the roof had caved in above.

Time to leave.

But that captain.

He might not make it out.

Why should he care?

A conscience was such a hindrance.

He stuffed the gun back into his holster
and the key and journal into an inside coat
pocket. Then, against his better judgment, he
reclimbed the stairs, found the captain's
unconscious body, and heaved him onto one
shoulder. He carried the man down and out
into the daylight just as steam-powered fire
trucks rolled onto the grounds.

By now quite a crowd had gathered.

Smoke and flames poured from the Castle's upper reaches, curling around the stonework, licking out through the arches and trefoils. Books rained down from the windows, where volunteers were desperately trying to save what they could. A tower collapsed amid a storm of smoke and embers. He deposited the captain away from the building, near where others, choking from smoke, were being examined.

He stared back at the disaster.

The picture gallery, with its tall arched windows and walls lined with majestic Indian portraits, seemed lost, as was Henry's office. Upper-story windows exploded outward, raining down glass. The fire engines began to work, their job compounded by the cold. Remarkably, the east side of the building, where Henry lived with his family, seemed okay, the fire localized to the west portion of the second floor.

None of this was his problem, though. That would be for others to handle, most prominent among them Secretary Henry, the tall ascetic man, huddled inside a shapeless black coat, who scurried about the grounds giving orders. He caught Henry's eye and gave a discreet pat to a coat pocket, which indicated that all remained safe. Henry nodded, confirming that he understood. Then a slight jerk of Henry's head, angled off to one side, signaled that he should leave.

Excellent advice.

Without question, Joseph Henry was playing a dangerous game. On the one hand he served on the Navy Department's Permanent Commission, advising the Union on topics such as the use of balloons in warfare, new armaments, even the mining of coal in Central America. But on the other he held a deep belief in his responsibility to universal knowledge and to his duties as Smithsonian secretary. Keeping with that, he'd refused to fly the American flag over the Castle and resisted quartering Union troops, asserting that the Smithsonian was a neutral international scientific organization. His prewar friendship with Jefferson Davis was no secret, and today's meeting had been arranged by Henry directly with Richmond, the coded messages carried back and forth by pigeon posts.

He noticed a contingent of Union soldiers arriving.

Definitely time to leave.

He melted into the crowd and slowly eased away. He recognized some of the faces that had gathered to watch the spectacle and realized that Congress itself had adjourned. Many familiar Northern Republican politicians stood in the cold. His journal remained safe beneath his coat, close to his breast. He was one man, on a mission.

Just the way he liked it.

The soldiers had fanned out and were now

surveying the crowd. Odd, considering they should be dealing with the fire. Then he saw the captain from inside, roused to his feet, leading the search.

Several carriages were parked nearby, their occupants gazing at the burning building in the dim afternoon. He zeroed in on one where the pretty oval face of a middle-aged woman, framed by shoulder-length brown hair, could be seen. Around her neck she wore a necklace, the gold medallion standing out in stark contrast with her black coat, buttoned tight to the cold.

He studied the symbol.

A cross inside a circle.

Soldiers were drawing closer, but he kept easing toward the carriage, keeping his head down, his throat raw from deep, dragged-in breaths of freezing air.

He arrived and said, *"All you young people that pass by, as you are now so once was I."*

She smiled at his lyric. "So poetic."

"Might you be able to add to my prose?"

"As I am now so must you be, therefore prepare to follow me."

The precise words, spoken correctly. It was an epitaph he'd seen once on an old grave, the lines stuck in his brain. Things were like that for him. He had a hard time forgetting anything. Details stayed forever, a talent that had come in handy these past few years. Originally he was supposed to have found this attractive woman once he'd left the Castle, the plan being for her to pass by on 10th Street at precisely 4:00 P.M.

"Please, join me," she said.

He climbed in and closed the carriage door, sitting back out of view across from her.

"A few more moments and you might have been discovered," she whispered.

"That I might."

He rarely possessed any tangible sense of fear, able to stay calm in the face of intense danger. But once that peril faded there always seemed a momentary pause, a sense of release that signaled both relief and safety.

Like now.

She stuffed the necklace back beneath her coat, out of sight. Then she called out for the driver to leave and the horse moved ahead. The idea had been for him to conclude his business with Secretary Henry and, during the coming evening, join this woman for the second part of his mission. The Washington social season had already started — a time

24

for parties, receptions, and levees. The gathering tonight, at Navy Secretary Gideon Welles' home, would be its usual grand, influential event. Nearly 75,000 people lived in the Federal city, one-third of whom leaned toward the South. His job would have been to attend with this woman on his arm and keep his ears open. After all, that was a spy's main task. But that was no longer possible.

Things had changed.

At least he had the key and the journal.

Mentioning the encounter with the Union officer was not necessary. That report would be for Jefferson Davis' ears only. But he did owe his savior thanks, so he tipped his head and threw her a smile.

"Angus Adams, ma'am."

She smiled back. "Marianna McLoughlin. My friends call me Mary."

"A pleasure to meet you, Mary. My friends call me Cotton."

■ ■ ■ ■

PRESENT DAY

■ ■ ■ ■

CHAPTER ONE

Western Arkansas
Tuesday, May 25
1:06 P.M.

Cotton Malone focused on the treasure.

The hunt had started three hours ago when he'd left a nearby mountaintop lodge and been dropped off twenty miles away, on the northern outskirts of the Ouachita National Forest, amid 1.8 million acres of old-growth oak, beech, cedar, and elm. The wilderness was a magnet for nature enthusiasts, but 150 years ago it had been the haunt of outlaws, the hilly terrain and dense forests offering excellent hiding places for both loot and people.

He was assisting the National Museum of American History on an assignment that he'd been glad to accept. Usually his old boss Stephanie Nelle either roped him in or outright hired him, but this time the call had come from the Smithsonian chancellor himself, the chief justice of the United States, who explained the problem and provided enough information to pique his interest. The offered $25,000 fee had also been more than generous. Truth be known he would have done it for free, as he had a soft spot for the Smithsonian.

And who didn't like searching for buried treasure.

The woods that engulfed him stretched from the rugged plateaus of the Ozarks in the north end of the state to the rolling peaks of the Ouachitas in the south. In between lay valleys, overlooks, ridges, caves, and countless rivers and streams. All in all it was a paradise, one he'd never visited before, which was another reason he'd accepted the assignment.

He'd come equipped with 21st-century technology, both a magnetometer and a GPS tracker, along with starting coordinates. Using the GPS locator he was threading his way through the trees, approaching a point that, hopefully, a satellite thousands of miles overhead would signal as X-marked-the-spot.

The whole thing was intriguing.

A reference librarian named Martin Thomas, who worked inside the American history museum, had been studying a cache of old maps, notes, and diaries stored in the Smithsonian's vast archive. The documents were restricted, detailing a Smithsonian investigation conducted in 1909 that had involved a prior expedition to western Arkansas. Nothing had come of that journey, except that its lead researcher had been killed when a couple of hunters mistook him for a deer. It could have been an accident, but Cotton was not naive enough to think that a locally elected sheriff never looked after his constituents — and rural Arkansas at the turn of the 20th century seemed the precise definition of *local.*

Easy for things to be swept under the rug.

The GPS locator continued to flash off numbers.

He adjusted his direction and kept walking, searching through the trees. He'd spent the past three days in DC, shuffling through the same field notes, books, papers, maps, and files that had captured Martin Thomas' attention. His access, though, had come with the chancellor's blessing. He'd read at length as to what might be expected here on the ground in Arkansas. More recent notes, provided by Thomas himself, described a specific marker — what had been labeled long ago the map tree — along with its precise coordinates. A cooperative concierge at the lodge had told him even more, including the general vicinity of where to find the stately beech.

The locator beeped.

X marked the spot.

And there it was.

The tree stood at least fifty feet tall. Upon it were carved 65 inscriptions. He knew that because Thomas had been here a month ago and counted them. But there'd been an incident. A headless effigy, pockmarked with bullet holes, was suspended over the trail. Strung up from a tree like a lynching, dangling over a pile of spent shotgun shells. Inverted crosses had been painted on the trees all around. A line of string had led from the effigy down to the shells. The message clear.

Go away.

Which had worked.

Thomas had fled.

This time, though, a professional accustomed to trouble had come.

He approached the tree and noticed the carvings. He ran his fingers slowly over a bird, a bell, and what appeared to be a horse with no legs. He'd been told by a botanist at the natural history museum that a beech tree's thin, smooth bark grew slow, preventing cracking. So a mark made on a beech would still be there decades later. Many of the carvings were filled with moss, others warped from decades of growth. But most were legible. He'd brought along a soft nylon brush in his backpack, which he used to gently clear away the lichens, revealing additional letters and symbols. He wanted to study them further, along with their possible interpretations, but they weren't important at the moment. Instead, taking this as the point of beginning, he searched for another tree.

And saw it.

Ten yards away.

It was a tall red oak, its limbs trimmed long ago into an unnatural pattern, now grown tall like goalposts. He sighted a path past that tree and pointed the GPS. He needed to stay on a straight line, using where he stood as one point and the goalposts as another, keeping the longitudinal GPS number constant, and walking northward, shifting only latitude. He marveled at how, decades ago, this all would have been done by dead reckoning.

He stepped ahead, the underbrush sparse, the trees thick. Sunlight sieved through the leafy spring canopy, dappling the ground. Heat and humidity slid across his sticky skin, heavy as a towel, reminding him of boyhood days in middle Georgia.

A bit shy of twenty yards from the map tree he found a clump of rocks, heavily encrusted with more lichens. He'd been told to keep a lookout for just such a feature. He bent down and examined them, using the brush to clean away a green patina. On one, near the ground line, he found the number 7 chipped into the rock.

Faint. But there.

He lifted the softball-sized stone and turned it over. A quick swipe with the brush and he spotted two letters.

SE.

He'd learned that many markers had been intentionally placed within these woods. There, but not there, so obvious that no one would ever pay them any attention. This clump of rocks seemed the perfect example. Meaningless, unless you were actually paying attention. Something his grandfather once told him came to mind.

"Why hide loot and not have a way to find it?"

Exactly.

The assumption now became that *SE* meant "southeast." The *7*? Who knew? Probably just misdirection. Anyone who saw it would never think to turn the rock over. But for someone in the know, who'd come to retrieve whatever had been hidden, the *7* acted as a billboard to draw their attention. He also knew that for the clandestine group who'd supposedly hidden these caches, *7* was a symbolic number. One that said, "The drawbridge is down, the way ahead clear." All part of their secret, cryptic language.

He switched on the magnetometer. He'd been holding off using it to preserve battery power. He turned southeast, which would take him back toward the map tree, and readied himself. The 1909 field notes had talked of more hidden markers.

An ingenious security system.

Proof positive of human inventiveness.

34

He hovered the magnetometer just above the ground. The other hand held the GPS locator and he kept on a straight line to the southeast, sweeping the metal detector back and forth. Sixty feet later the instrument buzzed. He laid everything down and found a collapsible shovel in his backpack. Carefully, on his knees, he worked the ground above the find, the soft loamy soil coming away in moist clumps. Six inches down he located a heavily oxidized iron plow point. He knew not to disturb it. Instead, he must learn from it.

He cleared away the dirt and noted the direction the plow pointed.

Southwest.

He marveled that the object was even here. Information within the 1909 field notes had revealed how horseshoes, mule shoes, picks, ax-heads, and, sure enough, plow points had been buried about four to six inches deep. Enough to remain hidden, but not enough to be undetected by a compass needle. Pass a compass over buried iron and the needle will react, much as a paper clip when near a magnet will start to act like a magnet. Martin Thomas had tested the theory while here a month ago with a new plow point and had recorded that it worked. Not nearly as good as a magnetometer, but definitely its great-great-grandfather. Only time had not been factored into the equation. Oxidation degraded magnetic abilities, so it was doubtful a compass would be of any use today. Thank goodness for modern technology.

Expectancy clutched his chest.

This was exciting.

His grandfather would have loved it.

But it was also serious, as a man had died here long ago and Martin Thomas had been terrorized just recently.

So he stayed alert, re-gripped his instruments, and started walking southwest. Sixty more feet and he found another buried marker, this time an ax-head, still pointed southwest. He was careful with both his steps and his digging. This was rattlesnake country, and a few might be out enjoying the toasty afternoon. Which was another reason why his holstered Beretta rested within easy reach inside the backpack.

The vector he'd taken had led straight back to the map tree, forming a large triangle. Now he knew where to concentrate his efforts. No longer was the entire Arkansas countryside in play, only the space between the lines he'd just laid out.

He walked toward its center.

The reflective matte-black lenses of his sunglasses muted the harshness of the bright sun. The branches were full of noise from birds, squirrels, and insects. This part of Arkansas seemed a gorgeous gem tucked away in nearly the center of the country. It was remote a century and a half ago, and not much had changed, the biggest difference being that the National Park Service now made sure everything stayed pristine. He wasn't exactly sure if he was inside the park boundaries but, if not, he was awful close.

Historically, no substantial quantities of gold had ever been mined in Arkansas, but legends persisted of its existence. And not the kind that came from a clear stream or out of a vein. Instead, it had all been placed. The original hypothesis revolved around 16th-century Spaniards, who'd hidden hundreds of gold caches across the Midwest and West. But outlaws, too, had used these woods as their hideout. Then there was one other group. From the 19th century.

The Knights of the Golden Circle.

Who'd flourished here.

Ahead, nearly in the center of the triangle, he spotted a large maple with a long, vertical line ingrown in its bark.

Hardly noticeable.

Yet there.

He swept the magnetometer over the ground around the tree and it screamed a find. Back to his knees, he dug carefully. Six inches and nothing. He kept going. About a foot down, he felt something hard. An object placed deep enough that no compass would ever find it.

And he knew what that meant.

The prize, gained only after deciphering the other clues and knowing exactly where to dig.

Yes, definitely, this was the property of the Knights of the Golden Circle.

He cleared the soil away and realized that he'd located a glass jar with a metal lid that had long rusted through. He freed the jar, about the size of a half-gallon milk container. Once it was out in the light he saw that it contained a stash of gold coins, packed tight, time doing nearly nothing to dull them. He tried to estimate how many were inside. He'd been told to photograph anything before physically examining it, so he laid the jar on the ground, located his phone, and activated the camera.

He was about to snap a few images when he heard something.

Movement.

Quick.

Approaching.

He reached into his pack, found his Beretta, and pivoted. In a blur of sight and reason, all he caught was a dark figure and the familiar outline of a rifle.

Coming his way.

Then, there was nothing.

CHAPTER TWO

Danny Daniels hated funerals, avoiding them whenever possible. As president of the United States he'd attended precious few, delegating that solemn task to others. Now, as an ex-president, he had no one to send. No matter, though. This funeral was an exception to his usual rule.

He'd known the deceased ever since his own days as a Maryville city councilman, when Alex Sherwood served in the Tennessee state legislature. Ultimately, they'd risen together, he to the governor's mansion, Congress, and finally the White House — Sherwood to Speaker of the Tennessee legislature then on to the U.S. Senate. Two country boys, each finding his own path to success.

During two terms in the White House he'd always counted on Alex. He knew that his old friend would have liked to have been president. But it had not happened. Quick to praise, reluctant to find fault. That was Alex. Just too damn nice. To be president you had to own many moods, not only making decisions but also convincing everyone else that you knew what the hell you were doing. Sometimes that took an ass-chewing, which was not a skill his old pal had ever mastered. Instead, Alex used courtesy, kindness, and reason. Which many times just did not work.

A slow drizzle drained from the gray, spring sky. Umbrellas protected the mourners. He'd left his at home, donning only a raincoat to keep his suit dry. His time as president had ended four months ago and he'd returned home to Blount County, Tennessee.

To start a new life.

"Please join us," the minister said, urging the crowd forward to the grave site.

The church had been filled with over five hundred, that service open to the public. But here, in the old cemetery among the trees, with the Appalachian foothills off to the east, less than a hundred had been invited, all relatives or close friends. No press. The U.S. Senate was represented by the majority leader and eight of his colleagues. The House, too, had sent a contingent, headed by the Speaker himself. But he'd never cared for the current Speaker, a self-confident, pompous ass from South Carolina named Lucius Vance. They were of different parties, different states, different thinking. Vance, though, was a master at satisfying his colleagues, finagling support, and juggling the thousand chores needed to keep his seat. He was a man of the House, accustomed to biennial approval, acutely aware of how fast the public's love changed to hate. Nine years ago that experience, and over twenty years in office, finally accumulated enough political capital to elevate Vance to the Speaker's chair, making him the 62nd person to hold the job.

Once Danny had kept a close watch on the opposition, knowing their every move. And when was that? Oh, four months ago. But not anymore. What did it matter? Ex-presidents rarely amounted to much. Their one job was to fade away. Vance, though, was still going strong — pragmatic and precise — holding tight to the reins of power. For eight years Vance had been a thorn in the Daniels administration's side, trying every way possible to derail anything the White House proposed.

And succeeding more often than not.

But that was no longer Danny's problem.

That task now fell to President Warner Scott Fox, who had the advantage of being in the same party as Vance.

But that might not mean a thing.

Congress routinely ate its own.

The mourners scrummed together around a large tent erected near the grave. Alex's widow, Diane, sat beneath it with hands folded in her lap. The Sherwood marriage had lasted a long time. Unlike his own, which was now over. He and Pauline had already signed the divorce papers. They'd agreed that July 1 would be the day to file and end their relationship. By then people would have forgotten about the previous president of the United States and his First Lady.

Interesting how things had changed.

Not all that long ago he was the most important man in the world. Thousands worked around the clock to please him. He commanded the most powerful military on the planet. His decisions affected hundreds of millions. Now he was again an ordinary citizen. Of course, not that long ago Alex Sherwood had been alive. So he shouldn't complain. Pauline seemed happy with her new life and love. And he was happy with Stephanie Nelle. Some people might call the whole thing strange. He called it the way of the world. He'd done his duty and served his country. So had Pauline. Now it was time they served themselves.

He walked across the wet grass, pebbles crunching beneath his soles, hands inside his coat pockets. He stopped just inside the tent, where he could hear the minister over the patter of rain on canvas overhead. The governor was there, another friend, along with a state legislative delegation. Diane had not left out any of the key players, seemingly mindful of protocol.

The minister spoke in an impromptu manner, talking of death and resurrection, then of Alex, whom he'd known personally. That was another thing Danny hated about funerals. Preachers who pretended. This one, though, spoke from the heart. He suddenly felt old, though he shouldn't. He would soon be sixty-five, eligible for Social Security, which he would not accept, just as he'd refused the Secret Service protection offered to all ex-presidents. The last thing he wanted was more babysitters. The time had come to be free in every respect.

A small contingent of the Secret Service was here protecting the Speaker of the House. Vance stood outside the tent holding an umbrella, a dashing, handsome chunk of a man with a thick bush of black hair and eyes the color of pennies. Central casting could not have sent over a better physical specimen to be Speaker. Fifteen years separated them, which seemed more like fifteen hundred. Power both invigorated and eviscerated, especially the kind that came with two terms in the White House.

He caught Vance's unemotional stare, one that carried the pallid look of a mannequin, surely designed to convey nothing. Then the current Speaker of the House acknowledged the former president of the United States with a slight nod of the head. He was impressed. That was more courtesy than he'd been offered over the entire last eight years. Graciousness, though, was easy to extend to someone who could no longer cause you any harm.

And that made him feel even older.

He ought to form a support group. Something like NOLIP. No Longer Important People. Folks who could help one another through the withdrawal from being addicted to power. Some people who left public office were glad to go. Others channeled their energies into philanthropic work. A few just capitalized and made money. Then there were players, like himself, who knew how to do little else. For him *politician* was not a dirty word. It simply meant "compromiser." Which was exactly how things got done. The sine qua non of politics was not vision, but consensus. Nobody, not himself, not Lucius Vance, not Warner Fox — nobody got their way 100 percent of the time. The trick was to get as much as you could with each opportunity. *If the deal you want isn't possible, then make the best one you can.* That had been his motto. And his legislative success as president, despite the best efforts of men like Lucius Vance, had been respectable.

The minister finished and the mourners with their blank expressions began to file past the casket, paying their respects with heads bowed, gentle touches, and sincere looks of sympathy. He watched as Vance took his turn, gently shaking Diane's hand, then speaking with her for a few moments.

He waited, then joined the line.

A few old acquaintances said hello.

Blount County had been around since 1795, named for the local governor at the time — Maryville, the county seat, for the governor's wife. Talk about vanity. The land had once been Cherokee-owned, then was stolen away by farmers who'd migrated west from Virginia and North Carolina. His ancestors had been a few of those energetic settlers. The landscape was green and lush, the forested hills like ocean waves flowing off into the distance. The Blue Ridge Mountains defined everything, and several national parks had ended logging long ago. There were two hundred churches countywide, which had to be a record of some sort. Its most famous resident was probably himself, though Alex Sherwood ran a close second. But here, among friends, he was not a president, nor an ex-president. No one called him by his given name — Robert Edward Daniels Jr. He was just Danny, the guy who once served on the Maryville city council.

And he liked that.

His turn came and he approached Diane. She wore a stylish black dress with a lace veil and clutched a wad of tissue in an ungloved

45

hand. He stooped to her chair and she accepted his offer of condolence.

"Thank you for coming," she said.

He didn't really care for Diane. Never had. She didn't like him, either. He ought to clasp her hands or do something, but touchy-feely was not his thing. So he simply said, "I'm going to miss him."

"Please," she said. "Do come by the house."

He hadn't planned on going to any post-service gathering, hoping to avoid both her and the idle chitchat that came with an east Tennessee funeral. Not wanting to make a scene, though, he simply told her, "I'll definitely make the effort."

But he had no intention of it.

He fled the tent and walked back through the rain toward his car. This cemetery held a lot of memories. His uncles, grandparents, and parents were all here.

And one other grave.

His daughter.

She'd died in a fire decades ago. A part of both him and Pauline perished that night, too. She'd been their only child and there'd been no more after that. Not a day passed that he did not think of her. It had been years since he last visited the grave. And his refusal to deal with her tragic death had been a big part of his and Pauline's demise.

He angled away from the crowd and threaded a path through the rows of monuments and markers, the wet cemetery quiet and shadowy. He found the southern face of the treed knoll and his daughter's plot beneath the old oak. The turf was cut low and tight, in good repair. The stone lay flush with the earth, noting her full name, date of birth, date of death, and a simple statement. OUR BELOVED DAUGHTER. He stood, hands in his pockets, rain flattening his hair, and begged her one more time for forgiveness.

So much time had passed.

But the pain seemed as fresh as yesterday.

A familiar emptiness gnawed at his stomach. He closed his eyes and tried not to cry. His whole life had been spent projecting an image of toughness. Never had he let anything get to him.

Except this.

"I need to speak with you," a female voice said.

He grabbed hold of himself, not realizing anyone was near. When he turned he saw a woman, maybe late fifties, early sixties, with thick, tangled hair and wide brown eyes.

"Who are you?" he asked.

"A friend of Alex's."

"There are a lot of those here today."

"Mr. President —"

He held up a hand and cut her off. "My name is Danny."

She threw him a weak smile. "All right. Danny. There's something you need to know."

He waited.

"Alex was murdered."

Years of hand-to-hand politics had taught him the value of a poker face, especially when the person speaking was trying to get a reaction. So he kept his features frozen and allowed the rain to wash away the mistiness that had been forming in his eyes.

"You didn't answer my question," he said. "Who are you?"

"I have to talk with you. Privately."

Still no answer. So he asked, "Why do you believe Alex was murdered?"

"There's no other explanation that makes sense."

CHAPTER THREE

Arkansas

Cotton examined his prison. Different, he'd give it that. Some sort of old incinerator, built long ago of cast iron welded into a cylinder eight feet wide and stretching upward at least twenty feet. He'd studied every inch of the rusted interior and found no weak spots. At the bottom, where he now sat, the only escape came through a locked iron hatch that opened to the outside, but no amount of force he'd applied had caused it to budge. The stinking air hung clammy and close, filled with the fine soot of rusty corrosion. He'd woken inside, after being unconscious for probably a couple of hours. A knot the size of a half dollar had risen at his hairline.

Somebody had popped him hard.

The afternoon heat of a bright sun had turned the metallic confines into hell. Mosquitoes had found him through slits in the roof that re-formed into a latticework of shadows across the brown walls, and his body

itched. He'd been sitting, thinking about how he'd abandoned his bookshop in Copenhagen once again. He seemed to spend more and more time away than there. Luckily, the people who worked for him could handle things.

At least this time there'd been buried treasure.

Neither the gold coins, his backpack, phone, sunglasses, gun, nor any of his tools had been imprisoned with him. No surprise there. Whoever coldcocked him was probably enjoying those. Normally, enclosed spaces weren't his favorite, but here the afternoon sky was visible overhead, his physical movements unrestricted, so it wasn't entirely threatening. The great outdoors — albeit a bit confined.

His fingertips prickled with heat, and thirst had become a problem. A fly buzzed overhead, crossing through the slanted bars of sunlight and diving closer. It would not be long before this place became an unbearable oven — and he assumed that had been the whole idea. Just leave him out here. He could scream his lungs off and nobody would hear him, nothing but empty woods for miles in every direction. He drove that wonderful thought away with a flick of his hand at the fly that would not retreat. His temples throbbed and his head felt disoriented. He had a crick in his left shoulder and felt stiff all over.

Definitely getting a little old for all this.

A loud clang on the outside wall startled him. He'd grown accustomed to the silence. He waited for metal to grate metal and the lock for the hatch to be released.

But nothing.

Instead something hit the latticework above.

He stared up to see a thick rope find an opening between the slats and drop down toward him. Tied to its end was a rock, enough weight to allow gravity to feed out the slack.

It hit the floor a few feet away.

Bound between the rope and the rock was a handwritten note.

Miss me?

He shook his head and smiled, then freed the rock, yanking on the rope.

Tight.

Ready for action.

He knew what he had to do, so he braced his boots against the iron wall and leveraged his way up. His forearms and shoulders ached from the climb but he made it to the top, gripping one of the rusted iron girders, hoping it remained strong enough to support him. He swung his body upward and kicked the lattice away. He'd already noticed from below that the panels merely rested inside frames, most twisted with corrosion. The one

51

he assaulted squeaked in protest but flew skyward.

He clambered up through the opening and gripped another of the old girders, his eyes tracing from one side to another, satisfied it, too, remained secure. A small superstructure extended skyward a few yards, part of a chimney that once funneled smoke. He leveraged himself to his feet and scrambled across the warm metal, balancing like an acrobat, finding the edge where the rope disappeared downward.

Cassiopeia Vitt stood in the thick brush below. Trees engulfed the incinerator on all sides.

"You couldn't just open the door?" he asked her.

"It's padlocked."

"Why didn't you pick it?"

He knew she always carried the proper tools.

"It's a combination lock. So I had to go find some rope, and that wasn't easy."

"You could have called out and told me what you were doing."

She smiled up at him. "And what fun would that have been?"

They'd split up this morning. She dropped him off in the national forest, then drove to visit with park rangers trying to obtain more information. Finding him would have been easy since he wore a Magellan Billet–issued watch that contained a GPS tracker, her smartphone capable of accessing the signal.

"I assume there's a good story here?" she asked.

"It's a laugh a minute."

The drop was over twenty feet, so he reeled up the slack from inside the incinerator, discarded the rock, and tied the rope's end to one of the girders. His vantage point was high enough that he was able to spot the same chalky ridge he'd located earlier at the GPS coordinates that had started his search.

He was not all that far off.

A shot echoed and a bullet pinged off the iron a few feet away.

He dropped to the girder, lying flat, using the old superstructure chimney for cover. Sweat ran down his brow and stung his eyes. He blinked the moisture away and, through the trees, spotted a gunman with a rifle fifty yards away, perched atop another ridge, large boulders providing cover. The shooter was shifting positions, perhaps looking for a clearer line of fire.

"Darling."

He caught her condescending tone from below.

"Reel up the rope."

He did as she said.

Tied to its end was a nine-millimeter pistol. Not one to question a gift, he freed the gun and leveled the weapon, waiting for the rifleman to appear from behind another outcropping

He squeezed twice.

Rounds skipped off the distant rocks like flung stones.

His assailant ducked away from the line of fire toward a scatter of boulders. Which allowed him to stuff the gun inside his belt, then toss the rope over the side and slip down to the ground, the incinerator and trees now providing protection.

"You look terrible," she said as his feet hit the ground.

He was wet, unshaven, and odorous. Dirt and grime stained his clothes, especially his hands, red with rust. She actually looked great, though, moving with the ease and suppleness of someone quite comfortable in snug jeans. Her pitch-dark hair, normally cascading past her shoulders, sat coiled into a tight bun at the back of her neck. Her coffee-colored skin seemed accustomed to the heat, part of a Spanish ancestry, her sultry face full of beauty and candor, the type of woman who easily turned a glance into a stare. He calmed his breathing and tried to think beyond his adrenaline.

"Does that knot on your forehead hurt?" she asked.

He shook his head with a strained attempt at vigor. His mind was racing, ticking off possibilities. Number one on the list of things to do was finding out who attacked him, but common sense told him the answer to that inquiry lay on the ridge above.

"You move ahead and see if you can draw the shooter's attention," he said to her. "The brush is too thick for anyone to get a bead on you. Try and make enough noise to attract attention. I'm going to double around and get behind whoever it is."

"I think the people at the Smithsonian are oblivious to what's going on here."

"That's an understatement," he said. "I almost brought Gary into this."

His seventeen-year-old had begged to come, and he'd nearly given in, but the warning of trouble from Martin Thomas' earlier visit had cautioned otherwise. And school, too. Gary lived with his mother in Atlanta and still had another two weeks before summer break.

His head remained woozy and each breath tore his throat like a mouthful of broken glass. "Do you have some water?"

She produced a plastic bottle from her backpack. He unscrewed the top and swilled the tepid liquid in his mouth, trying to ignore the tinny taste. Somebody had been watching him in the woods, somebody who knew exactly where to be and possessed skills enough to get close. Then that somebody, or somebodies, had carried him here and tossed him inside an iron can.

That was a lot of effort.
But for what?
Time to find out.

CHAPTER FOUR

Danny parked the car in the empty parking lot for the Missionary Baptist Church. The woman from the cemetery sat across from him in the front passenger seat. A little insane for an ex-president to be alone with a total stranger, but instinct told him that this lady was no threat. Rain continued to tap the roof, hood, and windshield. They'd ridden in silence from the funeral, slipping away unnoticed.

"You plan to ever tell me your name?" he asked her.

"Alex said that you and he were best friends. Is that true?"

"How long were you and he *friends*?"

He'd never suspected Alex Sherwood was an adulterer.

"We've known each other six years," she said.

That shocked him even more. "How was it possible to keep that secret?"

"Because we truly were just friends. That's

57

all. Never once did he violate his marriage."

"And what did his wife think of this friendship?"

"I have no idea. She came to Washington only a few times a year. Her husband seemed to be the last thing on her mind."

He caught the contempt. But it wasn't unusual for congressional spouses to stay at home. Most had either jobs or children to care for, and living in DC was not cheap. Contrary to public opinion, the vast majority of people in Congress were not rich and the salary they were paid barely compensated for the costs of serving.

"I live across the hall from Alex," she said. "We were neighbors a long time. He was a darling man. I can see you don't believe me, but sex was not part of what we meant to each other."

He could understand his old friend's self-control. He and Stephanie were at first enemies, then friends, now something more, and all without him violating his marriage, either.

"We enjoyed spending time together," she said. "Having a meal, watching a movie, reading. He was talking about retiring from politics in two years."

Another surprise. "Then what would happen?"

"He told me he was going to divorce his wife."

"Because of you?"

"I don't know. We rarely spoke of her. But during the past few weeks he'd begun to say more. And he wasn't some miserable husband, complaining to another woman. He just seemed like an unhappy man who'd grown apart from his wife."

"And your presence had zero to do with that?"

"His telling me his intentions to divorce came as a total shock. But I won't say I didn't like the prospect. He said he would do it when he was no longer a public person. I know what you're thinking, that's self-serving. But he thought it would be easier, on all concerned, if it happened that way."

He could perfectly understand that philosophy, as it was exactly what he'd done. The only difference being that he and Pauline had mutually agreed to end their marriage.

"I want you to know that I wasn't with Alex to have him end his marriage and be with me. The two of us being together was never discussed. Not until recently, at least. I was with Alex because I came to love him, and I believe he loved me. The decision to end his marriage, though, was entirely his own. No pressure came from me."

Her face carried an anxious, worried look, the corners of her mouth drawn down. Nothing about this woman seemed flighty or emotional. He believed every word she was saying.

"You need to get to the point," he told her.

"Alex was really bothered in the weeks before he died. It all came from a notebook he was reading."

She had his attention.

"It was about so big." Her hands outlined a volume about seven inches tall and five inches wide. "He spent many an evening recently thumbing through it."

"Where did it come from?"

"His brother-in-law."

Whom Danny knew nothing about, other than a name, Kenneth Layne, and that he headed some political action committee associated with state legislators from around the country.

"I'm sure you know how Alex could be with his causes," she said.

Yes, he did. Especially the call for a 28th Amendment. Alex had long been a proponent of changing the Constitution to ensure that every federal statute also applied equally to members of Congress. He'd hated how the legislative branch liked to exempt itself from laws imposed on everyone else, elevating Congress into some sort of ruling class. *A government of the people, by the people, and for the people should live under the same rules it passes for the people.* How many times had the senior senator from Tennessee said that? Alex had tried repeatedly to introduce the amendment for floor approval, but had been batted down. He recalled two years ago when his friend tried to draw attention to the issue by introducing a bill to end overly generous congressional pensions, which was met with similar negative resistance. Alex's response — delivered on every cable news network — had been vintage. *"How can the American people trust Congress to fix a broken Washington when the people in Congress don't even live under the same rules as everybody else?"*

Indeed, how could they?

"His comments to me about that notebook," she said, "involved the Senate and some kind of radical change. A way to end all the problems that have been festering there lately. He talked about gridlock and never being able to get anything done, but said that what he was reading in the notebook was not the answer. I know I'm being cryptic, but he was equally so with me."

He knew all about the dysfunction of the U.S. Senate. Three terms there taught him how one senator, through a filibuster, could shut down the entire legislative process in *both* houses of Congress. He'd even used the tactic a few times himself to make a point. But efficiency had never been part of the Senate's playbook. The House of Representatives and the presidency had terrified the Founding Fathers, every one of them deathly afraid of popular excesses. So the Senate was created as an impediment against hasty lawmaking, designed to be an antagonist to both the House and president. That was why senators were originally chosen by state legislatures, not subject to general election. When that changed in the early part of the 20th century, with the adoption of the 17th Amendment, so, too, had the Senate, metamorphosing into something the Founders would definitely not recognize.

As president, he'd suffered its wrath.

During the last three years of his second term the Senate blocked a major financial package, a defense appropriations bill, and housing reform, all thanks to a handful of obstructionists who wanted unnecessary amendments attached that benefited only them. At one point or another, the Senate had even allowed several federal bureaus, including the National Labor Relations Board, to lapse into defunding, again so that one member could make his own particular point. And over his eight years as president the Senate confirmed only 70% of his judicial nominees, nowhere near the 90-plus-percent that Clinton, the Bushes, and Reagan enjoyed.

During the past four months, though, things had really escalated.

President Fox's cabinet choices to head Labor, the EPA, the Defense Department, and Transportation had all been filibustered with no confirmation votes ever taken. An unprecedented series of events, each championed by a different senator with a different agenda, none caring about the consequences. Even a former member of the House of Representatives, nominated to the Federal Housing Finance Agency, had been denied confirmation.

Talk about a slap in the face.

Only yesterday the press had reported that confirming a new head of the Federal Reserve might prove problematic. Which Wall Street had not liked to hear. The Dow Jones fell 5 percent just on the possibility of that happening. Since Inauguration Day the news channels, pundits, and social media had skewered all one hundred senators. A public opinion poll taken last week revealed that less than 12% of the country thought the Senate was doing a good job.

So what had grabbed Alex's attention?

He needed this woman to explain herself. "You said what he was reading came from Diane's brother?"

"That's what he told me. I know nothing about the man, but Alex was not himself over that notebook. It upset him to the point of anger, and that was something totally foreign to him. Then, two days ago, someone entered

Alex's apartment. I heard it happen and watched through my peephole."

"Who was it?"

"A middle-aged white man. I never saw his face, but I did get a look at the back of his neck. He had a port wine stain on one side that seemed to wrap around. He was inside the apartment only a few minutes." She paused. "He had a key."

"He could have been a staffer with Alex's office."

She shook her head. "He was no staffer, and he came out with the notebook in his hand. He also carried two tote bags full of books that related to what Alex was concerned about, not your ordinary reading material. They dealt with constitutional brinksmanship, constitutional conventions, filibusters, and the history of congress. He'd bought them all at Politics and Prose."

He knew the bookstore, a DC staple.

"I know that because I picked them up for him. He was definitely researching something specific."

"Alex didn't share a thing about what was written inside the notebook?"

She shook her head. "He kept that to himself. I think it was one of the things he really liked about me. I never pried. I knew my limits."

"You realize that there could be a logical explanation for what happened. Wouldn't his wife have a key to the apartment?"

"I'm sure she does. And there's this."

She reached into her coat pocket and removed a chain with a gold locket attached.

A cross within a circle.

She handed him the necklace. "I found this in his trash can."

Like himself, Alex hated jewelry, which explained why neither of them ever wore a wedding band. His refusal used to drive Pauline nuts, who never went anywhere without her rings. He meant no disrespect. It was just that jewelry aggravated him, so no ring, watch, or necklaces.

"Any idea what it is?" he asked.

She shook her head. "I found it the day after he left to come back here to Tennessee. About a week before he died. I kept the apartment up for him when he was gone. Tidied up, made sure there was food in the refrigerator when he returned. I saw it in the trash — I don't know why — but I fished it out. Why I kept it, I don't know. But I planned to ask him about it at the right moment."

"What about those limits?"

"I suppose they were violated."

He'd read the press accounts. Five days ago, Alex had taken a walk in the woods behind his house. By dusk, when he hadn't returned, Diane became worried. Two hours later a sheriff's search party found his body downriver where it had washed ashore. An autopsy revealed no evidence of foul play. Tennessee's senior U.S. senator had drowned after falling into the river. Where it happened was anybody's guess, the whole thing sudden, tragic, and senseless. And sure, there were no witnesses and the circumstances raised questions, but accidents in these hills happened all the time.

"Why do you think Alex was murdered?" he asked.

"The day before he left for Tennessee, he told me that he had to make sure something monumental didn't happen. So I stretched those boundaries again and asked."

He waited.

"His answer was cryptic. He told me that *if we make ourselves sheep, the wolves will eat us.*"

"Benjamin Franklin said that."

"I know. He told me. I pressed a little and he admitted it had to do with what he'd been reading. He left the notebook on his desk in the apartment, with all those books I mentioned." She pointed to the pendant. "The notebook was brown leather with that symbol embossed into its front cover. A bit too coincidental, don't you think?"

He did.

"The man who went inside the apartment took only the notebook and the books. Nothing else."

"And this is why you think Alex was murdered?"

"He didn't just fall off a cliff," she said. "It makes no sense. And that man, with a key to the apartment, might prove my point."

Hard to argue with the logic. "What do you want me to do?"

"He was your friend. He talked about you with great respect. I was his friend. We owe it to him to find out how and why he died."

"Diane has no idea about you?"

She shook her head. "Not to my knowledge. I never once spent the night, and we never were out in public together. It's a quiet building, where people stay to themselves, so we were never disturbed. And Alex wasn't what anyone would call overly controversial."

"Except that he wanted to overhaul Congress."

She smiled. "Who wouldn't? But he never got anywhere. You know that. I imagine he seemed more an amusement than a threat."

Another reason his old friend could have

never been president. Voters liked candidates who actually got things done.

"You still haven't told me your name."

"Taisley Forsberg."

"You realize that I may have to compromise you in order to look into this."

"I know, but we have to learn the truth about what happened to him."

Maybe so. Yet he had only this woman's word about the man in Alex's apartment. It could all be a lie. Still, Taisley Forsberg had tapped into his own lingering doubts, ones that had clouded his brain ever since he first heard the bad news. For the past few minutes his internal radar had been on red alert but he'd detected no lies, no embellishing flourishes to provide a stronger feeling of truth. In fact, everything he'd heard carried the strong odor of fact.

She was right.

Alex Sherwood just didn't fall off cliffs.

And that notebook from Diane's brother. About some monumental change? What the hell?

He'd been invited to the Sherwood house.

Maybe he should put in an appearance.

"How do I find you?" he asked.

She handed him a business card and he saw that she was a lawyer with a DC firm. One he knew. "My cell phone number is on the back."

He still held the necklace. "May I keep this

for a bit?"

"It's yours now."

She reached for the door handle to leave.

He grabbed her arm. "Where are you going?"

"It's better you and I aren't seen together."

"I'm a big boy, I can handle it. Tell me where I can drop you." Then he decided to treat her like a big girl, too. "I meant what I just said. Diane Sherwood may have to learn about you and Alex."

A sadness crept onto her face, the eyes shining, tears finally running down her cheeks. "Alex is gone, and regardless of what she thinks might have happened between us when he was alive, I would hope she would want to know how and why her husband died."

Chapter Five

Cassiopeia plunged into the thick Arkansas woods, doing as Cotton had asked, making enough noise to draw the sniper's attention.

Here they were, back in the fray.

Together.

Both she and Cotton seemed to thrive off excitement. They liked to say otherwise, but they were only kidding themselves. This assignment had particularly interested him, and he'd opened up a little about his middle Georgia family and their connections to both the American Civil War and the Smithsonian Institution. Learning about his past was important to her. So when he'd asked if she'd like to come along, she'd never hesitated.

A shot rang out.

She stopped her advance.

Acting as bait was a little foolish, since there was always the possibility that a stray round could find her or another shooter might be around. She regretted messing with Cotton, not telling him she was outside the incinerator and working to get him out. He'd obviously been assaulted, the knot on his forehead serious enough that a doctor should take a look. But she knew that wasn't going to happen. Not his way. On the plane trip from DC he'd told her about his mother's relatives, part of the old landed gentry who'd supported the antebellum South and fought with the Confederacy. His father's family had been from the northern part of Georgia, their loyalties divided between North and South, their history not as clear.

Her own parents had boasted a strong Iberian and European connection. She'd been raised to know and appreciate her heritage, though her parents eventually discarded some of it, choosing a path far different from their ancestors. Ultimately she, too, had made choices, some good, others bad, and had dealt with an assortment of lingering demons. Cotton had played a big part in some of that resolution. She'd resented and fought his involvement and tried to deny how she felt but, in the end, realized that her destiny seemed locked with his. Which now did not bother her one bit.

He was an extraordinary man.

They'd been through a lot together. Each had saved the other more than once. He showed her nothing but love and respect, and she did the same for him. If that was a sign of weakness, then weakness it would be.

She restarted her way through the under-brush, making noise, generating movement one way, then slipping quietly to another, hopefully leading the bullets to where she'd just been instead of where she was headed.

Another round cracked, the bullet whining through the trees behind her. The ploy seemed to be working. Cotton was headed for a trail leading up the ridge and she spot-ted another way up just ahead, one that also wound a path to the shooter. She decided to make her way there and climb from the other side. Together they could pincer their assail-ant.

Her life was definitely exciting. She lived in a French château, where she was rebuilding a 13th-century castle using only tools and materials available 800 years ago. Her family's business ventures were operating on a solid footing, generating hundreds of millions of euros annually. Her father had left her the company as his only heir, apparently confi-dent she could handle things. And she had. Occasionally she made an appearance to keep in touch, but by and large she allowed the managers freedom to operate.

She grabbed a couple of hand-sized rocks and heaved them off to her left. Both created the desired noise and attention. A shot came their way and she used the moment to hustle unnoticed for the base of the ridge. There was no defined trail, and the terrain was not steep enough to defeat a hasty climb. She hugged the ground and, using the trees and foliage for cover, headed up. This was not good for her clothes. But luckily she'd dressed in jeans, boots, and a durable shirt. Thankfully, she'd also piled her long, dark hair into a bun that kept the strands off her face. Her brow was slick, her eyes stinging from salty sweat. She'd passed on makeup today, but rarely used much anyway.

She considered herself lucky to have found someone like Cotton. He was a few years older, tall, broad-shouldered, sandy-blond hair, with a handsome face full of responsibility. No sags existed in his cheeks, no traces of a double chin. His green eyes danced with delight and always seemed to captivate her, as did his fight to keep the depth of his feelings to himself, which had clearly become harder for them both. Each move he made seemed judged and balanced, with no pretensions. Once there'd been a time when she'd wanted no one to invade her loneliness. When she became angry at her own weaknesses, and her heart rebelled. But after what had happened between them of late, she'd decided not to make the mistake again of thinking she could live without him.

Normally, it could be difficult to get him to leave Copenhagen. Saving the world was no longer his thing. He'd done his tour with the Magellan Billet, working twelve years as one

73

of Stephanie Nelle's Justice Department agents. As he liked to say, *That's someone else's problem now.* But there were issues that clearly attracted him. More and more it had become simply a matter of making money. Everyone had to eat, and his skill sets were definitely in demand. Here, though, the attraction had been a connection to his family's heritage.

And one ancestor in particular.

Angus Adams.

Who, she'd learned, had been a Confederate spy and also went by the moniker Cotton.

She shaded her eyes against the afternoon sun and kept to her crawl, the firing from above halted. Pinpricks of moisture glittered the fine hair on her arms. Cotton had to be making his way up the other side so she stopped and lay still, close to the warm ground, giving him time to take the lead.

She knew only a little about the Smithsonian Institution. One of the largest repositories of artifacts and information in the world, with a global reputation for excellence. Just to say the words invoked visions of history, mystery, and adventure.

And here they were.

Right in the middle of one.

But it wasn't quite as glamorous as books and movies liked to depict.

She was lying belly-first on parched dirt, among thick foliage heavy with heat and bugs, someone above her shooting with a rifle.

Would she marry Cotton?

A strange thought given the circumstances.

But lately she'd considered the possibility more and more. Perhaps it was just a fantasy. Everyone had them, right? Why would she be an exception? Marriage was not something she'd considered. But that was probably because no one had come along who'd offered her the possibility of long-term happiness.

She could not say that any longer.

At the moment, though, corralling this shooter was the priority. Where things led from there was anybody's guess. But that was the great thing about an adventure.

Whether it be in life or love.

You simply never knew how it would end.

CHAPTER SIX

Cotton scampered away from the incinerator, making his way toward where he could scoot up the ridge toward the shooter. He shook off a wave of tiredness and a gritty sensation that had settled behind his eyes. Cassiopeia was doing a good job of holding the sniper's attention, moving in the opposite direction. His sweaty clothes were stained by a cloying dampness, his nostrils filled with the waft of dry earth, reminding him of his grandfather's farm. His mother still lived there, having inherited the three hundred acres, which continued to produce Vidalia onions. Something about low sulfur in the soil made the onions fat and sweet. The official Georgia state vegetable, in fact. It reminded him he needed to go see his mother. He hadn't visited her in a long time and his calls of late had become less and less frequent. She never complained, that wasn't her nature, but he thought it was probably time she met the woman he loved.

He ducked beneath the stiff arms of a weathered tree and stopped his approach. More shots rang out toward Cassiopeia. He spotted a narrow track that wound up a sharpening slope. Trees, motionless in the heat, stood perched along its flanks. He wondered about more than one assailant but, so far, that didn't seem to be the case, as all the gunfire was concentrated from a single locale. Everything that had happened the past few hours made little sense. He'd followed the clues and found a cache of gold coins, supposedly buried sometime in the last half of the 19th century. The most logical conclusion was that someone else also had been searching for the same treasure, or maybe it was simply a case of being in the right place at the wrong time. But how could someone just happen to be near that map tree?

Unless he or she already knew about it.

No shots had echoed for a couple of minutes. So he grabbed that opportunity and hustled up the trail, staying down, moving with stealth across the loose rock and shale. He led with his gun, using the brush for cover. He felt like a sheriff from the Old West, closing in on an outlaw. This kind of pursuit was different from his usual tactics. He was more of an urban cowboy.

He stopped and allowed his eyes and ears to search for the shooter. Flies hummed all around him. Birds rustled in the nearby thatch. His nostrils still carried the scent of ferrous dust, the same stale, metallic taste remaining in his mouth. Movement came from his left, farther up the inclined path. He risked a look and spotted a litter of boulders that seemed to be providing excellent cover. Luckily he was approaching from the rear and should be able to surprise the sniper.

Another shot rang out.

Hopefully Cassiopeia was ahead of things. She knew how to handle herself and he trusted no one more than her. They'd been together long enough to know each other's strengths and weaknesses. Their ups and downs seemed epic, but things now seemed good between them. For all her unpredictability she had a tenacious quality that he admired. Both of them were card-carrying loners, adept at sidestepping emotions. She lived in southern France, her education and training in history and architecture. He lived in Copenhagen, above his bookshop on Højbro Plads, in a modest apartment. He made a decent living, supplemented by an occasional foray back into his old profession. Marriage had not been discussed between them. But if it ever was, one of them was going to have quite a lifestyle change.

A shadow loomed ahead against the scatter of rocks. He fled his position in a dodging run and kept climbing, staying down, trying not to scuff his boots on the dusty track.

Plenty of trees continued to offer cover, as did the underbrush. Sunlight lay everywhere, smooth as a carpet. The trail he was following seemed well worn, maybe a favorite of hikers. It led to the top of the ridge where surely there would be a wide panorama. Splashes of yellow jonquils lined the way. The buzz of a faraway airplane meshed with that of a nearby hornet. He crawled the final few feet, his fingernails filling with dirt. He found the top and safety against a thick, low, knurled branch.

To his left he caught sight of the shooter.

A dark-haired, slender female, tanned brown as a nut, dressed in jeans, sneakers, and a dull-green shirt. Not more than twenty, her body hard as a whipcord. She lay on her belly, facing away, cradling a long-barreled rifle of dull metal, concentrating on the scene below, oblivious to what may be behind her.

Big mistake.

"Just stay real still," he said to her.

The young woman froze.

"Don't turn around, until I tell you."

He cocked the hammer on his gun to make the point clear.

"Don't kill me, mister."

"Give me a good reason why I shouldn't."

"I wasn't tryin' to hit you. Just scare you."

To his right he saw Cassiopeia emerge from the woods on the other side of the ridge and approach where he stood. The look on her

79

face conveyed the same confusion he was experiencing.

"This just gets stranger and stranger," he whispered.

She nodded in agreement.

"Let the rifle go," he said. "Then turn around slowly. But keep those hands where I can see them."

The young woman did as instructed, now lying on her back, facing them, with her arms held high. They stepped closer and he asked, "Did you attack me this morning, then dump me into that old incinerator?"

"I helped."

"You're not going to make me ask, are you?"

"My grandfather. He tracked you, then knocked you out. He and I carried you to the can."

"Why would he do that?" Cassiopeia asked.

"It's his job."

He crouched down where the girl lay. "We're federal agents. Your grandfather assaulted me and you shot at us. Those are major felonies. You want to go to jail?"

The head shook quickly back and forth, the hands still in the air.

"Then I suggest you start talking."

"He's the sentinel. It's his job to protect the stash."

"The gold coins?"

She nodded. "That's part of it. His father

and his father before that were sentinels."

He glanced back at Cassiopeia. No question. This girl was telling the truth. Still. "Those coins have been in the ground a long time. A hundred thirty or forty years. You're telling me people have guarded them all that time?"

"That's what the sentinel does. I was goin' to be next."

"Did your grandfather tell you to shoot at us?"

"He told me to keep watch and if you got out, make sure you left real quick. I wasn't goin' to hurt you."

"And what would have happened if I hadn't gotten out?"

"I was goin' to unlock the hatch at sundown. That long a time usually does the trick."

"There've been others?" Cassiopeia asked before he could.

"Every once in a while. Mostly treasure hunters. A few hours in the can and they get real eager to leave."

"Does your grandfather have the coins and my stuff?"

The girl nodded. "Back at the house."

He stood and motioned for her to get up, too.

"Take us to him. Right now."

CHAPTER SEVEN

6:00 P.M.

Danny had always admired Alex Sherwood's home, which reminded him of old Tennessee mountain lodges. Most of those were long gone, but Alex's spacious incarnation remained with a rough brick-and-stone exterior, mixed with heavy timbers that seemed to emerge naturally from the wooded hillside. Its great room came with thick rugs scattered across dull wood floors, a tall ceiling, open rafters, and a fieldstone hearth large enough for several people to stand inside. Today no fire was lit, but in an Appalachian winter the room would be warm and cozy. A deck swept out from a wall of glass, dotted with a profusion of plants and ferns, high-backed rockers, a fire pit, and two swings, the view of the nearby Great Smokies like something off a postcard. Alex's grandfather bought the land a hundred years ago for pennies on the acre. Then his father built the house when costs were equally cheap. But time had changed all that, and Blount County real estate was no longer a bargain. The many manufacturing concerns, like Alcoa, Denso, and Toyota, that now called the area home had brought both prosperity and higher property values.

A rustic scheme dominated the décor, everything oozing grace, heritage, and elegance. He knew *Architectural Digest* had wanted to feature the stylish interior, but Alex had nixed that idea. *It's okay to have it,* his old friend liked to say, *but never flaunt it.*

The drive over, after leaving Taisley in Maryville, had taken half an hour, the spring rain still falling. No shortage of water existed in Blount County thanks to countless creeks, the Little Tennessee River, and a chain of man-made lakes that formed the county's western border.

About fifty people had returned for the private gathering. He noticed that Lucius Vance and the contingent from the House of Representatives were not there. Neither were the folks from the Senate. The governor, though, had come. He was an old friend, serving as Tennessee's secretary of state when Danny had occupied the state's chief executive mansion. They'd fought many a political battle together, some with Alex at their side.

He eased past the knots of mourners into the nearby dining room, not seeing Diane anywhere. He stopped, mingled, and spoke to a few acquaintances. Having an ex-president around had to be a novelty, but no one seemed overly impressed. A long oak table was laid out with covered dishes that he knew had been brought from people all around. More food than anyone could eat over the next week, much less this evening. He liked the fact that he no longer carried a cadre of aides in his wake. No men with guns watched his every move. No guy followed him around with a suitcase from which a nuclear war could be started. And no reporters were hanging on his every word. Just Danny Daniels, private citizen.

He shied away from the crowd's center of gravity. The governor ambled over and whispered, "How does it feel not to have to worry about elections anymore?"

"Not as good as you might think." And he meant that. He kept his voice low and close. "I need to talk to Diane. Do you know where her highness might be?"

"In her office, holding court."

He caught the sarcasm, knowing that Diane Sherwood was not on this man's Christmas card list, either.

Rain continued to thrum the roof.

"I'll catch you later," he said, and walked off.

He found her in a pine-paneled rectangle that reflected the tastes of a history enthusiast, which its owner fancied herself to be. Mountain art dotted the walls, and on the tables lay local memorabilia. Diane stood in front of the far windows, facing toward the wilderness, still wearing the black dress minus the veil from the funeral. The door was open, but he knocked lightly on the jamb anyway.

She turned and motioned for him to enter. Two other woman occupied the room. They excused themselves, leaving them alone. He was uncomfortable to say the least, since he could not recall their ever having a private conversation. Their chats had always occurred at gatherings, with spouses around, like insulation between them. Strange that he felt that way, considering how he and Alex were so close. But Pauline had never much cared for Diane, either.

"And to what do I owe this honor, Mr. President?" she said.

A miniature poodle rose from a corner bed and tried to get Diane's attention, then quickly scuttled in a cloud of *cluck-cluck*s to the hollow beneath a nearby chair.

"You invited me," he said.

"I didn't think you would come."

"My friend died."

Her eyes bore into him. "Yes, he did."

He got the message. *Get to the point.* "I'd like to ask you something. Are you satisfied with the official conclusions regarding Alex's death?"

A curious look came to her bluish eyes.

"You're not?"

"That's not an answer."

She sauntered away from the rain-smeared windows. "I suppose it's not. But that's an odd thing to ask a widow on the day she buries her husband."

"It's a simple question, one you seem to be having trouble answering."

She now tossed him a frosty glare. "Alex so admired you. To the point of it being sickening. You do know that I always thought you a fool."

A pulse of anger swept through him, but he'd learned long ago not to chase smelly bait like that. "I've been called worse."

She chuckled without any humor. "I'm sure you have. But twice I did not vote for you."

His spine stiffened in a familiar feeling of confrontation. "I don't really give a crap what you think of me. I just want to know if you have any doubts about Alex's death?"

She shrugged. "He fell off a cliff into a river and drowned. There's little to question. No one was there. Nothing points to anything suspicious. This has been all over the news for the past week. If someone knew or saw something he or she would have come forward by now."

All valid points, so he shifted gears. "I heard that Alex might not have run again in two years, when his term ended. Was that true?"

She nodded. "We talked about doing some

traveling. Enjoying ourselves. I think he was looking forward to retirement."

That's not what Taisley had said. "Then I assume everything was good between you two?"

Curiosity filled her face. "Why would it not be?"

He decided to drop the pretense. "I was just wondering if perhaps he might have finally tired of your bubbling personality."

She stepped toward an oak desk that sat catty-corner before one of the room's exterior corners, more blurry windows on either side. "Since it's just you and me here, and you seem to be speaking frankly, may I join you?"

"Absolutely."

"My husband loved me and I loved him. We've been married a long time and planned to stay that way. Contrary, I might add, to your own marriage, which Alex told me is over."

"Why is *my* marriage of interest to you?"

"The more relevant question is why mine interests you. As I recall, you never cared much about what I might want."

He knew what she was referring to. A sort of breaking point between them. It happened two years into his first term when a vacancy came to the Supreme Court. She'd wanted Alex to have the appointment and sent a personal note to the White House making the request, which he'd shown to his old friend.

"I know all about this. She's dead set on it," Alex said to him, handing back the note.

"And you?"

"You know how I feel about judges in their robes. Just a bunch of turkey buzzards. I don't care to be one."

He smiled at his friend's judicial cynicism, which mimicked his own. "What about what your wife wants?"

"She'll get over it."

"You do know that Alex had no desire to be a Supreme Court justice."

"Alex had little idea what he desired. He relied on me to make those choices for him."

He heard the change in timbre of her voice, from grief to challenge, and wondered about the observation. Alex Sherwood might have been too nice, but he wasn't weak. He did, though, have a soft spot for this woman, one they rarely discussed since the last thing you ever wanted to do was criticize another man's wife.

"None of that matters anymore," she said. "Alex is gone. I'm a widow. You're an *ex*-president. Politics is over. It's time for us both to fade away."

Her personal insults didn't matter, but the jab about him being irrelevant did get to him. So he decided to do a little irritating of his own. "How good was it between you and

Alex? I heard you've been scarce in DC for a long time."

"I didn't realize I was so high on your list of interests."

"You weren't, until your husband suddenly died."

She caught the accusation, and he was trying hard not to be confrontational, but this woman had a way of bringing out the worst in him. He'd wondered many times why a good, decent Tennessee mountain man like Alex Sherwood would have married a shrew like this. For money? Hardly. Her family had next to nothing. Influence? None existed. Personality? Not unless you preferred the surly type. Possibly looks. She offered a neatly carved profile with a short, fine nose, high curved cheeks, and an angled chin. Her complexion carried the clear, flawless hue of someone who definitely lived in clean air. Tendrils of thick red-brown hair brushed ever so slightly at the base of a slender neck. She was definitely a looker. Alex had been insufferably handsome, too, the sort of appearance few women aged well against. Yet Diane had held her own. Maybe it had been her confidence? She'd always cast the assurance of a movie star, and she was no dummy. He knew she held a master's degree in American history.

"I do have interests, apart from my husband's," she said. "I serve on several boards, the Smithsonian Libraries Advisory Board being one of those. Those took me away a lot. So it was hard to get to DC. Alex understood. He even encouraged me to do them."

Considering the presence of Taisley, that was the first thing he'd heard that made sense.

"I haven't been to Washington in several months," she said. "Contrary to your conclusion that I've been scarce, I go at least twice a year for the Smithsonian board meetings. I'm going tomorrow to see about his apartment. It's a task I'm not looking forward to."

Her face seemed as tight and stiff as a mask. He'd been trying to gauge her replies, wondering the whole time why he was even doing this. The last thing he wanted to do was reveal anything of another woman. Nothing about that would be positive. Especially for Alex. So maybe he should just excuse himself and leave. He was about to do that when he noticed something on the floor, beneath the windows, behind the desk. Two cloth tote bags full of books. He caught the odd title of the top volume in the left bag.

Brinksmanship: Amending the Constitution by National Convention.

What had Taisley said Alex was reading? *"Books that dealt with constitutional brinksmanship, constitutional conventions, filibusters, the history of Congress."*

At the top of the other bag lay a brown

leather notebook. About five by seven inches.

With a circle and cross etched into its cover.

Exactly as Taisley had described.

What were the odds?

But how did it get here? Considering that Diane, in her own words, had not been to DC *"in quite some time"* and the notebook had been left there on Alex's desk. What else had Taisley said about the intruder?

"The man had a key."

Okay, Columbo, calm down.

He decided to go the next step and found the necklace in his pocket, which he showed her.

Surprise filled her face. "Where did you get that?"

"Alex came by the house a day or so before he died. He dropped this. I was going to return it to him, but never got the chance."

The lie seemed plausible, since the visit had occurred. Their last time together. She reached up beneath the collar of her dress and fished out a chain. Attached to its end was the same gold cross within a circle.

"It's a wheel cross," she said. "Or a sun cross, as some call it. An ancient symbol for good luck. I liked it, so I had one made for each of us."

"Then I should return this to you."

And he handed it over.

She stared at the pendant.

"Now I see where you got your information," she said. "I should have known the two of you would talk."

He decided to let her believe what she wished.

"You realize," she said, "that there's no reason for us to have any animosity toward each other. It's doubtful we'll ever speak again, so why don't we part, not as friends, but as two people who loved Alex Sherwood?"

She wore her stature like a crown, standing before him with shoulders thrown back, chin tilted skyward. And though her words had been voiced with a mechanical lack of feeling, she was making a gesture, or maybe just practicing the old adage of rocking an enemy to sleep. No matter. He'd learned all he was going to learn.

"Consider it done," he said.

And he excused himself, leaving her alone.

Alex had maintained his own office farther down the hall, which Danny had visited many times. He'd like to see it one last time but doubted anything of substance would be there. The purge had already been accomplished, and it had reached all the way to Washington, DC. He had a bad feeling, one that came from years of political combat. He might be an ex-president, his public life over, but he wasn't dead.

Not yet, anyway.

He sauntered back to the great room and spent a few minutes chatting with old friends.

The governor stayed across the room, doing the same. Diane appeared and made her way outside to a group on the covered part of the deck, thanking people for coming and accepting more condolences. He watched her carefully and saw none of the dazed incomprehension that someone newly affected by grief would exhibit.

A crazy thought swirled through his brain.

Why not?

He excused himself and headed back down the hall, toward where both the bathroom and Diane's refuge sat. He approached the open door of her office and spied no one inside, not even the dog. He quickly entered, found the notebook in the tote bag, and stuffed it under his suit jacket between his belt and spine. If he kept the folds loose and was careful, no one would notice, and once he donned his raincoat he'd be fine.

He headed for the great room.

Out of office four months.

And already committing crimes.

CHAPTER EIGHT

Cotton drove, his prisoner sitting beside him in the front passenger seat. He'd learned her name. Lea Morse. Her grandfather was Terry Morse, who'd lived here all his life on land owned by Morses dating back 200 years. It was clear the granddaughter worshiped the older man, but it was equally clear that she did not want to go to jail.

"I try and tell him," she said. "All that stuff's over. It don't matter anymore. But he won't listen."

"What stuff is over?" he asked her.

"Secret things that Granddaddy lives for."

"But you love him, so you do as he asks?"

Lea nodded. "I've lived with him since I was a teenager. My mama and daddy were no good. Granddaddy takes care of me. But we have to stop all this sentinel stuff. He could have really hurt you today."

"Actually," he said, "my head's still spinning."

He was following Lea's directions, driving

the rental car. Cassiopeia sat in the rear seat, watching and listening. Lea led them east on a two-laned state highway, out of the national forest and into the rural Arkansas countryside. Her grandfather's land lay to the north of a small town, just off the highway, down a long dirt track lined with more forest. Cotton negotiated the road with care, the steering wheel struggling in his hands against the rutted washboard surface.

The clapboard house they found was single-story with tall, narrow windows, a covered porch, and a brick chimney. Thick-leaved trees crowded it on all sides. Chickens roamed free and he caught sight of the pink rump of a pig as it darted toward several wooden outbuildings, whose corrugated roofs flashed in the evening sun.

He'd decided on a direct approach and parked near a waist-high wooden fence that outlined the yard surrounding the house. He stepped from the car. The warm air carried the heady scent of manure. An older man bobbed out of the front door. He wore a faded blue shirt, worn dungarees, heavy boots, and a wide-brimmed hat that seemed fixed to his head with the permanence of hair. He carried a single-barreled shotgun — .410 gauge, if Cotton wasn't mistaken.

"No, Granddaddy," Lea yelled. "Put that down."

Terry Morse did not budge.

Cotton reached for his gun.

"Now," Lea screamed.

The weapon was lowered.

"These people are federal agents," Lea said. "You went too far this time."

Cotton admired the simple room. A light-colored bookcase filled with *Goosebumps* and Harry Potter novels lined one wall, a nondescript rug protected the plank floor. Six chairs were drawn near a pine table, the walls dotted with black-framed memories. Everything was clean and tidy. Expediency, not style, ruled. Not all that dissimilar from his mother's house back in Georgia. The only blemish was the acrid scent of nicotine and the mashed cigarette butts that filled several ashtrays.

He'd flashed his Magellan Billet badge and made it clear that he was working with the U.S. Justice Department. He'd also been glad to see his backpack, phone, and Beretta lying on the table. Even his sunglasses, along with the jar full of coins.

"You want to tell me about those," he said to Morse, pointing at the gold.

"Ain't nothin' to tell. It's buried treasure and you found it."

"What's a sentinel?" Cassiopeia asked.

"How do you know about that?"

"I told 'em," Lea said. "This has to end, Granddaddy. It makes no sense to keep it up anymore."

"And how do you know what makes sense?" Morse asked her.

"I know plenty. You taught me, remember?"

Morse folded his arms tightly across his chest and squirmed in a chair that creaked in resistance. He had to be pushing seventy, a bell of a man — short, stout, and rock-hard — with a flat pan of a face and a complexion, like Lea's, brown as tobacco. White hair sprang from every follicle on his scalp, ears, chin, neck, and eyebrows.

"I know," the older man said in a gravelly whisper. "I've known it a long time. But this is my life, all I've ever been. And I like bein' a sentinel."

"And you're good at it," Cotton said. "I have a knot on my head to prove it."

"We just wanted you to go away."

"We're not going anywhere," he said. "So tell us what this is all about."

The lid on the glass jar was gone. The old man grabbed the container and poured the dirty coins out onto the tabletop. Cotton considered himself somewhat of an amateur numismatist. Monetary currency had always intrigued him. Before him he saw 1861 $5 gold pieces, 1854 $20 gold pieces, and 1845

97

$10 gold pieces. The earliest coin was dated 1825, the latest 1865. About fifty all totaled, surely worth a fortune to collectors.

"Is this outlaw money?" he asked Morse.

Silence was the only reply.

"You certainly aren't going to make me ask again, are you? 'Cause the next time will be from the FBI office in Little Rock, with you both charged on a list of felonies."

"It's Confederate gold."

He had to admit, just hearing those words sent a chill down his spine. He was a Georgia boy, born and bred, his roots deeply southern. His father had been career navy, and though childhood until age ten had been spent traveling from one duty station to another, both his parents made sure that he understood where he came from. After his father died he and his mother moved back to Georgia, where he'd lived until age eighteen, finally going off to college, then the navy and law school. When he joined the Magellan Billet, Stephanie Nelle had headquartered the agency in Atlanta. He'd lived there until he retired out early, divorced, sold his house, and moved to Denmark, opening the bookshop. All his life he'd heard stories of how most Georgians had fervently believed in the Confederacy, fighting the North hard, but in the end most lost everything. His mother's family had been lucky and managed to keep their land, which still produced Vidalia onions by the thousands of bushels.

Middle and South Georgia were rife with tales of lost rebel gold. The vice president of the Confederacy, Alexander Stephens, had lived in Crawfordville, not far from his mother's family land. Jefferson Davis fled through the area, after the war, trying to avoid arrest. Even the Confederate treasury itself was said to have passed by on its way to disappearing into legend. Every one of those connections had come to mind when the call came from the Smithsonian's chancellor, asking for his help.

He glanced over at Cassiopeia, who seemed as interested as he was in what the old man had to say. But Morse's lips, hidden within the white sable of a wiry beard, appeared more a thin line of refusal than one of co-operation.

"Tell 'em, Granddaddy," Lea said. "If you don't, I will."

"Girls," the old man said, shaking his head. "So different from boys. I couldn't wait to take over for my pa. It was what we did as a son. But girls. They're much smarter than we ever were."

"Granddaddy is a knight," Lea said. "Show them."

Morse rolled up his right sleeve to reveal a faded tattoo.

"The cross and circle," Cotton muttered.

"You know it?" the old man asked.

How long had it been since he'd last seen that symbol? Twenty years? At least. His mind raced, as it had back in DC at the American history museum when he'd studied the 1909 records. A clock with brass movement hanging on the wall dinged for the half hour.

"You know what he's talking about," Cassiopeia asked. "Don't you?"

He nodded.

"I know all about the Knights of the Golden Circle."

CHAPTER NINE

Danny Daniels woke from a sound sleep and smelled smoke.

The darkened bedroom was thick with an acrid fog, enough that he choked on his next breath, coughing away a mouthful of carbon. He shook Pauline, waking her, then tossed the covers away. His mind came fully awake and he realized the worst.

The house was on fire.

He heard the flames, the old wood structure crackling as it disintegrated. Their bedroom was on the second floor, as was their daughter's.

"Oh, my God," Pauline said. "Mary."

"Mary," he called out through the open doorway. "Mary."

The second floor was a mass of flames, the stairway leading down engulfed in orange. It seemed the whole house had succumbed save for their bedroom.

"Mary," he yelled. "Answer me. Mary."

Pauline was now beside him, screaming for their nine-year-old daughter.

"I'm going after her," she said.

He grabbed her arm. "There's no way. You won't make it. The flooring is gone."

"I'm not going to stand here while she's in there."

Neither was he, but he had to use his brain.

"Mary," Pauline shrieked. "Answer me."

His wife was bordering on hysterical. Smoke continued to build. He bolted to the window and opened it. The bedside clock read 3:15 A.M. He heard no sirens. His farm sat three miles outside of the center of town, on family land, the nearest neighbor half a mile away.

He grabbed a lungful of fresh air.

"Dammit, Danny," Pauline blurted out. "Do something."

He made a decision.

He stepped back inside, grabbed his wife, and yanked her toward the window. The drop down was about fifteen feet into a line of shrubs. There was no way they could escape out the bedroom door. This was their only avenue out and he knew she would not go voluntarily.

"Get some air," he said.

She was coughing bad and saw the wisdom in his advice. She leaned out the window to clear her throat. He grabbed her legs and shoved her body through the open frame, twisting her once so she'd land sideways in the branches. She might break a bone, but she wasn't going to die in the fire. She was no help to him here. He had to do this on his own.

He saw that shrubbery had broken her fall and she came to her feet.

"Get away from the house," he called out.

Then he rushed back to the bedroom door.

"Daddy. Help me."

Mary's voice.

"Honey. I'm here," he called out, into the fire. "Are you in your room?"

"Daddy. What's happening? Everything's burning. I can't breathe."

He had to get to her, but there was no way. The second-floor hall was gone, fifty feet of air loomed between the doorway and his daughter's room. No time to jump out the window, find a ladder, and climb to Mary's window. In a few more minutes the bedroom where he stood would be gone. The smoke and heat were becoming unbearable, stinging his eyes, choking his lungs.

The little girl had to jump herself.

"Mary. You still there." He waited. "Mary."

He had to get to her.

He rushed to the window and stared below. Pauline was nowhere to be seen. He climbed out through the window and hung from the sill. He released his grip and fell the nine feet, penetrating the shrubbery, landing on his feet. He pushed through the branches and ran around to the other side of the house. His worst fears were immediately confirmed. The entire second floor was engulfed, including his daughter's room. Flames roared out the exterior walls and obliterated the roof.

Pauline stood, staring upward, holding one arm with the other.

"She's gone," his wife wailed, tears in her voice. "My baby is gone."

Danny closed his eyes and fought the horrible memory that had haunted him for forty years.

And the fire's cause?

His cigar, left on the corner of his desk.

At the time he was a city councilman in Maryville and liked a good smoke. Pauline had begged him to quit, but he'd refused. Back then, smoke detectors were not commonplace. Still, the official report noted the fire as *accidental, but preventable.*

Visiting Mary's grave had brought it all back.

Which explained why he stayed away.

He stood outside the front door to his house and tried to calm himself. The drive back from the Sherwood place, through the rain, had been uneventful. He lived alone. Pauline had not returned here after the inauguration. Instead, she now lived in Nashville, starting her new life. The idea had been for him to return home and do the same.

And he was trying.

He opened the door and entered.

He'd never bothered with locks. Useless. If

people wanted to break in they would. So why have a door to repair, too? The land around him was the same as forty years ago, but the house was different. He'd razed the other structure and built new. Eventually, life went on and he ended up first in the governor's mansion, then the White House. He'd tried hard to forget, then forgive himself, but had never accomplished either. Eventually the guilt cost him his marriage, as his wife could never forget or forgive. Thankfully, they'd finally made peace between themselves. He wanted Pauline to be happy. God knows she deserved it.

But didn't he, too?

He laid the stolen notebook on a table, then removed his wet coat and hung it on the oak coatrack that filled the entryway. No one had paid him any mind while he was leaving. Diane might eventually notice the volume was gone, but why would she suspect him?

His encounter with her still bothered him.

Apparently she'd had Alex's apartment searched and specific items removed. Why? Did that mean she also knew about Taisley? Hard to say. And what was Alex concerned about? *Something monumental. It involved the Senate and some kind of radical change. A way to end all the problems that have been happening there lately.*

Tall order.

Many had tried that feat and failed.

If we make ourselves sheep, the wolves will eat us.

Ben Franklin had been right on with that. But James Madison had expressed a thought, too. *If men were angels, no government would be necessary.*

Everyone hated Congress. Its approval rating stayed in the toilet. But what did you expect when 535 people tried to get something done. What had Twain said? *A camel was a horse made by a committee.* Just too many egos, too many agendas, and too little compromise. Incredibly, though, the first branch of government had always managed to acquit itself, stepping up to the plate and hitting home runs exactly when the United States of America really needed it. Two world wars. A Great Depression. Countless recessions. Social Security. Fair labor. Civil rights. Health care. You name it. All had been dealt with by Congress. People tended to forget that. He never had, constantly reminding himself that naysayers had their own agendas, too.

He grabbed the notebook and wandered into the front parlor, sitting in one of the rocking chairs. His mother's house had contained a parlor, as had her mother's, so he'd included one even though the room was hardly ever used. Pauline called it a waste of space but indulged his whim, decorating it in proper Tennessee fashion. They hadn't visited the house much while in the White House since the Secret Service would have demanded too many security changes. He'd always known that, once out of office, this would be his home, so he'd wanted it to remain inviolate.

And it had.

Now it was his alone.

He stared down at the notebook in his lap, the circle and cross visible in the leather. *"It's a wheel cross,"* Diane had said. *"Or a sun cross. An ancient symbol of the sun, for good luck."* Last week Alex had been here, in the house, during their last visit together. He'd been glad to see his old friend, but they'd talked little about politics and more about doing some hiking and fishing. Not once had Alex mentioned retiring from the Senate. Not a word about *something monumental*. No comments, either, about marital discord. And Danny had sensed nothing wrong. Misdirection? Possibly. But anyone who managed to get elected multiple times to the U.S. Senate knew how to keep things close. Was it none of his business? Maybe. But he and Alex had been friends. They'd shared a lot. Apparently not everything. Still, who was he to criticize. He'd never once mentioned his feelings toward Stephanie Nelle, though he had told

Alex that his marriage to Pauline was over.

He had to know if Taisley's fears were justified. It still amazed him that Alex had maintained a six-year connection with another woman and no one, not even his wife, had ever suspected a thing. But wasn't that exactly what he'd done with Stephanie? Their interaction for eight years had been out in the open, only fleeting opportunities here and there to speak alone. And no one had ever suspected that they harbored feelings toward each other.

Not even Pauline.

Rain pattered gently on the windows.

Outside, he heard cars approach, then stop on the graveled drive.

They were early.

Doors slammed closed.

The old boards of the front porch creaked beneath heavy footfalls.

He glanced out through the screen door and saw the governor of Tennessee. While here, the governor planned on meeting with local industry leaders and had called a few days ago and asked if he might bum a night in one of the spare bedrooms. Nashville was only a hundred and eighty miles away, and his old friend could have easily gone back to the state mansion, but he'd been glad for the company.

He slid open a drawer in a table beside the rocker and dropped the notebook inside.

No use involving another co-conspirator.
Then he rose and called out, "Come on in."

CHAPTER TEN

Diane Sherwood sat at her desk.

People remained in the house, still mingling and reflecting among themselves on their grief. The time was pushing 7:00 P.M. She expected the gathering would end soon. Afterward, the help would clean things up and restore the house to order. In a few weeks it would go on the market, the story being that she could not bear to live there any longer without her husband. They'd built the place long ago using Alex's money and, being childless, their last wills and testaments left everything they owned to each other.

The rain outside still fell.

She'd asked for a few minutes alone and everyone had understood. A widow with her grief. She and Alex had been married a long time. She'd met him back when they both were barely thirty and there'd been so much promise to his future. He'd been headed for the Tennessee state legislature, but people were already talking about the U.S. Senate, maybe even a presidential run down the road. Instead, another man from east Tennessee claimed the White House. A pompous, arrogant, self-righteous fool.

Danny Daniels.

His visit earlier had nauseated her.

But she'd learned long ago that there was nothing stupid about Danny Daniels. That good ol' boy façade shielded a shrewd mind. She'd invited him out of courtesy since not to do so would have raised questions. At the graveside, where he hadn't seemed eager to come, she'd been thrilled. Duty done and refused. But instead he'd showed his face and asked disturbing questions. Hopefully her offer of peace, which he'd accepted, would be the last time the two of them ever spoke.

She felt reassured enough to pour herself a Scotch, sipping it slowly, allowing the alcohol to soothe her nerves.

The door eased open and her brother entered.

She'd asked one of the ladies to have him join her. Nothing unusual should arise from the request, as she'd want family near her at such a difficult time.

"Close it," she said to him. "And sit down."

Her tone conveyed the extent of her sour mood, but a few more sips of Scotch made her feel better.

Kenneth Layne was not much of a man, either mentally or physically. He stood tall and thin, with the tawny hair of their father and a mustache to match. He had an expressionless quality about him that all her life had been irritating. Most of that detachment came from their mother, a docile, placid woman with few convictions and even less purpose. Thankfully, those weak genes had avoided her and she'd favored their father, a man of strength and élan, tough as a hickory stick. But it was Kenneth's lack of courage that she most detested. Her brother was more a man of reflection than action. He'd take bold steps, but never alone. And risks? Those terrified him. She, on the other hand, enjoyed pushing the envelope.

He sat in one of the club chairs across the room.

She walked closer to him, her eyes turning narrow, her cold lips taut. "Do you have any idea how much trouble you caused?"

The problem started a few weeks ago with a call from Alex. Kenneth had come to see him in Washington, explaining what they were planning and seeking help.

"What you and Kenneth want to do would change the course of this country," Alex said to her.

"Which is precisely what you've talked about for the past twenty years. Maybe it's time we actually do something about it."

"I'm not sure that's a decision for you or me or Kenneth to make. It's something the people themselves have to choose, after open debate."

"Be real, Alex. That's never going to happen. The people don't have a clue what they want. We have an opportunity here. Why not take it?"

"Is the Speaker of the House with you?"

"Definitely."

"He told you that?"

"In no uncertain terms. He's ready to make history."

"I bet he is, considering the incredible benefits he'll accrue. I've been reading Kenneth's notebook, and I've ordered some books. Amazingly, what you're proposing seems perfectly legal, and entirely consistent with the Constitution."

"People have known that since before the Civil War. This is not a new idea. Frankly, I would not have involved you in any of this. Kenneth made that decision, on his own, without consulting me."

"Which only illustrates how far you and I have drifted apart."

"We both know that our marriage is in name only."

"And I can see now what you've been busy with these past couple of years. More than I ever realized."

"I want to actually do something, Alex. And here's the chance."

"I'm not as convinced as you."

Those last words had sent a chill down her spine. Containment was everything, and her brother's unilateral decision to involve her husband had jeopardized their success. Alex was a dreamer who believed too much in the system as it existed. Like so many others, he screamed change but did little to nothing to make it happen.

"You made a big mistake," she said to her brother. "If I'd wanted Alex part of this, I would have included him."

"Who died and left you in charge?"

"You did, when you came seeking *my* help."

He did not challenge that statement, because she'd told him at the time that the price of her participation was that she make all the critical decisions.

"Alex was needed," he said. "There'll be hard resistance in the Senate, and he could have worked to lessen that. Now we'll have to find someone else."

Her eyes locked on his. "Who gives a damn what the United States Senate thinks? It lost its ability to have an opinion on this when it decided it was better than everyone else. I don't care about their resistance. In fact, I welcome it."

Never had *she* shied away from a fight.

They were fraternal twins, formed from two separate eggs, fertilized by two distinct sperm cells, which thankfully grew into two vastly different people. They neither looked nor acted alike. She acquired a love of history and an appreciation for conscientious study, while he favored politics and shortcuts. He ran a citizen's action group known as the Committee to Save America, which boasted a membership that included nearly 60% of state legislators from around the country. Its primary agenda based on a demand, by two-thirds of the states, for a new Article V constitutional convention. So far thirty of the thirty-four states needed had made the official request of Congress. Four more and Congress then would have no choice but to call for a national convention to consider amendments to the Constitution. Through those efforts, Kenneth had acquired the ear of Lucius Vance and eventually introduced her to the Speaker of the House.

Which had led them to this moment.

"It was foolish to give Alex your notebook," she said again.

A look of surprise invaded her brother's face. "He told you about that?"

"Oh, yes. And why did you even write all that crap down? My God, you even had the cross and circle stamped on its cover."

"I gave those notes to Alex to show him we weren't crazy. That there's a solid, legal basis to what we're doing. I've researched it carefully, and I genuinely wanted his take on things. And who cares what's on the cover? It's meaningless to 99.99% of the people."

"Alex actually did some research of his own," she said. "And, as I would have suspected, he had major reservations. He told me in no uncertain terms that he would not be a part of what was about to happen."

He shook his head. "I don't believe you. That's your whole problem. You think no one is as smart as you. You always underestimated Alex."

As usual, her words seemed to wash over him without registering. She stepped back to the desk and found the cross-and-circle necklace returned by Danny Daniels. "Why did you give him this?"

Kenneth shrugged. "To make him feel included. He appreciated the gesture."

"He played you. How much did you tell him?"

"Enough for him to know that what we're doing isn't original. It goes way back. People smarter than us came up with the idea."

"You told him about the Order?"

"Of course. He was fascinated. How did you get that necklace?"

"How *much* did you tell him?"

"Enough for him to know that this might be the way to finally accomplish what he'd talked about for years. Change Congress, change the country."

What an idiot.

"He was just learning all he could from you, saying what you wanted to hear. You really didn't know Alex all that well, did you? He liked to make speeches, go on TV, and say how awful things were. But he never actually did anything about it. You never found that strange? It's actually quite common in today's world. People will talk about how terrible a McDonald's hamburger tastes, but they keep buying them by the millions, over and over. Why? Because they're safe. A sure bet. You know exactly what you're getting. Good and bad. No surprises. It's the same in politics. Men like Alex get reelected over and over because everyone knows what they're getting. They're safe. Mavericks rarely win elections and never get reelected. Alex would not have changed the government." She paused. "Nor would you, I might add, if I had not come into the picture."

He pointed an accusatory finger at her. "I'm the one connected to Vance. I'm the one who's working with the state legislatures. Those petitions calling for a second constitutional convention are not appearing out of thin air. I make those happen. You're the one who upped the ante in this game to include a change in Congress."

True.

But why not take advantage of every opportunity.

All her life she'd heard stories about the Knights of the Golden Circle. Her master's thesis had dealt with 19th-century clandestine organizations. Groups like the Brotherhood of the Union, the Freedom Societies, and the

Circle of Honor. Advisers who read it called her work brilliant and urged her to publish it as a book, but she'd refused. Instead, for the past three years she'd been working quietly trying to implement a plan first conceived 170 years ago. Then the imbecile sitting before her, with whom regrettably she'd shared a womb for nine months, decided for once in his life to make a decision on his own.

She, too, had involved Alex once, but not to the extent Kenneth had chosen, and certainly not as obviously.

When the Smithsonian Institution was created in 1846, a seventeen-member board of regents was charged with its management. Presently that board was composed of three senators, appointed by the president pro tempore of the Senate, three House members, appointed by the Speaker of the House, and nine ordinary citizens. The chief justice and vice president of the United States acted as ex officio members, the chief justice being the institution's chancellor. Alex had served as one of the regent senators for the past five years. Two years ago she'd used that connection and had him secure her an appointment onto one of the many Smithsonian advisory boards. The one that interested her worked with the libraries. She'd used her love of books and history to convince him to speak on her behalf, which he'd been more than happy to do. Nothing raised any alarms or concerns. Just a husband helping out his highly qualified wife.

And she'd used that position to maximum advantage.

Right now, it was working on two fronts.

One in Arkansas, the other in Washington, DC.

"I'm tired of arguing," Kenneth said. "And it's all moot now anyway. Alex is gone. But Vance will be by later. He called a little while ago and confirmed."

"Make it late. After everyone has left. We don't need any more containment problems."

"We still have one big problem," Kenneth said. "Running wild and loose."

She knew who he meant.

The fourth person in their circle.

"He's going into the Smithsonian tonight," she told him. "Doing his job, I might add."

Kenneth shook his head. "You say I'm a problem? Grant Breckinridge is a loose cannon. I'm not in that bastard's league when it comes to trouble."

She glared at her brother. "There are things that have to be done, most of which involve breaking laws. Are you prepared to take those risks? To make those things happen? Because if you are, Kenneth, I'll get rid of Grant right now and turn it all over to you. But if you're not, then shut your damn mouth and leave this to me."

And she meant it.

They needed Grant, an intriguing combination of charm, promise, and assurance. Sharp as a swindler. His strength an asset, his confidence a sound counter to Kenneth's whining and complaining. True, Grant had taken chances, and she was aware of what he was overseeing in Arkansas and about to do in DC, but as she'd just said, there were messy things that had to be done and somebody had to do them.

She stepped away, finished with the conversation. Her brother had a way of turning her stomach. Thankfully, Grant had gone into Alex's apartment and retrieved the notebook along with some books. She'd known nothing about the necklace or that would have been located, too. Behind her desk, below the study's windows, sat the two tote bags Grant had delivered.

She glanced that way and immediately noticed something wrong.

Lying atop one of the bags for the past few days had been Kenneth's notebook, the cross and circle visible on its leather cover.

But it was not there.

She glanced over at her poodle, sleeping in his bed. Perhaps he was the culprit? Or maybe it just had fallen inside the tote.

Kenneth stood from his chair. "I'll call Vance and confirm a time. I'm going to rest a little while before he gets here."

"You do that. And try not to screw any

more things up."

He ignored her insult and left.

Quickly, she checked the tote bags and found nothing but books. There'd been people in and out of here all day, but no one would have had any interest in that notebook.

Or would they?

She still held the cross and circle returned to her by Danny Daniels. His explanation of how he acquired the necklace had sounded plausible. She recalled Alex going over for a visit. Had they discussed more than Alex's political future? Had Alex confided in Daniels? Or was it as Daniels had said, the necklace had simply been lost?

An uncomfortable paranoia swept through her.

Which she did not like.

She reached for the phone.

And called Grant.

CHAPTER ELEVEN

Grant Breckinridge cared little about his surname, which harked back to the 19th century. John C. Breckinridge served as vice president of the United States under James Buchanan, the youngest man ever to hold that position, then ran for president in 1860, finishing second to Lincoln. When war broke out he sided with his native Kentucky and became a Confederate general, fighting at Shiloh, Stones River, and Chickamauga before taking command of Southern forces in the Shenandoah Valley. Late in the conflict he became the last Confederate secretary of war. After all was lost he fled abroad, eventually returning when Andrew Johnson granted universal clemency. Since childhood Grant had been told that he was related to that Breckinridge. But who the hell cared? He wasn't one of those who longed for the antebellum South, lamenting over the unforgivable War of Northern Aggression. None of that mattered.

Except one thing from that time.

Treasure. Confederate gold and silver.

That interested him.

He had a primal need for massive wealth, brought on by a life that had enjoyed precious little of that commodity. He'd been a disappointment to his parents, not given to serious study. His father had been an academic who eventually found a career at the Smithsonian Institution. Now the old man was little more than a babbling idiot.

Talk about disappointment.

"How are you tonight?" he asked his father.

James Breckinridge was pushing eighty. And though the body had survived relatively intact, the mind had slipped away. The old man lived alone, still able, though, to care for himself. Somehow meals were cooked and the house kept reasonably clean. But it was only a matter of time before a retirement home would have to be found.

"Do I know you?" his father asked.

He could see that tonight was going to be difficult. Which was not good. He had no time for nonsense. He needed answers. The house sat on the Virginia side of the Potomac, just beyond the DC Beltway. It had been paid for long ago, which allowed his father to live comfortably off a Smithsonian pension and Social Security.

"It's Grant. Your son. Think hard. Remember me."

"My boy is off to college. He wants to be a teacher. That's a good job, being a teacher."

"No, I'm here. I'm Grant. I need you to concentrate. Can you do that for me?"

"Julie. Julie," his father called out.

He shook his head. His mother died years ago. "Mother's gone. She's dead. I've told you this before."

His father stared at him with a puzzled look. "Why do you say such mean things? If my boy Grant was here, he'd smack you in the face. That's his mother you're talking about. She's right here. I just saw her a few minutes ago. Julie."

Repetition was another annoyance that he'd learned to endure.

He stared around the den. Once books filled every available space, floor-to-ceiling. But he'd moved most of the important stuff to his own apartment and sold the rest to used-book shops. The old man could not read anymore. Nothing registered. All he did was sit in front of the television, flicking through the channels, watching nothing.

"Listen to me," he said, voice rising. "I need you to focus. I'm going to the Smithsonian tonight. You remember that place."

"I work there. I was there today."

"No, you weren't. You haven't been there in a long time. Listen to me. I need you to tell me some things."

"Young man, I'm the head curator for the

Castle, and I don't like your attitude. Not one bit."

His father had indeed held the coveted position of Castle curator, which meant he was in charge of maintaining the Smithsonian's centerpiece. Only three men had ever held that job, his father the first, in charge from 1969 to 1992. He and his mother had been there on retirement day, when the Smithsonian's secretary thanked his father publicly for his service and co-workers gathered to wish him a long life. He recalled a momentary feeling of pride, one any young boy should have about his father. But those moments had always been few and far between. Tonight his father's sick mind was apparently back twenty-five years ago. So he decided to use that fantasy to his advantage.

"I meant no disrespect, but I have to ask you about one of your exhibits."

"Oh, gosh, we have so many of them."

"The key. I need to know about the ceremonial key."

The old man's brow furrowed. "What key? I have many keys. Too damn many. I've tried to tell people we need to eliminate locks, but they just keep adding new ones. I have to have a key to every lock. Secretary's orders. The curator must have access to everything. No exceptions."

Some progress. The sick mind was staying focused on one subject.

"Listen to me. It's the ceremonial key. I need to ask you about that."

"That's an odd thing to bring up."

"No, it's not. Think hard."

A swipe from a withered hand dismissed any further thought. "You're talking nonsense. A key is a key is a key. It's just a key."

"No, it's not."

He'd tried the easy way, realizing that it would probably be useless. But at least he'd tried. Time now to do what always worked. He reached down and grabbed the old man by the throat, yanking the scrawny body upward from the chair. Breath squeezed out through the constricted airway. With a vise-lock grip he slammed his father into the wall, keeping him there, feet off the ground, the pressure to the throat just enough to allow only minimal air to the lungs.

"I don't have time for this," he said. "You have to focus and listen to me."

His father did not move. He never did. Rarely had simple communication achieved results. But something about violence stimulated the diseased mind. Perhaps it was a primitive survival mode. Or maybe some defensive chemical or hormone was generated. Grant had no idea. All he knew was that force made its way through the fog.

"I'll ask you again. The ceremonial key. It's the original that I need, correct?"

They'd talked on this subject before.

"I found it, you know. I'm the one who found the key."

He did know that. Learned through another encounter just like this one.

"It was in the attic, at the Castle. In the rafters. Just lying there. All brass. Good as the day it was forged. I gave it to the secretary."

Which he also knew.

He increased the pressure to the throat and the old man's eyes widened as breathing became more difficult.

A signal that his patience was drawing to a close.

Nothing remained in the worn-out muscles that could offer any resistance. So he lifted the feet farther off the floor, which added more pressure to the throat, keeping his father's spine tight to the wall.

"Will. It. Open. The. Lock?"

The breaths came in spurts, the lungs now choking for air.

"I swear, Colonel . . . I'm loyal to the South. I'm . . . no spy."

Damn. The Civil War delusions had begun. He was hoping to avoid those.

"The lock is . . . only for the . . . righteous. Those of the . . . Order. Those who pledged their . . . loyalty to the cause. Are . . . you one of those, Colonel?"

He knew the right answer. "I am."

The look in his father's eyes softened, as if

a light had switched on in the dark corners of his brain.

"Then . . . I shall tell you."

He loosened his grip enough to allow the feet to touch the floor and his father to breathe unimpeded.

"When at last you need your rest . . . the South will face its greatest test. Oh elder Knights . . . all clad in grey, lead the charge into the fray."

He stared at the crazy old man and shook his head.

Dammit.

More gibberish.

Why didn't the old bastard just die? No. This fool planned to live forever. And if he could somehow communicate anything of value that fact might not be so bad. Instead, Grant had to endure fantasies and delusions, anything useful coming only in drips and dribbles from micro-moments of clarity. But time was running out. Which explained why he had to take a big chance tonight. Success hinged on two things, both of which were locked away inside the Smithsonian.

"Near and far in warrior's grey, the final conflict will come our way. Sounds of battle draw ever near, ye gallant knights we need not fear."

He'd listened to this crap all his life. As a young boy it had at first been enthralling, but it eventually played on his nerves. Nobody gave a damn about the Civil War anymore. But billions of dollars in lost gold and silver? That would interest anyone.

"The gold, you stupid idiot," he spit out. "Can't you tell me anything about the gold? Do we need the key?"

"The servant of faith, I shepherd to the north of the river. This path is dangerous. Go to 18 places. Seek the map. Seek the heart."

A hard knot of anger balled within him.

He popped a fist into the old man's gut. Not hard enough to break anything, but sufficient to make his point. Breath rushed from his father's lungs and he allowed the limp body to crumple to the floor. He should take the gun nestled inside his shoulder harness and shoot the moron, like a wounded horse no longer capable of doing much of anything but whining.

He had no more patience.

A massive treasure awaited.

Hidden for over a hundred years.

About the only thing of any value he'd ever acquired from his father was a knowledge of its existence. He was thirty-five years old and tired of failure lying as a foul taste on his tongue. School was not his thing. Neither was a nine-to-five job. Both bored him. He'd been married twice and thankfully fathered no children. He suspected he may be sterile, since he'd never really practiced any form of contraception. He was so tired of wanting. Finally, for the past two years he'd been actively involved in something that could possibly change his life. A fast track to the top. But that outcome hinged on the pathetic excuse for a human being that lay wheezing before him.

"You're not going to tell me, are you?"

His father remained on all fours, face toward the floor, choking.

"The South will rise again . . . once more, on honored fields . . . just like before. Heavenly Father we plead our case . . . our Southern nation before thy face."

Puzzles were not his thing. Solving them never came easy. Thankfully, Diane had learned the secrets of the sentinels, which had proved fruitful. Hopefully, by the end of the night they would have what they needed, both here and in Arkansas. He'd hoped to obtain a little more clarity before heading into town. A way to make sure that the risks were worth it. But now he'd just have to hope they were. He was expected at the National Museum of Natural History in a little over an hour.

His father cowered on the floor.

He kicked the old man in the chest. Again, only hard enough to express his irritation. The great thing was that his father never remembered a thing. Not a single blow ever registered in the old man's memory.

Each time he visited was like the first.

Thankfully, he knew enough to move forward. He'd spent the past few years combing through books, manuscripts, letters, and old documents. The people at the American Civil War Museum in Richmond knew him on sight. One thing he was good at was retrieving things.

Amazing how time leveled the playing field. Once there were tens of thousands of Knights of the Golden Circle. But all that remained were men like the old sentinel out in Arkansas and the man coughing on the floor before him. Who, for all intents and purposes, was dead, too. He'd hired men and sent them to Arkansas, paying them with Confederate gold he'd personally retrieved, following Diane's instructions. And, yes, himself, Diane, and her brother all wore the cross and circle as a show of unity, but they were not knights. Especially Diane. Women would have never been allowed to take the oath. Nonetheless, like the knights, the three of them were bound together in a common purpose.

Of which he was a vital part.

His cell phone vibrated.

He checked the display. Diane.

He debated answering, but decided to let her wait.

No time.

The call he really wanted was the one from Arkansas.

CHAPTER TWELVE

The Knights of the Golden Circle sprang from the Southern Rights Clubs of the 1830s that openly advocated a reestablishment of the African slave trade, which Congress had banned in 1807. More inspiration came courtesy of the Order of the Lone Star, which helped orchestrate Texas' independence from Mexico in 1836. Some even have argued that the Order's roots stretched all the way back to the Sons of Liberty during the American Revolution.

The Order was officially organized in Lexington, Kentucky, on July 4, 1854, by five men whose names have been lost to history. It was heavy on ritual, most borrowed from the Masons. Local chapters were called castles, and collectively the Knights of the Golden Circle became the largest, most dangerous subversive organization in American history. By 1860 it boasted 48,000 members across every state and territory. Its economic and political goals were to create a prosperous, slaveholding southern empire extending in the shape of a circle from their proposed capital at Havana, Cuba, through the southern United States, the Caribbean, and Central America. The plan also called for the acquisition of Mexico, which was to be divided into fifteen new slaveholding states, a move designed to shift the balance of power in Congress in favor of slavery. Facing the Gulf of Mexico, these new states would form a crescent, the entire expansion a golden circle, its planned robust economy fueled by cotton, sugar, tobacco, rice, coffee, indigo, and mining, all employing slave labor.

In early 1860 newspapers across the country reported that the Order was recruiting troops for a planned invasion of Mexico. It's unclear what went wrong, but the invasion never happened. Some say it was because of inadequate manpower and supplies, but with civil war looming, the more logical conclusion was that the Order did not want to fight on two fronts. So they postponed their plans for Mexico and started preparing to fight the North.

In January 1861 the South began to secede. By February seven former states had ratified a new Constitution and named Jefferson Davis their provisional president. The Knights of the Golden Circle immediately abandoned their expansionist policies and became an ally of the newly created Confederate States of America.

And flourished.

Many Southern military groups were composed either totally or in large part by knights. They infiltrated Federal arsenals, mints, navy yards, army posts, and local governments, playing a major role in the Northwest Conspiracy, designed to foster revolution across Indiana, Illinois, and Ohio. In rural areas they ran off horses, driving them away from any possible Union service. They took control of small towns and newspapers, collecting guns, ammunition, armaments, uniforms, and supplies. Burning, plundering, and terror were their main tools. They were essentially a clandestine paramilitary unit engaged in counterintelligence operations. Little is known of their specific activities since most of the records kept by the Confederate secretary of state dealing with the Order disappeared when Richmond fell in April 1865. But when Lee surrendered at Appomattox and the war officially ended, the Order did not disband. What had been a shadowy society became even more secretive, going fully underground, using aliases to hide its activities, which included preparations for a second civil war. Legend spoke of how it invested in mining, railroads, and shipping, amassing fortunes that were eventually converted into gold and silver, then systematically buried across the country.

Supposedly the Knights of the Golden Circle ceased all operations around 1916.

By then the United States was fighting World War I, and most of the fanatical rebels had died.

No new civil war was coming.

"The Order doesn't exist," Cotton said to Terry Morse.

" 'Cause you say so?" the old man fired back. "That's exactly what they want you to think. But they're still out there."

Cotton had heard the stories since he was a little boy. His great-great-grandfather on his mother's side, Angus Adams — who'd fought in the Civil War as a spy for the Confederacy — had also been a knight of the Golden Circle. Letters and papers in his grandfather's attic talked of a conference held in 1859 at the Greenbrier resort in what was then Virginia. Nearly 1200 came, including cabinet members, governors, and congressmen. They approved a sixty-page booklet — *Rules, Regulations and Principles of the American Legion of the Knights of the Golden Circle* — which expressed the organization's intents and purposes. He'd read the copy that had been in the attic, and recalled its opening lines. *Let their be no strife between mine and thine, for we be brethren. To maintain the Constitution as it is, and to restore the Union as it was.* The oak, the tree of the acorn, became one of their many symbols, representing strength, growth, and diversity. Most men of influence in the South, including his own ancestors, joined. They wanted not a simple confederacy, but a grandiose empire.

And Morse's tattoo.

The circle and cross.

One of his mother's family heirlooms had included a gold cross inside a gold circle.

"What is it?" he asked his mother.

"A remembrance of something long gone."

He was now more curious than ever. "Of what?"

"A time when men believed in things we now find disgusting. When an entire race was enslaved. When women meant little to nothing, and the South thought itself invincible."

"You mean the Civil War?"

He was in only the fifth grade, just beginning to learn about Abraham Lincoln and all that had happened between 1860 and 1865. But the medallion his mother held seemed fascinating. "Why do you keep it?"

"My grandfather gave it to me and told me to give it to my child one day. He wanted us to remember. But I think the tradition will stop with me."

He didn't like that. "Why?"

She dropped the locket back into the jewelry box and replaced the case on the top shelf in her closet. "Because it's time those memories end."

His mind snapped back to Morse. "The knights were definitely a force before, during, and shortly after the Civil War. But by World War I they'd faded away, their purpose gone."

"All I know is that I got a duty and I gave my word to my pa that I'd do it until the day I died."

Cassiopeia had sat quiet, watching Lea and her grandfather. Cotton caught her gaze and could see she had questions for him. A month ago they'd made a pact. No more bullshit between them. That also meant no more secrets. So he winked, signaling that later he'd offer more of an explanation.

"He's a knight and a sentinel," Lea said. "Those are people who watch over the treasure. They keep folks away and protect it."

"For how long?" Cassiopeia asked.

"Generations. It's a family duty." The young girl said the words with pride. "They say the woods here are filled with gold."

"Belonging to the Golden Circle?" Cotton asked.

"That's right," Morse said. "They hid it and left markers in the trees, on the ground, all over. You followed 'em today. Did real good, too. People like to say it's outlaw money. But it ain't. It's Confederate."

His own grandfather told him that the knights had been *real good at hiding things in plain sight.*

Today he proved that observation true.

Past the windows, a warm and seasonal twilight was thickening into night. His watch read 7:40 P.M. It had been a long day, one that had unfolded much differently than he'd

137

imagined this morning. The idea had been to investigate the site, check out the markers, then ask around to see what the locals knew. Two days on the ground, tops, then back to DC.

"What did you mean when you said the knights just wanted us to think they were gone?" he asked Morse.

"Some men came to see me, about a month ago. They gave me the handshake."

The older man extended his right hand, which Cotton shook. Morse's grip was firm, but only with two fingers and the thumb. The third and little finger stayed free and Cotton locked his two fingers with Morses.'

A familiar feel.

"Why did you do that?" he asked his grandfather.

They were in the attic, the dusty air cool from a Georgia autumn morning.

"You're old enough to understand now," his grandfather said.

"I'm only eleven."

The old man chuckled. "But real smart. So I wanted you to see this stuff."

Usually the attic was off limits. He and his mother had lived back at her father's house for over a year now, ever since his own father disappeared, presumed dead, on a naval mission. They knew little to nothing about what happened, only that his submarine had sunk with all hands lost. His mother had taken the loss hard, eventually finding refuge in running the day-to-day operations of the onion farm. He'd done what he always did and kept the pain to himself, but he and his papa spent a lot of time together.

Today they'd come up into the attic.

He stood grasping the older man in a strange handshake, two of his grandfather's fingers locked with his own.

"You feel that? That was the Order's grip. One member would do that to another, in public. Then ask, 'Are you on it?' The correct reply was 'I am on it.' That meant they were both knights."

His grandfather had told him stories about the Knights of the Golden Circle and how his great-grandfather and great-great-grandfather had been members. He'd even gone to the library and tried to find some books on the subject but had come up empty. He'd asked his history teacher, who knew nothing.

Which made him wonder if the whole thing was even true.

"They had a castle, right here in Toombs County," his grandfather said. "That's what they called their local chapters. Castles. My father served as an officer, as did his father before him. They were devils, those knights."

His mind returned to the lit room around him, and he released Morse's grip.

The older man watched him with curious eyes. "You know what I'm sayin' is real, don't you?"

He wasn't going to admit anything. "What did the men want who came to see you?"

"It was right after I scared off the last guy who was snoopin' around the map tree. And he wasn't no treasure hunter. Not sure what he was, but he didn't care for the woods. He was easy to spook. I just hung a dummy and off he went."

Exactly as had been reported by Martin Thomas.

"But he did bury a plow point in the ground and used a compass to locate it," Morse said. "That told me he knew things. Just like you today. I watched you. Somebody taught you, didn't they?"

He was beginning to see that this old man was far smarter than he wanted people to think.

"The men who came to see me knew I was a sentinel," Morse said. "They also knew what I was protectin'. But I told 'em nothin.' Didn't trust a word they said."

"Even though they were knights?"

"I'm not sure what they were. So I kept quiet."

"Here's the thing," he said to Morse. "You don't have a choice with us. So are you going to tell me what they wanted?"

"Better than that. I can show you."

CHAPTER THIRTEEN

Tennessee
8:00 P.M

Danny sat in his battered recliner, huddled among his favorite things, a lamp burning to his right, the notebook open in his lap. He'd carefully read every page. He was inside his second-floor bedroom with the door closed. The governor was down for the night. They'd had dinner together, pizza delivered from a local eatery. It had been fun catching up. He hadn't had many visitors the past four months. Only Alex and a literary agent, pestering him about starting to write his memoirs. Apparently it was some sort of mandatory duty that all ex-presidents had to write a book. His story seemed to be a hot commodity, as three publishers had already offered seven figures for the manuscript. A ghostwriter had to be hired and dictation started, but the simple thought of doing that turned his stomach. It almost seemed like an admission that his life was over, time now to write everything down before he died. He didn't need the money and he certainly did not want the aggravation that would come from remembering every detail of his life.

Reading the notebook, though, had piqued his curiosity.

Alex had clearly been up to something.

For a second time he scanned through the handwritten pages, at paragraphs here and there, committing the sentences to memory.

The U.S. Senate met in secret from 1789 to 1795. No public sessions and no one paid it any mind. It was deemed a political black hole from which no career would emerge. It had no affect on any legislation. Did little to nothing. Conversely, the House held its sessions in public and dominated Congress. Everything was done there, the Senate all but forgotten. Henry Clay called the Senate's atmosphere a "solemn stillness."

1806. Aaron Burr, as vice president, convinced the Senate that its rule allowing members to vote an end to debate was unnecessary. His colleagues agreed and, henceforth, senators carried the right of unlimited monologue, not stoppable by the other members. They had no idea what they had stumbled upon.

1820s. Things started to change. House had grown to 181 members, while Senate stayed small at 48. House members elected by the people. Senators came from state legislatures. Different rules governed each body. The House limited members on time and length of debate. Not so in the Senate. Debate actually encouraged there. No limit on how long a senator could talk. Again, they still had no idea of the potential.

1830s. Southern senators discovered that Senate rules allowed them to refuse to yield the floor once they began to speak. Combine that with no way for other senators to stop the debate, and no time limit on how long a senator could talk, senators realized they could hold the floor forever. Filibuster was born. Webster, Calhoun, Clay, and others used it to paralyze the Senate and stall or kill any legislation they did not like.

The notes were listed under a header that read REBUTTAL REMARKS, as if the author had been preparing either for a speech or for a paper. He was familiar with Alex's handwriting and he'd immediately noticed that the journal was not penned by his friend.

He riffled through the pages.

Many dealt with observations about obscure Senate rules, things nearly no one would care about.

But they should.

Procedural rules determined how and when laws were passed. Smart representatives gained a tactical advantage by studying those in detail. During his three terms in the Senate Danny had learned every nuance of the 1500-page procedural manual.

Since 1789 nearly 2000 men and women had served in the U.S. Senate. Those folks could be divided into two broad classes — workhorses and show horses. One got things done, the other took the credit or assigned blame. Of late, that dichotomy had been brought into sharp focus, as the Senate seemed overrun by show horses.

Everyone clamored for the limelight.

Television and newspapers had been consumed for the past four months with the Senate's refusal to confirm President Fox's cabinet appointments. First one Senator, then another, had blocked a floor vote, effectively stopping the will of the other 99. True, cloture now allowed 60 votes to end a filibuster, a safeguard implemented in the early 20th century, but getting three-fifths of the Senate to agree on anything was next to impossible. Especially when it came to ending debate. It was like a courtesy. If one Senator wanted to filibuster, the others simply allowed it since next time they could be the one in the hot seat.

He scanned more of the notes.

Article I, Section 5, Clause 2 of Constitution provides that the House and Senate are the sole judge of their procedural rules. The Supreme Court has held that House rules are adopted by each new Congress, every two years. Senate rules, though, stay in effect until otherwise changed. In 1892, United States v. Ballin, the Supreme Court said that there must be only a reasonable relation between an established rule and the result sought to be attained. That's pretty wide open, meaning that the power of Congress to make procedural rules is unlimited. It is continuous, absolute, and beyond challenge by any other body or court.

He looked up from the notebook.

What in the world?

Taisely had told him that all of this had come from Diane's brother, Kenneth Layne. The pages seemed some sort of a research summary on the subject of Senate and House rules, containing references and notes from various court opinions. Other parts dealt with Article V, which provided the means and method of how the Constitution could be amended — another rather obscure subject, but one that had apparently consumed Kenneth Layne's attention. What was Layne up to? And why had Alex soured on it, as Taisley had said?

The last few pages of the notebook were particularly intriguing.

Jefferson Davis and Alexander Stephens hated each other. Though they served as president and vice president of the Confederate States, their philosophies differed. Davis favored war. Stephens preferred constitutional change. Stephens never wanted war, but stayed loyal to Georgia and supported his state when it seceded. But where initially Davis had thought legal change impossible, by April 1865 he came to believe it may be the only course left since war had failed.

Stephens served in the House of Representatives from 1843 to 1859. Just as the Senate was growing in stature, the filibuster was coming of age. By the 1850s little could be done in Congress without placating every member of the Senate. One senator was enough as an enemy. Fed up, Representative Alexander Stephens from Georgia devised a way to strip the Senate of its power, but could never gain enough momentum to have the idea implemented. Then war intervened. From 1873 to 1882 Stephens once again served in the House of Representatives. By then the Senate had become the dominant chamber in Congress. Changing anything was out of the question.

He had no idea what to make of the observations. What had Alexander Stephens devised to corral the Senate? He'd never heard of that observation before.

Only about three-quarters of the notebook's pages were written upon. On the final page appeared a name.

Knights of the Golden Circle.

Which he knew about, vaguely, from old stories.

Then a written statement.

I consider a nation with a king, as a man who takes a lion as a guard dog. If he knocks out his teeth, he renders the lion useless. While if he leaves the lion his teeth, the lion eats him.

A notation indicated that the quote was attributable to James Smithson, the man who left the initial seed money that ultimately created the Smithsonian Institution. Alex had served as a Smithsonian regent, so he'd be familiar with Smithson. But the single word written at the bottom of the page was what really drew Danny's attention.

Exactly.

The ink for all three entries was in a different color, written by a different hand.

Alex's, which he recognized.

As if a point was being made.

He had a bad feeling.

And unfortunately there was only one play left on the board.

Diane.

Sure, she'd be pissed at what he'd done, but she'd get over it. That was one thing about being an ex-president. People cut you a lot of slack. He recalled something one of his old political nemeses liked to say. *Observe, remember, compare, read, confer, listen, and question.*

He'd already worked the first six.

Time now to question.

He sat a few moments, sucking in the waft of old comforts around him. The silence pressed on his ears, palpable as the pressure from an explosion. Rain peppered the window, sounding like mice scurrying on the floor. He glanced over, the curtains not drawn. Pauline had hated to be in a lighted room, at night, with the windows unshaded. But he'd never seemed to mind. How would Diane react to the fact that her husband may have loved another woman? That he planned to divorce her? He'd keep those tidbits to himself for as long as possible. Though he may not have cared for Diane through the years, there seemed no reason to hurt her outright.

With the notebook in hand he stood, found his car keys, then headed downstairs. Outside, the governor's security team kept watch on the front porch.

"I'll be back," he said.

"It's awful late. Do you need an escort?" the man asked.

That was the last thing he required.

"Nope. I got it."

CHAPTER FOURTEEN

Cotton followed Morse outside. Cassiopeia and Lea came, too. He was learning things, like with his own grandfather, in tiny doses. From ages ten to sixteen he'd been enthralled by stories. His mother's family had all been Confederates, proud Georgians who'd stood with their state when it abandoned the Union. Clearly a different time and place. But no Adams had ever owned slaves. Instead, they'd worked the land as a family. Thankfully, there'd been a lot of them in and around Vidalia, Georgia. No onions then, though. Those didn't start until the 1930s. Corn and cotton had been big business then.

They all stopped on the porch.

"I been doin' this a long time," Morse said. "Sentinels were once stationed all over Arkansas. We each had a slice of land to look after. My pa showed me the map tree that you found. I was younger than Lea when he explained about it. It's my main marker. That's why it's there. Like a boundary line. I keep a watch over the woods for fifty miles in every direction from it. Not all the time. Just when people come snooping."

"And how do you know where things are buried?" Cassiopeia asked.

"I don't. But the markers lead the way. I was told only a few exact locations by my pa. But those are paycheck holes."

God bless his grandfather. Cotton knew what that meant. Of the caches that were buried, some were made known to those who guarded over them. Small amounts of gold and silver hidden as periodic payment for their services.

"We'd get instructions sent to us where to dig. Then we'd go and get us a little gold for ourselves," Morse said.

"You ever dig one up?" he asked.

The old man shook his head. "Never got the opportunity. No instructions ever came to me. But that jar you found today was mighty small. I'd say it was a paycheck hole, meant for my pa."

"So you've worked for free?" Cassiopeia asked.

"I guess so. I watch for people who get interested in certain spots, then I work to change their interest."

The knot on his forehead still hurt from that persuasion. "Has there been a lot of interest?"

"That's the funny thing. Nothin' for a long

151

time. A while back there were some books put out on the subject that brought in treasure hunters. Mostly amateurs. They came lookin' for the trees, diggin' for markers. But I scared 'em off. Then, a month ago, the one fellow came, then the group of fellows, then you. Been busy lately."

"There was a Smithsonian expedition here back in 1909. Did your father or grandfather ever mention it?"

Morse threw him a curious look. "That one was a big deal. My pa told me about it. Fellow died, I believe. Huntin' accident. That kind of stuff happened around here sometimes."

"Your pa ever kill anybody who got too close?"

Morse clearly did not like the question. "My uncle did. Two in fact. Shot 'em and buried 'em up in the hills."

"Which is murder."

"I guess it is, but what the crap does it matter anymore? My uncle and all the sentinels from back then are dead."

"It matters, Mr. Morse," Cassiopeia said. "Because it *was* murder."

"You ever kill anybody?" the older man asked her.

"I have."

"I bet you have, too," Morse said to Cotton. He nodded.

"I would imagine you had a reason. They

did, too. That gold didn't belong to those people searchin' for it."

Cotton decided that this debate would lead nowhere so he changed tack. "You never learned to read the markers in the woods?"

Morse shook his head. "Never had to. Not my job. You seem to know a lot about us. You sure you ain't a knight?"

He actually could have been. His grandfather had told him a lot about the Order and how they hid their loot. So-called hoot owl trees, like he'd seen earlier, either purposefully bent or unusual looking, mainly three or more in a straight line, there to tag the site from a distance. Or trees planted in rows, sometimes with one missing, that spot most likely where a hoard lay buried. Other trees were trimmed in unnatural patterns, like the goalposts today, or into T's or cross-shaped, molded for years from saplings. A few had knobs knitted into their trunks, or gauges down the bark. To make sure magnetism survived as long as possible, large ferrous objects like stoves, wash pots, milk cans, strongboxes, and plows were buried. More markers included diamond-shaped clusters of stones, holes drilled into rocks, and cryptic carvings, each an indicator of direction and distance, referring either to compass headings, topographic features, or a linear geometric grid.

There'd been a logic to it all. A silent

language spoken by only a precious few — which, as Morse noted, had not included sentinels. Thankfully his grandfather had learned some of it, which made him wonder. Had he been a sentinel, too?

"I found that cache today thanks to what I know personally and notes made back in 1909," Cotton said. "The guy who died in the hunting accident" — his sarcasm was clear — "his notes survived. Whoever killed him missed those. Granted, it's taken over a hundred years to make use of them, but we made it back. That guy a month ago you scared off? He came to do what I did today."

He'd always thought it all just stories. A way for a grandfather to entertain a grandson. Not anymore. Not since he'd found a jar of Confederate gold and met a real, live, third-generation sentinel.

"Follow me," Morse finally said.

They stepped from the porch and rounded the house, heading for one of the outbuildings. Three stood in the nearly gone daylight, all made of notched logs. He heard a steady, low purr in the quiet air.

"What's that? Machinery?"

A derisive cackle burst from Morse's mouth. "Bees."

Morse opened a nail-studded door and switched on the lights. The persistent murmur inside was much louder, the air clotted with a sweet smell. About a dozen wooden boxes sat on stout tables, each one humming like a transformer. A long wooden workbench ran the length of one wall, its scarred surface littered with tools and a vise.

"The bees stay in here for safety," Morse said. "Keeps the rustlers away."

"People steal them?" Cassiopeia asked.

"All the time. I rent these out to farmers so they can get their fruit trees pollinated. Rustlers steal 'em, then rent 'em out themsleves. No way to brand a bee. No way to prove it's yours. So you lose 'em. It's a big problem."

Cotton noticed slits in the walls overhead that allowed the insects to come and go.

"Those men who came to see me," Morse said. "They were after somethin' special. Somehow they knew that I was the one guardin'. The fellow who came a month ago didn't seem to know much about it. He never asked the right questions in town."

"How did you learn about us?" Cassiopeia asked.

"Friend at the lodge where you're stayin'. He calls and tells me about any treasure hunters. You were askin' around about things and it caught his ear. It's what we do for each other around here."

Which was the same in middle Georgia.

If the stories he'd heard were true, it meant that the Knights of the Golden Circle had accumulated an enormous amount of gold and silver. Some had been legitimately earned, while other parts most likely came from the Confederate treasury, which some said was found in 1865, but others believed it had been hoarded away. Nobody knew anything for sure. History also noted that three U.S. mints were looted in the early days of the Civil War of their gold and coin reserves. Much more wealth was simply appropriated during and after the war, stolen from banks, companies, and individuals. A ton of lost-treasure stories existed across every Southern state, the version different depending on the locale. Book after book had been written on the subject. The only consistent element to it all was that the knights did in fact hide their wealth in the ground, which explained why treasure hunters had been searching for so long.

"My pa told me we were extra special," Morse said. "We guarded somethin' real important. Sure, there's gold hidden in our stake. You found some of it today. There's more out there, too. But the real important thing we protected wasn't metal."

Morse approached one of the tables with hives and bent down beneath to a shelf. Something lay sheathed in a dirty green canvas. About two feet long, nearly that wide. And apparently heavy, as Morse strained to slide it free of the shelf and lay it on the table between the hives. Removing the canvas revealed a stone, about three inches thick, with carvings.

"It's the Witch's Stone," Morse said. "Or at least that's what my pa called it."

Cotton was fluent in several languages, another benefit of an eidetic memory, so he was able to translate the Spanish. The top line read, *Esta bereda es peligroza*. This *bereda* is dangerous? The word *bereda* meant nothing to him. But *vereda* meant "path."

This path is dangerous?

The second line, *yo boy 18 lugares,* I go 18 places. Again *boy* was not a word in Spanish, but *voy,* to, seemed to fit and was consistent with the *b* for *v* from the first line.

I go to 18 places.

The third line, *busca el mapa,* was easy.

Seek the map.

The same was true with the final line, *busca el coazon,* which had to be *busca el corazón.*

Seek the heart.

This path is dangerous. I go to 18 places. Seek the map. Seek the heart.

Cassiopeia snapped some pictures with her phone.

"I don't want you doin' that," Morse said.

"Then why show it to us?" Cotton asked.

Morse did not answer him.

The door creaked open.

Three men entered.

Each armed.

Cassiopeia reached for her weapon but the lead man cut her off with a shake of his index finger.

"Don't do that. You wouldn't want the girl hurt, would you? Toss the gun to the floor."

Cassiopeia glanced Cotton's way and he nodded that there was no choice. She released the weapon and one of the men quickly retrieved it.

"You got a gun?" the man asked him.

He found his Beretta and dropped it to the floor, too.

"Good work," the lead man said to Morse, and the old man acknowledged the compliment with a nod.

Lea seemed shocked.

But Cotton was pissed.

CHAPTER FIFTEEN

Washington, DC
8:50 P.M.

Stephanie Nelle stood beside Constitution Avenue, just outside the National Museum of Natural History. The call had come half an hour ago and she'd come straight over from the Mandarin Oriental, the hotel where she always stayed while visiting the capital.

The building that stood before her was part of the expansive Smithsonian Institution, which owned and operated museums on both sides of the National Mall. The American Indian, Air and Space, and the famous Romanesque Castle lined the south side, while natural, American, and African American history dominated the north. Together they formed the largest museum complex in the world. 140,000,000 objects. Every item regarded as a national treasure. Tonight, though, the natural history museum loomed quiet, closed to visitors.

She entered through street-side doors held

open by a security guard and was directed to a windowless room that contained a wall of LCD monitors, each displaying a different slice of the museum's interior. Six floors, over 1.5 million square feet of space. A lot of territory to watch over. Waiting for her was Rick Stamm, the current curator of the Smithsonian Castle, albeit a little out of his element here in natural history. They'd been friends a long time. Recently he'd helped her out in a pinch. She owed him one. So an hour ago, when he called, she could not tell him no.

"Lucky for you I was in town," she said.

"Yes, it was. I really appreciate your coming."

He pointed to one of the monitors where two men stood inside what looked like a library. "That's the Cullman Library. They've been there since before I called you."

She was familiar with the Smithsonian Libraries, comprising separate locations scattered across the twenty-one museums and research facilities. Together they were regarded as one of the greatest repositories of knowledge in the world. The Cullman was situated on the natural history museum's ground floor. She knew all about its collection of rare books on anthropology and natural sciences.

"The light-haired man is Martin Thomas," Rick said. "He's one of our reference librarians, with a spotless ten-year employment history. I'm told he's at the head of the list to succeed to the top spot when the current administrator of the American history library retires."

"Why is he in the Cullman at this hour?" she asked. "That place has nothing to do with American history."

He shook his head. "We don't have audio. The guy arrived and Martin took him straight there."

The other man on the monitor was tall and muscular, with a thick head of tight brown curls. He fidgeted a lot, his hands constantly groping for something to occupy them. He stood with his back to the camera, offering no view at his face. He wore a dark sport coat, slacks, and an open-collared button-down shirt.

"What's that on the back of his neck?" she asked.

They both stared closely at the screen.

"Looks like a port wine stain," Rick noted. "A good-sized one, too."

She wanted to know, "Why is all this a problem? I assume staff comes in a lot at night."

"Martin has been working with us on a special project. The problem is he never reported to us that he was coming here tonight. We're supposed to be on the same team. Yet we had no idea, until he showed up with this man. Security caught it and called

161

me. I decided to call you."

"You going to tell me why?"

Two other security guards sat in the dark room, working the monitors, and she caught her friend's gaze that indicated this was not the time or the place. But he did offer, "One problem is they came in through the staff entrance."

Which probably meant no metal detectors and little security.

"You have no idea who that other man is, or what he's doing here?"

Rick shook his head.

"You have a security force and the police."

"I prefer you."

She got the message.

Payback could sometimes be a pain in the ass.

He gestured for them to walk outside into the corridor. There he quickly explained that it had all started a few months before when some confidential records, not available for general inspection without administrative approval, were violated in the museum archives.

"I didn't realize the Smithsonian had a secret archive," she said.

"We don't. It's just that some materials are held in trust, not for general inspection."

Video surveillance had quickly targeted Martin Thomas. When confronted, he'd confessed that a member of the library's citizen advisory board, the wife of a Smithsonian regent, a woman named Diane Sherwood, had requested he examine the information.

"Senator Sherwood's widow?" she asked.

He nodded. "That's right."

She was beginning to appreciate the delicacy of the situation.

Aiming to please, Thomas had accommodated Mrs. Sherwood. Interestingly, instead of confronting either offender, or shutting off access, Rick told her that further views into the confidential files had been allowed.

"We thought, what better way to find out what was going on than to allow her to show us the way. Martin was, by then, working with us, so we let it ride."

"What happened?"

"Something we didn't expect. Martin flew to Arkansas, returned rattled and scared, reporting on a threat to his life. That's when we called Cotton Malone."

That shocked her. "How do you know Cotton?"

"I didn't. But the chancellor knew about him and had me make some inquiries. I found out he once worked for you, but is now retired. So we called him at his Copenhagen bookstore and hired him."

"Cotton is here? Working with you?"

"Actually he's in Arkansas with a Ms. Vitt,

going behind Martin Thomas to see what's there."

Usually it was the other way around, with her calling Cotton and either corralling or hiring him. He'd been her first recruit at the Magellan Billet and worked for her a dozen years before opting out early and moving to Denmark. At the moment all twelve of her current agents were either on assignment or busy helping her restart the Magellan Billet after its recent temporary shutdown by the new president and attorney general. She'd come to DC to meet with the new AG, trying to forge some sort of working relationship with someone who had no desire to work with her.

"Rick, it seems you have quite a mess. But you also have Cotton and Cassiopeia on this. They're really good. So why am I here?"

"We're going to take this new guy and Martin Thomas down. I need your assistance with that. Then I want you to help me find out what's going on. This kind of thing is a little out of my area of expertise."

The door to the security room opened and one of the technicians told them that the two men were on the move. They rushed back inside and watched the screen as the two left the library. Thomas was talking and gesturing toward the visitor, who still kept his back to them.

"He knows there are cameras," she said.

"I see that."

Thomas left through the exit doors. His guest followed. But as the man turned for the door his jacket swept open for an instant. He quickly caught it and rebuttoned it, but not before the lens captured a disturbing sight.

"Go back and replay that," Rick said.

She'd seen it, too.

One of the men working the monitors typed on his keyboard. A frozen image appeared on one of the screens. Where the jacket gaped open the metallic butt end of a pistol could be seen in a shoulder harness.

"That's not good," she said. "You need to stop this now."

"I have to see what they're after."

"You could be putting that librarian's life in danger." She could see his dilemma. "And you're still not telling me everything, are you?"

"Will you trust me on this a little longer?"

That went without question. She'd known this man a long time.

On the monitor the two men left the Cullman Library and the lights extinguished. Another camera captured them in the hallway, walking down the corridors, finally entering a set of metal doors.

"That opens into a closed-off area that's under construction," Rick said.

She knew what had to be done.

"Tell me how to get there, undetected."

■ ■ ■ ■

She eased the metal door shut without a sound. A small radio was clipped to her waist, an ear fob and lapel mic providing her with hands-free communications.

"They're still there," Rick said in her ear. "Walk straight ahead and take the first right."

She stood in a dim corridor, only occasional lights illuminating the cavernous space around her. Shadows hung thick but she could see the construction. Rick had told her that this part of the museum had once been used as a storage basement, though it actually sat at ground level. It had been closed for over a year, undergoing a renovation to add additional office space. Her entry point had been on the far side, away from where the two men had entered, the idea being to allow her to weave a path close and find out more about what was going on before they took anyone into custody. Security guards were waiting for her signal, posted at all the exit doors.

There was nowhere for anyone to run.

No working cameras existed inside the work site. Barricades prevented anyone from wandering into the area, but her two targets had ignored those. It seemed that whatever they were after must be here. She was concerned about the situation but assumed Martin Thomas was in no real danger since the other man was here for a reason and apparently needed Thomas to accomplish that.

Or at least that's what she kept telling herself.

Carefully she wove her way through the maze of wires, pipes, ducts, and machinery to where Rick had told her to turn. She could hear the two men talking, their voices echoing thanks to the unfinished walls. Perhaps they'd come to this part of the building to further avoid the cameras? The presence of the gun, though, still hung in her mind. Thankfully she, too, was armed, her Magellan Billet–issued Beretta snug in a shoulder harness beneath her jacket. There was a time when she hadn't carried a weapon. But she'd learned that it was better to be safe than sorry.

It should have been easy to keep her steps silent on the concrete floor, but a layer of sawdust, drywall shavings, and dirt challenged her footing. She marveled at how resilient places like this could be. This building had stood since 1910, remodeled over and over, each time adapting to an ever-changing world.

She closed the gap to the voices, finally stopping at a corner with bare Sheetrock walls.

"— appreciate what you've done. I truly do," a male voice said.

"I've worked here a long time, but I have to

167

tell you, the pay is not why you stay," another voice said, which she assumed was Thomas.

"Those gold pieces I gave you should come in handy. Here's three more for your trouble tonight."

She heard the clink of metal.

"These are really rare," Thomas said. "I've been looking into all this. You're after more gold, aren't you?"

A few seconds of silence passed.

"I can help you," Thomas said.

"What is it exactly you want?"

"Part of the lost Confederate treasure you're after."

CHAPTER SIXTEEN

Grant appraised Martin Thomas. Perhaps he'd underestimated this librarian. Diane had assured him that the man would be fully co-operative, enamored by the fact that she was the wife of a U.S. senator and a Smithsonian regent. And so far Thomas had been nothing but compliant, accessing the right records, providing needed information, even going to Arkansas to investigate things firsthand.

That had been important. Sentinels were still out there. Where? Nobody knew for sure. Only bits and pieces of the Order's records had survived, though enough for Diane to learn that the Witch's Stone might be under the care of a man named Terry Morse, whose family had longtime ties to the knights. So she'd suggested to Thomas that he have a look, which the librarian had done. They'd thought that a trip by someone from the Smithsonian might open doors that would have otherwise remained closed, but that had not been the case. They did learn, however, that a sentinel was still there.

The warning with the hanging effigy, the bullets, and the string was an old Order ploy. It rattled Thomas enough that he fled the state without finding much of anything. They'd wanted him to follow the leads from the 1909 expedition to see if a gold cache could be located. But Terry Morse seemed to still take his job seriously. So professionals had been hired, told to use loyalty to its maximum effect, convincing Morse they were of the Order. Seemed like a smart play, and he was hoping that he'd soon receive a phone call that the Witch's Stone had been found. Right now his problem was the mousy little annoyance standing before him.

And those three words he'd just heard.

"Lost Confederate treasure."

"What is it you think you know?" he asked Thomas.

"I've been studying all of this in great detail. The Smithsonian archives have a lot of information on this subject. Millions of dollars in gold and silver disappeared after the Civil War. Nobody has any idea how much." Thomas displayed the three pieces he'd given him. "Much of it like these coins. A strange way to pay someone, wouldn't you say?"

"I thought you might appreciate the historical aspects."

Thomas chuckled. "I do. More than you realize. From what I've already read, it looks

170

as though the Smithsonian itself figures prominently in finding the treasure you're after. They did a lot of work on this back in 1909, then again in the 1970s."

"Really? Concerning what?"

"Oh, I get it. This is a test. To see how much I really know. Okay. I have five words for you. Knights. Of. The. Golden. Circle."

"And just how much do you know about that?"

"Enough to write a book. Which I plan to do. It's going to sell a lot of copies."

Diane should have known better than to trust this opportunist. But if all went well tonight, they would not have any further need of Martin Thomas. All they required from him at the moment was a little covert access to the buildings. The plan had been to pay him off, then cut him off. According to her, he would be an easy matter to handle.

Now this.

"You have been busy," he said.

"I've spent many hours reading. It's quite a story."

He'd heard enough.

"All right. I'll cut you in."

Stephanie listened in amazement. Martin Thomas hadn't reported the visit tonight because he didn't want anyone to know. He was making his own deal and, for some inexplicable reason, thought he could sneak

171

in unnoticed, except by the night security detail who wouldn't pay him much attention. Surely staff worked all the time after hours. It was nothing unusual, and Rick had told her that they were allowed to bring people into the building.

She wondered about Thomas' declaration on writing a book about lost Confederate treasure. And what was the Knights of the Golden Circle?

"I tell you what," the other man said. "Let's get to the Castle, do what I have to do, then come back. I need to take a look at something else, back over here, before I leave. After that, we'll discuss your share."

She debated whether to act now since a deal like that never, ever worked out well for the recipient.

"Why are we going to the Castle?" Thomas asked. "And what is it you need to see here?"

"I'll explain as we walk."

Apparently Thomas did not know either objective and, if she moved now, neither would Rick.

So she stayed put.

"The hatch is there," Thomas said. "I've never been down it before."

Footsteps scuffled across the dirty concrete. Then she heard the squeak of hinges and the clang of banging metal.

"What's happening?" Rick asked in her ear.

"I don't know," she whispered. "They seem

to be leaving."

"There's no way out, except past you. All of the other exit doors are sealed for the construction."

She stood still and listened, hearing only silence.

Finally, she risked a look.

The space beyond was maybe fifty feet square. Two of the interior walls were half built with exposed conduits and wires, the ceiling bare concrete from the floor above. The room nestled against the museum's exterior wall, facing the Mall side, a line of transom windows dark to the night. The only light came from two incandescent fixtures. Near the exterior she spotted the source of the noise earlier.

An open iron door in the floor.

She crept closer.

No one was in sight.

She spotted a metal ladder that stretched down a few feet into the ground. Insulated pipes, ducts, and wires were visible, as was light at the bottom from another opening into the earth.

"They crawled down to a tunnel," she whispered to Rick.

"It leads across, under the Mall, to the Castle," he said in her ear. "It's mainly for heating and cooling pipes that go back and forth. It's hardly an exit, but it can be walked."

There seemed to be no choice. "I'm going after them."

"That tunnel is full of creatures. We go in there only if we have to. Besides, we can be there on the other end, when they come out."

"I thought you wanted to know what they were after."

"I do."

Her psyche screamed that this was a job for one of her agents. But there were none around. And Thomas was leading that man to something. Time to do what she always told her own people to do.

Suck it up and get the job done.

She tucked the gun away and eased herself down the ladder.

Grant admired the tunnel. He knew all of its particulars. 730 feet long, 4 feet wide, 5.5 feet high. Built in 1909, its concrete interior had been sloped and troweled to a smooth surface. Waterproofing had not seemed a priority, the walls and floor pregnant with age and damp, the confines tight. Definitely not for claustrophobics, but he'd never been prone to such weakness. Lights shone every twenty feet. Without them you probably would not be able to see your finger touch your nose, and there'd be a real threat from rats. He'd heard the stories as a kid of how the maintenance people would go on hunts, and he'd even once ventured a little way in

174

from the Castle entrance, where they were now headed. That was the one good thing about growing up as the child of a Smithsonian curator.

Lots of cool perks.

Of course, Martin Thomas knew none of this. To this reference librarian he was simply a friend of Diane Sherwood's who paid in gold. How many coins so far? At least ten, not counting the expense money for the trip to Arkansas. He wondered how Diane would react to Thomas' blackmail attempt. Knowing her, she probably would say to give him what he wanted. There was plenty for all. But just the thought of such a sellout turned his stomach. He'd found this payday on his own and had no intention of allowing a newcomer to dilute the prize.

"How did you know about the tunnel?" Thomas asked him, leading the way. "That's not something many know exist."

"My father once worked here."

"You've never mentioned that. But that explains why you know so much about the Smithsonian."

He estimated they were at least three hundred feet into the passage. Plenty of privacy.

No more talk.

He withdrew his gun.

And fired.

■ ■ ■

Stephanie worked her way through the tunnel, not all that pleased with its confines or smell. Definitely things were dead down here. The air bordered on acrid hot, and sweat was forming across her brow. A tangle of wires and pipes made the journey back and forth between the Castle and the natural history museum. She was careful not to touch any of them.

A loud bang rattled her ears.

She stopped.

A bend in the path ahead kept the two men out of sight. The route was lit with bulbs enclosed in metal cages, more thick pipes and wires disappearing into the distance.

"Can you hear me?" she whispered into the lapel mike, using one hand to cup her mouth and keep her voice down.

No reply.

Which she'd expected, being sealed underground within concrete.

Her ears rang from the loud noise. She checked her gun and continued moving, not sure what to expect. How far was it across the Mall? Several hundred feet, at least.

She came to the bend and peered around. A hundred feet away lay a body. She rushed forward and found Martin Thomas lying facedown. Blood oozed from a hole in the back of his head. No need to check for a pulse. He was dead.

Dammit.

She'd pressed too far, believing Thomas' best insurance was the fact that the other man needed him.

But apparently that was not the case.

In the distance she heard a metal bolt release, followed by a clank.

Like a gate closing.

Then the lights extinguished and absolute darkness engulfed her. For an instant she panicked, then grabbed hold of herself, not moving. She could feel Thomas' body beside her, but could not see him. Nor could she see any of the pipes or wires, especially the bulky and sharp-collared brackets she'd noticed that held things together every few feet. Then there were the local residents, who surely loved the dark. Her mind started clicking off options. She could use her phone for light, but that might reveal her presence to the shooter, who could still be lurking. All of the mechanical equipment for the tunnel had been confined to one side, so she could feel her way back to natural history, using the clear side as a guide.

The lights came back on.

She blinked away the burning as her pupils adjusted.

A noise disturbed the silence.

Echoes made it hard to know from which

direction.

Ahead? Or behind?

She pointed the Beretta, readying herself.

Someone was coming her way.

But from where?

CHAPTER SEVENTEEN

Cassiopeia watched the three men as they assumed positions around the room. Not with any purpose or plan, just here and there, none of them all that attentive. Which told her these guys were amateurs. Hired help. But they'd managed to use Terry Morse to lure her and Cotton into their clutches, so she had to give them credit for effort.

"You know these people?" Lea asked her grandfather.

"They're knights."

Cassiopeia heard the pride.

"No, they're not," Cotton said, who'd apparently come to the same "hired help" conclusion.

One of the men signaled to a compatriot to snap a few cell phone photos of the stone. The one giving the orders was squat, heavily built, with a squashed nose, gap-toothed mouth and a thick mat of black hair.

"That what you came for?" Cotton asked.

"Absolutely. But you two kind of changed things."

Nothing about this seemed okay. And the fact that Lea was in the middle concerned her even more. Terry Morse had not a clue who or what he was dealing with.

The man finished taking his pictures. She concluded that getting their hands on all the cell phones in the room might be the quickest route to where this led.

"I did what you wanted," Morse said. "I got 'em here."

"Yes, you did," Black Hair said. "Good work. So tell me, why are you two here?"

Cotton shrugged. "Never visited this part of the country, so we thought a trip would be fun."

The leader chuckled. "We got ourselves a comedian."

"I'll be doing two shows a night at the lodge where we're staying. I can get you tickets."

"I heard you talking in the house," Black Hair said. "What are two federal agents doing here?"

Cotton smiled. "We're with the Census Bureau, just gathering some information."

Black Hair lunged to his right, grabbed Lea, and jammed his gun into the side of her neck. Shock flooded the young girl's eyes.

"Get your damn hands off my granddaughter," Morse yelled.

"Shut up, old man."

Morse leaped forward. "Who the hell you callin' old."

But one of the other men cut him off, slamming the butt of his pistol into Morse's left temple, sending him to the floor, groaning.

Lea gasped.

Cotton held up his hands in mock surrender. "No need for that. We can work this through."

"Then answer my question."

The gun on Lea remained unchanged.

Cassiopeia decided to go with the truth. "Like you heard, we're federal agents, here investigating on behalf of the U.S. government. And you're in a lot of trouble."

"That still doesn't answer my question."

Morse tried to stand, his head clearly woozy, but the man beside him returned him to the floor with a shove. The bees maintained a steady hum, not all that concerned with their presence.

Cassiopeia could imagine what had happened. These men appeared, provided the supposed handshake, used the right words, then talked of the Order and the past. She hardly knew Terry Morse, who seemed like a decent person, the one constant in his life the duty his father had passed down. Sure, it bordered on ridiculous, but it was still something tangible that provided him a sense of belonging. At times, she'd wrestled with her own past, trying to decide exactly where she belonged, and those demons had proven formidable. Luckily, she'd had Cotton there to help. Morse seemed to be on his own, except for Lea.

"I'm not going to ask again," Black Hair said. "Why are you here?"

The gun remained tight to Lea's neck. She stared into the girl's eyes and surprisingly saw more resolve than fear.

Lea had guts.

Like her granddaddy.

"We came for that stone, too," Cotton said, pointing.

A lie, but it seemed like a plausible explanation. In fact, she firmly believed that it was the right answer to the question.

"Who sent you?"

"The Smithsonian."

She watched them all carefully, then caught Cotton's gaze, a current of complicity passing between them, his green eyes crinkling assent. It was as if they could read each other's minds and she knew what he wanted done. An old trick, for sure, but one that nearly always worked. So she blurted out, "I don't want anyone to get hurt."

Black Hair swung around and faced her, keeping hold of Lea.

"I'll tell you what you want to know," she said to him.

She stood near one of the hives, a three-foot-tall rectangle slotted with openings. The boxes were made of thin wood and would not survive much jostling.

"I'm no hero," she said. "Just a paid employee. I can tell you all about why we're here."

"I like your attitude," Black Hair said, and he shoved Lea away, aiming the gun directly at Cassiopeia. "Let's hear it."

"I talk better without a gun aimed at me."

Not a hint of concern laced her voice, which the fool listening to her should have noticed.

But he didn't.

Cotton used the moment of distraction to inch his way closer to the tables.

The gun slowly lowered.

Cotton's leg swung up, the sole of his right boot slamming into one of the hives. She took his cue and thrust both of her elbows backward, sending two more of the fragile boxes to the floor. The paper-thin wood shattered, the tops on all three flying off, the honey frames spewing across the floor. The bees, crushed together and stunned for a moment, crawled about in a great furry brown blob, then took to the air.

The humming grew louder.

As did the insects' agitation.

She knew a little about bees. They'd swarm and aggravate, though they wouldn't sting unless threatened. But the three men didn't help matters by vainly swatting at the marauders with their guns.

The first sting came on the intruder to her left, who shrieked in pain. She stiff-armed him hard against the wall, his head slapping the thick wood with a thump. He slumped, feet skidding on the earthen floor, hands clawing for support, fingers caught on the edge of one of the hive tables. Instead of supporting, the table tipped over, more boxes crashing open, releasing a new cloud of bees. She noticed that Lea had immediately hit the floor, lying prone beside her grandfather.

She still wanted that cell phone the one guy had used to snap pictures and darted that way, bees everywhere. She knew once they decided to attack they would not discriminate between friend and foe. The three men staggered for the door, slapping their faces, necks, ears, and scalps.

"Get down," Lea yelled. "Lie still."

Cassiopeia dropped to the floor, beside the Morses.

Two of the men fled.

Cotton cut off Black Hair before he could escape. The hand with the gun swung around. Black Hair feinted right, then swung from the left, delivering only a glancing blow, lunging through the bees. Cotton brought his right elbow up with a sharp thrust to the throat. He then wrenched the gun arm down and over his hip, using his weight, twisting and flipping the man in a somersault to the floor.

The gun jarred free.

But Black Hair was quick, rolling through his fall, then rebounding to his feet and bursting out the door.

The bees, now fully stimulated, seemed to have decided that everyone was a threat. A few began to land and she brushed them away. Lea and Morse started crawling to the door.

She followed.

Cotton retrieved the gun and moved for the exit, too.

Shots rang out.

Bullets came through the open doorway, thudding into the walls beyond.

"Stay down," Cotton yelled.

The bees were becoming an ever-denser shadow. She swiped a few away as carefully as possible, trying not to make matters worse. Cotton belly-crawled to the doorway. She heard the drone of a car engine, then the scrunch of tires on loose dirt.

"They're gone," Cotton said. "Let's get out of here."

And they did, rushing away toward the house.

"That didn't go well," she said to Cotton. "Should we go after them?"

He shook his head. "They're not our problem."

She agreed.

"I really screwed up," Terry Morse said, his voice shaking.

And she could not argue with that conclusion.

Cotton seemed to grab his breath. "Listen good," he said to Morse, the voice hard. "You've only got one more chance to make this right. If not, then you're both going to need a real good lawyer to stay out of prison."

CHAPTER EIGHTEEN

Danny drove across Blount County, navigating roads he'd known since childhood. The windshield wipers ticked a slow, symmetrical beat, keeping the view ahead clear. So much had changed, some of the county nearly unrecognizable, a lot like his own life. He'd risen to what many regarded as the highest office on earth, and now his career was over. Yet he was barely eligible for Social Security and mentally he felt like a man of fifty. There was so much more he could do. But how? Nobody gave a damn about an ex-president. Courtesy demanded that he never criticize either his successors or Congress. Something about *preserving the integrity of the office.* So if history was any judge all he would do was write his memoirs, build a library, adopt some charitable cause, then charge a god-awful fee to people who wanted him to come and impart upon them his accumulated wisdom. In short, a slow, painful fade to oblivion.

And what wisdom would he charge those people to hear? He was just an east Tennessee boy who'd had a knack for politics. Campaigning ran in his blood. No one had ever defeated him at the polls. His two runs for president had been landslide wins in both the popular and the electoral vote. He'd miss campaigning. He loved connecting with voters. He'd always been a straight shooter, staring the public square in the eye and saying what he meant. Sure, that had gotten him into trouble over the years, but it had also forged him a reputation. He'd been called a lot of things. Stubborn. Arrogant. Overbearing. Even a bastard once by a fool congressman. But never had he been labeled a hypocrite or a liar. His friends loved him and his enemies feared him, which was precisely how he liked things.

Only two failures haunted him.

That night in the fire with Mary, and his inability to make Pauline happy.

And both were irretrievable.

The time was approaching 9:00 P.M. The woods around him towered as a thick mass of impenetrable shadow. He'd encountered no one on the highway, which was not unusual for rural Blount County at night. He eased up and stopped at the intersection with the route to the Sherwood place. A pair of headlights to his right signaled an approaching car, which sped through the junction, headed in the direction he was about to take.

The vehicle caught his attention.

A black Lincoln sedan.

Cars were his thing. He loved them. Always had. While in the White House he'd maintained subscriptions to *Hot Rod, Car and Driver, Road & Track,* and several other auto magazines. They'd been his escape from the job. And if in the coming years he could swing a few special invites to some antique-car shows — now, that would not be so bad.

He turned and drove toward his destination.

The notebook lay on the passenger seat. Explaining to Diane why he'd stolen it was not going to be easy, but he'd cautioned Taisley that her secret may have to be revealed. A part of him wanted to tell Diane the truth just to wipe all the smugness from her face. She'd seemed to have enjoyed digging into him about his own divorce. But that would mean truly hurting her, and no matter how he might feel about her personally, that was not his style.

It seemed really odd tooling around by himself, on a dark highway. The only place he'd been alone for the past eight years was his bedroom at the White House. That had been his sanctuary, breached only by his chief of staff. Pauline had adhered to tradition and kept her own room down the hall. Presidents and First Ladies rarely slept together, their

189

schedules so different and rest so needed that separate accommodations had proved a necessity. There'd been exceptions, but life in the White House was not conducive to sound marital relations. The Former Presidents Act gave him a pension, an office allowance, health care, and bodyguards for life. He'd kept the pension — splitting it with Pauline, God knows she'd earned it — and the health care, then declined the rest. If somebody wanted to kill him, bring it on. But he doubted that anyone really gave a damn about ex-president Danny Daniels. It would be like going to the trouble of shooting a piece of roadkill.

He approached the driveway for the Sherwood residence. Through the trees he noticed that lights still burned inside. Floodlights washed the front and sides, burning through the steady mist. Surely the wake was not still happening? One car was parked in front along the circular drive, a Lincoln sedan like the one he'd just seen. He eased his own car into a long driveway across the highway and doused the headlights, buying himself a few moments to think about what to do.

He hadn't expected Diane to still have visitors.

So this would have to wait.

He reached for the gearshift, intent on backing out and heading home. He'd deal with this tomorrow. But another set of headlights caused him to pause. They came from his left and he watched in the rearview mirror as a second sedan turned into the Sherwood driveway. Rain transformed the back windshield into a watery kaleidoscope of blurred images. So he lowered the driver's-side window and stuck his head out, able to see through the trees as the car rounded to the front and stopped. The rear door opened and a man stepped out, the silhouette distinctive — the face clear in the front-porch lights.

Lucius Vance.

What was the Speaker of the House of Representatives doing here at this hour?

Two other men emerged from the car.

Secret Service.

The Speaker of the House, like the president and vice president, had long been afforded protection. They'd been at Vance's side earlier at the funeral. One of the agents entered the house with Vance, the other stayed outside with the car.

Alex and Lucius Vance had never been friends. One was of the House, the other the Senate. And though the two bodies were, in theory, equals, everyone knew that wasn't the case. One senator possessed as much raw political power as the Speaker himself. No Speaker liked to acknowledge that, but it was true. So no senators gave a rat's ass what the Speaker of the House thought of them. And he certainly knew of no connection between

191

Vance and Diane.

So what was Vance doing here?

Years ago, when he first sat on the Maryville city council, a constituent complained about how some employees with the city road department were not working a full day. Instead, they'd take their truck out into the woods, where they'd smoke and drink beer for at least a couple of hours. That post had been his first experience in public office and he'd wanted to make a good impression, so one day he hid himself in the woods and waited. Sure enough, as advertised, those employees came, smoked their cigarettes, and drank their beer. He'd brought a camera and snapped a few choice shots. What really shocked him was that their supervisor was there with them, a man he'd managed to get hired as a favor to another supporter. It would have been easy to have them all fired, but instead he just stepped out, popped open one of their beers, and had a chat about what wasn't going to happen anymore. After that, they were the best workers the city ever had, and forever grateful to Councilman Danny Daniels.

Try to make a point and a friend.

That was his motto.

He doubted Lucius Vance would ever be a friend, but he could make a point. So he left the notebook in the car and stepped out into the rain. He crossed the street and avoided

192

the two entrances for the rounded drive. The house sat about twenty yards off the highway, among trees and underbrush. Alex used to complain how much trouble it was to keep the green stuff out of the brown.

Ten yards beyond the Sherwood mailbox he left the roadway. If he recalled, the trail should be no more than a few yards in. He knew this path. It led up a ridge toward the rear of the property, where the Little River cut a swath across the county. Somewhere up there his old friend had fallen to his death. Alex used to call the woods his office, a place away from the scrutiny of the public and press, where he could smoke his pipe and do his best thinking. Presidents had a spot like that, too. Camp David.

As a kid and teenager Danny had spent many a night in the Smoky Mountains. His father had been a devoted hunter, his mother born and raised in Appalachia. He liked the sodden, gloomy world of a dark forest, the air pungent with the waft of damp earth. He'd learned a long time ago not to be afraid — instead to be aware. That advice had also served him faithfully in politics.

He found the trail, his coat wet from the underbrush, and curbed his pace to a slow walk. Pine needles underfoot cushioned each step as he slowly worked up the incline toward the rear of the Sherwood house. It wasn't all that difficult to make out the twisting, turning track in the surrounding gloom. Thankfully, his night vision had survived the years of public service.

A gentle breeze soughed among the trees, the river could be heard in the distance. A dog barked and the mountains caught the sound and threw it back with an echo. Crickets pulsated, but more under than over the other sounds. In the White House he'd loved the night's solitude, his early-morning phone calls to sleepy aides legendary. He spotted the house's interior lights through the trees and hoped the wall of glass in the great room had been left unsheathed. That would not be unusual, considering there was nothing but woods for miles.

He came to a point where he thought his view would be unobstructed and plunged into a mass of ferns. There he edged forward, careful with his steps, aware of his vulnerability. He was mindful, too, of the security detail, who might decide to check out the rear of the property. Luckily the foliage, though wet, seemed moderate. It was an easy matter to make it to the trunk of a thick pine, where he could clearly see the rear deck. This was nuts, but he couldn't help himself. As with those workers all those years ago, something drove him forward. A need to solve a problem. But he was not a city councilman. He was a former president of the United States.

194

And for the first time in a month he actually felt alive.

Rain fell in more of a mist than a drizzle, the spring foliage overhead keeping most of it off him. His hopes were raised when he saw that the rear glass doors and windows were unobstructed by drapes or shutters. He could see straight into the great room and counted three people.

Diane.

Vance.

And one other man. Middle-aged, dark-haired, mustache, dressed in a suit but no tie. The face was not familiar. He could hear nothing, but he watched as they each took a seat, drinks in hand. Every political alarm inside his head screamed *Trouble*. Not a single reasonable explanation for this gathering occurred to him. Still, he told himself to be calm. All his life he'd thought like a person surrounded by enemies. *Justifiable paranoia*, he called it. But that fear had kept him sharp. And there was no denying that a clear sense of menace hung in this wet air.

Along with a jumble of unanswered questions.

CHAPTER NINETEEN

Stephanie stared down the tunnel in both directions, her head whipping back and forth, the gun following her gaze. Someone rounded the bend from the natural history side and headed her way.

Rick Stamm.

She relaxed.

"We lost you on the radio," he whispered, approaching close. "Oh, no," he said, seeing Thomas' body. "It can't be."

She saw the panic in his eyes.

"This is awful," he said.

"You have to forget it for right now. He's dead. We have to deal with the shooter."

He nodded, took a moment, gathered himself, then they stepped over the body. He led her down the tunnel at a brisk pace until they found an unlocked iron grate at the far end. He opened the portal and they walked through into a lit space. The block walls here were all whitewashed, the ceiling lined with pipes, ducts, and wires, the floor a polished tile.

"We're below the Castle," he whispered. "In the basement. My office is right over here."

He led her into a room cluttered with display cabinets, bookshelves, and a desk stacked with files and paper. The décor consisted of artifacts that clearly had come from the Smithsonian collections, the walls dotted with historic paintings and pictures, most of the Castle.

"Are there cameras in this building?" she asked in a low voice.

"Only a few on the ground floor, in the main hall, where the public goes. This is generally an admin building. There's not much of value to worry with security."

"So what's this guy doing here?"

"I truly don't know."

She could see he was upset over Martin Thomas. But she was as much to blame as him. "Maybe we should alert security as to what's happening."

"Not yet."

That answer came too quick.

"Why not?"

"You can handle this, right? This is what you do."

"It's actually what my agents do."

"I called you because I need your expertise. Let's find the guy and see what he's after."

"Without security?"

He seemed to steel himself. "For the moment. Can you do it?"

"I can handle it."

His attention was suddenly diverted and he darted toward one of the exterior walls where a metal panel hung ajar. He swung it open to reveal a spiral staircase that wound a path upward inside the confines of rough brick.

"I keep this door closed at all times," he said. "He must have gone up through here. This guy definitely knows his way around."

Grant climbed the spiral stairs. Nine towers were the Castle's trademark. They were built primarily to hold staircases like this one, and later elevators, but eventually they came to house offices, laboratories, and storage. A few even served as sleeping quarters for 19th-century interns. One once held an aviary for falcons, and the tall north tower had served as an observation perch during the Civil War. The most famous residents were owls, who came uninvited, keeping the National Mall clear of swallows. When those squatters disappeared, two similar birds from the National Zoo were relocated. But eventually they flew away, too.

He knew all about the stairway he was climbing, put here so scientists could get from their labs above down to the wet collections storage area below. The door he'd entered through in the curator's office was sealed shut back in the 1970s, reopened in the early 1990s. He was there the day his father cracked the seal.

He stopped his corkscrew ascent and eased open a wooden door on the Castle's second floor, in what would have long ago been the original picture gallery. The great fire of 1865 had started right here. Now it was a dimly lit space, part of the administrative areas that dominated the second floor, off limits to the general public. As best he could recall, this floor was a maze of nooks and crannies, all from decades of haphazard remodeling. Though the outside remained inviolate, the Castle's inside was nothing like the original.

He hustled through the former picture gallery and came to a long, narrow corridor. Paintings and sculptures graced the walls. Carpet lined the floor. Display cases stood full of objects. Offices lined either side. Originally the second floor had accommodated an enormous two-tiered lecture hall, an apparatus museum, and a picture gallery. The Smithsonian's first secretary, Joseph Henry, had his office up here, too. But all that changed after the fire, when the lecture hall was eliminated and the floor converted to other uses.

He made his way down the corridor, past the dark offices.

Into the rotunda.

■ ■ ■ ■

Stephanie exited the spiral staircase into a second-floor gallery. Rick had explained that the hidden staircase once offered employees a quick way up and down, away from visitors. Now it was used mainly by him to gain access to the upper reaches.

She stopped and gestured that they should move quietly. She gripped her Beretta, ready for what might come their way, allowing Rick to lead, not knowing where she was going.

He approached an open doorway that led out and peeked around the edge, jerking his head back quickly.

"He's in the rotunda, just outside the Regents' Room," he whispered in her ear. "There's nothing there of any historical value. Zero to steal. I prepared those exhibits myself."

But apparently he was wrong.

Grant marveled at the rotunda, recalling how he'd once explored this area as a child. Twenty-five years ago the octagonal-shaped, windowless space had also been secretarial, filled then, as now, with desks, sofas, and chairs, serving as an anteroom for the adjacent office of the secretary and the prestigious Regents' Room. Back then, though, there'd been few display cases. Especially not the oversized one, sheathed in gold leaf, that now dominated one wall. An antique lamp on a wooden table burned as a night-light. He approached the gold case and read the placard at the top.

S. Dillon Ripley, 8th Smithsonian Secretary, was once eloquently lauded for "his almost magical sense for the perfect symbolic gesture." The importance of symbolism and ceremony was never lost on him. For Ripley's induction as Secretary, in 1964, outgoing Secretary Leonard Carmichael originated the custom of presenting a ceremonial key to the new Secretary, a symbolic tradition at many universities. Ripley further commissioned the creation of two more symbolic ceremonial devices commonly found in institutions of higher learning. The Mace and the Badge of Office. These three special objects, imbued with symbolism, are uniquely associated with the Smithsonian.

He stared at the mace, the badge, and, most important, the ceremonial key, gently tapping on the sheet of glass that protected the case front. Maybe five feet wide and at least that much, or more, tall. Thick, too.

But breakable.

He stepped back, aimed his gun.

And pulled the trigger.

■ ■ ■ ■

Stephanie snuck her own look at what lay down the corridor. Their target had disappeared from view, somewhere in a spacious room at the end that Rick had called the rotunda. Then the man reappeared with his gun leveled at something.

And fired.

She heard a crackle of glass breaking.

Apparently he'd found what he was after.

She nodded at Rick, and he agreed.

Do it.

She called out, "I'm a United States Justice Department agent. I need you to toss out your weapon and stay where you are."

Her target turned toward her, seemed to consider the command for an instant, then fired two rounds her way.

Grant retreated, until he was no longer visible from down the corridor.

"We have the building sealed," a female voice said. "There's nowhere to go. Toss your weapon down the hall."

He clenched his teeth and all restraint vanished from his composure.

This big risk had turned treacherous.

Justice Department?

He retrieved what he'd come for, then stepped back to peer down the hall, toward where the voice seemed centered, and caught a quick glimpse of a face disappearing around the edge of the far doorway.

He sent two more bullets to that spot.

Stephanie whirled back and slammed herself and Rick to the carpet. Rounds found the Sheetrock where she'd just been standing, piercing the wall and whizzing into the gallery beyond.

"Stay here," she told Rick. "On the floor."

He nodded his understanding and she sprang to her knees, risking a low-level look back down the corridor.

No one in sight.

She came to her feet and headed toward the rotunda. More open doors to dark offices on either side of the corridor offered her a refuge, if need be. Ten more feet and she'd be there. She cursed herself again for allowing this to go as far as it had. She came to the end of the corridor and saw no one in the rotunda. A glass-fronted display case stood shattered against the wall, a bullet hole in its rear panel.

Multiple doorways led out of the octagonal-shaped space.

"No argument this time," she yelled back to Rick. "Alert security and call the police. I assume the double doors I'm looking at are the only way out of here."

"That's right. All of the other exits go to

offices or meeting rooms."

"You stay put."

She rushed after the killer, following the only route the man could have taken, finding a vestibule with white walls, a checkerboard floor, and a staircase leading down. She descended quickly and quietly, staying close to the iron railing, finding the ground floor where everything was enveloped in a spooky semi-darkness. To her right was the building's Mall entrance. Across the way on the far side was the street entrance. He hadn't fled through either set of doors — fire alarms would have sounded. So she turned left and, with her gaze, searched the ground floor, main hall.

Movement caught her attention.

She focused through the shadows and caught sight of her man as he swung into view and leveled his weapon.

Grant had heard a woman's voice tell someone to alert security and call the police. Then he'd spotted his pursuer. Older. Silver-blondish hair. Armed, taking cover behind a half wall, in the foyer at the bottom of the staircase, near the building's Mall-side exit.

He was huddled in the Great Hall, among a line of faux-marble columns that held up the second floor, three tall windows behind him, which offered no escape as they were locked and barred. He knew every inch of the building's geography. The only escape would come to his left, through an arched doorway, down a short connecting corridor into Schermer Hall.

His pursuer had assumed a position fifty feet away, and he would have to navigate thirty feet from where he stood behind the column to the beginning of the corridor. Once there, he'd be safe. Getting there was the problem. Lots of open space, plenty of opportunity to be shot. He heard the bleating wail of a siren in the distance and assumed the worst.

He leveled his gun and sent two rounds in her direction, the bullets whizzing past an arched half wall, ricocheting in all directions.

Then he rushed toward his escape.

Stephanie kept down, using the thick masonry for protection as bullets came her way. The rounds raced by overhead through an archway that opened into the main gallery, lead pinging off the iron railing of the staircase behind her. She hoped she had this guy contained, or at least occupied enough until help arrived. Sirens in the distance offered hope. A quick look and she saw the man vanish through a set of double doors marked TO SCHERMER HALL & THE COMMONS.

She fled her position and ran.

An enclosed corridor led to the Gothic-like Schermer Hall.

A klaxon filled the air.

Fire alarm?

Not good.

To her left a lighted sign identified a fire exit and a cocked-open door signaled a route. She rushed over and saw a metal staircase leading one flight down to an outside door.

He was gone.

Luckily, she'd caught a look. Mid-thirties. Straight nose, square chin, wide jaw, same curly hair. She returned to the main hall. To her right doors opened and Smithsonian security guards burst inside.

The fire alarm stopped.

She told them what had happened and men fanned out, several heading for the street side of the building and the gardens, others back toward the Mall. But she knew there was little chance of finding their target. He'd known from the start what he wanted and how to get away.

She climbed the stairs, back to where Rick waited in the rotunda.

Two security guards joined them.

She again noticed the display case, a huge gold monstrosity, its glass front in pieces scattered on the floor.

"Do you know what he was after?" she asked.

Rick nodded.

"I see exactly what he came for."

CHAPTER TWENTY

Diane remained irritated at her brother, who greeted Lucius Vance as if they were long-lost cousins. His pandering sickened her. Vance was just an elected official, susceptible to the polls and owned by big-money contributors. Any grasp on power he possessed was tenuous, at best. How many Speakers of the House had fallen to scandal? A lot. Nearly half served little more than a year in the job. One for only a few hours. They were, as her father used to say, "comers and goers." She had little respect for politicians. Especially the 21st-century variety, who seemed more concerned with their own survival than making any kind of difference. In theory Vance was no better than the others, but there was definitely something attractive about his raw ambition, a quality Alex had never much coveted.

"Have a seat," her brother said. "We have a lot to talk about."

Vance had requested the meeting, once he

realized he would be attending the funeral, and she'd agreed. The clock on the far wall read 11:20 P.M. The help was gone, the house restored to order. Only she and Kenneth were here, along with Vance and his two security people, who both now waited outside.

"I want to say again, Diane, that I offer my sincere condolences. Though we were never friends, Alex and I weren't enemies, either. He served this state for a long time, and will surely be missed. I really hate that this happened."

Vance was ensconced comfortably in one of the club chairs. She and Kenneth sat in their own facing him. He had a habit of barely moving his lips when he spoke, like some ventriloquist with his dummy.

"I'm also glad we have this chance to speak privately," Vance said. "I have good news. We're moving forward. Immediately."

She was surprised. "You're ready?"

"I've studied this from every angle. I even had some lawyers I trust look at it. They see no problem. The House parliamentarian also says the concept is constitutional."

"You discussed this with him?" she asked.

"Nothing is going to get out of the Rules Committee unless the parliamentarian stamps his okay. Not to worry, he's my guy, loyal to a fault, and I've been working with him quietly for nearly a month now. I have the votes to make this happen."

Magical words, for sure.

She imagined the many times throughout American history meetings just like this had been held in nondescript places, outside the public eye where momentous decisions were made. One that came to mind was the famous 1790 dinner among Jefferson, Madison, and Hamilton where Hamilton convinced two political rivals to support his plan for debt reduction in return for Virginia being the location of the proposed new capital city. Another was the meeting in 1861 when Francis Blair conveyed to Robert E. Lee Lincoln's request that Lee assume command of the Union army. Lee refused, instead resigning his commission and standing with his native Virginia.

"This is great," Kenneth said, his face beaming. "It's exactly what we've been working for."

She did not share that enthusiasm. Not yet, anyway. She wanted to hear more. "Is the Rules Committee primed?"

"We wouldn't be having this conversation if it weren't."

Any change to procedures in the House of Representatives first had to be approved by the Committee on Rules, one of the oldest standing committees in Congress, currently comprising thirteen members. Nine appointed by the Speaker, the other four from the minority. Its nickname was the Speaker's

Committee, since it was how the leadership controlled the House. Every single measure, before heading to a floor vote, had to pass through Rules.

"No one opposes you?" she asked.

Vance sipped on a glass of Evian with a squeeze of lime. "No one that matters. My nine votes will do as I say. The other four?" He shrugged. "Who cares? But if they think about it, they'll be with me, too. This is to everyone's advantage."

"This action will be revolutionary," she said. "Highly controversial. There'll be consequences we have to consider."

Vance gave a shrug. "It's the perfect time. The press is skewering the Senate for its failure to confirm Fox's cabinet appointees. Even the holier-than-thou *New York Times* is calling for change. The House is furious with the Senate for rejecting one of our former members for a cabinet position. The people of this country are fed up with this crap. We're fed up. So enough already. There's no reason to wait. Let's end it."

She understood why he could not have moved prior to this point. A change had been needed in the White House, which came in the last election. A new president, untested, unsure, seemed perfect to exploit. An old warrior like Danny Daniels would have proved difficult to challenge. He might even have mustered enough public support to quell things. As it was, the Senate's natural obstructionism had played right into their hands, and the White House had even joined the chorus for change, expressing its own frustrations.

Everything seemed primed.

She sipped on the whiskey she'd poured herself. "Okay, let's do it."

Vance tossed her a smile. "I think in three days. Tops. This has to happen quick, with no delays. There's a one-day-layover rule in effect. So once the Rules Committee reports the proposed change, we have to wait one day before the committee can vote. Then we'll go straight from committee to a floor vote. Within an hour or so. The press will get wind of it during the one-day layover, but it'll be over and done before they can do anything."

"And once we get to the House floor, will it pass?" she asked.

Vance sat forward on the chair and turned his handsome face her way. "My people will do what needs to be done. We have nearly a 60 percent majority. But you might be surprised at how many from the other side join us."

Vance's party controlled both the House and the presidency. But the other side of the aisle would have to be considered. Luckily, few in Congress possessed the tenacity to fight. Instead, they preferred to posture. This issue, though, left no wiggle room. You were either with it or against it. And Vance was right, there was a lot here for both sides to embrace.

"I'm the Speaker of the House," Vance said. "That means I live by results. Those are achieved by getting the people under me to do what I want. I wouldn't be here talking to you if I didn't have this under control. We'll sell this by making it not a political issue, but one of common sense. Thankfully, the Senate's arrogance over the past few months will make that an easy sell."

Kenneth seemed elated.

She was glad, too. She'd listened to Alex rant for years about Congress and its abuses, how the Senate had become more and more dysfunctional, and how there was little to nothing that could be done about it.

Actually, there was something.

An idea that wise men from the South conceived long ago but never had the chance to implement. Instead, those same wise men had been goaded into foolishly seceding from the Union and starting a civil war — one they lost badly. Thomas Jefferson said, *A little rebellion now and then is a good thing, as necessary in the political world as storms in the physical.*

And he was right.

But it all depended on the form of rebellion.

"How does it feel?" she asked. "You're about to become the most powerful man in the country."

Vance nodded and gave her a wide, confident grin.

"That I am. And all thanks to you."

They talked for another twenty minutes, then her brother left to drive to Nashville. Kenneth had never cared for Blount County, and she hadn't offered him a room for the night. She preferred him two hundred miles away. Vance was still there, the hour approaching 1:00 A.M.

"Let's walk outside," he said to her.

They stepped out onto the wet deck.

The rain had finally stopped.

"It's really lovely here," he said. "A little piece of paradise."

"I'm going to sell this place."

"Really? I didn't realize you hated it that much."

"That part of my life is over. Alex is gone. Time to move on."

She heard movement below and stared out beyond the railing. In the penumbra of the deck lights she saw a man wandering in the short grass of the rear yard, near the tree line. A wall of impenetrable black signified the start of the forest, which she knew continued unabated for miles.

Vance saw the man, too, and called out, "Is there a problem?"

She realized that the figure below was one of the Secret Service agents, patrolling the grounds.

"No, sir," a voice said from below. "I just wanted to have a look."

"Any reason why?"

"I thought I heard something."

CHAPTER TWENTY-ONE

Danny froze against the wet tree.

Vance's Secret Service agent stood twenty feet away, at the edge of the light and yard, just beyond the woods line. If he coughed or sneezed or even breathed too loud he'd be found. He'd heard the agent's explanation as to why he was there — *"I thought I heard something"* — and wondered how far the man would go to satisfy his suspicions.

"What's causing your concern?" Vance asked from the deck.

"It's too dark. There's no way to know what's out there. You really should go back inside."

"This is the way it always is," Diane said. "It's the mountains. I'm sure you heard a raccoon or a deer out after the rain. Could even be a bear. We have lots of those."

The agent said nothing. As he should. Danny knew the drill. The Secret Service wasn't there to chitchat or engage in a debate. They simply did their job. Protection detail required a special type of personality, equal parts bodyguard, diplomat, and confidant. Having Secret Service protection meant that other people were constantly in your business. No longer could you go wherever you pleased, whenever you pleased. Instead you had to ask, preparations had to be made. He wondered if this visit here, tonight, had been planned or happened on a whim. It made a difference when it came to security.

He watched as the agent continued to stand in the yard facing his way. A wall of blackness loomed between them. He was safe so long as he didn't make a sound and the man ventured no closer.

"It's fine," Vance said. "Go back around front. We'll be leaving shortly."

The agent retreated.

He exhaled, realizing he'd been holding his breath.

Diane stood beside Vance.

"I've missed you," he said to her.

It had been a few months since they were last together. Their affair started two years ago. Kenneth had introduced them so she could explain what she knew, and Vance had been immediately intrigued at the possibilities. At first she'd thought Vance was only humoring her, a chance to work his way closer, but she came to see that his curiosity was genuine. Her husband had long ago lost all physical interest in her, their marriage no longer intimate. Her liaisons with Vance had numbered only a few, and always in places far from Washington or Blount County. And she harbored no illusions. The man was married, with three children, a nine-term veteran of Congress, now Speaker of the House. He wouldn't discard all that. Nor would she want him to.

"I wish I had time to stay," he said.

"That would not be a good idea."

"I meant what I said earlier. You have my sincere condolences on Alex's death. It's a terrible thing that happened."

"And I appreciate that. Yet you wouldn't mind sleeping with the widow."

"Come on, Diane. Don't get moral on me. You made that choice long ago, when your husband was still alive."

That she had.

Interesting how easy it had been, crossing the morality line. Five years ago if someone had said she would become a multiple adulteress she would have slapped the person down. But as she'd grown older, she'd also grown restless. Alex satisfied his passions with politics. She had nothing. Until rediscovering all her father's old papers and the dreams of men long dead.

"I think we should keep this proper," she said. "Especially with what's happening. Like I said, you're about to become the most powerful man in this country, and powerful men need wives and children. Not mistresses."

"Changing history can be quite an aphrodisiac."

He was standing close, her skin tingling under his warm breath. She couldn't argue with that observation, which more than anything else explained her liaisons with him.

This man definitely wanted to make a name for himself.

And what did Kenneth want?

Power and credibility. And her?

She wanted wealth.

She'd lived off a public salary nearly her entire adult life. First from what Alex made in the Tennessee state government, then as a U.S. senator. Luckily, he'd inherited assets that had kept them debt-free. But they'd never lived a life of leisure or privilege. Alex was always careful with donor contributions and gifts, never breaching any ethical lines. Not once during his tenure had he ever accepted a paid trip anywhere. He barely allowed anyone to buy him a meal. *Don't take it and you don't owe it.* She'd heard that a million times. Her philosophy was vastly different. What she sought could be worth in the hundreds of billions of dollars. More than enough wealth to provide her with a comfortable life. Only on his deathbed had her father told her about the possibility of locating the gold.

"You're a million miles away," Vance said to her.

That she was.

An odd play of emotions swirled inside her. Pride, greed, ambition, guilt. A strange combination she'd only recently learned to master.

"You and I won't be sleeping together again," she told him.

He didn't seem bothered. "As I recall, you were the one who started that in the first place."

"I did. So I'll be the one to end it."

"Somebody else?"

"You could say that."

"I hope he appreciates what he has."

That remained to be seen.

"Go home to your family. Be a good boy, Lucius. Don't screw this up."

"I have no intention of failing. You gave me a gift, which I plan to use wisely."

"Nearly all men can stand adversity, but if you want to test a man's character, give him power."

"Your words?"

She shook her head. His lack of knowledge of history was embarrassing. "Lincoln's. And he was right. You're about to be put to that test. Don't fail."

"I have no intention of that happening."

She knew Vance had wanted to be president. Before last fall's election he'd thrown out feelers and tested the water. But no one had jumped to his call. Not the press, the public, or the party. His ignorance of history again worked to his disadvantage. Only one person had ever moved from Speaker of the House to president. James Polk in 1845. A long, long time ago. In modern times the post represented the end of a legislator's career. Vance had held that seat of power for nine years, a lifetime in Speaker's terms. He'd used the post wisely, making far more friends than enemies. But she knew how he'd resented being shunned, especially when the party had turned to a political lightweight like Warner Fox for president. So he'd jumped when she'd offered him a way to move from number two in the line of succession to, in essence, being president, and all without facing a national election.

"I'm going to change this country, forever," he said. "But I could not have done it without you."

She appreciated the graciousness, but knew that, soon, she would be the last thought on his mind. Which was okay. She had other interests, too.

"One last kiss?" he asked. "For the warrior about to do battle?'

She smiled. He was impossible.

But what was the harm?

■ ■ ■ ■

Danny watched with rapt fascination as the Speaker of the House of Representatives kissed the widow of one of his closest friends. Not a peck on the cheek, either. An embrace, their lips crushed against each other, with no resistance from either side. He could hardly believe his eyes or his ears, as he'd been close enough to hear their entire conversation.

Something big was definitely in the works.

"You're about to become the most powerful man in this country."

Diane's words to Vance.

The two lovers parted, then walked together from the deck back into the house. A few minutes later a car left the driveway. He assumed Vance was gone, along with his two minders.

So he fled the woods.

He drove back to his house, his thoughts swirling. Being president of the United States had been a continuous mental task, there'd never been a moment when a thousand different things weren't raging through his brain. That might be a problem for most people. Not him. He'd loved every second of it and missed it more than he'd ever thought possible. What had another Tennessean, Andrew Jackson, said?

I was born for the storm, and a calm does not suit me.

Damn straight.

And he seemed to have stumbled right into the middle of a hurricane. Silently, he weighed the pluses and minuses, seeking a loophole, some straw to grasp, a reasonable explanation.

But found nothing.

The wipers continued to squeak against the rain. Droplets, like silver bullets, revealed themselves in the headlights, the damp road glistening like black ice.

Unfortunately, no nagging toothache of doubt existed here.

Only bad thoughts crawled around in his mind.

He'd watched the gathering inside the Sherwood home, noting a jollity among the three participants that suggested familiarity. Then the encounter on the deck. That was almost too much to believe. Nobody would believe him. He barely believed it himself.

But what to do now?

He had an idea, crazy in its scope, unique in its approach.

So he rattled off its pros and cons.

His divorce from Pauline was scheduled to be filed in July and, after the mandatory sixty-day waiting period, finalized in September. That would be eight months after leaving office. They'd agreed to issue a joint statement expressing regret, then not to speak publicly on the matter ever again. To friends the explanation would be that *things happen,* but those closest would not be surprised. The pain from Mary's tragic death had hung between them for a long time. His daughter would have been a grown woman now, probably married with children of her own. Music had been her love, and he could still hear her, as a child, playing the flute. Visiting her grave had been a start at his personal reconciliation with that past.

But more work remained to be done.

Ego, of course, would be raised by his enemies, along with *enough is enough.* But before leaving the White House he'd been privy to polling numbers that indicated he was popular in Tennessee. The data had been gathered as part of the research concerning the location of his presidential library. Private donors would be needed to make it a reality, and having the building located in friendly territory always helped with contributions.

Beyond that, he could think of no other deal-breaker con to his plan.

Sure, objections would come, but the naysayers could go to hell. His dearest friend was dead, and he'd been unwittingly drawn into finding out how and why. He owed that to Alex Sherwood, so he'd take whatever heat might come his way. Never once had he ever been afraid of a fight. And it was unfettered courage that had made him a decisive president. The military had respected him, Congress feared him, and the people, by and large, liked him. That same poll taken late last year had also revealed that he left office with a 65% approval rating, which no other modern president could claim. So was he letting all that go to his head? Was he overplaying his hand? Maybe.

But he had to do it.

For Alex.

He kept driving through the rain. No sleep had settled in his eyes. Instead his mind worked at an Olympic pace.

"No, Danny," he whispered, "you're doing this for you, too."

Being honest with himself had always served him well. He knew his strengths and weaknesses, conscious of both, oblivious to neither.

He wanted this. No. He needed this.

He turned off the highway and cruised down the drive, parking in front of his house. The security team was still ensconced on the front porch.

"Anything we can get you, Mr. President?" one of the men asked as he climbed the steps.

"A third term would have been good."

And he tossed the man a smile as he headed inside, shedding his wet coat. Pauline would have made him take it off outside. Now he could do as he pleased. Whether that was a good thing or not remained to be seen. He'd brought the notebook inside with him. Upstairs, he bypassed the closed door to his room and opened the one where his friend lay sleeping. He sat on the edge of the bed, switched on the tasseled lamp, and roused him.

"You do realize that I am the governor of this state," his pal said, sleep still in his voice.

"But I outrank you."

The governor sat up in the bed. "How do you figure? You're a private citizen."

"We've got trouble."

And he told his friend everything, including the details concerning Taisley, Lucius Vance, and Diane. "I'm tellin' you, that gathering I just witnessed was like something from *Seven Days in May.*"

He'd always loved both the book and the original black-and-white movie, which dealt with a military-political cabal's attempt to take over the government.

"They were plotting," he said. "No question."

"Is that the notebook?"

He nodded and handed it over. "Diane lied straight to my face. She had someone go into Alex's apartment and get this."

"She is his wife and, I assume, sole heir?"

"Then why lie?"

"Because she doesn't like you? And considers it none of your business?"

225

"I wish it were that simple. No. They're about to do something big. So big that she was warning Vance about the effects of power."

"What can you or I do about it?"

"I have an idea."

The governor stared at him, waiting.

"Alex had two years left. You're the one who appoints someone to serve out that Senate term. We both know the score. The person has to be totally uninterested in keeping the job two years from now. He or she is a caretaker. Nothing more. A seat warmer. But the person also has to be competent." He saw the dots were already connecting. "I know this appointment could be a minefield for you. People from everywhere will call in favors to get it, even for only two years just to keep the seat warm. No matter what you do, you're goin' to piss somebody off. So screw 'em all and give me the job."

The governor grinned. "It does have a ring of sentimentality."

That it did. Only one other man had ever served as president then been chosen for the U.S. Senate.

Andrew Johnson.

Who hailed from just up the road in Greene County, Tennessee.

"You'll be the second."

"And it's a good play for you," he said. "I'll keep things quiet until the voters can pick

226

who they want to be their next senator in two years. You can't get in trouble for that."

"Except you've never kept anything quiet in your life."

"I do plan to snoop around. I'm going to find out what the hell's goin' on here. But I promise, I'll be a good boy."

"You do realize that ex-presidents are supposed to go away."

"I never liked that prefix. It has an awful ring to it. But I'm doing this for Alex." He paused, realizing he shouldn't kid a kidder. "And for me."

"I knew there was no way you were just going to sit around and write your memoirs."

A fierce, predatory concern had enveloped him. One that had never left him during eight years in the White House, but had quelled four months ago as he'd watched a new president take the oath.

"I need this," he admitted again. "I really do."

"I remember a time when I needed things. And you made sure I got them. So no problem, Danny. I'll do it. For Alex — and you."

In an instant the fear and isolation he'd been feeling of late transformed into a focused desire for action.

And a realization.

He was back in the game.

Plan your work and work your plan.

His mantra.

He knew his eyes held both a brassy glint of mischief and a touch of relief, so he told his old friend, "There's somethin' dead up this creek. I can feel it. So I'm gonna paddle up and see what we find."

Chapter Twenty-Two

Cotton stared across the table at Terry Morse, his patience at an end. They sat in the kitchen, Morse's gaze out toward the open windows. A few of the bees hovered with a murmur just outside the screen, beneath the eaves.

"They'll head back to the hive soon," Morse said. "After they calm."

Morse had uprighted and repaired the shattered boxes, then used smokers to herd most of the insects back to their homes.

"Bees live by order," the older man said. "They like things organized. There are rules in the hive."

Cassiopeia and Lea sat at the table with them. Cassiopeia kept a watch out the windows, too, holding her gun, which the men had left behind.

"What did they tell you?" Cotton asked, his Beretta on the table before him. "That you'd be doing your duty by leading us on?"

Morse nodded. "They showed up right

before you came. Parked out back, out of sight. They knew the handshake and the right words. My pa told me to always respect men who knew those things. When you appeared with Lea, they waited in the bedroom and listened. I was plannin' on showin' them the stone, so I just led you out there, too."

"Your father lived in another time," Cotton said. "Things have changed. Those men don't give a damn about the Knights of the Golden Circle."

"I see that now. I made a mistake." Morse stared at his granddaughter. "I'm sorry, honey."

"It's okay. I'm fine."

"Tell me about that stone," Cotton said to Morse. "And for your own sake, give it to me straight."

"You realize I've kept this secret a long time."

"Like I said, different time. A lot of crimes have been committed here, and it's judgment day."

A look of defeat swept across Morse's face. He felt for the old man, but he had a job to do.

"It's one of five," Morse said. "My pa told me that his father was specially chosen to guard this one. That was an honor he was really proud of, and he passed it on to me."

"So how did the stone end up in your bee house?" Cassiopeia asked.

He wanted to know the answer to that question, too.

"It goes back a long time, when I wasn't much younger than Lea."

Morse followed his father through the forest of oak, beech, hickory, and pine, careful to keep a watch for rattlesnakes and hogs. He loved the woods. The streams yielded not only fresh water but also fish. The woods had deer, walnuts, berries, and — his personal favorite — cherries. The Ozark and Ouachita Mountains were his home, and he imagined that would be the case for his entire life.

His father was a powerful man other men treated with great respect. He raised pigs and trapped furs. When people were starving during the Depression he brought many of them game and made sure no one went hungry. His moonshine was legendary with both the locals and the revenuers. People came to him for both help and advice.

"Where we goin'?' " he asked his father.

"Huntin' cows."

He'd heard the term before and, when younger, actually thought that's what his father meant. But he'd come to know that the term had another meaning. Usually, his father had saddled up his horse and headed into the woods alone, huntin' cows. Today he'd been brought along, riding his own horse, toting his own rifle.

His father stopped and he came up beside him.

"Take a look at that twisty beech tree, there by the stream?"

He followed his father's pointed finger.

"We call 'em treasure trees. They're loaded with carvin's. Read 'em right they lead you to gold."

His father had never spoken of this before.

"You're the firstborn. That means you're the next sentinel. I'm goin' to teach you all you have to know, but that's only if you want to learn."

A thrill rushed through him, like water down the stream, connecting him to his father like never before. Was there any better feeling?

"I want to learn," he said.

"I thought you might. See that hollow, beyond the creek?"

He did.

"Someone's buried up there. He was in places he shouldn't be and ended up dead. It was a long time ago. But that's what it takes sometimes. You have to hunt the cows."

And he suddenly realized what the term meant. "Did you shoot him?"

"My father did. But I was there. Just like you're here today."

The connection became stronger, back another generation. "I can do whatever I have to."

His father smiled. "I believe you can."

They kept riding, deeper into the woods,

heading south, away from their cabin, following the stream. He'd explored this region of the woods many times and had seen the carved animal figures, the cryptic letters, the dates notched into trees and rocks. But he'd never understood their significance. He'd thought they were just graffiti. He wanted to ask more questions but knew that was not a good idea. His father would tell him what he wanted him to know when ready.

But he realized what was happening.

His education had begun.

"My pa was a tough man," Morse said. "I learned later that he killed three people while huntin' cows."

"That's not what you said earlier," Cassiopeia noted.

"I lied."

Lea seemed surprised by the revelation. "You never told me anything about people dyin'."

" 'Cause I never expected you to ever kill anybody. So you didn't need to know."

"Did you kill anyone?" she asked her grandfather.

Morse shook his head. "I never could. I just scare 'em away."

"What happened with your father?" Cotton asked. "That day by the creek."

"We went somewhere."

He kept riding up the narrow trail, the horses' footing sure, but kept a wary eye out just in case.

"There's a lot of gold buried up here," his father said. "More than any of us could ever spend. But it ain't ours. Others own it. Our job is to protect it."

He considered that. It seemed important.

"And besides," his father said, "I don't know how to find the hidin' places."

They crested the ridge and the ground leveled off.

His father stopped his horse before a holly tree. "Look there."

He'd already spotted the carving. A snake of some sort, in the bark.

"I can't read the signs," his father said. "I have no idea what they mean. That was on purpose. We just watch over 'em. Protect 'em. Make sure they last. So before I pass, I'll show you all of 'em I know."

"But he never did," Morse said. "He died a year later from a fall off his horse, while huntin' more cows."

"What about the stone?" Cotton asked, getting back to the original question.

"He showed me. That first day, when we found the snake on the tree."

"There are sentinels, then there are special ones, like us," his father said. "Sure, there's lots of gold all around here in the ground, but there's also somethin' extra important. And that I do know how to find."

They rode for a few minutes in silence. Then his father stopped and dismounted. He did, too. In the underbrush, near a stand of elm, he saw the rusted remnants of an iron strongbox.

"That came off a stage robbed near Hot Springs back in the 1870s."

On one side, visible through the rust were the faint letters WELLS FARGO.

"Jesse James left that here when he hid the gold it contained. He was a knight of the Golden Circle. All those banks he robbed. That gold ended up in these hills, hidden away, belongin' to the Order. But there's somethin' else you need to know. Somethin' real special I was told by my pa."

"Most of that gold is gone," Morse said.

Cotton stared at the older man.

"They came and got it."

"Who came?" Cassiopeia asked.

"Knights. They went all around everywhere and collected the gold, leavin' only some."

"And did what with it?" Cotton asked.

"Took it to one place. They called it the

235

vault. We never knew where, just that it was all bein' brought together. A few of the smaller hidin' places were all they left. But my grandpa and my pa were given a extra-special job. One that passed to me. We guarded that stone out there."

"And why is it so important?"

"It leads to the vault."

CHAPTER TWENTY-THREE

Washington, DC
10:45 P.M.

Stephanie retreated from the rotunda as Smithsonian security and the local police examined the shattered display case. Rick had gone silent, professing to know nothing. One of the DC police approached her and wanted some information. Her first inclination was to tell them about Thomas' murder, but a plea from Rick's eyes asked her to stay silent. So she just flashed her Magellan Billet badge and told the officers to take it up with the U.S. attorney general.

"What about Thomas' body?" she whispered to Rick as they stood off to one side in the rotunda.

"At the moment, only a couple of people know about that."

"What in the world have you brought me into?"

She drifted away, taking another look at the shattered wooden display case. The inside housed the institution's ceremonial objects, each described by a printed card. On the rear wall hung a mace made of gold, silver, diamonds, rubies, and polished Smithsonite, a mineral first identified by James Smithson and named for him after his death. From the placard she also learned that the mace was encrusted with symbolism relating to Smithson. She knew that universities employed a mace to represent jurisdiction, authority, and academic independence. She assumed those same ideals applied here, and she read how the mace was presented to each incoming secretary. Also displayed was a sterling-silver salver and badge of office.

Lying at the bottom, a printed card described the ceremonial key.

The tradition of passing this key to the incoming Secretary originated with the 1964 induction of S. Dillon Ripley, as eighth Secretary of the Smithsonian. In lieu of the administration of an oath of office, outgoing secretary Leonard Carmichael proposed instead a key-passing ceremony based on similar ones frequently used in the inauguration of university presidents. Chief Justice Earl Warren, Chancellor of the Smithsonian at the time, presented the key to Ripley prior to the January 23, 1964, meeting of the Board of Regents. The key, as a representation of knowledge and of guardianship, is an appropriate Smithsonian symbol. Dating to 1849, this large brass key may have opened one of the original massive oak doors of the building.

Beside the card sat a small wooden box, hinged open, lined with blue velvet. An indentation outlined what appeared to be a skeleton key.

Gone.

"What about the key that's not here?" one of the DC police asked, noticing the empty container, too.

"It's been out of there for a while," Rick said. "We're duplicating it."

"You have any idea why this case is the only thing destroyed?"

"Could have been an accident," she said. "He was in a hurry to leave."

"And you were here because — ?"

"Just helping out a friend."

She turned and faced Rick, who stood on the far side of the rotunda. He slowly nodded, both agreeing with her statement and thanking her for the partial lie.

A cell phone buzzed and she watched as Rick answered, then drifted down the hall for privacy. What was so important about a ceremonial key that it cost Martin Thomas his life?

"Stephanie."

She turned.

239

Rick motioned for her to come.

She left the police and approached.

"Someone wants to speak with you."

They descended the spiral staircase back to Rick's basement office. There he led her into the tunnel beneath the Mall and over to the natural history museum. When they came to Thomas' body she saw that it had been covered with a sheet and a security guard stood watch. Rick had locked the gate on the Castle side when they entered, and another guard was on sentry at the portal inside natural history.

"No one will come in here," he told her.

They made their way up to the Cullman Library, where an hour ago all this had begun. Everything inside the natural history museum loomed cemetery-quiet. During the day this was a place of people, light, and noise. Rick had told her that no cleaning crews worked inside any of the buildings after hours. All that work was done during the day. So at night the exhibits slumbered alone, in a surreal silence. Easy to see why books and films liked to dramatize the tranquility.

A man waited for them inside the library. A monk's ring of white hair, like a halo, encircled a bald pate. He carried some girth at his waistline, beef to his limbs, and puffiness around the eyes, but this gentleman had a reputation for brilliance.

240

Warren Weston.

Chief Justice of the United States.

Chancellor of the Smithsonian Institution.

"It's a pleasure to meet you," the jurist said, rising as she came into the library.

Rick turned to leave.

"No. Please stay."

"I need to see about Martin. I'll be back."

And he left.

"I'm afraid I'm the reason you're involved in this," Weston said to her. "We needed help, and I learned that you and Rick were friends, so I asked him to call you."

"After you involved Cotton Malone. Mind telling me why?"

"That's a long story."

She nearly smiled. Exactly what Cotton liked to say when people asked him about his name.

"We have a serious situation here," Weston said. "One that seems to have taken a tragic turn. I was informed about what happened, so I thought it best to speak with you directly."

"No disrespect, sir. But this is not my problem. I'm here only because Rick asked for my help. I came into this blind and allowed it to escalate far past what was prudent. My agency deals with issues of national security. This is now a job for the FBI or the DC Police."

"Before I arrived, I spoke with the attorney

241

general. He told me the Magellan Billet was at my disposal."

She resented the end run. "That was quite presumptuous of you."

"I realize that, and apologize. But it's necessary."

She knew what was happening. The new AG cared nothing about the Magellan Billet, originally wanting it eliminated. But on Inauguration Day, Danny had stopped that from happening, forcing President Fox to keep the agency in place. True, it had been reconstituted with the same personnel and funding as under previous administrations, but she harbored no illusions. No longer would it be the White House's go-to agency. In fact, it would probably do little to nothing. So they were occupying her time. Keeping her busy. Not that this wasn't important. And not to discount what had just happened with Martin Thomas' death. But it was as she'd noted. The local police and the FBI were more than capable of handling this.

"I require absolute discretion," Weston said to her. "Your agency can provide that. And for the moment, I need Martin Thomas' body secured somewhere for a couple of days, until we sort this out."

"You realize that's a crime. He was murdered. We'd be tampering with evidence."

"Which I'm sure your agency does routinely, while handling *issues of national security.*"

She caught the mocking. "How are you going to explain Thomas being gone?"

"Let that be my concern."

With no choice, she found her cell phone and entered a code. The unit was specially made for the Billet, preprogrammed, able to dial straight into a secure line. When it was answered she said, "I have a priority cleanup situation at the National Museum of Natural History." She listened a moment, then said, "On my authority. You'll be met at the building entrance on Constitution Avenue with further instructions. Do it now."

She clicked the phone off.

"That's impressive," he said. "I assume in your line of work people die all the time."

"Not too many civilians drafted into service. We prefer to kill only the trained ones."

She saw on his face that her sarcasm was noted. "I suppose I deserve that." He motioned for her to sit, which he did, too.

She decided to switch to diplomacy. "You'll have to forgive my surliness but, unlike you, I'm operating in the dark. And you've yet to tell me why Cotton is involved."

"I share your frustration. I've served as chief justice for over thirty years, and probably have lingered longer than I should. When I retire I really won't miss being a judge, but I will miss being chancellor of this great institution. I've never missed a regents' meeting. Few of my predecessors can say that."

"And the point of me knowing that?"

A look of irritation swept over the older man's face.

"I get it," she said. "I'm being difficult. Probably not something you're accustomed to dealing with. But I'm not one of your clerks, or a lawyer standing before you at oral argument. And I haven't had a good evening."

"Martin Thomas' death was not your fault."

"Then whose fault was it?"

The meaning of the question was clear.

He shook his head. "We had no idea Thomas was coming here tonight with that man. None at all. He placed himself in that danger."

"But we saw the gun and allowed it to continue. It should have been stopped, and I blame myself for that omission."

"Please don't. I take full responsibility. I'm not looking for a scapegoat here. I'm looking for help."

And she heard the desperation. "All right. I'll shut up and listen."

He seemed to appreciate the gesture.

"This all started a long time ago, during the Civil War. The Smithsonian played a dangerous game. Our secretary at the time, Joseph Henry, wanted us to remain neutral as an international science organization supposedly above politics. But that noble gesture angered a lot of people. And it didn't help that Henry and Jeff Davis were close friends. We barely had enough funds during the war to operate. By its end we were broke, operating on a deficit. That situation led to choices. Martin Thomas managed to learn about some of these, and Diane Sherwood has shown a disproportionate interest in them, too."

There was that name again. "Did you ever speak to Senator Sherwood about this?"

"I did. About two weeks before he died. I told him that his wife was pressuring one of our employees and misusing her position. I told him that she should resign her position on the libraries' advisory board. He told me he would speak with her. But apparently that conversation never took place, or she didn't listen, and now both the senator and Martin Thomas are dead."

She had to say, "Thomas was not up front with you." And she told him what she'd heard about lost Confederate treasure, the book Thomas wanted to write, and the cut he'd demanded. "That's why he told no one he was coming here tonight, and bringing a guest."

The chief justice sighed.

They sat in silence for a few moments.

Finally, he said, "I need to tell you some things. In confidence."

CHAPTER TWENTY-FOUR

Grant slowed his pace to a brisk walk. He'd made it out of the Castle, utilizing a fire escape door that he'd many times gone in and out of as a kid. It opened to the building's south side and the gardens, paved walks leading from there to the streets beyond. He knew there were precious few exterior cameras on Smithsonian buildings, its security all concentrated on what was stored inside. So once he crossed Independence Avenue and disappeared into the maze of government buildings beyond, he should be fine. The fact that no one was following made him feel better. The sirens he'd heard had gone toward the Castle but, as he suspected, the woman chasing him had come alone. He'd caught a quick glimpse of her face and wondered if she really was with the Justice Department.

Killing Martin Thomas had been the only option. If Thomas had done his job, accepted their generous payment without becoming greedy, he would have let him be.

But that had not been the case.

And writing a book?

That was the last thing he could allow to happen.

He wondered if his subterranean route into the Castle had been discovered. Could the Justice Department woman have come that way? Or was she waiting in the Castle? But how would she have known to be there? From Thomas? No way. During a call earlier arranging the visit no mention had been made of where he planned to go, only that he needed access into the buildings. He hadn't told Thomas where they were headed until they left the Cullman. So there was no way anyone, including Thomas, could have known that he planned to use the old tunnel. No. They'd been followed across the Mall through the tunnel, which meant the corpse had been found.

Diane would not be pleased with what he'd done. She'd been the one who'd greased his path into the Smithsonian, connecting him with Thomas. Questions would surely come her way, but that was assuming they knew of any links among the three of them. He had to hope that they did not. If so, then this would all be over soon with his arrest. Connecting the dots would not take long. But something told him that the other side was working blind.

Unfortunately, he'd needed to make two

stops tonight. One in the Castle, the other back in the natural history museum. He'd retrieved Thomas' Smithsonian badge and swipe card, intent on using them for access back into the natural history museum once he'd obtained the ceremonial key. But that second errand had not been possible.

Which raised issues.

He slowed his pace and his breathing.

The whole thing had been close.

Too close.

He kept walking, following a procession of streetlamps, his shirt clammy with sweat. Finally, he found 14th Street, where he crossed, hailed a cab near the Holocaust Museum, then rode to Dupont Circle. Traffic and the sidewalks were light with people and cars. He walked a few blocks, avoiding Embassy Row where there'd be more cameras, keeping to the quiet residential neighborhoods. Only an occasional car jolted past. Eventually he crossed the river into Georgetown. He'd ignored his phone during all the excitement, the unit set on silent, but now he checked its display.

An email had come from Arkansas.

Found the stone with Morse and took pictures, which are attached. Unable to get the stone as two federal agents showed up. We tried to find out why they were here, but learned nothing. They don't know who we are. We got away from them, but we're done. Goodbye.

Now they tell him.

That information would have been welcomed a few hours ago — or maybe not. He might have lost his nerve. But a Justice Department agent here? More federal agents in Arkansas?

He viewed the photo that had been sent.

The Witch's Stone.

And stopped walking.

Damn. Terry Morse really had been its keeper. Thankfully, the scant few records he and Diane had managed to find among their fathers' papers had proved correct and the right sentinel had been found. So if one stone was real, the other four might be, too.

Diane would be thrilled.

Perhaps thrilled enough to overlook the unfortunate death of Martin Thomas.

Short of Diane, nothing linked him to Thomas, as all calls to the librarian had been made from the few remaining pay phones around town. Their face-to-face meetings had taken place at Thomas' apartment, with no witnesses. And he'd been careful with the cameras inside the buildings tonight. Unless Thomas himself had ratted him out, which he doubted, nothing should lead back to him.

The gold coins clinked in his pocket.

Face value $10.

Worth a few thousand dollars each today. Three had done the trick tonight, which he'd retrieved from Thomas' corpse. No sense leaving that evidence to be found. He'd unearthed those himself from a cache hidden in western Kentucky. One of the paycheck holes was meant as payment for a sentinel. Records his father had kept for decades had led the way, and Diane had deciphered the clues, pinpointing the location of a decayed iron pail full of gold. That money had helped finance everything to this point, but those funds were dwindling. Unfortunately, the remaining records they had did not provide good leads on other caches.

They had to find the vault.

He had to find the vault.

The rest of his life seemed predicated on that success. He'd met Diane two years ago after she tracked his father down. Her father and his had worked at the Smithsonian at the same time, first as friends, later as enemies. Twenty years in age separated him and Diane, he being the younger. His father had been more lucid then, talking of his days at the Castle, reminiscing about her father and their feud. They'd struck up a conversation after her first visit to the house, having dinner that same night. A month later they were lovers. She was an amazing woman, different from any he'd ever known.

The image of the stone on the screen

continued to glare at him.

He noticed the wording.

Spanish?

Seemed so. Foreign languages were not his thing. And the images? Random. Seemingly unrelated. But he knew better.

The Order's success had lain in its cleverness. An ability to create traps, diversions, and false trails. Hiding in plain sight became an art form. His father long ago had told him that hidden away in the continental United States was a place loaded with immense wealth, all accumulated by the Knights of the Golden Circle. Over the past few years there'd been renewed interest in the Order. Several books had been published about its supposed treasure. One by a fellow in Arkansas had been way too close for comfort. Like himself and Diane, that man had learned secrets from his family, then managed to piece together even more, deciphering the signs in the woods and finding a few of the remaining caches. But he'd noticed no mention of the vault in that book, which meant that man's ancestors, who most likely had acted as sentinels, were not privy to the stones.

Now one had been located.

Four remained.

He found Thomas' security swipe card in his pocket. His ticket back in. He'd have to go, no matter the risk.

Something Martin Thomas said kept ringing in his brain. About writing a book. Which *would* include the vault. That could be a problem. Thankfully, he'd kept his head about him and also relieved the corpse of a ring of keys, one of which surely opened Thomas' apartment.

Good.

He needed to do some cleanup.

CHAPTER TWENTY-FIVE

Stephanie listened to what Chief Justice Weston was telling her, fascinated by the subject matter.

"In 1846 President James Polk decided that the fastest way to increase the size of the United States was to have a war with Mexico. Which wasn't all that hard to manufacture — Mexico had been begging for a fight ever since it lost Texas in the 1830s. So Polk provoked a conflict and, after two years of fighting, defeated Mexico. The Treaty of Guadalupe Hidalgo gave the United States what would later become Arizona, New Mexico, Utah, Nevada, and California.

"In 1854 the Smithsonian Institution sent a team to the newly acquired American Southwest for mapping and geological research, one of our first scientific expeditions. At the time Jefferson Davis served as secretary of war under President Franklin Pierce. Davis was secretly approached by a newly formed group called the Knights of the

Golden Circle."

"Thomas mentioned them earlier."

"And he would know, as that's what he's been looking into. The Order had a specific interest in Mexico and the Caribbean, wanting to acquire them to form a new southern empire. It talked of political reform and changing the country by creating new states, altering the balance of power in Congress. It spoke of a new constitutional convention and amendments to secure southern rights. Jefferson Davis thought the whole idea intriguing. The Order thought the Smithsonian expedition would provide an excellent opportunity to covertly reconnoiter the newly acquired lands, which they hoped to organize into slave states."

"Sounds grandiose."

"It was. While serving in the U.S. Senate in the late 1840s, Jefferson Davis also served as a Smithsonian regent. That's when he and our secretary, Joseph Henry, became close. In 1854, as secretary of war for Franklin Pierce, Davis used that connection to have a man added to the Smithsonian expedition. Eventually that man reconnoitered the entire Southwest region, gathering vital geographic, geological, and political information, recording everything within a journal that was delivered back to Davis. The young man sent with the expedition was named Angus Adams, who worked at the Smithsonian. Seven years later, Adams quit his job and joined the Confederate army, becoming a renowned spy. He even acquired a moniker." Weston paused. "Cotton."

"He's related to Malone?"

"His great-great-grandfather."

"And you know all of this, how?"

"I did extensive genealogical research on Malone," said Rick Stamm, who'd returned about halfway through Weston's recitation.

Which raised a host of questions, but she decided to ask, "Whatever happened to that journal?"

"Originally Angus Adams delivered it to the Castle on the day the building burned in January 1865, along with a key."

She knew. "The same key that was stolen tonight."

"Correct. But both objects vanished during the fire. The key was found in the late 1950s in the Castle attic, quite by accident. The journal is gone."

"So much for this institution remaining above politics and staying neutral."

"We do a good job of that now," Weston said. "Not so much 160 years ago. The Civil War was a trying time for everyone. Loyalties were tested across families, governments, even here, within these supposed hallowed halls."

"Where exactly is Cotton?" she asked.

"In Arkansas," Weston said. "Checking out

some information."

"I'm assuming you plan to explain what and why."

Weston smiled. "Absolutely. Right now, let's focus on Diane Sherwood, as it was her interest in all this that drew our attention. What you don't know is that back in the 1960s to the mid-1990s, her father, Davis Layne, served as head of the American history museum. He accumulated a respectable amount of research on the Knights of the Golden Circle. Mr. Malone spent a couple of days here reading that research and some other materials from our restricted archive. From a 1909 expedition to Arkansas and the 1854 expedition to the Southwest."

"Any idea why Layne's daughter is so intent on this now?" she asked.

"We truly don't know."

"I'm assuming there is a treasure. As Thomas mentioned. *Lost Confederate gold.*'"

The chief justice nodded. "That there is, which this institution has long had an interest in acquiring."

She looked at Rick. "Is there a link between our killer tonight and Mrs. Sherwood?"

"Only Martin could have made that connection, and he said nothing to us about it."

"We all know there has to be a connection," the chief justice said. "But we do need to proceed with caution. She is the widow of a regent. There is a chance that this could all begin and end with Martin Thomas. As you say, he was making a bargain on his own, without our knowledge. But we can't forget that she did recruit Thomas to breach our restricted archives."

"Why is any of this information restricted? It seems like ancient history."

"The last thing we want is for this institution to become the haunt of treasure hunters."

She decided to cut to the chase. "Not to mention, one, the scandal, and, two, that you'd like to keep that treasure for yourself?"

The chief justice shifted in his chair. "Ms. Nelle, it's important that you appreciate the situation we find ourselves in. It takes over a billion dollars a year to keep the Smithsonian running, and everything here is free to the public. We've never charged a user or admission fee and never will. People think the federal government pays all of our bills. It doesn't. Congress pays about 70% of the costs. We have to raise the other 30%, which amounts to several hundred million dollars each year, just to balance the budget. You can imagine how daunting a task that is. Those funds come from donors, all around the world, large and small, mainly small. If that flow of money is disrupted in any way, this institution is doomed. So yes, we'd like to have those funds. And yes, we cannot afford a major scandal."

"Let's see where we are," she said, "First, the Smithsonian played both ends against the middle during the Civil War. Then you have the wife of a dead regent, a woman who serves on one of your advisory boards, who may be an accessory to murder. Then there's a reference librarian who got himself killed, a man who was allowed into harm's way, all so that you can keep secret the fact that you have information leading to some lost Confederate treasure."

"Are you always so surly to people who seek your help?" Weston asked.

"Only the ones who hold back on me, which you're still doing. At least tell me about the ceremonial key that was stolen."

Weston nodded at Rick, who said, "Nobody has a clue what it opens. Once, the locks on all of the Castle doors took skeleton keys just like it. A couple of those locks remain, but the key doesn't open them. Like the placard in the display case said, Secretary Ripley decided to make it part of the installation ceremony. For a long time, while a secretary served, the original was displayed in his office. But that stopped about thirty years ago when it was placed in the display case. Now it's used only at induction, then a copy is given to the secretary for him or her to keep."

"How many copies exist?"

Rick did a count with his fingers. "Three for past secretaries, one for the current, and I have four in the safe in my office, to be used in the future."

"All identical?"

Rick nodded. "I had them made myself."

"So tell me, why did this guy want the original? He took an enormous chance coming in here to get it."

Weston shrugged. "Unfortunately, that is something you're going to have to learn for us."

"Mr. Chief Justice, regardless of what the attorney general has said, this is a matter for law enforcement, not an intelligence agency. A murder has been committed. You should involve the police and the FBI and cooperate fully with them."

"From a legal standpoint, the Castle is within the federal district. The locals have jurisdiction only if we cede it to them. And the FBI comes only if we call them. I prefer not to involve either. We have to keep this contained — for a little while longer."

She could refuse to help, but that would just start another feud with her new bosses. The new attorney general was nothing short of a presidential lapdog, so she knew who'd lose that battle. She could not afford to fight about everything, so she decided to suck this one up.

"What is it you want me to do?"

"Conduct a thorough investigation. Help Rick find some answers and, above all, find

Martin Thomas' killer."

"You do realize that other people are more qualified than me to handle this. Cotton being one."

"I do," Weston said. "And we'll involve him, once he returns from Arkansas. For now, could you get things started?"

"Any suggestions?" she asked, since both men had been thinking about this a lot longer than she had.

"Begin with a search of Martin Thomas' apartment," the chief justice said. "Things are missing from our archives that are not in his office. We need them returned."

"And how will I know what these things are?"

"I'll go with you," Rick said.

She should have known. "How do we get into his apartment?"

"I'm assuming you can pick a lock," Weston said.

"I have some talent in that area."

Rick smiled. "Once everything had finished here tonight, you and I were going to go over there with Martin and have a look anyway."

"So you did suspect he was not being straight with you."

"Not until I saw him with the guy in the Cullman Library, which is another reason I called you."

"All right. Let's see if there's anything there."

CHAPTER TWENTY-SIX

Cotton checked his watch. Tuesday was about to become Wednesday. What a day. It had started early this morning in a lovely room at a mountaintop lodge. Now it was ending in the heat and humidity of an Arkansas spring night, after he'd been twice assaulted, shot at, then chased by bees.

"What's the vault?" he asked Terry Morse.

"It's where they took all the gold and silver."

He and Cassiopeia listened as Morse told them what happened starting in the latter part of the 19th century. Hundreds of caches were dug from the ground, their sentinels told to stand down. The Knights of the Golden Circle was fading into oblivion. A loyal core still existed, but their number was too small to be effective. The idea of a second secessionist movement seemed no more than a dream. So the decision was made to consolidate the Order's wealth, where it could be more easily managed and retrieved, if the time ever came.

"Those were the days of the Klan," Morse said. "Everybody focused on them and their cross burnin's and lynchin's. They were bad people. That wasn't the knights. The KKK was somethin' else entirely."

His own grandfather had issued a similar disclaimer.

"My pa helped transport a lot of the gold from here to Kansas City, where it was given to other knights," Morse said. "He told me they dug it slow and quiet. Took thirty years to get most of it, so nobody would notice."

"I thought you said your father couldn't read the signs in the woods," Cassiopeia said.

"He couldn't. But knights came who could."

"Were there hoards buried all over the country?" Cotton asked.

"Best I know they're scattered everywhere, but heavy in Arkansas, Tennessee, and Kentucky. The farther away from the carpetbaggers, the easier to hide."

Which made sense. The fewer Federal troops around after the war, enforcing Reconstruction, the more freedom of movement an organization like the Knights of the Golden Circle could enjoy.

"You still haven't told me about the vault," Cotton said.

" 'Cause I don't know much. Only that it exists and that the stone out there with the

262

bees helps lead the way to it. It's called the Witch's Stone because of the figure on the front and the hat."

Cassiopeia produced her phone and Cotton saw again the image of the carved face.

"Where did the stone come from?" he asked Morse.

"That's a tale my pa did tell me, as his grandpa told him."

The wagon stopped on the dirt track, just beyond the split-rail fence. Trees lined the rutted route that led six miles east, back to town. A few days ago a tornado had cut a path across the road, dropping limbs, which had obviously been cleared, allowing the three-horse hitch to make its way into the Arkansas woods.

"That's a fine-lookin' council tree you got there," the young driver called out.

The towering oak sitting off to one side of the front yard had been there when Morses first came nearly seventy years ago. Its trunk measured a good six feet in diameter, the height and breadth of its massive limbs signaling age and strength.

"It is that," Grady Morse called out. "The Cherokees themselves sat beneath that tree with the governor of this territory, back in 1818, and bargained. That's how we got all the woods north of the river."

Council trees were common in Arkansas, shaded places where men gathered. Grady Morse was particularly proud of his. He studied his two visitors. The driver was a young, tough, healthy buck, the other man more like himself. Older, with pallid features, scarred and cratered, thin as a corpse, a white beard sprouting from a narrow jaw.

"I need to speak with you," the older man said, the voice hard and sharp, resonant with authority.

Grady held his rifle, which was the prudent thing to do when strangers appeared. "About what?"

"Your duties, sir, as a sentinel."

The older man climbed down from the wagon and stepped through the opening in the rail fence. As he approached, Grady noticed the watery eyes, red-rimmed, with dark crescents

264

that cast a haunted look. One seemed sharp and watchful. The other not so much, more clouded with pain. Wrinkles on the neck and liver spots on the back of the hands betrayed an advanced age. The thinning gray hair was nearly a perfect match for the wool suit he wore.

"May I shake your hand?" his visitor asked.

They did, the grip tight, the palm moist, and he felt the familiar grasp of the third and little fingers with his own.

"Are you on it?" the man said.

"I'm on it."

"They sat under the council tree for an hour and the old man told my great-grandpa about the Witch's Stone," Morse said. "He'd brought it with him in the wagon."

"You never told me any of this," Lea said to her grandfather.

"Wasn't the time. You had to accept the duty, which I kinda figured you weren't goin' to. So I kept quiet."

"Why are you telling these people?"

" 'Cause I don't want either of us to go to jail."

"What happened?" Cotton asked. "With the stone."

"The driver and the older man headed off into the woods. They came back two days later and told my great-grandpa that they hid it in the woods and left markers, like always."

265

"You're special," the older man said to Grady. "You were chosen for this duty because of your family's dedication to the cause."

"I fought in the war and killed my share of Federals."

"That's what I was told. So we want you to guard the stone, as you've done our gold."

Then the older man climbed atop the wagon beside the young driver.

"I do have one question," Grady said.

"I was wondering when you'd get around to that. I applaud you for your patience. That, and your discretion are reasons you were chosen for this great duty. You wish to know my name. Right?"

Grady nodded.

"I am Jefferson Davis, formerly the president of the Confederate States of America, now an unpardoned rebel, still loyal to our great cause."

"That was 1877," Morse said.

"Jefferson Davis himself brought that stone here?"

"As God is my witness."

And Cotton believed him.

It was no different from the stories his own grandfather had told him about what happened in middle Georgia after the war, things only a few were privileged to know. Back then men could actually keep a secret, harboring a duty to both principle and cause.

"Jeff Davis was a knight, high up in the

Order," Morse said. "May have been the head man himself. I don't know. But there were five stones. That's what he told my great-grandpa. We had one. But we weren't told a thing about the other four."

"So how did it get out of the ground and into your bee hut?" Cotton asked.

Morse chuckled. "My great-grandpa cheated. He followed 'em into the woods and watched for two days. He knew exactly where they buried it. And he told my pa."

"So who dug it up?" Cassiopeia asked.

"I did. About forty years ago. We'd had some interest then. Folks had come around again. One time my scarin' barely worked and I thought I was goin' to have to hurt somebody. Luckily, I didn't need to, and they went away. After that, I decided it would be safer under the hives."

He stared at the image on Cassiopeia's phone. The hooded figure on the left, wearing a flowing robe with a cross emblazoned on the sleeve, had the look of a Klansman. The long, pointed hat with a band across it, though, seemed to indicate something different. And the backward grip on the cross. Odd. He again read the fractured Spanish at the upper right. *This path is dangerous. I go to 18 places. Seek the map. Seek the heart.* He looked closely at the flurry of symbols and numbers floating next to the robed figure. A curved line, followed by a ringed *O.* A rectangle with a cross. Another curved line, another ringed *O,* all leading to a heart with a *4* inscribed inside. Then *8–N–P.* It all ran together, linked, arcing from the cross above to the letters below, as if signifying a path.

Or a message.

Chapter Twenty-Seven

Stephanie noted the time. After midnight. She'd left the National Museum of Natural History with Rick, the two of them taking Rick's car to an apartment complex north of town where Martin Thomas had lived. There, they climbed two flights of stairs to a door marked 2F.

"Martin lived here alone," Rick said. "He's divorced, with three kids." He shook his head. "Which might explain his greed. I still can't believe this has happened."

She could sympathize. Many times she'd ordered her own people into harm's way, and the vast majority of them had emerged unscathed. But there'd been plenty of instances when the opposite had happened, and each one of those mishaps still kept her up at night.

They'd found a couple of pieces of wire at the natural history museum. Over the years she'd acquired a few of the skills her agents knew intimately, lock picking being one.

She'd attended a class at Quantico, where her people trained alongside other intelligence officers. She grasped the knob and worked her makeshift picks. It took a little longer than she expected, but finally the tumblers released.

She opened the door and pushed it inward. Rick found a light switch and flicked it on. Another thing she'd learned. If at all possible, never enter a room without first switching on a light. Only idiots prowled around in the dark. Inside was a picture of order. A quick reconnoiter showed a den, a kitchen, two small bedrooms, and two baths. More than enough space for a man living alone. What they sought seemed waiting for them in the den, which was cluttered with books scattered across the furniture and with bulky, dark-green folders, faded with age and fastened with string. A laptop computer sat atop a fold-out table.

"These folders are from our archives," Rick said. "They have our stamp."

"Is this what's missing?"

He nodded. "It looks like it. I'll need a minute."

She studied the documents as he did. Some of the papers were brown with age, while others were fresh white copies. A quick scan showed them to be field notes, reports, correspondence, and newspaper clippings, lots of single-spaced typescript and well-thumbed edges.

"These are the 1909 materials," he said. "We definitely need these returned."

"You allowed him to take them."

Rick nodded. "It seemed like the best way to find out what Mrs. Sherwood was after. Martin knew how to care for them."

The books dealt with the Civil War and bore a stamp for the Smithsonian's American history museum library. Three travel guides for Arkansas carried a discount Barnes & Noble sticker.

"Has to be for the trip he took out there," Rick said, lifting the guides.

Across the room, on a side table abutting the wall, stood framed pictures of Thomas and three children of varying ages, the oldest a teenager. Soon they would learn that their father was dead. She recalled the pain her own son had experienced when they learned of her late husband's suicide. That agony she did not wish on her worst enemy.

"We can't keep his death secret for long," she said. "It's not fair to the family, and the longer it goes the more questions it will raise."

"We'll put it out that Martin is working on something special, indisposed, that sort of thing. Then, in a day or so, we can reveal the truth. Hopefully by then we'll have caught the guy who killed him. I know you're aggravated with the chief justice. But he has his reasons, and I'm sure they're good ones. Can we give it twenty-four hours?"

She smiled. "You do remember that you're the curator of the Castle, not James Bond."

"I've reminded myself of the same thing — several times lately."

She noticed maps of western Arkansas and the southwest United States, along with a copy of an old newspaper article, tucked inside a plastic sleeve.

From the *Los Angeles Herald Examiner.*
Dated June 1, 1973.
Headlined in big letters.

DEAN'S "BURIED GOLD" STORY ISN'T NEW

Everything seems to be turning up these days in the Watergate hearings. Last week, fired White House counsel John Dean III raised the matter of buried treasure.

Dean testified that former attorney general John Mitchell told H. R. Haldeman, former White House chief of staff, at a luncheon Dean attended that "criminal lawyer F. Lee Bailey has a client who has an enormous amount of gold in his possession and would like to make arrangements with the government whereby the gold could be turned over without the client being prosecuted for holding gold." Dean termed Haldeman "nonresponsive."

According to Dean, Bailey's client proposed to deliver hundreds of gold bars to the Treasury Department, the treasure allegedly part of "an old Aztec cache" hidden in the American Southwest. Federal law prohibits U.S. private citizens from possessing gold.

Davis Layne, head of the Smithsonian's National Museum of American History, questions the claim.

"In the first place," Layne told the *Herald-Examiner,* "it would not be pure gold because the bars would contain some zinc, copper, and other trace minerals. But the treasure could still be worth many billions, thanks to gold at $42 an ounce. And it's not Aztec."

Layne explained that the treasure belonged to the Knights of the Golden Circle, a Confederate spy organization, which existed from before the Civil War to around 1916 and amassed somewhere around $100 billion in treasure, burying it in depositories and caches all across the South and West. The hoard was intended to finance a second civil war, which never came.

She looked up. "Is this for real?"

Rick nodded. "Absolutely. Layne is the one who fed that story to the media. That actually happened with Dean, Haldeman, and F. Lee Bailey."

273

She gestured with the article inside the plastic. "This relates to what's happening here?"

"Definitely."

She finished reading the article.

In a reply to attorney Bailey, the Treasury Department reportedly said it must be informed of the gold's location and the circumstances of its discovery before it can pursue the case. Layne, as a historian, sympathized with Bailey and his clients.

"So they have to reveal where the treasure is before the government will even discuss any turnover? I think Bailey was trying to do the right thing, and I think Haldeman was wrong in giving him short shrift. It set a dangerous precedent. Now anybody who finds gold will do their best to smuggle it out of the U.S. because they know their government is hard-nosed and intractable. It will become the Boston Tea Party in reverse."

She searched her memory for more facts.

Roosevelt did in fact ban the private holding of gold. Executive Order 6102. May 1933. Congress ratified that action in 1934 with the Gold Reserve Act. All of that changed, though, in 1974 when Congress again legalized the private holding of gold.

Long after the article she was holding had been written.

"Finding gold before 1974 would have been foolish," she said. "There was nothing legal that could have been done with it. But after Gerald Ford made gold possession okay again, that's another matter."

Her friend stayed silent and she saw the frustration in his eyes. They'd known each other a long time. "Rick, sooner or later you're going to have to trust me and talk."

"Tell you what. Let's gather all this up and head back to the Castle. We can talk there in private. There's some additional material you'll need to see."

It sounded like the veil of secrecy might be lifting.

Or at least she hoped that was the case.

"Give me an armful," she said, "and I'll take the first load out to the car."

Grant sat in his car and watched Martin Thomas' residence. Once he'd decided what to do, he'd headed straight back to his apartment, found his car, then driven here. He'd arrived just as the woman from the Castle and Rick Stamm arrived. They'd been inside the apartment for the past twenty minutes.

Containment was becoming a problem.

He had to do something.

But what?

The lights for 2F still burned.

He waited, and a few moments later the Justice Department woman appeared, carrying a stack of folders. Materials he'd surely need. Rick Stamm he knew — he'd worked the same job his father had once held. They'd never met, but he'd routinely consulted Stamm's book *The Castle,* an excellent guide to the building's history and geography. What was he doing here with this woman?

A mild panic overcame him, like when he was a kid and his mother caught him doing something he shouldn't.

He hated that helpless feeling.

There was still the question of whether he was openly linked with Diane, who *was* linked to Martin Thomas. That remained to be seen, but something told him Thomas had kept their relationship private — and that shakedown back at the museum was real. Perhaps the people at the Smithsonian had secretly targeted Thomas?

The woman followed one of the concrete walks that led toward the car that had brought her. He was parked deeper in the maze of buildings in one of the spaces provided for residents. No way they knew he was there.

He reached beneath his jacket and found his gun.

As with Thomas.

This had to be handled.

Now.

Stephanie heard a car start. Odd considering the late hour. The engine revved and she whirled to see a small sedan emerge from one of the parking spaces. The car came straight for her and she noticed that the passenger-side window was down. Only one silhouette could be seen, the driver, and she caught the dark outline of his right arm coming up, holding a gun.

Fifty feet away.

She dropped the folders and reached for her own weapon.

Twenty feet.

Her right hand gripped the gun.

Ten feet.

She withdrew the Beretta, but never got the chance to fire. The car overtook her. Two rounds spit out the open window and slammed into her chest. The car kept going, wheeling to the exit. She tried to read the license plate but her eyes refused to focus.

Her world began to blur.

Blood poured from two wounds.

Her left hand reached down to stem the flow. She tipped stiffly to one side, every muscle involuntarily relaxing.

She collapsed.

Red brake lights of the car glared angrily in the distance, then disappeared around a corner.

Sounds of the gunning engine receded.

She fought to stay alert.

But a terrible darkness blinded her eyes.

Then swallowed her.

CHAPTER TWENTY-EIGHT

Western Arkansas
Wednesday, May 26
2:06 A.M.

Cotton lay in bed and listened to Terry Morse's snoring. He and Cassiopeia were back at the lodge, having brought both the old man and Lea with them. They'd secured a second room, their original for Lea and Cassiopeia, the new one for him and Morse. Thankfully, this one came with two queen beds. Everyone was tired, particularly Morse, who'd drifted right off. What to do with these two posed a problem, but Morse had told him that they could head upstate to family in the morning where they'd be more than safe. And he doubted the men from tonight would return anyway. He'd sensed that a picture of the stone would be enough for their needs. If not, then they would have made a greater effort to fight the bees and take it with them. The stone itself rested safely beneath his bed, wrapped in towels.

He'd enjoyed a long shower, welcomed after yesterday. Some food would have been good, too, but it was entirely too late for room service. Though stylish, the lodge wasn't the Four Seasons. The cool sheets felt good, but sleep was proving elusive, thanks to the sound of the freight train in the bed next to him.

All that happened had brought back a lot of childhood memories.

As an adult he'd finally learned the truth about the Knights of the Golden Circle. Contrary to any romantic notions, both before, during, and after the Civil War it had been a subversive organization that openly supported slavery and engaged in murder, sabotage, and terror. Enough accounts had been written by men who'd been part of various local castles to know that violence had been an integral part of its modus operandi. And not only against outsiders, but against its own members, too. Today, with no hesitation, it would be labeled a dangerous terrorist organization.

It was what happened after 1865 that remained murky. From his reading he recalled that the Order lingered for about a decade, taking on new names. Eventually, more militant branches became the Ku Klux Klan, but the main line seemed to have disappeared from history.

Now he wasn't so sure.

If Morse was to be believed, starting in the

1870s the Order's wealth had been systematically collected and taken to a place known as the vault. But that wealth could also have been accumulated simply to line the pockets of a precious few, men in the know who played off other men's loyalty to get rich. That would not have been a hard thing to accomplish back then. Little government, weak law enforcement, no oversight. The Gilded Age. A time when immense fortunes were amassed off greed and ruthlessness. No one would have noticed another few multimillionaires rising from nothing.

He lay in bed with his clothes on, trying to let sleep steal up on him. Unfortunately, he'd passed that point and his body had clicked into overdrive with no off switch. During his time at the Magellan Billet he'd lived for weeks off less than three hours of sleep a night.

That part of the job he did not miss.

His cell phone vibrated.

He'd switched off the ringer once Morse had fallen asleep. His thoughts dissolved into a haze as he groped for the phone.

The display indicated an unfamiliar number.

He stepped into the bathroom and closed the door, answering with a feeling of terrible anticipation.

"It's Rick Stamm. I have some bad news."

■ ■ ■ ■

Cassiopeia woke.

Somebody was knocking on the door.

She rolled off the bed and gripped the gun from the nightstand. Lea was sound asleep. One glance out the peephole and she saw Cotton in the hall. She found the key card, left the gun, then stepped outside. The look on his face told her something had happened.

"Stephanie's been shot."

Shock swept through her. "How bad?"

"Not good. She's in surgery. Two slugs in the chest. Rick Stamm just called."

She gently touched his shoulder. "Any idea if she's going to be okay?"

"He said she was ambushed. She was barely alive when the ambulance got there. Martin Thomas is dead, too."

She'd had her differences with Stephanie, both of them strong-willed women with equally strong opinions. Never, though, would she wish any harm on her.

"I'm going back tonight," he said. "I want you to stay here and see where this leads. We need to know more about that stone."

"I've been trying to gain Lea's confidence. I think she could use a friend."

"Work on that. I'll let you know what's happening as soon as I know something."

She wrapped her arms around his neck. He

was hurting, that was obvious, but he'd never admit it. He and Stephanie went back a long way. They were more than employer and employee. They were close friends, and Cotton had precious few of those.

Like her, he was a loner.

"I took a few bullets during my time," he said. "But that was part of the job. Not her. She's front office."

"An office she never stays in."

"I know. She's been taking more and more chances of late. But you can only cheat fate for so long."

She kissed him in a long, lingering embrace.

Which he seemed to like.

She drew back and said, "I want you to remember what you just said about cheating fate."

"Same for you."

"Deal."

"I'll take the rental car to the airport," he said. "The Justice Department plane is waiting for me."

The same jet that had brought them to Arkansas.

"Pick up the rental car tomorrow to use. I'll leave the keys in the glove compartment. We'll worry about getting you out of here later."

She nodded. "I'll make do."

"Of that I have no doubt."

She watched as he headed back to his

room. "Cotton."

He stopped and turned.

She caught the look of consternation on his face.

"Call Danny Daniels. He needs to know."

She reentered her room to find Lea awake in bed.

"Are you two a thing?" the younger girl asked.

"Were you spying through the peephole?"

"I heard voices and looked out to see who it was. That was quite a kiss."

She nodded and smiled. "We have a thing."

"He's handsome."

"He's headed back to Washington, DC. Some things there have to be handled. I'm going to stay here and make sure you two are okay."

"We don't need a babysitter. Me and Grandpa have gotten along real fine on our own."

She noted that the declaration did not carry any anger or resentment, more just a statement of fact. "I realize that. But this is a little above and beyond what the two of you are accustomed to handling."

"Where are you from?"

She decided to go with the abrupt change of subject. "I live in France, but I was born and raised in Spain. My father's ancestry goes back to the Moors, my mother was European."

"You have nice clothes. Are you rich?"

She was impressed with the girl's powers of observation. "I'm not poor. My father left me a company that makes a great deal of money."

"I look at the fashion sites online. I like fashion, though I don't get to wear much of it."

Walls were definitely cracking so she decided to see if she could break them down further. She grabbed her laptop and accessed the website for her castle reconstruction project. Lea came close and they scanned through the pages, which were loaded with photos and information.

"This is my passion," she told Lea.

"We have one of those here."

Which she knew about, as her project had been its inspiration. The Ozark Medieval Fortress. Like her own, it was to be a reproduction of a French castle. Unlike her own, which she personally funded, that project had closed for lack of money.

"It's up in the northern part of the state," Lea said. "I heard about it from some people who went and saw it."

She'd already sensed that this girl had too few female influences in her life. She loved her grandfather, but sometimes that wasn't enough. So she kept the conversation going and they talked more about each other.

"If you're rich and buildin' a castle, why are you workin' with the feds?"

"Cotton and I help them out sometimes. Of course, we had no idea it was going to turn into all this. It was supposed to be a simple fact-finding mission."

"I'm ashamed of what Grandpa did with those men," she said. "Trickin' you. He was actin' stupid."

"I think he knows that."

"Can I tell you somethin'? Between you and me?"

She nodded.

"I have a special fella."

She smiled. "Like Cotton is to me?"

"Yep. We like each other. But I know how Grandpa feels about that. He says boys are bad."

"He's just looking after you."

"I guess. But he really thinks all boys are bad. I get it. He just wants me to be careful and sure, and I am."

There was a lot of maturity in this young woman, evidenced by how she'd earlier handled a gun to her neck.

"My fella's uncle was a sentinel, too, who guarded some important stuff, like the stone. We've talked about it, tryin' to figure things out."

"And what did you decide?"

"That my grandpa and his uncle were not crazy."

She could sense there was more.

"I can show you somethin', if you want."

CHAPTER TWENTY-NINE

Tennessee

Diane could not sleep. She'd lain down after Vance had left, switching off all the lights in the house and enveloping herself in a welcomed darkness. Her brother's missing notebook weighed heavy on her mind. Somebody had taken it from the study, of that she was sure. But who? And why? Tops on her list was Danny Daniels, especially since he'd possessed the cross-and-circle necklace. He'd acted as though he knew nothing of its significance, but that was coming from a man who knew how to lie. Did he know what the cross and circle meant? Were all the questions about Alex's death just curiosity or something else?

She had to stop.

Damn this paranoia.

Danny Daniels could not care less about what she was doing. Why would he? He was nothing more than Alex's friend and had returned the necklace. So she asked herself once again, who could have taken the note-book? It was there two days ago after Grant delivered it, when she'd read every word. Luckily, most of it was shorthand reflections, bullet points and legal citations, meaningless to almost everyone and certainly not threatening. The cross and circle on the front would probably not even be noticed. Just some manufacturer's decoration. She'd debated whether to tell Vance about Kenneth's breach of secrecy with Alex and the notebook being gone, but decided to keep that to herself.

Like everything else.

"You can't do this," Alex said to her, his voice rising.

They were sitting alone in the great room.

"I won't allow you to do any of this," he said.

That, she resented. "I don't require your permission."

"No, you don't. But I am the senior senator from this state, and I can stop you, Kenneth, and Lucius Vance."

She shook her head. "What a hypocrite. All your preaching about changing the government. All your complaining. Here you have a way to fix it, and you don't want to take it."

"This is not a fix. It's a revolution. One the people should decide for themselves."

"They will, through their duly elected representatives. If they don't like it, they can un-elect them. They get that opportunity, in the House of

288

Representatives, every two years."

"It's not that simple and you know it. Once done, this will be tough to undo. And once power is tasted, people have a tendency to keep on eating it. Even the minority in the House, who will oppose the change by the majority, will see the political advantages."

"What's the matter, Alex? Afraid you and your Senate cronies will lose your clout? Right now you take every molecule of oxygen from the room. Senators get the local party money, the local party support. House candidates fight for the scraps, and most times they don't even get those. They have to go out and raise every dime for their campaigns, while you prima donnas in the Senate have everything handed to you. That will all change, won't it?"

"You don't have a clue what you're about to unleash. Lucius Vance is no benign statesman. He's ambitious and arrogant and wanted to be president. Now he will essentially become an autocrat. More powerful than any president. That kind of concentration was never meant for one man. This country was not founded on that principle."

"That's where you're wrong, Alex. This plan is exactly how this country was governed for its first thirty years. The House dominated, and the Senate followed. And we survived. We're just going back to our roots."

"We were a tiny nation, with a tiny central government that did little to nothing. The world has changed. This plan, as you call it, was designed by men to strip the North of its ability to hold the South in check. It was meant to be a declaration of political war — which by the way was never implemented. Perhaps they realized, as I do, it's a risk too great to take."

"Where is Kenneth's notebook?"

"I left it in DC. It will make for good evidence, if needed."

"You can't stop this, Alex. If you don't agree, then just stay out of the way. Let Vance do what he has to do."

"There'll be strong opposition to what he proposes."

"Of course there will. But that's far different from you, a sitting senator, my husband, screaming conspiracy. Leave it be."

"You should have told me about this. Not Kenneth. You."

"The way you told me about your girlfriend?"

He stared at her. "How did you know?"

"I didn't. I only suspected. Until this moment."

He shook his head and chuckled bitterly. "That's one for you. You ran that bluff like a pro."

"I am a pro. Who is she?"

"A woman I met in DC. But whether you believe me or not, I've done nothing I'm ashamed of."

"Except, maybe, fall in love with her."

"I won't deny that we enjoy our time together."

"Which actually hurts worse."

"And what about you, Diane? Have you been a saint?"

"Actually, no. I've been with two other men."

She said it to hurt him. Not a lie, either. Strange how love so quickly evolved into hate.

"I didn't realize," Alex said, surprise in his voice. "But we've been strangers a long time."

"So leave this alone. Let me have this moment. My father would be so proud. He studied the Order all his life, learned its secret language, found what documents he could, and searched for what was lost. He passed that passion on to me. Alex, let me do this, without your interference."

"I wish I could, but I can't."

He'd left the house, heading out for a midafternoon walk. She knew where he went, up the path at the rear of the property, into the foothills, to his thinking place. He would stay a couple of hours, smoke his pipe, then return, ready for supper and bed. That night, though, they were scheduled to have dinner in Knoxville with some supporters. One thing she would not miss was the constant pandering for money and votes.

She'd sat there that day in the great room, alone, and thought about what to do. Everything seemed to hinge on her. First with Kenneth recruiting her assistance, then her finding Grant, then the moves at the Smithsonian with Martin Thomas, and finally Alex.

A wheel with many spokes, her at the center.

And she had indeed slept with two men.

Lucius Vance and Grant Breckinridge.

One was part of the moment, an intoxicating reaction to power and influence. The other stemmed from a deep longing. Kenneth thought Grant reckless. She considered him passionate. He'd seemed so lost that day when she'd visited with his father. He worked as a paralegal for a DC firm. He'd thought about law school, but considered the profession more word pushing than anything else. Grant craved excitement. Which explained his many job moves among the DC firms, eking out a living until she came along.

How much gold was out there? Many billions of dollars' worth, for sure. Just waiting for a new set of revolutionaries to claim it in the name of freedom. Long ago passionate men had tried to alter the course of the United States by violently dividing it. They'd been wrong. Instead, the smarter path was to simply use what the Constitution itself provided. Work *within* its parameters. People tended to follow that which seemed to make the most sense. And what she and Lucius Vance were planning certainly fit into that category.

It almost seemed too perfect. But that was its beauty. The men who conceived the original idea had marveled at its simplicity.

They just hadn't been able to stave off the waves of radicalism that eventually consumed the South. It had taken hundreds of thousands of deaths and the total destruction of a way of life to show the error of their ways.

But a few of those visionaries had been right about one thing.

Change things from within.

She lay in bed and stared at the ceiling.

A part of her missed Alex. He'd brought comfort to her life. Never had he raised a hand to her. Rarely had they argued. She'd lived a life of privilege and importance. He'd always treated her with courtesy and respect, and there was something to be said for that. But she'd come to resent the pained politeness between them, and realized there was something wrong with never daring, never risking, never being willing to take a blind leap with no safety net.

Never living.

She'd finally done that.

By sleeping with two men. Then she went a step further and showed one of them how to create a new United States of America. For the other, she pointed him down a path that could make him rich. She was proud of both endeavors, the results of which would soon be known.

Alex would have denied her all that.

Thank God he was dead.

CHAPTER THIRTY

Cassiopeia was not pleased with having to bring Lea along, but the price of directions had been her inclusion. They'd left the lodge quietly, a note slipped under the door telling Terry Morse they'd be back soon. Neither one of them had wanted to wait around until morning. She'd learned that Lea's special friend lived about twenty miles away. They'd get together when she went into town, or to the store, or running errands. Most of their relationship was electronic — text, emails, FaceTime — which seemed the way of the modern world. Her grandfather was not all that tech-savvy, so a measure of privacy existed there, something Lea seemed to like.

They'd taken Terry Morse's truck, which Lea and her grandfather had brought from the house earlier. Luckily, Lea had driven and had the keys. The time was approaching 3:30 in the morning, a half-moon illuminating a landscape of forested hills and dark valleys. Their route took them deep into the woods northwest of the lodge. Lea explained that she'd visited the location a few times with her special friend. His uncle had died years ago, leaving behind a trunk full of maps and papers, many in code. Her friend had spent a few years trying to decipher them, especially after Lea explained to him about sentinels. Apparently his uncle had never volunteered anything on that subject, and allowed the duty to die with him.

"We came up here one night," Lea said as she drove. "Grandpa was gone. There was nobody around, so we had things to ourselves."

That she could see, since there was not a light in sight. "And what did you do, up here, with things to yourselves?"

Lea did not immediately reply. Finally the girl said, "Nothing all that bad."

"I was your age once. I get it."

"I really like him."

"And that's fine. But be careful how far you go. If he truly likes you, too, *that* won't matter."

"He does really like me, 'cause it didn't matter."

"Good girl. Your grandpa would be proud."

"No. Grandpa would have shot him."

Lea turned off the highway and followed a rutted path, wood fences on either side, most nearly hidden by a jungle of weeds and wildflowers springing from the ditches.

"All this land belongs to his family," Lea said. "Like us, they've owned it a long, long time."

They bucked down the narrow track, headlights swaying and jolting. The road ended at a rocky incline protected by a heavy ring of pine and elm. A gate blocked the path ahead, but Cassiopeia saw that it was not locked shut. Instead, a short length of chain lay in the dirt, the gate half open. Lea eased the front of the truck forward and pushed the panel out of the way.

"It's usually locked," Lea said, "and you have to walk from here."

"How far?"

"About a quarter mile."

She didn't like the feel of things.

Why? She wasn't sure. But her internal alarms were chiming.

"Shut the lights off and park up in the trees."

She led, with Lea behind her, the road dry as a desert. A flashlight found under the front seat illuminated the path. Tall trees and dense underbrush lined the way, the terrain more mountainous than yesterday, loose shale crunching beneath their soles. Ragged clouds scuttled across gaps of stars. The buzz of a cicada masked their steps.

Shadowy hulks appeared ahead.

She counted the remnants of six derelict

buildings, all in a state of ruin, every window smashed, walls collapsed, roofs swaybacked with neglect. There was also what looked like a collapsed conveyer.

"What is this?" she asked.

"An old silver mine. There are lots of 'em around here. This one's been closed a long time."

"Your special friend's family owns this?"

"They leased it out once. But nobody comes up here now except his family to hunt."

"All right. Show me what's here."

The camp sat among a chain of tree-covered hills that ran from west to east, dipping and tapering into a trough-shaped hollow that stretched black into the night. She could hear a fast-moving stream. Which made sense. Any mining operation would need a water source.

They entered one of the collapsed buildings. The flashlight beam wove through a yard of battered blocks, slabs of rock, and rusted metal, all piled onto one another in a solid mass. Time had clamped the debris down, flowering weeds springing up among the rubble. Little remained of the structure besides three partial walls and patches of roof. The building had once abutted the base of the mound, and at its far end she saw an opening into the earth.

"That's not the same," Lea said.

An archway rose three meters and stretched nearly the same distance wide. Loose rock packed its confines, as if a landslide had sealed it long ago. But a neat hole had been dug through its center, big enough to walk through.

"Always before that was closed off," Lea said. "Once, we picked out some of the larger boulders and made a squeeze point. It was tight to get through, but we could make it. I was going to show you what's on the other side. There's never been an opening like that."

They approached and carefully entered the tunnel, swallowed by a yawing darkness. A shaft stretched before them that angled slightly upward into the hillside, the walls bearing evidence of the picks that had long ago been used to chop through. The air hung close and stale.

"I know the story of this place," Lea said. "Back in the 1840s the locals mined lead and silver that they shipped off to England. They made good money. Then the Confederates came and took over, mining silver during the war. Union troops blew it up after, and it's been empty ever since."

"Except for who?"

"My friend's uncle. He guarded this place real careful, like Grandpa does the woods. He wouldn't let anyone get too close. But he's been dead a long time and there hasn't been a sentinel since."

They continued their walk up the incline. Overhead ran a frayed cable of old-fashioned braided ceramic fiber wiring, with corroded empty sockets every five meters. Once, this whole thing had been electrically lit. She felt no drafts, which meant this was probably a one-way route. About thirty meters in, the way became blocked by an iron gate, bars thick as her thumbs drilled directly into the stone at the top and sides. At its center was a barred door fitted with hinges and a built-in lock. The iron was coated with a crusted layer of rust, but the lock and hinges were aged brass. Ordinarily it would be a formidable portcullis, but the door hung half open.

"It's never been unlocked before," Lea said. "We tried to open it, but never could. I was going to see if you could do it."

More alarm bells rang.

The lock looked like many she'd seen in castles all across Europe, opening only by a skeleton key. Was this one of the Knights of the Golden Circle's caches? If so, something she'd read back at the American history museum urged caution. Booby traps. Explosives were their favorite. But something told her that whatever danger might have existed did not any longer.

After a few meters she noticed a black line on the dirt floor. The bobbing puddle of the flashlight beam revealed the end of an electrical cord with a three-pronged male plug. She traced the wire's path ahead and saw that it disappeared down the tunnel. They followed the cord as it wound its way toward a large gash. The main shaft continued farther into the mound, but here somebody had dug sideways into the tunnel wall, where the electrical cord headed, too.

She stepped through and saw that it was a short connector to another tunnel. It would be easy to become disoriented in the blackness. Thankfully, they had the cord to lead them back to where they came from. The new tunnel was narrower, about two persons wide and tall enough that that they could stand.

"Somebody knew exactly where to dig," she said to Lea, "to get where they wanted to be."

The new tunnel wound a path that she estimated to be perpendicular with the main shaft, with several twists and turns. Luckily, no offshoots. It ended at a wooden door, the hinges coated in rust. Once, a hasp had held it closed, but no lock was there. It swung inward on a wood frame. The electrical cord slipped past through a crack.

She handed the flashlight to Lea and shoved at the door.

The hinges squealed but held.

She threw her shoulder into it.

The door creaked inward a fraction, but it remained wedged tight. She backed up and drove her body into it hard. The hinges released and the thick slab of wood burst inward. Momentum drove her down to the earthen floor.

"That was harder than it needed to be," she said, rising to her feet and brushing the dirt from her clothes.

The flashlight revealed a spacious chamber with a vaulted roof carved from the rock. The electrical cord ended at a stand for two large floodlights. Wooden trunks of various sizes lay across the floor, each covered in dust and fused together by decades of grime.

She did a quick count.

Nineteen.

Two-thirds of which were open and empty.

Seven were still closed.

She approached one and hinged open its lid, which resisted but gave way.

Gold bars lay stacked inside.

She heard a distant engine coughing, then the lights sprang to life and the chamber was flooded with brightness, which burned her pupils.

A generator?

They had to leave.

But there was only one way out.

A man appeared. Then three more in the doorway.

Not the same people from earlier at the Morses'.

Different.

And far more threatening.

CHAPTER THIRTY-ONE

Tennessee
5:40 A.M.

Danny stood at his bedroom window, his mind tangled with scattered images. Daylight was breaking, the first pale rays of silver streaks thrusting above the eastern mountains growing in intensity, the events of the night before seemingly far away, as if a dream.

But they weren't.

The governor was already up and gone, headed for an early breakfast with business leaders. They'd agreed last night that the announcement of his Senate appointment would be made later in the morning, giving Danny time to get to DC so the vice president could immediately administer the oath of office. Once he was sworn in, for the next two years he'd be the junior senator from Tennessee. He'd already decided to keep Alex's staff in place and make do with what he had. Their former boss had been a close friend, so he assumed that there would not be a whole lot

302

of enemies there.

His number one job would be to look after the people of Tennessee. But in the short term, his goal was to find out what had happened to Alex, along with discovering what Lucius Vance was up to. Thankfully, he was a world-class practitioner of multitasking. Damn, it would feel good to be wanted again. He'd known he would miss it, but the extent had actually surprised him.

He was a power addict.

Pure and simple.

Not the kind of power, though, that brought personal gain or pain to others. His addiction was more to the process of getting things done, making a difference. He loved the tense, theatrical atmosphere of DC, one that echoed conflict and confidence. Constituent service was the linchpin of any good public servant. People elected their representatives to take care of their problems, and he liked being a solver. He'd never been one to go with the flow. Instead he'd swum upstream, bucking the system, loving every minute of it.

Finally, he felt alive again.

The house phone rang and he stepped toward the bed and answered.

"Mr. President, it's Cotton Malone."

His spine stiffened.

Nothing about this call was going to be good. "You finding out how to get a hold of me means there's a big problem."

"The Magellan Billet had your home number on file. And you're right, this is bad news."

He knew instantly.

"What's happened to Stephanie?"

Cotton tapped off his cell phone.

He stood in an empty hospital waiting room, on the sixth floor, near the intensive care unit. He'd arrived in DC by jet at Reagan National a little over an hour ago and had come straight here. Stephanie was out of surgery, which had taken several hours and had been touch and go, the two bullets doing some internal damage. With its leader down, the Magellan Billet was being operated by procedures she'd long ago set into place. There was no formal second in command, the Billet strapped with as little bureaucracy as possible. Everything was centered on Stephanie, which was good and bad. Her administrative assistant was as close to a vice commander as the Billet got, and she was now directing the agents in the field, withholding that Stephanie had been injured.

Danny Daniels had taken the news hard, saying he'd been on his way to Washington anyway this morning and would accelerate his travel plans.

"But by God keep me informed," Daniels ordered.

They'd exchanged cell phone numbers and

Daniels had said he'd text the number where he could be reached. Cotton knew about the connection between Daniels and Stephanie. Not the details, nor the particulars, but enough to know that they cared for each other. Cassiopeia knew far more, which she'd kept to herself. Earlier, when she'd encouraged him to call Daniels, he'd understood. The exact nature of their relationship was none of his business, but what had happened to Stephanie was definitely Daniels' concern. So he'd opted to break with Billet rules and make the call. Per her standing command, no one was to be alerted to the situation. Not unless she died. Then the attorney general was to be told first, and he or she would decide what happened next. But as long as she breathed, silence reigned. Those procedures were all part of Billet training, designed to keep things flowing uninterrupted by what might or might not happen to her.

A strange mixture of emotion swirled through him. Seeing Stephanie so tied to tubes, wires, and oxygen was more than disconcerting. He had few close friends in the world. Most of the people he met were around for a short while, then gone. Sure, some relationships lasted, but they were more acquaintances than friends. Henrik Thorvaldsen, perhaps the person closest to him in recent years, got himself killed in Paris. Cotton had arrived a few moments too late to prevent it from happening, and the guilt from that had never left him. Even worse, they'd been estranged at the time, Henrik taking a path that he hadn't agreed with, which friends did sometimes. Now his other closest friend, a woman he'd known for a long time, someone who'd altered the course of his life, lay in critical condition.

Why had this happened?

What was she doing working with the Smithsonian? No mention had been made of her when the chief justice asked for his assistance. Nor had her name come up the past few days.

Rick Stamm waited down the hall, just outside Stephanie's room, which was now guarded by a Magellan Billet agent. That wasn't part of Stephanie's contingency plan, but Cotton had insisted, and no one in Atlanta disagreed. So an agent had been diverted and two more were on their way.

He walked back to where Stamm stood alone. "Talk to me. What happened?"

"I called her for help. She's an old friend. This is my fault. Thomas is dead and Stephanie is fighting for her life, thanks to me."

He laid a hand on the curator's shoulder. "Look, we don't have time for the blame game. Tell me what happened."

Stamm told him how he had been inside Martin Thomas' apartment when he heard two shots. He ran outside to find Stephanie on the ground, bleeding, a car racing away.

"Was she there when Thomas was killed?"

Stamm nodded, then recounted the rest of the evening's events.

"Do you think the person who shot Stephanie was the same man from the Castle?" he asked.

"Who knows? I didn't see a thing."

He told Stamm what he and Cassiopeia had found in Arkansas.

The Witch's Stone.

Which seemed to get the curator's attention.

"Is that what the chancellor is after?" The inquiry was met with silence, and Cotton did not like the hedging. "I assure you, this is no time to be coy."

"We need to get back to the American history museum," Stamm said. "We can talk there. In private. That's where Stephanie and I were headed before . . . this happened."

Fair enough.

The doctors had said she would be out for a few hours in a medically induced coma.

And he'd already compartmentalized his worry and turned his focus to the mission.

Not always a good thing, but necessary under the circumstances.

"Lead the way."

Danny drove to the Knoxville airport, which sat on the far-east side of Blount County,

307

where the state's jet would be waiting. The governor had offered the ride, which he'd accepted. He was thinking back to the first time he and Stephanie actually had a face-to-face conversation, not in a formal meeting, but private. Just between them.

A few years ago.

At Camp David. During another crisis.

"Contrary to what you might think, I'm not an idiot," he said.

They were sitting on the front porch of the cabin, each in a high-backed wooden rocker. He worked his with vigor, the floorboards straining from his tall frame.

"I don't think I ever called you an idiot."

"My daddy used to tell my mama that he never called her a bitch to her face. Which was also true. I have a problem, Stephanie. A serious one."

"That makes two of us. According to your deputy national security adviser I'm under arrest. And didn't you fire me?"

"Both had to be done, so you could be here now."

He recalled how unimpressed she'd seemed with her predicament. So he'd told her a story.

"One of my uncles used to say, want to kill snakes? Simple. Don't give 'em a chance to bite you. Make 'em come to you. Just set fire to the underbrush and wait for them to slither out. Then you just whack their heads off. That's what we're going to do. Set some fires. I need your help."

"To do what?"

"Find my traitor."

And that was exactly what she'd done.

In fine style.

As she always did, she'd yanked his butt out of trouble. The Magellan Billet had been the one agency he could trust to get the job done, headed by a remarkable woman whom he'd hoped to spend the rest of his days with.

Now she was fighting for her life.

He'd originally planned to head to Washington and set some fires, chase out the snakes, then whack their heads off.

But he added one other task to his list.

God help the bastard who shot his girl.

CHAPTER THIRTY-TWO

Cassiopeia kept blinking, allowing her eyes to adjust to the sudden burst of harsh blue-white light. Lea was doing the same.

"Who are you?" the man in front asked.

He was lean and drawn, with an almost military bearing about him. Maybe mid-forties, handsome features, the eyes a deep, striking brown beneath a tousled mop of shaggy, grayish hair. She decided to use the truth, which might be their only weapon.

"I'm Cassiopeia Vitt. I work with the U.S. Justice Department."

"And the young lady?"

"Lea Morse. She lives around here."

"Are you related to Terry Morse?"

"I'm his granddaughter."

He seemed impressed. "Do you know of the Witch's Stone?"

And apparently informed.

"What if we do?" Cassiopeia said, answering for Lea. "And you never mentioned your name."

"James Proctor."

His accent was decidedly southern, like Cotton's, both men using the soft drawl as a measure of control. The fact that he revealed his name brought her no comfort, nor did his tone. Neutral. Businesslike. Unwelcoming.

"Why are you here?" he asked.

"Same reason you are." She motioned to the open trunk. "The gold."

"But it doesn't belong to you."

"And it does to you?"

"In a sense. We are its keeper."

"Is this the vault?"

A slight smile came to his lips. "I see you're familiar with us."

"I'm not the only one."

She hoped he got the message that people back in Washington were aware of things — which, sadly, wasn't exactly true.

They were on their own.

Proctor stepped close to where she and Lea stood. "This gold has waited here a long time. But no, this is not the vault. Just one of a few remaining repositories we made use of."

"You can't be serious. The Knights of the Golden Circle still exist?"

She'd already concluded that these men bore no relation to the three imposters from earlier at the Morse place.

"We are knights," Proctor said.

He was deadly serious, so she decided not to antagonize him.

"Were all these trunks filled with gold?"

He nodded. "We've been removing it for the past several days. You arrived while we were carting off the next-to-last load. One of my colleagues was standing guard outside in the woods and saw you approach. Now tell me, are you really here for the gold?"

"We know about sentinels," Lea said. "My grandpa is one."

"That he is, and an excellent one, too. He held to his duty for a long time. His grandfather, your great-grandfather, was specially chosen to guard the Witch's Stone."

This man had access to some precise information.

"Were you being trained to assume the duty?" Proctor asked.

Lea nodded. "I was."

Smart girl, she knew a lie was better than the truth.

"I assume there are no grandsons?"

"Not a one."

"Women can't serve?" Cassiopeia asked.

"It's not usual. But if you were being trained, why would you violate this place?" Proctor asked Lea. "A sentinel's job is to protect."

"Why'd you send those men to hurt my grandpa?"

For the first time Proctor seemed surprised. So it was just as Cassiopeia had thought.

There were two different factions at work here.

"I sent no men," Proctor declared.

She seized the moment. "Which means others are onto you. They also claimed to be knights and knew the handshake and the right words of greeting."

A look of concern came to Proctor's face. "That's disturbing to hear. But I assure you, those men were not with us."

She needed a diversion. "There's a lot of gold here."

He nodded. "Somewhere in the range of $50 million worth, depending on the purity, which is usually quite good."

She still had her gun, tucked tight to her spine. With the warm night she'd worn no jacket so, if she turned around, its bulge would be exposed. She could reach for it, but the men standing before her were surely armed, too. The ensuing firefight would be no fight at all, and Lea could get killed.

"I pride myself on being a gentleman," Proctor said. "So it's most unfortunate that you came. I must apologize for what I have to do."

He motioned and two of the men surged forward.

She did reach for her gun then, but Proctor's right hand whipped up, holding a semi-automatic.

"That weapon behind your back will do you

no good," he said.

His eyes momentarily drifted downward, to her shirt, unbuttoned just enough to expose the rim of her breasts.

"I thought you were a gentleman?" she asked.

"That doesn't mean I'm blind."

He gestured with his free hand and one of the men grabbed Lea, who started to kick. The second man gripped her ankles and together they hauled her across the chamber. Cassiopeia had already noticed a rectangular yaw in the floor about three meters long and two meters wide.

They tossed Lea in.

She started to rush over, but was stopped by the gun only millimeters away. She faced down Proctor's penetrating stare with open hostility.

"Go ahead," he said. "But first."

He reached around behind her and claimed the pistol with a smile of superior, mocking pleasure.

She ran over and saw that the opening was a vertical connector, like an elevator shaft, down. A wooden ladder stood propped to one side. Darkness filled the cavity.

"Lea, are you all right?"

Nothing.

"Lea."

"I'm okay," a voice said from below. "The bottom is real soft."

Proctor came up close behind her and she caught the garlicky bouquet of a recent meal. "As I said, I'm a gentleman. Your turn. You may jump on your own."

"Move to one side, Lea, near the ladder. I'm coming down."

"By the way, that ladder is of no use. Rotten. The rungs are all gone."

She leaped into the blackness, the world dropping out from under her feet. The plunge was maybe five meters and she landed hard, rolling to one side. But Lea had been right. The ground was thick with powdery earth, which absorbed the impact like a sponge.

Her eyes searched for Lea but could not see the girl.

"You okay?" Lea asked.

She pinpointed the voice.

"Here," Lea said. "Crawl."

"It's a shame we have to part like this," Proctor said from above. "But it's important neither one of you is ever found."

She knew what was about to come, so she scampered toward Lea, who was huddled at the base of the shaft. When dug, the walls at the pit's bottom had been flared out. Niches had formed, either from the digging or cave-ins. Lea was inside one and she quickly nestled tight to her, forcing both of them into the slit as far as possible, protecting the girl with her body.

Three shots rained down.

Lead thumped into the sandy earth. She knew what the bastard was doing. Aiming all around, knowing one or more would find their mark. So she gave him what he wanted and moaned in feigned agony.

Four more shots came down.

She went silent.

"Do it," Proctor said from above.

And something whooshed down the shaft, crashing to the floor. Her pupils had dilated enough that the outline was clear.

One of the trunks.

Another followed, then more, each disintegrating atop the other.

She realized what was happening.

They were filling the shaft.

CHAPTER THIRTY-THREE

Cotton entered the National Museum of American History after being waved through a security checkpoint thanks to Rick Stamm being with him. The building would not open to the public for another two hours, so its halls were vacant. They made their way across the empty ground floor to a set of stairs, then up one level, past the Star-Spangled Banner display and into a foyer that led to more exhibits. Stamm bypassed those and led him through a closed door that required a security key card.

One swipe and they were inside.

The slick elegance of the public areas gave way to the employee-only portion, where plain white walls and shiny terrazzo floors dominated. They climbed a steep staircase, then Stamm used the swipe card again to gain access to a carpeted, windowless space filled with tracked shelves. Fluorescent lights illuminated everything, the flowing air cool, clean, and dry.

317

"This is one of several American history archives we have in the building," Stamm said. "It deals specifically with the 19th century, and most of this stuff has never been displayed."

The repository where he and Cassiopeia had spent a couple of days reading had been located on the fifth floor, near the main history library where Martin Thomas had worked.

Stamm had explained how the chief justice had drafted Stephanie's assistance in hiding Martin Thomas's body for a day or so while they found the man's killer. Now, Cotton supposed, that duty had fallen to him.

"This is all way out of my league," Stamm said.

"And yet here you are, right in the middle of things."

He hoped the message was received. His bullshit-tolerance level had dropped to zero. Time to shoot straight.

The room was about thirty feet square. Painted pipes and conduits ran close to the gray concrete above. No sounds save for the muted hum of the air-conditioning. No luxury, either, only functionality. A single metal desk supported a computer monitor.

He decided to come to the point. "I want to know how my ancestor, Angus Adams, figures into this. Why was I specially recruited?"

He listened as Stamm told him about an 1854 Smithsonian expedition to the newly acquired American Southwest that also involved some covert reconnaissance by the Knights of the Golden Circle.

"Your great-great-grandfather was part of the expedition, working secretly with the Order," Stamm said. "How much do you know about Adams?"

Quite a bit actually.

And all thanks to his grandfather.

Angus Adams had been one of the Smithsonian's early hires, a painter who evolved into a first-rate illustrator. A trunk in his grandfather's attic contained several lithographs Adams created while working at the Smithsonian. In the time before photography, art was the only way specimens could be memorialized. At the outset of the Civil War, Adams quit his job and obtained a lieutenant's commission, becoming part of Georgia's famed Cobb's Legion. In 1862 he was promoted to major and reassigned to spying. Cotton had seen several grainy, black-and-white photographs of Adams, who'd been short and slender with a bushy head of light hair and a thick mustache, both common for the time. More letters revealed a soft, talkative man with a rash of pessimism, reflected in his constant carrying of both a gun and a knife. Friends called him dedicated, enemies labeled him a zealot. Nobody thought him

319

stupid. He seemed to prefer nature over people, music to books, and ideas to silence. Most remarkable was the resemblance he bore to Cotton, there in the chin, eyes, nose, and mouth.

As a spy, Adams had led the first covert incursion into Pennsylvania with twenty other Confederates, posing as a Union unit in search of deserters. He obtained vital intelligence on troop movements, which Lee used in his march toward Gettysburg. He was then sent to Indiana to stir up insurrection as a way to entice that state to join the Confederacy.

And he almost succeeded.

But he was captured and imprisoned in Ohio.

What happened after that evolved into legend.

Supposedly, while in jail, Adams was reading *Les Misérables* and became inspired by Jean Valjean's escapes through the Paris underground. He then noticed how dry the lower prison cells were, with no mold, though they remained in perpetual darkness. That might indicate a constant source of fresh air. Sure enough, he dug down and found a masonry-lined tunnel, probably used for drainage. Adams and five others eventually made their escape through it, and he left a note for the warden.

Castle Merion, Cell No. 20. November 27, 1863. Commencement of digging, November 4, 1863. Conclusion, November 20, 1863. Hours for labor per day, three. Tools, two small knives. La patience est amère, mais son fruit est doux. By order of six honorable Confederates.

That was the thing about an eidetic memory. Hard to forget anything. He remembered every word of the note. His grandfather told him that Adams had possessed the same advantage. And what a character, as the brazen note and French phrase illustrated.

Patience is bitter, but its fruit is sweet.

The warden had not appreciated having his face rubbed in the insult of an escape, so a massive manhunt ensued. Adams fled south, heading for Kentucky. Near the Ohio River, Union troops cornered him in a small border town. He found refuge inside a farmhouse where the owner lay ill with delirium. Escape was impossible, so he hid himself inside the mattress upon which the sick man lay. When soldiers inspected the house, they checked to see if Adams was the man in the bed, but never thought to look beneath the man, inside the mattress. They left, but posted guards at the door. The following day it rained, but visitors still came to see the sick farmer. Thankfully, the soldiers paid little attention to the faces under the umbrellas, which allowed Adams the opportunity to sneak away. When he made his report to his superiors they were both impressed and amused. One of them made a comment. Something to the effect that Adams was apparently soft as cotton, since no one, not even the sick soul in the bed, had known he was there.

And the name stuck.

Cotton.

"I know a lot about him," he said to Stamm. "What I don't know is how he figures into all of this today. Enough for the chief justice of the United States to hire me to help."

Stamm explained how Adams had recorded his observations from the 1854 expedition in a journal, which had disappeared a long time ago.

"We were hoping your family might have it," Stamm said.

"If they do, no one ever said a word about it, and I never saw it. Why is it important?"

"I truly don't know. All I was told was that the chancellor wants to locate it. He'll be disappointed, but we still need your help." Stamm walked over to the computer and sat at the screen, tapping on the keyboard, calling up images of a brass skeleton key. "This is what was stolen last night. We catalog everything."

He studied the images that showed both sides and each end of an old brass key. Stamm told him what he knew about it, and how it had become one of the institution's ceremonial objects.

"Any idea why the guy wanted this so bad?"

"That's something else we don't know. But there might be someone who does."

He was listening.

"There were two men who once worked here. One was Diane Sherwood's father, Davis Layne. He headed up this museum. He also accumulated much of the restricted archive you read. Unfortunately, he died about fifteen years ago. The other is Frank Breckinridge. He once had my job as Castle curator. He's the man who found the key in the attic back in the 1950s. He, too, was an expert on the Knights of the Golden Circle. Luckily, he's still alive."

"You familiar with him?"

Stamm shook his head. "He was before my time."

Cotton's mind raced and he rubbed at the stubble on his chin. "Adams is from my mother's side of the family. He left the South after the war and moved out west."

A curtain of time parted in his mind and he began to recall everything his grandfather had told him about Angus Adams.

A cell phone rang, startling him from his thoughts.

Not his.

Stamm's.

The curator answered, listened for a moment, then ended the call with a perplexed look on his face.

"I had Martin Thomas' key card flagged. I didn't find it last night on his body, so I was going to cancel it this morning. But it was just used to gain access inside the natural history museum."

CHAPTER THIRTY-FOUR

Cassiopeia huddled tight in the earthen crevice, Lea beside her farther inside. The wooden trunks kept raining down, obliterating and filling the shaft. Dust and dirt clouded the air and made breathing hard, but she swallowed the urge to cough or make a sound, not wanting to alert anyone above that they were still alive. She'd whispered to Lea that she should do the same and was pleased that the young girl had stayed silent. Luckily, none of the bullets had found either of them and the men above were most likely more occupied with the retrieval of the gold than worrying about if they were dead.

The crashing stopped, but the air remained fouled. She used her shirttail as a filter and tried to breathe short and shallow. Only a few feeble rays of light penetrated from above.

"Are you okay?" she whispered to Lea.

"I'm fine, but we need to get out of here. It's hard to breathe."

She agreed. But there was still the problem

of the men. She kept listening, hearing nothing. Were they gone, or just waiting?

Time to find out.

She wiggled free and kicked at the old wood, which gave way to her assault. Luckily, the debris had not packed tight and there were plenty of air pockets. More kicks and she was able to squirm out, feeling her way with outstretched hands. A claustrophobic wave swept through her but, thankfully, unlike Cotton, she was not susceptible to that phobia. High-speed-moving heights were her weakness. Airplanes and helicopters, particularly.

She pushed and prodded, creating enough space that she could rise to her knees, her back against the shaft wall. Her breath continued to congeal in her throat, and she swallowed dust. More chunks of the shattered containers were piled above her, but not tightly. She told herself to be careful of rusted nails.

"Stay where you are," she whispered to Lea. "I'm going to see if I can get us out of here."

Hands planted on the debris, she hoisted her body up, shoving more of the dark obstacles out of the way. Her cell phone remained in her pocket and she found the unit. It was useless for calling, considering her location, but it generated enough light for her to study the mess around her.

Not insurmountable.

In fact, only a few meters above her head was nothing but air to the top of the shaft. She replaced the phone and climbed atop the pile, which groaned, then settled from her weight.

"I need you to come out and watch what I do," she told Lea.

The young girl appeared below.

She estimated it was five meters to the top where a rectangular-shaped slab of weak light waited. Not much leaked below. The shaft was narrow, the sides rough, offering plenty of ridges and crevices for her feet and hands. She could scale it chimney-style, legs braced on the opposite wall.

The climb was tough but not impossible, since her legs and arms were in terrific shape. She came to the top, planted her hands, and pivoted herself up and out of the shaft. Her breathing was harder than she'd like, so she rested a moment, gathering her strength. She was about to help Lea out when a noise caught her attention. To her right. At the doorway leading from the chamber.

A tramp of footsteps.

Approaching.

"We have company," she told Lea. "Stay there and be quiet."

The chamber was bare except for two remaining trunks. She'd thought the men had completed their extraction, but apparently that was not the case. How many were returning was unknown and there was no place to hide, so she assumed a position near the doorway, her spine pressed to the rock wall.

One man entered.

Bald, jeans, boots, late twenties.

But that didn't mean she couldn't take him.

He moved toward the two trunks and began to dismantle them with solid kicks. The old wood easily gave way and the noise he generated provided the perfect distraction. Two quick steps and she was on him. A swift swipe from her boots to his kidneys sent him reeling. She then drove her shoulder into the man's chest, forcing him against the wall. He seemed to momentarily recover his composure, but a pop to his knee buckled his right leg. She was mad and planned to take out her anger on this idiot, but before she could finish him off a pair of arms wrapped her chest, pinioning her from behind.

Another of the men had returned.

She knew better than to resist.

Instead she allowed her body to go limp, which provided an instant of wiggle room, enough for her to slip from the bear hug, the heel of her right boot snapping the other knee.

The man shrieked.

She whirled and with caution forgotten threw one punch after another, fists a blur, each one a full swing with every ounce of strength she had behind it. The man dropped to the ground and tumbled onto his back, writhing. One more sweeping kick to the side of his head rendered him still.

"That's enough," a male voice said.

She turned.

The other man had recovered enough to now have a revolver aimed at her. He lay on the dirt, his eyes cool and unreadable, the face a mask of rage.

"Sit your ass down on the ground," he told her.

She decided to comply.

He was hurting, unable to stand from her assault, but not incapacitated enough not to pull a trigger. Two meters lay between them, more than enough distance to provide him with the advantage.

"What now?" she asked, her eyes not leaving his.

He struggled up on his side. She'd apparently broken something in his leg. "We wait."

That meant others would be returning.

Behind her captor she spotted the shaft from below and saw two hands on one edge. A head slowly appeared, then eyes, as Lea assessed the situation. Cassiopeia wanted to tell her to stay put, but realized that would place her in even more danger.

So she watched as the young girl silently emerged.

It took guts and nerve to deal with a situation like this. She recalled her first few times in battle. She'd always been frightened, but that feeling had never paralyzed her. Instead, fear sharpened her determination. Her initial forays into risky extracurricular activities had come at the request of an old friend, Henrik Thorvaldsen, who'd needed her assistance from time to time. That was how she first met Cotton a few years ago in southern France. Henrik was gone, God rest his soul, but she was still here, right in the thick of things. She'd learned a lot from Henrik, especially how to handle pressure. Lea seemed to have the same innate ability, though her grandfather would not have approved.

The girl was now free of the shaft, on all fours, her face streaked with sweat and grime. Lea was too small to attack the man holding the gun. So Cassiopeia decided to send a message, pointing across the room and saying, "Did you plan on throwing those busted crates down on us, too?"

"You broke my damn leg," the man spit out.

Lea understood and inched her way toward a large piece of one of the demolished containers.

"What are we waiting for?" she asked, trying to provide more distraction.

"Shut up."

Lea froze, her eyes focused on something behind Cassiopeia. Her assailant saw it, too, readjusting his aim.

A gun exploded.

And not the pistol.

Much louder.

The chest of the man across the chamber erupted as lead slapped into flesh. A death rattle seeped from the man's mouth, along with rivers of blood. Then the body doubled over, jerking in unnatural, ugly movements.

Lea gasped in shock.

Cassiopeia turned, cold shivers prickling her skin.

Terry Morse stood with a shotgun in hand.

"There's no time for me to be angry right now," Morse said. "We have to go."

CHAPTER THIRTY-FIVE

Grant had weighed the options and decided making a move now was the smart play. Sure, they may have found Martin Thomas' body, but if he was fast he might be able to find the other part of what he was after before anyone knew he'd even looked. There'd been no news reports or anything in the media about a death at the Smithsonian. And if they could link him to Diane and Diane to Thomas, then why had he not heard from her or the police? Instead, there was only silence. Hopefully the Justice Department lady was dead, and Richard Stamm should not be a problem. True, those records the lady had been cradling would have been nice to have, but there'd been no way to stop and get them.

He'd casually entered the natural history museum with the day's first wave of visitors, which included schoolchildren on a field trip and a smattering of early-bird tourists. As a kid he'd spent a lot of time inside the museums lining the Mall, especially American and natural history. There really was no slow time. Millions flooded through the doors each year, thanks in large part to everything being free. He'd listened to his father babble about that perk too many times to count. Those were stories he would not miss. But the other ones — where his old man had used a quick, vivid turn of a phrase, one that breathed life into something from the past that could have easily been dull and boring — those he'd liked.

He stood inside the famous marble rotunda with its trademarked African elephant, heavy with tusks, dominating the center. Ocean Hall opened straight ahead, the Mammals Room off to his left. To the right loomed Fossil Hall, which was closed for renovations.

His destination.

He did not want to draw any undue attention to his incursion. There could be workers on the other side of the closed doors. If so, he'd just flash Thomas' ID badge, one finger over the librarian's picture, and hope no one asked too many questions. He glanced around and noticed no museum attendants in sight, and only one security person. There were cameras, so he told himself to keep his head down and blend into the crowd. Children raced about, as new arrivals washed past him to mingle with the previous tide of visitors. He wove a path through the bobbing heads to a security reader adjacent to Fossil Hall and swiped the card. The electronic lock clicked open and he quickly stepped through, the doors shutting behind him.

Silence returned.

Thankfully, the space beyond was empty, the hall in a state of demolition. Ceiling spotlights, here and there, provided partial illumination. All the carpet was gone from the concrete floor. Placards and writing still adorned the walls where exhibits had once hung, but no artifacts remained. Construction materials lay stacked everywhere. Cement blocks, lumber, scaffolding, debris. A couple of the larger exhibits still stood, yet to be removed.

One in particular drew his gaze.

The Permian coral reef exhibit, illustrating the diversity of sea life in the Permian Sea, from 250 million years ago, when all of the continents were assembled together in one giant landmass and western Texas and New Mexico lay underwater. The display had been there since he was a kid. Two months ago Martin Thomas had told him that it was on the list to be replaced during the renovations. He hadn't taken a look then, thinking he had plenty of opportunity.

But things had changed.

Cotton raced out the doors into a warm May morning and headed for the American history museum. Rick Stamm followed. They ran to Constitution Avenue, then down the sidewalk, crossing 12th Street and continuing on to the entrance for the natural history museum. He'd decided not to involve any of the Smithsonian security people, preferring to handle this situation himself so no one else would be placed in harm's way. He had a feeling that this intruder was the man who'd killed Martin Thomas and shot Stephanie.

No word had come from the hospital, which could be good or bad. He'd shaken death's hand a few times himself and viewed the Reaper as less an enemy and more an equal. But he'd never imagined that Stephanie would garner an introduction so soon. He also wondered about Cassiopeia and how she was doing in Arkansas.

He'd have to check in with her shortly.

But not before determining just who was using Martin Thomas' ID.

Grant stopped and made absolutely sure no one else was in the hall. The silence assured him he was alone, but that might not be the case for long. So he hurried to his left and found the reef exhibit, which loomed as large as he remembered, maybe ten feet long, that much high, and half that deep. Glass had once enclosed it on all sides, but the front and side panels were gone, exposing the colorfully crafted corals, sponges, sea fans, plants, and shells. Everything appeared exactly as it would have been hundreds of millions of years ago.

A few days ago, after another violent encounter, his father had told him the secret the exhibit held. In the 1960s his father had found what was known as the Trail Stone within the Smithsonian's collections. There it had been cataloged and stored away, just one more of the millions of curiosities the institution harbored. In 1974 it became necessary to hide the stone away, so his father chose the newly created reef exhibit, a safe bet since its funding had come from a special gift by a wealthy family with the condition that the exhibit remain standing for at least thirty years.

It lasted over forty.

But its time had expired.

Cotton and Stamm swept into the natural history museum, bypassing the metal detectors and entering through the staff line.

"He's in Fossil Hall," one of the security people waiting for them said. "It's closed off, under a total renovation. Everything's been removed."

"I'm assuming there are no cameras in

there," Cotton asked.

Stamm shook his head. "Not a one."

"Okay, I'll handle this. Just point the way."

Grant studied the Permian reef exhibit, marveling at the detail and the fact that, forty years ago, his father had used the opportunity of its construction to hide the Trail Stone.

But where?

He decided subtlety would accomplish nothing, and the thing was about to be destroyed anyway. To his right, metal supports for the scaffolding stood propped against the wall. He grabbed one of the iron struts and used it to gash into the exhibit, scraping away the fake coral, seabed, and an assortment of plants and shells. He had to be careful not to gouge too deep, as it could damage the Trail Stone's face, and he had no idea how or where it had been incorporated. Everything was fashioned from polyurethane, epoxy, and foam, and the surfaces gave way easily. Beneath the artistic exterior was a substructure of wood and stone. He saw that some actual rock had been positioned so its leading edges were exposed, becoming part of the towering faux reef wall.

And then he saw it.

Lying on its side, about two feet long and three inches thick, tucked into a wooden niche. Plywood sheathed the exhibit's rear, encasing the Trail Stone inside a safe cocoon.

He set the strut aside and slid it free.

Carefully, he laid the stone on the concrete floor.

It looked just as Diane had described. Davis Layne had seen the stone back in the 1970s, before the feud between the fathers gestated out of control. A carved dagger on the left, squiggly lines etched into the face, an *R* in the upper right. A concave, heart-shaped indentation, about two inches deep, dominated the center, with *1847, 10,* and two other symbols inscribed into its bottom. That niche was where another piece of the puzzle fit.

The Heart Stone.

There was no need to carry it out, which

was good since leaving with something that large could prove difficult. Instead, he found his phone and snapped several photos from varying distances for different sizes and perspective.

Modern technology would do the rest.

Cotton slipped quietly into Fossil Hall.

Stamm had told him that the place was a wreck, everything gone, the walls stripped down to the studs. It was a huge space with several rooms and offshoots, no telling where the man he sought might be. But they knew he was still inside as none of the doors had electronically recorded an exit.

He found his target, facing away, crouched over something lying on the floor, snapping pictures with his phone.

He aimed his Beretta.

"Nice and slow. Stand up and turn around."

CHAPTER THIRTY-SIX

Danny entered Stephanie's hospital room. The doctors had not wanted her to have any visitors, but being the ex-president of the United States still carried some clout. He also liked the fact that the door was guarded by an armed Magellan Billet agent.

She lay with wires connecting her to a variety of machines monitoring vital signs. Surgery had taken three hours and all the damage had supposedly been repaired. Tubes periscoped into her nostrils and she was breathing with the help of a ventilator, the rhythmic pulse of its ins and outs hypnotic. More tubes sent medicine and blood, and the fact that she needed so much technology did not seem good.

He stood beside the bed.

He'd loved two women in his life. He and Pauline had been together a long time, ever since high school. Their marriage had been inevitable and relatively happy until Mary died. Nothing was ever the same after that, though they each tried to pretend otherwise. Why they stayed married was easy. Both of them were ambitious. He admitted to the sham, Pauline liked to deny it. But he knew better. She'd enjoyed being the First Lady of both Tennessee and the United States. True, neither honor brought her happiness, but each may have provided a small respite from the enormous pain he never could cleanse from her.

Now he loved another woman.

Who lay before him with two bullet wounds.

He'd never told her exactly how he felt. As president and her boss, that had seemed inappropriate. Since his leaving office they hadn't spent a whole lot of time alone.

He reached down and grasped her hand.

Her breaths were so shallow that it was nearly impossible to detect the rise and fall of her chest. The doctor had told him that she should make it, but there was a serious risk of infection since the injuries had been so extensive. They were pumping her full of antibiotics and decided a short-term, medically induced coma would aid the process, which also explained the ventilator. But a coma was not without risk, either, since the brain would have to be overloaded with dangerous barbiturates. Nothing about any of this was good, except for the fact that she was still alive.

He wondered what her reaction would be

when she learned that he was about to become a U.S. senator. She probably would not be surprised, since she knew him better than he knew himself.

He gently squeezed her fingers, trying to quell a consuming anger, one that kept demanding revenge. Nearly his entire adult life had been spent keeping his emotions in check. Only alone with Pauline had he ever let his guard down. But even with her, there hadn't been full openness. Both of them had held back. The last fifteen years of their relationship had been totally platonic, and he'd grown accustomed to the lack of physical intimacy. Politics and power had become his aphrodisiacs, but both of those vanished on January 20. Perhaps that further explained why he'd been so depressed the past few months. Only the prospects of a new life, with a new love, had kept him optimistic.

Yet here he was, about to be sworn into public office once again.

It had taken the death of an old friend and the duplicity of his widow to make that happen.

Timing wasn't everything, it was *absolutely* everything.

And his had been impeccable.

Nothing about Alex's death had rung right from the moment he'd heard the news. And now, with what he'd seen last night, he knew trouble was brewing. As president he'd had to treat Lucius Vance with kid gloves, since the Speaker of the House could cause the executive branch lots of problems. As a senator no such caution would be necessary. That was the great thing about the U.S. Senate. Members could do whatever they wanted, with few repercussions besides what their voters might think. And what an arsenal at his disposal. Unlimited debate, on any topic, without censorship. And without stoppage, except by a vote of sixty members, which was nearly impossible to obtain.

A hell of a pulpit.

So if what Vance was planning needed Senate approval, good damn luck with that.

He'd kill it dead.

He continued to hold Stephanie's hand, grateful they were alone. He'd told the guard outside to let no one other than doctors and nurses inside.

Appearances be damned. If she pulled through this there'd be no more delays, no more denials. Time for them both to live life out in the open.

His anger started to wane, replaced by a hollow, deflated feeling of loneliness.

"I love you," he whispered.

Cassiopeia, Lea, and Terry Morse fled the mine shaft through the archway dug from the rubble at the exit. Cassiopeia moved ahead, armed with a weapon from one of the men back in the chamber, Morse still carrying his shotgun. The steady hum of a generator, loud inside the cavern, faded as they rushed away. Morning had arrived over the trees to the east. They stopped among the rubble, staring out at the clearing that lay between the camp and the beginnings of the forest, where the dirt road led back to the highway. To their right was a black tarp covering something and she quickly checked what was underneath.

Gold bars.

Maybe fifty or more.

"Their last load," she said. "That means people are coming back."

"I figured you'd be here," Morse said to Lea.

"How did you know?"

" 'Cause the daddy of that boyfriend of yours is a sentinel."

"That can't be. His uncle was, not his daddy."

"That's what a good sentinel does. He never lets people know what he is. But he's got arthritis and isn't able to do much anymore, so I've been coverin' for him. And don't think we don't know about you and his boy. We do. But we let it go, since you're both good kids."

Cassiopeia was impressed with the old man's style.

"I woke up and everyone was gone," Morse

said. "I heard when Malone left. But you two? Where else would she have taken you? Sentinels keep each other informed. I've been knowin' somethin' was happening out here for days. So I took a guess."

"How'd you get here?" Cassiopeia asked him.

"Borrowed a car from a friend at the lodge, the same one that told me about you and Malone."

Morse was watching the woods, as was she, both of them alert for any signs of movement.

"These men are the real deal," she told Morse.

"Not like dumb me and those fakes?"

"That's not what I meant."

"I get what you meant," Morse said, his attention remaining on the rapidly dissipating darkness.

"You killed a man," Lea said to her grandfather, concern in her voice.

"It had to be done, child."

Cassiopeia agreed, but wanted to know, "Is the Witch's Stone safe?"

Morse nodded. "I made sure."

"Then take Lea and head back to the lodge."

"Where are you goin'?" he asked.

"To find the man who just tried to kill me."

CHAPTER THIRTY-SEVEN

Grant remained still, stunned that someone was here. It could simply be one of the security guards or a construction worker, surprised to see an intruder. He had Thomas' ID and he might be able to bluff his way out. Then again, why take the chance?

A door opened off to his right and voices could be heard. More people had entered the demolished hall. He used that moment of distraction to regrip the iron strut, which lay at his feet beside the Trail Stone.

"Get up," came the command from behind him.

Conversation continued in the distance, echoing through the hall. He had to move fast. So he rose, with the strut in hand, pivoted his body to the right, and flung the iron bar sideways like a Frisbee. At the same time he dropped back to the floor and rolled, still holding his cell phone, and managed a look back. The strut swooshed through the air, then slid across the concrete. The man who'd been there had leaped out of the way, offering him a moment where escape might be possible.

But he saw a gun in the man's hand.

This was no construction worker.

He scampered right, using a Sheetrock partition for protection, which blocked any shot coming his way. The source of the voices he'd heard was just ahead. Three people in hard hats who'd entered from a far door.

He knew where that exit led.

Into the research wings, for staff only.

Cotton dodged the strut.

He'd seen the man grip the iron bar, so he was ready. What he hadn't anticipated was other people entering the hall. He'd told Stamm to seal the place off, but apparently not everyone had gotten the memo.

His target was trying to flee, walls blocking both his view and any shot. Whatever the man had been after had apparently been concealed within an exhibit. Some sort of coral reef, now demolished, a huge slash marring the fake wall. Another stone lay on the concrete floor, its face loaded with etchings, similar to the one in Arkansas. But that was not his primary concern at the moment. Instead, he had to corral the man trying to escape.

He ran.

A large space loomed before him, thirty feet wide, over twice that long, an interior wall stretching on one side, an exterior one on the other. Surely it had once been filled with dinosaur skeletons and other fossils. Now it was empty, except for debris and three people in hard hats.

With another man beyond them.

Racing away.

Grant decided to use the three new people as cover, slowing his pace and passing by them, Thomas' ID hanging from around his neck. No one would notice the photo, just having the badge was all that mattered. He placed the men squarely between himself and the pursuer. If he could make it to the exit door, he could lose himself within the labyrinth of offices that he knew filled the other side. There would also be no cameras there, as the Smithsonian rarely monitored the staff-only sections of the buildings.

He readied the swipe card.

"Get down," he heard a voice command. "Out of the way."

Cotton ordered the three workers to hit the floor, waving his arm and signaling for them to move. His target was beyond them, heading for a door lit as an exit. The three looked at him strangely, then apparently noticed the gun and dropped to the concrete.

He leveled the weapon.

■ ■ ■ ■

Grant kept his cool, never slowing his approach to the door. He slipped the cell phone into his pocket and slid the card's magnetic strip through the slot in the reader. The lock immediately released and he yanked open the metal door. He bolted out and helped the hydraulic closer by yanking on the lever, closing it shut behind him.

Just as a gun fired.

Cotton sent a round straight at the door, where the man had stood one moment, gone the next.

He'd been an instant too late.

The bullet pinged off the metal door.

The three workers were sprawled on the floor, hands covering their heads, clearly in a panic.

"Get up," he said. He spotted an electronic reader at the door. "I'm with the Justice Department. Do any of you have a key card to open that door?"

One of the men said yes and found it.

He rushed over and grabbed the card.

Grant loved the adrenaline flowing through him. He knew everything that he'd done the past few hours was foolish, but God help him, he loved it. There was something intensely satisfying about defying the odds. He'd even managed by a split second to avoid getting shot, which should have generated fear. But in him it created only resolve.

And a need for more.

His mind recalled the details of this part of the museum. It had been a couple of decades since he was last inside, which probably meant that things had changed. But the stairway he recalled was just ahead. He could go up or down. He decided to descend, two steps at a time, slowing near the bottom and opening another metal door that led to more staff space on the ground floor. The museum sat between the Mall and Constitution Avenue, which came with a height difference. So the first-floor entrance opened to the Mall, while the ground-floor entrance led out to the street. Beyond the staff-only portions, where quiet and simplicity reigned, were the busy public areas, the street side particularly so since it contained gift shops, a café, restrooms, and a large auditorium.

And there'd be cameras.

He left the stairwell and entered a hallway where more offices opened on either side. He walked slow and confident, his badge dangling from his neck. No one challenged him.

He found the exit door and slowly opened it.

With his head down, he stepped out into a busy foyer throbbing with activity and alive with sound.

And he made a beeline for the street exit.

Cotton realized immediately that he'd lost the man. Before him, past the metal door, was nothing but labs and offices. There were also stairs that led up and down. His target could have gone anywhere. But he wondered. Did the man know his way around? Was he familiar with the building? It seemed possible.

The door from Fossil Hall opened and Rick Stamm appeared.

"This way."

He followed the curator down the stairs.

"An exit door opened a couple of minutes after the guy entered using Martin's key card. He didn't need the card to get out, so there's no way to know if it was him. But it had to be."

They quickly descended, then left the museum's back spaces through another metal door. Before them stretched a crowded, noisy public area.

"Did you get a look at him?" Stamm asked.

He nodded. "Enough that I won't forget him. He had brown, curly hair and a port wine stain on the left side of his neck."

"That's the guy who killed Martin Thomas."

They searched the crowds.

But saw nothing.
The man was gone.

CHAPTER THIRTY-EIGHT

Diane arrived at Alex's apartment. She'd taken the first flight of the day from Knoxville to Reagan National, a short one-hour hop. On landing she'd texted Grant and told him that they should meet at the apartment. She hadn't visited since last summer and the June Smithsonian Libraries Advisory Board meeting. The board tended to vary its meeting locations across the country, returning to DC usually for only one of the three annual gatherings. She liked that habit, as she hated Washington, a city of opportunists filled with people either wanting power or wanting to be close to power, Alex no exception. On the one hand he'd possessed the clout of a U.S. senator. On the other he did little with that power except cling to those who possessed even more, like Danny Daniels. So different from the 19th century, when lone senators faced down both the House and the president, afraid of neither. What a time that must have been. Bitter political battles constantly raging over tariffs, whether new territories would be free or slave, the annexation of Texas, the war with Mexico. At one point a member of the House, Preston Brooks from South Carolina, beat Senator Charles Sumner nearly to death with a walking stick right on the Senate floor.

Talk about passion.

That was a time when opinions mattered.

And people were not afraid to express them.

Political warfare today had turned entirely guerrilla, the assaults all coming from the shadows, making it hard to ever identify the culprit.

Especially in the Senate.

"Alexander Stephens' plan is not workable," Alex had said to her that last day. *"The Founders never intended for Congress to work that way. If they had, they would have written Article I differently."*

Not necessarily.

What a huge idea from such a small man.

Stephens had stood barely five and a half feet tall, weighing less than a hundred pounds. He stayed sickly all of his life, many times bedridden, though he lived to be seventy-two. He served nearly twenty-five years as a congressman, off and on both before and after the Civil War, making a name for himself as a skilled orator. During the war he acted as vice president of the Confederacy.

He died in 1883, while serving as governor of Georgia. Long before leaving this world, though, he devised a way to make the U.S. Senate irrelevant, just as it had been prior to 1800. Let the blowhards command the Senate floor and talk to their hearts' content. Filibuster away. Who cared? None of it would matter. The House of Representatives was the true American political body, elected every two years, responsible only to the people. To Stephens it was no accident that the first words of the first article of the Constitution dealt with the House of Representatives. And the first government official mentioned anywhere in the Constitution was the Speaker of the House. To him, those were messages from the Founders he believed the country had come to ignore.

But thanks to her, Lucius Vance was about to provide a reminder.

Inside the apartment she noticed its usual order. Alex had never liked things out of place. She was the same, so that was one fault she could not hold against him. She'd never felt comfortable here. This had been all *his* place. And something she'd noticed long ago now made much more sense. Nothing personal was displayed anywhere. No photos, accolades, or any mementos from a lifetime of marriage and service. His Senate office was part museum, part hall of fame. Here nothing reminded him, or anyone else, of his life.

She'd run a bluff that day, long suspecting another woman. What was the cliché? The wife can always tell. That's provided the wife actually gave a damn enough to pay attention. For her, that had happened only recently. They hadn't been intimate in years, which partly explained her own infidelity. But sex had never been all that important to Alex. What really hurt was his declaration that he'd not broken his marriage vows.

Because she believed him.

Which meant he'd really cared for the other woman.

Right here.

In this place.

The thought turned her stomach.

"Damn you, Alex," she whispered to the silence. "Why couldn't you just walk away and leave it alone? The way you did everything else."

For once in his mundane life Alex Sherwood had decided to take a stand and fight the fight. And all because her idiot brother thought they needed help.

She'd already decided that the lease on the apartment would be allowed to lapse and everything would be donated to the Salvation Army. Nothing would leave with her. She'd come today only to make sure that there was no lingering evidence that pointed toward anything she was doing. That would require a thorough search, which she and Grant would do together. Perhaps she might even learn a clue or two as to Alex's mysterious woman.

But what did it matter?

He was dead, which made her irrelevant.

She took a quick look around and noticed no accumulated mail, old newspapers, or magazines. Even the refrigerator had been cleared of perishables. Odd, considering that Alex lived here alone. On a whiteboard beside the phone there was no list of groceries, or reminder to pick up the dry cleaning, or anything to indicate an occupant.

A knock disturbed the silence.

She walked across and opened the door, which creaked to the sound of dry hinges.

Grant stood outside.

He stepped in, took her in his arms, and kissed her. Hard and intense. The way she'd become accustomed to from him.

"I've missed you," he said.

"It's been a tough few days."

"Why are you even here?" he asked.

"We need to make sure there's nothing left from Kenneth's mistake."

He let her go and closed the door.

"I also need to hear about your visit to the Castle last night."

"You might not like what I have to say. But I did get this."

His hand slipped into his jean pocket and

came out with the ceremonial key.

She smiled.

"And I also found the Trail Stone."

All good.

So she was curious.

"What is it I don't want to hear?"

CHAPTER THIRTY-NINE

Danny entered the Vice President's Room inside the Capitol, just outside the Senate Chamber. Its official designation was S-214, once the only government space in Washington assigned solely to the vice president. Times had changed, but not this room. The marble mantel, floor tiles, gilded mirror, and matching Victorian cornices all dated to the 19th century. The room's double-pedestal mahogany desk had certainly made the rounds. Nearly every vice president used it until 1969, when it went to the Oval Office for Nixon and Ford, coming back here with Jimmy Carter. Since the Civil War the room had been a place for work, ceremony, caucuses, press conferences, and private meetings, a few of which altered the course of American history.

The floor clock sounded 10:00 A.M.

Vice President Theodore Solomon had been alerted that a new member of the Senate was coming, so he waited behind the desk. Contrary to what people thought, though the Constitution vested the VP as the Senate's presiding officer, rarely did a vice president ever attend a session, voting only to break a 50-50 tie. Not like the old days, when vice presidents were a constant presence on the Senate floor. Today they came only if the majority leadership sensed that a tie-breaking vote might be required.

Which was rare.

The governor had made the official announcement of his Senate appointment thirty minutes ago at a Knoxville press conference. As expected, there'd been some immediate backlash, particularly since no other candidates had been solicited. All had been explained, just as they'd agreed, stressing that it was merely a caretaker appointment until the people could choose their own senator. And who better to keep the seat warm than Tennessee's favorite son. It sounded so good, even he almost believed it.

"Mr. President," Solomon said, standing and offering his hand to shake.

Danny liked this man.

Teddy Solomon was old school, a financial conservative but a closet social liberal, most likely brought on by the fact that his eldest son was gay. They'd served together in the Senate, Solomon a straight shooter from Missouri who'd run against Warner Fox in the primaries, coming up short and having to withdraw early. Fox, acting smart like his name, ultimately decided to bring this potential enemy into the fold and offered him the second seat. The surprising thing was that Solomon had agreed to the gig. Danny loved what Woodrow Wilson's VP once said. *Being vice president is comparable to a man in a cataleptic fit. He cannot speak. He cannot move. He suffers no pain. He is perfectly conscious of all that goes on, but has no part in it.* Then again, what John Adams said when he served as Washington's number two made more sense. *In this I am nothing, but I may be everything.*

What was it? One heartbeat away?

Which had happened eight times. Nine, if you counted Ford taking over for Nixon. Death or resignation seemed the only way any vice president ever became president. Only one in the last 125 years had managed to move to the top spot through election.

The first George Bush.

And he earned only one term.

Solomon stood tall, with a wide face to match his size that cast a weary, wary kindness that somehow managed to avoid softness. The jaw had yet to sag, the lips still firm, the features sturdy. He was a few years older than Danny, his hair smoothly brushed and surprisingly dark, occasionally inviting comparisons to Ronald Reagan's lack of gray. As always, he wore a pressed dark suit with a stiff-collared shirt and a striking silk tie.

"You sure about this?" Solomon asked.

He nodded. "Retirement was a bitch."

"It's been only a few months."

"Long enough for me to know that I don't like it."

He listened to the basso tick of the clock and knew its story. It arrived during McKinley's term, but gained prominence during FDR's time when his vice president used it to time his entrance into the Senate. As the chimes began to ring fifteen seconds before the clock struck twelve, John Garner would stop whatever he was doing and march into the chamber, reaching his seat on the podium precisely at noon.

"I want to be sworn in here, in private," he said to Solomon. "Then I want to get to work."

"The press is clamoring for us to do this outside for the cameras. After all, it is a bit of history in the making."

He knew Solomon felt the way he did about journalists. They were there only to be used. At the moment he had no need for their services. Decades back, when he first served in the Senate, reporters had been some of his closest friends. There was a code then, rules, an honor system, along with a different breed of man and woman who'd reported the news. He'd liked those journalists. Now it was all about money and ratings. Nobody gave a damn about being right. Just be first. Or even better, be controversial. There were so few journalists anymore. Entertainers now dominated the news channels. And he could imagine their present quandary. They'd all received the news of his appointment at the same time from the governor's announcement. Nobody had any advantage. They'd need an angle, a chance to pepper him with polecat questions about the whats, whens, whys, and hows. Better to let 'em wonder.

"That's the great thing about being a seat warmer," he said. "I won't be around all that long, so I don't have to answer a thing."

And he added a broad smile.

Solomon's gray-to-colorless eyes, ageless as salt water, flashed a boyish glance.

"What does your boss have to say about my return?"

"I just got off the phone with him. Shocked is the best way to put it. Fox was hoping to be rid of you. Truth be told I'm sure he'd like to be rid of me, too."

The words came in a cultivated, Midwest drawl. Though of opposite parties, he and Solomon had always seen eye-to-eye. This man had been a big assist during his time in the White House. And he'd returned the favor, making sure Missouri was never forgotten in the federal budget.

"I want to know, Danny, between you and

me. Here, with the door closed. What *are* you doing here?"

"Making a little history. Me and Andrew Johnson. Two presidents, from Tennessee, who became senators."

Solomon perched his lean frame on the edge of the desk, crossing one shiny shoe over another and folding his arms. "It's just us. What's going on, Danny?"

He knew he might need an ally, and what better one than this tall glass of water from Missouri. And though the VP and Lucius Vance *were* of the same party, he knew there was not a speck of love between them.

"Vance is up to something."

"I'm listening."

"I don't know much, just enough that I had to come and find out more. But I might need your help." He paused. "Before this is through."

"Sounds serious."

"I'm not sure. But every political alarm inside my brain is screaming trouble."

"Could this affect the president?"

"I don't know that, either. But Vance is no team player, and he did want Fox's job."

"Like me, he had no chance. But he sealed his fate a long time ago when he took the Speaker's job."

"You and I know that he's a danger. I hope Fox does, too."

Solomon chuckled. "Let's just say that our

364

new president is not as schooled on the lay of the land as you and I."

"And I doubt he'll be listening to his seasoned vice president."

"That's putting it mildly. Since January 20 I've talked with him a grand total of" — Solomon held up a finger — "one time. Just now."

A huge mistake on Fox's part. Solomon, like himself, was skilled in deciphering the silences between words, the thoughts obtuse speech many times disguised. From everything Danny had seen and read, the Fox administration seemed a nervous coalition of doves, hawks, and activists, each with their own idea of what might be best for the country. Teddy Solomon was far more pragmatic, a tried-and-true warrior. A man with an encyclopedic knowledge of Washington, DC. Information that a novice in the White House, like Warner Fox, could make good use of. Unfortunately, pride and stupidity usually kept the rookies from asking for help, which ultimately cost them.

One name proved his point.

Jimmy Carter.

"You knew they would ignore you," he said. "So why take the job?"

"I'm sixty-nine years old, Danny. I could have served in the Senate forever. But I've always wanted to be president. You know that. I can't explain why, I just wanted the job.

The people, though, had other ideas." Solomon shrugged. "This is as close as I can get. So you take the good with the bad."

This was a smart man, a pro who'd learned long ago, as he had, that the country was only what the people wanted it to be. If they made their decisions in ignorance, or off the cuff, or even in stupidity, so be it, it was their republic. *We the people* meant just that. His job, and that of everyone else in public office, was to serve the country — not mold it. Clever politicians understood that duty. Great ones, like Teddy Solomon, believed it in their heart.

This man would have made a terrific president.

"Can you snoop around on your side of the aisle and see if anything's brewing in the House? I've got a bad feelin', Teddy."

"Bad enough to come back in the line of fire? When you could have been off fishing somewhere?"

"Somethin' like that. It may be up to two broken-down old geezers like us to stop whatever it is."

"Sounds awful melodramatic. But I like it."

"And let's keep this between us. Just in case I'm totally full of crap."

"That's one thing you never were." Solomon extended his hand again. "Welcome back, Senator."

They shook.

"It's time to make you official," the vice president said.

He'd taken oaths as a city councilman, a governor, senator, and president. All before crowds, part of the spectacle. Now, with just him and a good friend present, he raised his right hand and repeated the words he'd said three times before.

"I do solemnly swear that I will support and defend the Constitution of the United States against all enemies, foreign and domestic. That I will bear true faith and allegiance to the same. That I take this obligation freely, without any mental reservation or purpose of evasion, and that I will well and faithfully discharge the duties of the office on which I am about to enter.

"So help me God."

CHAPTER FORTY

Cotton was back in the windowless archive at the American history museum, the engraved stone from Fossil Hall lying on the table.

"That guy took a huge chance coming back for this," he said.

Which meant it was really important. He was hoping that Stamm got the message. Time for more information, especially about Angus Adams. But the curator seemed to be waiting for something.

The silence within the archive was suddenly disturbed by a door opening at the other end, then closing. The rows of track shelves blocked any view, so he waited. And was not surprised when the visitor appeared.

The chief justice of the United States.

Warren Weston.

The jurist introduced himself and they shook hands, their attention immediately drawn to the stone.

"So it really was right here," Weston muttered. "All this time. Incredible."

The older man lightly caressed the pale-white limestone surface.

"You knew it might be?" Cotton asked.

"All the information available pointed to one of the museums as the hiding place. We just didn't know which one. Thankfully, we were led straight to it."

"With one person dead, and another in the hospital."

"I'm truly sorry for both of those," Weston said. "None of that was ever intended, but this whole thing has escalated. We need your help now, more than ever."

"This isn't the Supreme Court and I'm not some lawyer standing before you. And I mean no disrespect, but I'm going to ask you a question and you better give me a real good answer."

"Or what?" Weston asked.

"Or I'm pulling the plug on this entire thing."

"The attorney general may not like that."

"I don't work for him, either. I can do whatever the hell I want. And one call to the DC Police, then another to the *Washington Post* should do the trick."

"Ask your question."

"Why did you involve me in this?"

"Because your ancestor, Angus Adams, is key, and we were hoping you, or your family, might be able to add to our knowledge. The fact that you are a trained intelligence operative — one of the best, I'm told — seemed an added bonus. I considered it a win–win."

"How is Adams the *key*?"

"Can I answer that by asking you something?"

He decided to indulge the man and nodded.

"Do you understand what's depicted there, on that stone?"

To the uneducated it seemed there was little rhyme or reason to the squiggly lines, the dagger, and the numbers.

But not to him.

He nodded. "My granddaddy taught me some of the Order's hidden language. We used to play coded games with it."

"I was hoping that was the case. What does it tell you?"

"It seems incomplete. Like it's only part of something else. Something more. There are too few symbols to gather any meaning."

"You're absolutely right. This Trail Stone *is* part of something else."

He'd actually cheated a little, since Morse had told him about five stones. But one thing did jump out. The heart-shaped indentation. And something his grandfather taught him. *Hearts meant gold to the Spanish, and to the knights.*

"I'm assuming there's another stone," he said. "Heart-shaped, that fits into that recessed cavity."

"There is, aptly called the Heart Stone."

"Which leads to the gold."

Weston smiled. "I see you do understand the language. There were five stones all totaled. The Witch's, which I'm told you've already seen. The Trail Stone here. The Heart Stone." Weston turned to Stamm and nodded. The curator worked the keyboard for the computer, then turned the screen Cotton's way.

"Here's the fourth," Weston said. "The Horse Stone."

"Found sometime near the turn of the 20th century, along with the Trail Stone," Stamm said. "Both were kept in our collections. Unfortunately, around 1920, the Horse Stone was destroyed in what the records say was an *accident at one of the warehouses.* But these

371

photos survive."

He studied the black-and-white images.

A horse faced left, with its tail to the right, but cocked left. Within the torso was what looked like the number *3,* or, if viewed at an angle, a double-bump sign, which he knew was the Order's symbol for a bird, indicating movement and direction. Below the tail was what looked like the letter *E* and another double bump.

He noticed more letters and symbols, their meanings speaking to him. A *5* in the upper left with three equally spaced dots surrounding could be viewed on its side to be an inverted *U.*

Which meant a mine.

Below that stretched an uneven line with the word *rio*. Spanish for "river." Between the line marked *rio* and the wavy line to the horse's face were two more circles with dots and another inverted *U*. Below the wavy midline, near the left edge, was a solitary cross, then a Spanish expression *el cobollo de santafe*. He knew of no word *cobollo*. But *caballo* was a different story, so this might be similar to what was on the Witch's Stone.

An intentional error.

El caballo de santafe.

The horse of faith.

At the upper right, another expression. *Yo pasto al norte del rio.* This one was easy. *I graze to the north of the river.* Below that was what looked like a *G* or maybe the number *6*.

"You understand, don't you?" Weston said.

He nodded. "It talks about the horse of faith, who grazes or shepherds north of the river." He pointed to the cross. "That could mark the location of a church, or a mission. There are mine symbols all over it. And that horse wasn't placed there for decoration. What about the fifth stone?"

He could ask now, without compromising Morse, since Weston had noted there were five.

"It's said that the head of the Order kept that one for himself. Like a fail-safe. The Alpha Stone. And without it, the map is useless, as that one provides the starting point. Supposedly you need all five stones to form the map. Forty years ago Davis Layne thought he could get around that. In 1973 we knew the world far better than it was known at the turn of the 20th century. Today GPS technology is even better. Layne believed that with only four stones the treasure could be found, omitting the Alpha Stone. I'm thinking that whoever is looking now believes the same thing."

"Our killer with the curly hair and the port wine stain?"

"That's right."

"You know a lot about this subject," Cotton noted.

"I was a close friend of Davis Layne's. At the time I served on the DC Court of Appeals, and he and I talked about this subject in detail. The Knights of the Golden Circle may have been the greatest crime syndicate ever formed, though they would have called themselves patriots. During the Civil War they stole countless millions in gold and silver, robbing people, banks, trains, boats, and even a couple of U.S. mints. After the war they stole even more, mainly from Reconstructionists."

He explained what Terry Morse had told him, then said, "The Witch's Stone is safe in Arkansas."

Or at least he still hoped so. He still had

not heard a word from Cassiopeia.

"We sent you out there," the chief justice said, "hoping you could decipher the symbols in the woods and find that cache. I thought you might. Your locating the Witch's Stone is an added bonus."

"And we have digital images," he said.

On Cassiopeia's phone.

"To answer your original question," Weston said, "your ancestor, Angus Adams, was the sentinel who both created and guarded the vault. Show him, Rick."

Stamm found something in the computer data bank and pointed to the screen. The image was of a man in a mid-19th-century dress suit, slender, no more than 150 pounds, standing with his head held high, back straight. Cotton noticed the square jaw, piercing eyes, and light hair.

And in the face he saw himself.

"That was taken in 1877, long after Angus Adams achieved notoriety as a spy," Weston said. "I found it in the Smithsonian archives. Adams had come here, on a visit to see his friend Joseph Henry, and posed for the picture. A few months ago Rick researched the Adams lineage, which led us to your mother, then to you. Quite to our amazement, we came to learn that you were a former intelligence officer. One of some renown, like Adams. You even have his nickname. Can I ask how that happened?"

375

Ordinarily he'd be coy but, he had to admit, the photo cast a spell. People liked to ask him about the name Cotton and his answer was always the same. *Long story.* But not this time.

"When I was seven, my grandfather showed my dad a picture of Adams. Not as crisp as this one, but discernible. In ours he was younger, with a carefree look about him, grinning at the camera. We all noticed that I look just like him."

"You do," Stamm said.

"But that's only partly how I got the nickname."

So he explained how, shortly after seeing the old photo, he was being babysat by a neighbor he did not like. She had a disgusting habit of heaping cottage cheese over a slice of bread, then dripping honey on top, the sight of which turned his stomach. She also was a hard-ass. To show his displeasure at both her and her eating habits, he spiked her cottage cheese with cotton from his mother's medicine cabinet, lacing it in so it was hardly noticeable until she tried to swallow. The woman nearly choked. Of course, his father tanned his hide, but the act of defiance cemented his connection to Angus Adams.

"From that day on, my father called me Cotton," he said. "Three years later he died, but I kept the nickname. And every time I hear it, I think of him."

"I learned about your father," Weston said. "A navy submarine commander, lost at sea."

Which was still the official version, though now he knew better.

"I know about the vault," he decided to say.

"From Morse?"

He nodded.

"Most of the Order's hierarchy, Angus Adams included, were dead by the turn of the 20th century. Unfortunately, they died without passing on much in the way of information. Only bits and pieces survived. The Smithsonian made two efforts to find the vault. One around 1909, the other in the 1970s. Both failed."

He told Weston what Morse had related about Jefferson Davis coming to Arkansas to hide the Witch's Stone.

"Davis was of the Order," Weston said. "He was a southerner through and through until the day he died. It's good to hear that he was the one who helped protect the vault."

He caught the implacable eye of authority from eyes that were accustomed to exuding power, determination, and purpose.

"Mr. Malone, all of this is far above our expertise. We desperately need your help."

"To do what?"

"Find the vault."

"For the government? Or the Smithsonian?"

"Does it matter?"

"That wealth is stolen property."

Weston shrugged. "With no way to prove a thing."

He decided to let that one hang and shifted tack. "You realize that Diane Sherwood is more than likely connected to our killer with the port wine stain. A man who probably also shot Stephanie Nelle. Forgive me, but finding him is more important to me than any gold."

"But I believe that by finding the vault you'll also be able to solve both of those crimes. I would caution that speaking to Mrs. Sherwood now would be a waste of time. She'll have a perfect explanation ready, one that leads you nowhere. The better way is to stay quiet and keep digging. Approach her when we know the answers to all of the questions."

"Spoken like a lawyer."

"I'm assuming you, too, learned that lesson."

Absolutely. Never ask a witness a question you did not know the answer to.

"It's not like she's going anywhere," Weston said. "And we have a couple of days, thanks to Ms. Nelle, who secreted Martin Thomas' body away. Can we use that time wisely?"

He wondered exactly for what, but decided to heed the advice he'd just been given.

And not ask any more questions — until he had the answers.

CHAPTER FORTY-ONE

Danny had slipped out of the Vice President's Room in the Capitol, ignoring the media that had congregated beyond the restricted area. He further avoided the press by taking the underground subway over to the Dirksen Office Building. The tunnels beneath the Capitol were for senators and their staff, the subway just for senators. Seventeen senators worked out of the Dirksen building, including Alex Sherwood, who'd occupied a suite of fourth-floor offices befitting his seniority and influence. The building was named for the long-serving senator from Illinois, Everett Dirksen, who died in the late 1960s when Danny was still a teenager. Dirksen had been noted for his witticisms, one of which had worked its way into Danny's personal mantra. *I'm a man of fixed and unbending principles, the first of which is to be flexible at all times.*

Damn right.

Like now.

His swearing-in had probably caught every

member of Alex's staff off guard. They suddenly had a new boss. And not just any boss. An ex-president of the United States, who surely possessed his own inner circle of confidants that did not include them. So as he walked off the elevator on the fourth floor and made his way down the long, gleaming corridor, he told himself to be extra flexible.

He'd made a quick call to the hospital and was told by the Magellan Billet agent that there'd been no change. Stephanie was stable but still out. He'd head back over there in a few hours. But he'd told the agent to call the second anything changed.

At the end of the corridor a simple bronze plaque announced: SENATOR ALEX SHERWOOD — TENNESSEE. Sadly, that would have to be changed. But maybe not. Perhaps he'd leave it right there as a tribute to his friend. That was another thing about being an ex-president.

Accolades mattered little anymore.

He entered through an open door, flanked on either side by flags, one of the United States, the other Tennessee. There was no knob to turn. Instead, the door hung wide open. The message clear. *We're here to serve. Come on in.*

Inside opened to a comfortable reception area and he immediately noticed the wall to his left, which displayed from top to bottom tools, fiddles, guitars, and other Tennessee memorabilia, all mounted atop aged pine planks that left no doubt which part of the country this office called home.

A young lady sat at a desk.

She stood as he came into the room.

His eye caught a red-and-black-plaid shirt, inside a glass case, hanging from the wall. He stepped around the young woman's desk and approached the display. A card at the bottom right explained.

IN HIS FIRST CAMPAIGN FOR THE SENATE, ALEX SHERWOOD WALKED ACROSS THE STATE OF TENNESSEE. EVERY DAY OF HIS 1,000-MILE TREK HE WORE A TRADITIONAL RED-AND-BLACK-PLAID LEVI'S SHIRT. THEY WERE MANUFACTURED IN TENNESSEE AND PURCHASED FROM FRIEDMAN'S DEPARTMENT STORE ON HILLSBORO ROAD IN NASHVILLE.

He recalled when he and Alex first conceived that idea as the perfect way to connect with voters.

And it worked.

Alex won with a huge vote.

He heard people approaching from behind him and turned to see more of the staff.

"Mr. President," one of them said. "I'm sorry, I mean, Senator Daniels."

He smiled and started the process of winning these folks over.

"I know what you mean. It's confusing as

hell to me, too. But we'll both adjust."

Grant flung himself off the bed and scooped up his trousers. Diane had already risen and was out in the other room. She'd wanted a full report, but he'd wanted other things, which a part of her had seemed to want, too. So they'd both been distracted for a little while. Now it was time to get down to business. He hoped their passionate interlude would cushion the bad news. He walked out of the bedroom, pulling on his pants but leaving his shirt off.

"You don't find it weird, you and me, here?" he asked her. "I mean it doesn't matter to me, but it should to you."

"Why? It's not a shrine. And I assure you, nothing ever happened here between me and my husband. So I'm not filled with any touching memories. Now tell me, what happened last night?"

"When I went to get the key, Thomas tried blackmail. He figured out what we're after and wanted a cut. If not, he was planning on writing a book. I decided his dying was better."

"Excuse me?"

"I shot him." Might as well give it to her straight.

"Inside the Smithsonian?"

"Technically, it was under it. But not to worry, nobody saw me."

He omitted the confrontation in the Castle, the Justice Department lady, and the fact that he'd shot her, too. No sense begging for trouble. And besides, he was reasonably sure nothing could be traced back to him.

"You do realize that I was connected to Thomas," she said. "What happens if someone starts asking questions?"

Which was a possibility. One he'd deal with, if and when it arose. As much as he liked Diane, both in and out of the sack, he liked the prospects of billions of dollars in lost gold more. "Your connection to him was innocent, right?"

"Of course, and he may not have told a soul about it."

But he knew that was not the case. The Justice Department lady had been right there, all over him, and afterward had gone straight to Thomas' apartment. That meant she *was* informed. But hopefully she was now dead. And if Richard Stamm, or anyone else, could connect Diane, Thomas, and himself, why had they not already tried to contact Diane? She certainly would be easy to find. Which made him think that he'd been right all along. Thomas had kept the details of that relationship to himself.

He decided to move on to another subject. "The Trail Stone was exactly where it was supposed to be inside the natural history museum. My father's memory was right on that one." He reached into his pants pocket and found the ceremonial key. "And we have this, too. Combined with the Witch's Stone from Arkansas my men found, we're nearly there. I have photos of all the stones we've found so far. You need to work on decipher-ing them."

Her value came from being able to under-stand the Order's cryptic language. To find the gold, he would need that expertise.

"Things are about to happen in Congress," she told him. "Vance is moving ahead."

He shrugged. "Doesn't concern us. But I'm sure your brother's panties are all in a wad with excitement. He wants to change the country. You and I? We just want to be rich."

Greed was truly one of the simplest of mo-tives. And it wasn't like he was taking some-thing that belonged to other living people. This treasure had been hidden for a long time. The people who stole it were all dead, their cause long forgotten. Sure, Kenneth Layne and the Speaker of the House planned to resurrect some of the old ideas, but who cared.

"It's happening," she whispered.

That it was. They'd definitely made prog-ress.

He stepped over to a wall mirror.

Though no one may have seen his face, his curly hair could be a problem. And the port wine stain. He'd never given it much thought,

385

there since birth, not all that noticeable to him.

But to others?

"I'll email you photos of the stones," he said, studying himself in the mirror. "You work on them. I have to go out."

He headed for the bedroom to find his shirt.

"Where are you going?" she asked.

"I need a haircut."

Danny met each of the fourteen people who worked out of Alex's main office, including its chief of staff. Every senator had a DC headquarters, then satellite offices scattered throughout their respective states, usually one in each congressional district. All total, across ten separate offices, Alex employed 34 people, which was about average. But if you multiply those costs by 100, it added up to a serious line item in the federal budget. Something else Everett Dirksen once said came to mind. *A billion here, a billion there, and pretty soon you're talking about real money.*

He stood in Alex's inner sanctum, a bright, warm space decorated with more Tennessee memorabilia, the walls filled with dozens of framed photos, a visual reminder of a storied political career. There were presidents, senators, kings, queens, movie stars, singers. You name it, Alex had shaken their hand. Danny understood the importance of displaying those connections. The images sent a subtle, but clear, message that the man who occupied this office could get things done. So trust him. Vote for him. Once, long ago, when he'd been the senior senator from Tennessee, another suite of offices, on another floor in another building, had been littered with images of him. Interesting how presidents had no need for such pandering. It was so different in the White House. Your stock rose and fell by the hour and no amount of braggadocio photographs helped. Of course, everything here would have to eventually go to Diane. But something about that really bothered him. She'd had Alex's apartment searched. Then she'd met privately with Lucius Vance and some other man, smooching on Vance afterward. Giving these precious memories to her seemed wrong. So for now, everything would stay right where it was.

"Nobody loses their job," he said to the chief of staff, standing beside him.

She was a competent Capitol Hill veteran. Alex had never had anything but good words to say about her.

"If anyone feels they can't work for me, they're welcome to leave with a good recommendation and my blessing. But I don't want any of 'em to go. It's their call. This is hard enough without making things harder."

"I speak for everyone," she said, "when I say we're here for you, ready to go to work."

He already liked this woman.

CHAPTER FORTY-TWO

Cotton waited for more answers from the chief justice, deciding to let Weston set the tone. This man was on a mission. After something. What? He wasn't sure. The one thing that rang clear, though, was that he was not hearing everything. Experience had taught him that the ears were always more attentive than the mouth, so he kept quiet and listened.

"We had quite a civil war going on at this institution, back in 1973," Weston told him. "Davis Layne was interested in finding the Order's lost gold. Frank Breckinridge thought it best that the Smithsonian stay out of it. He argued that we made enough mistakes during, and after, the Civil War, so we should just leave it alone. That gold wasn't ours. His position is the one that ultimately prevailed."

"And Diane Sherwood?"

"She surely knows about what happened with her father back then. That's probably how she was able to steer Martin Thomas to the restricted archives, which are mainly her father's papers. And it's safe to assume that she would be sympathetic to him. She's apparently trying to finish what her father started and find the gold."

"Which Martin Thomas complicated by trying to make his own deal with our curly-haired killer."

"I told him about Thomas' duplicity," Stamm said.

"It appears we trusted Mr. Thomas far too much," Weston noted.

Cotton's mind was racing. "I still have Cassiopeia Vitt on the ground, in Arkansas. I assume you'd like the Witch's Stone returned here?"

"Definitely," Weston said.

That should not be a problem.

He again examined the Trail Stone, and decided to pose a question of his own. "How does the ceremonial key fit in? It has to be quite important."

And he caught the twinkle in Weston's eye.

"Actually, I was hoping you might have the answer to that question."

Cassiopeia hid in the trees, near Terry Morse's truck. Morning had arrived, the sun cresting the forested hills to the east. Morse and Lea had left in the car that had brought Morse to the mine. She'd stayed, waiting for whoever planned to come back for the gold and the two acolytes. Her patience was rewarded about two and a half hours after Morse and Lea left when a Toyota pickup rumbled down the road toward the mine.

She hadn't disturbed Morse's truck, as it was there when the men left earlier and needed to be there when they returned. Only the driver filled the truck cab, so three of the four men from earlier were accounted for. She'd also managed to grab a quick peek at the face, and it wasn't Proctor.

The driver disappeared toward the mine and she settled in, chafing with impatience, eyes gritty with fatigue. A dry breeze tapped loose soil against the truck's flank. The driver would have to find out what happened to his compatriots, then help the one guy out of the mine. What to do with the other body might be a problem. Leave it in the pit? Most likely. Would he load the gold onto the truck? Probably not, considering the situation. So thirty minutes, tops.

Sure enough, less than an hour later she heard the thrum of an approaching vehicle and saw the Toyota swing around a curve in the road, blurred by the swirl of accompanying dust.

Two people sat inside.

And no black tarp in the truck bed as it rushed by.

The time was approaching 9:00 A.M.

She emerged from the woods and hopped

391

into Morse's truck.

Cotton wasn't sure how to take what the chief justice had said. "Why do you think I know anything about that key?"

"Angus Adams is your ancestor. I was hoping there were family stories."

"There were. But not about the Knights of the Golden Circle or any skeleton key."

That wasn't exactly true, but two could play the quiet game.

"We know that Adams moved west after the war," Weston said. "We think it was intentional. Both the Confederate and the Union claimed ownership over the Southwest. Early in the war the Confederacy waged an ambitious New Mexico campaign, trying to open up unrestricted access to California."

Which he knew from reading.

"That covert reconnoiter Adams did back during the 1854 Smithsonian expedition, at Jefferson Davis and the Order's request, was utilized by the Confederacy to wage that war," Weston said.

That, he did not know.

"His journal provided a wealth of geographic information and local knowledge. Unfortunately, Confederate influence in the New Mexico territory ended after the Battle of Glorieta Pass, in 1862. In 1865 Adams went west. But not before he visited the Smithsonian on January 24. The day of the great fire."

He listened as Weston told him how Adams smuggled himself into the capital that day to make a delivery.

"Jefferson Davis feared that once Richmond fell, the Union army would destroy all the Confederate records. Nothing would survive the war, and he did not want the history of the South written by the victors. So he ordered the most important documents hidden. He wanted them to go to the Smithsonian, believing that was the best place to preserve them. Davis and Joseph Henry were close friends. He would have trusted Henry to do the right thing. But those records never made it here and have never surfaced."

"Is that also what you're after?"

"We're not actually *after* anything," Weston made clear. "Diane Sherwood started this by using Martin Thomas to access our restricted archives. We're merely investigating that breach."

"You keep telling yourself that and you might actually start to believe it."

"Might I tell you a story?" Weston asked, seemingly ignoring his insult.

"Why not."

He listened as Weston explained what happened the day of the great fire. Adams had come to bring the key to Joseph Henry and retrieve his 1854 field journal, which the Smithsonian still possessed. But the fire intervened, along with a Union officer, who'd been sent to thwart Adams' mission.

"Adams managed to escape with both the key and the journal," Weston said. "There were questions afterward, but Joseph Henry's close relationship with Lincoln prevented anything of ever coming of it." Weston paused, as if gathering himself. "Then, in 1877, Adams visited the Smithsonian again and met with Henry for the last time. The photo you just saw was taken while he was here. On that day he returned his field journal to our collections on loan for seventy-five years, then it was to be returned to his family. We have a record of the journal coming in that day, but not one of it ever leaving. We thought perhaps it might have been returned unrecorded, and survived in your family."

"Rick mentioned this earlier. But nothing like that was at my family's home in Georgia. And my grandfather never mentioned anything about a journal. He spoke of Adams, but nothing on that subject."

And unfortunately, his grandfather had been gone a long time, his grand-uncles likewise dead.

"Let's return to that civil war we had here at the Smithsonian," Weston said. "In 1973 Frank Breckinridge lodged a formal ethics complaint against Davis Layne, one the secretary at the time had to investigate. Breckinridge claimed Layne had breached our internal rules for personal gain. The investigation proved inconclusive, but Layne and Breckinridge emerged from the battle bitter enemies."

"Relations between the Castle and the American history museum were still frosty a decade later," Stamm said, "when I became curator. It took a lot of work to ease those tensions, though both men were long gone."

"You told me Layne is dead. What about Frank Breckinridge?"

"He lives not far from here," Weston said.

He got the message.

The chief justice wanted him to go there.

"I need an address."

CHAPTER FORTY-THREE

Cassiopeia stayed back and followed the Toyota pickup using a loose tail. Its driver seemed unconcerned. Just a casual pace, right at the speed limit, not drawing any attention. Proctor had surely wanted to handle all of this under the cover of darkness, but her appearance at the mine had clearly thrown off his schedule.

They were headed back toward town, on the same state highway that eventually led to the lodge. She'd told Terry Morse to take Lea and stay out of sight until she returned. Her best route to Proctor was the two guys in the truck ahead of her, and she intended to play this lead out. Her cell phone remained without reception. At the first opportunity, she would call Cotton, tell him about what was happening, and find out about Stephanie.

A sign indicated that they were entering town, the speed limit gradually reduced. A river ran right through the middle of the business district, the quaint row buildings fronting the wide street all of brick and wood. Mainly cafés, gift shops, a grocer, and sporting goods, clustered together like meat on a skewer. Everything seemed to cater to tourism and outdoor recreational activities. Bed-and-breakfast inns dominated. The Toyota was parked on the street in an angled space before one of them.

The driver hopped from the pickup and headed off down the sidewalk, leaving the injured man inside. Bushy trees lined the sidewalks, and bright geraniums filled sill boxes. People were already out for the day, the town buzzing with life. The driver headed straight for a diner, this one occupying the ground floor of a three-story brick building. A plate-glass window announced SOUTHERN BITS & BITES.

She parked down the street from the bed-and-breakfast, stuffed the gun she'd retrieved in the mine into her jean pocket, and draped her shirttail for concealment. She then made her way down the sidewalk, opposite the diner, using parked cars for cover. She passed the diner and kept going, before crossing the street, then backtracking toward it. A peek through that plate-glass window would be good, but the front door was half glass, too. Approaching, she risked a quick look and spotted the driver, sitting at a booth, another man across from him with his back to her.

397

But she recognized the head and hair.

Proctor.

Apparently having breakfast.

She was deciding what to do when the driver slid from the booth and headed toward the door. She retreated to the shop next door and watched from a recessed doorway as the man emerged, turned, and headed back to where the Toyota waited.

She eased out of the shop and hustled to the diner's door, entering, then walking straight for the booth, slipping the gun from her back pocket as she eased onto the bench seat opposite Proctor, who glanced up from his food, no look of surprise on his face.

She nestled the weapon's barrel to his right kneecap.

"I'd like nothing more than to pull this trigger and make you a cripple," she whispered, her tone at variance with her smile.

"I see I made a mistake not shooting you *before* tossing you into that hole."

"Add that to your growing list of errors."

He returned his attention to the ham and eggs on his plate. "And what other mistakes have I made?"

"One of your men is dead. I assume the *knight* who was just here reported that. Then there's another knight with probably a destroyed knee out in the truck. And don't forget about the stack of gold still waiting out in the open back at the mine. That's a lot of problems. Not to mention that your men led me straight here."

He motioned with his knife and fork. "Did you ever think I might have wanted that to happen?"

"I can't imagine why."

She pressed the gun firmer to his kneecap to make her point clear.

His eyes locked on hers and she saw, for the first time, a touch of annoyance. And she doubted that face ever relaxed into a smile, except to deceive.

"Give it a try," she said, reading his mind as he seemed to be deciding whether to challenge her. "Please. I want you to."

And her right thumb cocked the gun's hammer, which clicked into place, adding an exclamation point to her request.

"What do you want?" he calmly asked her.

"Answers."

He returned to his food and stuffed a fork full of runny eggs into his mouth. "I was assuming you'd be soon dead, so I didn't mind providing you information back in the mine. Now is a different story."

"And I'm sure, at the moment, you're trying to decide how you can get out of here with both legs intact."

He chewed. "The thought had occurred to me."

"Do the Knights of the Golden Circle really still exist?"

"I can't answer that."

She pressed again with the gun.

"But I can take you to someone who can."

"Nice try. But I never give up a position of advantage."

He reached for a piece of toast and buttered it. "You must forgive my manners, but I haven't eaten since yesterday afternoon. It was a long night."

"Moving all that gold works up an appetite?"

"Your name, Cassiopeia Vitt, it sounds mysterious."

"More Spanish."

"You're a beautiful woman."

"You can't honestly think that's going to distract me."

"I didn't say it to distract. I just spoke the truth."

"You do this all the time?"

He motioned to his plate. "Have breakfast? Of course. Every day. It's the day's most important meal." He grinned at his own joke, and she told herself to be careful. "If it matters, I took no pleasure in tossing you down that hole."

"I feel so much better. Thank you for sharing that." She'd been around Cotton too long, now mimicking his sarcasm. "You clearly don't understand. I am with the federal government and you're coming into custody."

"On what charge?"

"Murder."

He chuckled. "Who did I kill? From what I was told, Terry Morse shot my man. Do you plan to take him into custody, too?"

"What do you think?"

"It doesn't matter. I'll deal with him. A knight does not kill another knight."

"I thought he was a sentinel."

"He is. But he's also a knight."

She decided to point out, "This is an intelligence operation."

He seemed to consider that for a moment. "I feel honored."

"Don't be. But prosecuting you is not what the people I work for will want."

He got the message. No rules. "You'll learn nothing from me."

She shrugged. "There's a dead man in Washington, DC, and another woman fighting for her life. She's head of a major U.S. intelligence agency, the one who sent me here. I'm betting there's a connection between that murder, what happened to her, and you. Her agency is going to want to talk to you, and they're not going to be subtle about how they get answers."

Proctor pushed his plate aside and patted at his mouth with a napkin. A sinister expression swept over his face, which deepened into a look of cruelty. "That all depends."

"On what?"

"You getting out of this town alive."

CHAPTER FORTY-FOUR

Danny stepped from the taxi. His new chief of staff had learned that Lucius Vance was having lunch near the White House at the Willard Hotel. He knew the place. A city landmark since before the Civil War, it liked to brag that every president since Franklin Pierce had either slept or attended an event there at least once, himself no exception. He'd visited several times, even staying there in the days leading up to his first inauguration.

All of the hype was correct. A lot had happened at the Willard, its halls always thick with ambassadors, politicos, and celebrities. "The Battle Hymn of the Republic" had been composed in one of its rooms. Martin Luther King Jr. polished off his "I Have a Dream" speech while a guest. Dickens and Hawthorne had frequented. Lincoln and Coolidge even lived there awhile. If legend was to be believed, Ulysses Grant liked to sit in the elegant lobby, drink whiskey, and smoke a cigar. Folks would approach him and ask political favors, which supposedly led to the term *lobbying*.

Danny entered through the front doors, the atmosphere rich in ambience, the walls and floor adorned with veined marble, mosaics, and glass. He'd always thought it looked more like a museum than a hotel, exuding the same timeless feel. It was definitely one of the finest hotels in the country. They simply were not made like this anymore.

He followed a palm-lined promenade called Peacock Alley back to the Willard Room. What was the brag? The best dining space in DC. No question. And it came with all the bells and whistles. Two stories high, walnut-paneled, green-veined marble columns, bold fabrics. He'd always liked how the tables were spaced apart with lots of elbow room, offering an element of privacy that wasn't often found in such a grand space. As president, he'd attended a couple of diplomatic luncheons there.

The paneled doors leading into the dining room were swung open and two Secret Service agents stood guard, as he would expect given the Speaker of House was nearby. He recognized both from Alex's funeral and last night at Diane's house. He could hear a murmur of conversation and the tinkle of cutlery to china. He caught sight of the tables, and it appeared this was a small private gathering. Only three were adorned in white tablecloths beneath dimly lit chandeliers. Stewards fussed around, serving a cozy midday meal. He took a quick count. Twelve diners. His new chief of staff had learned that Vance was having a working lunch.

"Hastily called," the source had privately noted.

And conspicuously away from the Capitol.

Vance sat at one of the tables, talking to a few other congressmen, all of whom Danny recognized. He surveyed the remaining faces and was pleased he recalled nearly all of them, too. Thankfully, he'd been blessed with a good memory for faces.

He took a step to enter and one of the agents stopped him. "This is a closed lunch, Mr. President."

He threw the man a glare. "At least you still recognize me."

"I do, sir. And this is awkward, to say the least."

"Not really. I need to see the Speaker."

"He instructed us that this was to be a closed gathering. No one allowed in."

He'd always been irritated with how the Secret Service took everything literally. "You're not serious, are you? Do you really want to have this fight? I'll tell you now, you'll lose."

For eight years he'd had to do exactly what his protection detail required. So many rules and procedures, all aggravating. At first he'd bucked the system. Eventually, he just gave in and did what he was told. But that had not meant he'd liked it. So he sure as hell wasn't going to be told what to do now.

He allowed the agent time to consider the gravity of his challenge and a chance to make the right call.

Which the man did.

Stepping aside.

"Good move," Danny said.

He entered the dining room and walked straight over to Lucius Vance. He noticed that the others present instantly recognized him, tossing that look he'd grown accustomed to while in the White House. The *there's the president of the United States* stare. Several had given it to him out in the lobby, including the doorman, but he'd just kept smiling and walking.

Vance saw him coming and stopped talking, rising from his seat. "Our newest senator from Tennessee. What brings you here?"

The Speaker extended a hand to shake, which he did not accept. Normally, he would have, rocking his enemy to sleep, adhering to what Vito Corleone told his eldest. *Never let anyone know what you're thinking.* But this was different. He'd come to set a fire and drive snakes from the bushes. No use mincing words or actions. Vance clearly did not appreciate the rebuke, especially in front of his peers.

"We need to talk," he said to the Speaker.

"You can see I'm engaged in a lunch, with House members."

Fair enough. He'd embarrassed him, so a little pushback. To be expected. So he turned his attention to the others, who might not be willing to be so brazen toward a former president of the United States and new senator from Tennessee. "You folks care if I borrow him for a few minutes?"

No one said a word.

He extended his hands in a gesture of conciliation. "See, they don't mind."

This was fun. Like back in Maryville on the city council when you made your plays upfront, right in the face of your enemy. Toe-to-toe. Not like the hit-or-miss warfare-from-the-bushes practiced around this town. He was betting Vance would be too curious to know what was going on to refuse his invitation, and he was right.

The Speaker nodded and motioned. "Let's step outside."

They exited through the doorway and turned left.

The protection detail started to follow.

"You don't want them hearing what we're about to say," he whispered as they walked.

"Maybe I do."

He shrugged. "Your call. But don't say I

didn't warn you."

Vance stopped and stared at him, as though trying to read something, anything. But a lifetime of hardball politics had taught Danny the value of a poker face.

Vance turned to the agents. "Wait back at the Willard Room. We'll be right here, at the end of the hall, in sight."

The agents nodded and retreated.

Vance faced him. "What's this about?"

"It's not going to work."

A curious look came to the younger man's face. "I don't understand."

"What you're planning. It's not going to work."

He was running a huge bluff. On the Sherwood deck Diane had told Vance that, from now on, she thought they should keep their relationship proper. *"Especially with what's about to happen."* Then she'd made clear, *"You're about to become the most powerful man in this country, and powerful men need wives and children. Not mistresses."*

"I have not the slightest inkling what you are talking about."

" 'Changing history can be quite an aphrodisiac.' "

Exactly what Vance had said to Diane on the deck. He'd decided a quote, one only Vance would know he'd uttered, would be the quickest, clearest and most decisive way to start a fire.

And it worked.

"You can't stop me," Vance whispered.

"Want to bet?"

"You couldn't as president, and you sure as hell won't from the Senate."

God, he felt alive. To be back in the saddle, engaged in a meaningful fight, with a worthy adversary, the stakes surely high — there was nothing better. His whole psyche seemed geared for just this. Was it a sickness? An addiction? Probably. But it was a malady that he had no intention of ever being rid of. He was definitely *born to a storm.*

"How did it feel when your own party shunned you for the presidential nomination," he asked Vance.

"There are many ways to achieve power. Being president is but one."

A hint. Whatever it was would affect the White House.

"The people said no to you."

Vance chuckled. "The people have no idea what they want. They just want."

"Spoken like a true opportunist."

"I do appreciate the warning, though," Vance said. "I know now who to watch carefully."

"And you're going to have to ask yourself, why would I give you a heads-up? Why not just keep what I know to myself until I was ready to strike? Believe me, you're going to love the answer to both questions."

"Is that why you asked your pal in the governor's mansion to give you the appointment?"

"That, and other reasons. You better hope to God you had nothing to do with Alex Sherwood's death. The governor of Tennessee was a friend of Alex's, too."

The solemnity in Danny's voice seemed to give Vance pause and he watched for a reaction. Anything. But none came.

Which told him something.

Out of the corner of his eye he caught the agents keeping a close eye on them.

Vance noticed their interest, too. "Threatening the Speaker of the House is a dangerous thing."

"Screwin' with this country, and my friends, is even worse."

"I had nothing to do with Alex Sherwood's death. Which I understand was an accident. But this country needs changing. The time has come. And I plan to do it."

"One congressman from a small district in the middle of nowhere. You're going to be our savior?"

"Something like that."

He'd pushed this as a far as he could.

One last jab.

"Nearly all men can stand adversity, but if you want to test a man's character, give him power."

Lincoln's words, as quoted by Diane right

before she and Vance had kissed. One thought had to be shooting through Vance's brain.

How could he possibly know that?

"You have a good lunch, Mr. Speaker."

He walked away. No need to look back.

The fire in the bushes had started.

And the snakes would scurry soon.

CHAPTER FORTY-FIVE

Cassiopeia assessed the situation. She had a gun nestled to Proctor's knee. Though he was surely armed, both of his hands were visible on the table. The diner was crowded, and the last thing she wanted was a shoot-out, but she was puzzled by Proctor's confidence.

He settled back in the booth. "Let me put this in perspective for you. You're here and, yes, you can make me a cripple. But I have men all around you."

She knew of only four, including Proctor, one of whom was dead, another incapacitated. The waitress sauntered over and asked if they wanted anything else.

"I'm good," Proctor said. "How about you?"

"He'll take the check," she said.

And she noticed when Proctor gave the woman a playful wink before she walked away.

"Are you always a flirt?" she asked.

"Only when I think I have a chance."

"And what made you think you had one with me?"

He shrugged. "Women have been known to offer things — when backed into a corner."

"Not the women I know."

A chuckle slipped from his thin lips. There it was again. That deception.

"That wasn't a flirt to that woman," he said. "She's the daughter of the owner of this place. And you're about to have a whole lot of trouble."

Her gaze darted right as a man in a white body apron emerged through a swinging door, shotgun in hand. She swung her gun out from beneath the table and fired one shot into the ceiling, which had the desired effect. People panicked, rushing from their chairs and booths, heading for the door. The confusion stopped the owner's approach, and she doubted he was going to fire into the crowd. She slid from the booth and decided to join the mass exodus. But before leaving, she swiped the butt of her pistol hard into Proctor's right temple, which send the bastard's head down to the tabletop.

The owner was trying to get to her, but she managed to fall in with the patrons, jamming the gun into the waistband beneath her shirt-tail and emerging into the late-morning sun. Morse's truck was parked fifty meters away. Most of the people who'd fled the diner had run across the street to the opposite sidewalk.

She joined them, keeping quiet and trying to blend in. Hopefully no one would identify her as the person who'd fired the shot.

The man in the apron appeared from the diner, without his shotgun. She hid herself behind a wooden column that held up a canvas awning. The people around her were all talking with excitement. A police car sped down the street and stopped at the diner. A uniformed officer emerged and talked with the café owner. She could imagine what was being said. *A woman fired into the ceiling. Dark hair. Spanish looking. Dressed in jeans, boots, and a long-sleeved shirt.* Not too many of those around. No mention would be made of the shotgun appearing first. No reference to a man named Jim Proctor.

The uniformed officer and the owner disappeared inside the diner.

That was her cue to leave.

She hustled down the street toward the truck. The other men who'd come from the mine in the Toyota were nowhere to be seen. She needed to find out where that gold had been taken. The quickest way would be to follow Proctor. Right now, though, she had to get out of town. All the excitement had attracted a crowd, people streaming out of the shops and other eateries onto the sidewalk.

Her cell phone vibrated.

She checked the display. Lea.

They'd exchanged numbers back at the

mine to be able to communicate.

She answered.

"Some men just came," the young girl quickly said. "Grandpa told me to hide when they drove up. They took him with them. At gunpoint."

"Where are you?"

"At home.

"Stay there. I'm coming."

She wheeled up to the picket fence and braked to a stop. Lea bounded off the front porch and ran her way. She hopped out of the vehicle and saw the anxiety on the young woman's face.

"Tell me what happened."

Two men with guns had appeared. There was some heated talk, then Morse went along without resistance. Cassiopeia assumed the old man had done that to protect Lea.

"They also wanted the Witch's Stone."

"They took it?"

Lea nodded.

Apparently, Proctor was tying up loose ends. And he definitely had more help around.

"I heard where they were going," she said. "Grandpa asked them why they were taking him back to the mine."

Smart move on Morse's part sending that message.

"You stay here," she said. "I'll take care of it."

"I'm going with you."

The look of determination on Lea's face was hard to ignore and, besides, she needed some help with directions back to the site.

"Okay," she said.

CHAPTER FORTY-SIX

Cotton stood beside Stephanie's hospital bed. He'd left the American history museum and decided to stop by here on his way to where Frank Breckinridge lived. Rick Stamm had provided him with a car and told him that the retired curator was pushing eighty and lived alone, so he decided his visit could wait another hour. It was Stephanie's condition that concerned him.

She lay motionless amid tubes, dripping bags, and bandages, arms at her sides. They'd been through so much together, good and bad. He owed her more than he could ever repay. He'd been a JAG lawyer, headed for a mundane legal career, all at the insistence of others, men who'd known his dead father and thought that flying fighter jets was not his best career move. He'd really loved flying. Nothing better. But back then he'd carried a blind worship of his missing father that included listening to those other men, and doing what they thought best. Then everything changed the day he met Stephanie Nelle. And he found out what those friends of his father really had in mind. He became a Magellan Billet agent, permanently assigned to the Justice Department. He never lost his rank of lieutenant commander and kept his commission until the day he quit both the Billet and the navy and moved to Denmark.

Now he was a bookseller.

Sort of.

What would his father think?

He could only hope he'd be proud.

The door to the hospital room opened and Danny Daniels entered. Cotton hadn't seen him since Inauguration Day, when he, Cassiopeia, Daniels, and Stephanie left the White House for the last time. The former president was dressed in a suit and tie, looking every bit presidential.

"How is she?" Daniels asked.

"The nurse told me there's been no change. She's still in a coma."

"Any leads on who shot her?"

"I just had him in my sights, but he got away."

Daniels faced him. "Talk to me. Tell me everything."

He told Daniels about the Smithsonian, the Knights of the Golden Circle, what happened in Arkansas, and what had occurred over the past few hours.

"This started thanks to one of the Smithso-

418

nian Libraries Advisory Board members. A woman named Diane Sherwood. The widow of Senator Sherwood," Cotton said. "He was a Smithsonian regent, which makes this real touchy over there. I assume you knew Senator Sherwood?"

"He was a close friend. And by the way, you're looking at the newest junior senator from Tennessee. I was sworn in a little while ago to serve out Alex's term."

He was impressed. "I can only imagine how you pulled that off. And why do I get the feeling that's connected to what's happening here?"

"Because it is. You and I seem to be in the same mess."

And he listened as Daniels explained what he'd witnessed over the past twenty-four hours, ending with, "Alex's girlfriend told me that the guy who went into his apartment and took the journal was middle-aged, white, with a port wine stain on the back of his neck."

"The same guy who killed Martin Thomas and probably shot Stephanie."

"Who had a key to the apartment, which means Diane gave it to him. That ties her to the murder of that librarian and probably the attempt on Stephanie. I'd say you need to rattle her cage real good."

"The chancellor specifically told me not to do that."

He explained the chief justice's angle.

419

"Warren Weston is a friggin' blowhard," Daniels said. "He should have retired a long time ago, but he stayed on the Supreme Court just so I couldn't appoint his successor. We sent feelers his way several times that it might be time for him to leave, but he sent 'em right back with a polite go-to-hell."

"He's all over this. Personally overseeing things. He also deliberately involved me, then Stephanie."

They moved away from the bed, as if she could be listening.

Which they could only hope.

Daniels ran his fingers through his thick mane of silvery hair. "Weston could be right, though. If you spook 'em by going to Diane, they'll just go to ground. Better to let 'em keep runnin', thinking they're in the clear. But what the Speaker of the House is working on — that needs some brakes on it right now. He's a few steps ahead of me, and I need to catch up."

He now understood more about the temporary appointment. "Being a senator opens a lot of doors, doesn't it?"

"Damn right. But we're coming into this game late. I hope to God not too late. I knew Diane's father once worked at the Smithsonian. I just never knew about his fascination with the Golden Circle. I don't know anything about her brother, but I'm about to find out. I have to confess, the Knights of the

Golden Circle are pretty unknown to me. My granddaddy told me about 'em once. They were big in Tennessee. There was even a castle in Blount County, back at the end of the 19th century. But beyond that I don't know beans about 'em."

"I suggest you get familiar, since they're front and center here."

"Is a cross within a circle important to them?"

He nodded. "It was one of their symbols."

And Daniels told him about a necklace that Alex Sherwood's mistress had given him. "Diane told me she had it made. One for her, another for Alex."

"That woman is in this up to her eyeballs."

Daniels nodded. "That she is. And that same symbol was etched on the front of her brother's notebook. That's not a coincidence."

No. It wasn't.

They both stared over at Stephanie, who continued to breathe with help from a ventilator.

"She's important to you, isn't she?" he asked Daniels.

"I love her. And she loves me."

"You sound almost relieved to say that."

"I am. About time, too. She can't die on me now."

Daniels walked back to the bed and took Stephanie's hand into his own. Cotton re-

421

alized that this man would never do that with just anyone in the room, and he appreciated the confidence the former president was showing in him. He also saw the eyes. Wet with anxiety.

And maybe a little fear.

He was scared himself.

"One thing, Cotton," Daniels said, his gaze still on Stephanie. "When you find the guy with the port wine stain, I want in on taking him down."

"You mean you want to kill him."

"If the opportunity presents itself."

"You do know that would be the last thing Stephanie would want you to do."

"She'll get over it."

"Weston thinks this other man, Frank Breckinridge, might be able to fill in some gaps."

"Careful with Warren Weston. I never found him to be particularly trustworthy. But I hate all judges, so it might just be me."

Cotton had never been much of a fan, either. He could count on one hand the number of black robes that had earned his respect.

"I have to go," Daniels said. "I'll be back later. I plan to spend the night here."

"I'll check in with you when I know more."

"Diane Sherwood and Lucius Vance are up to no good," Daniels said. "Her brother, too. It's up to us to find out what that is. Tread carefully, Cotton. And one thing. I have Alex's Senate seat and everything that goes with it. So I'm now a Smithsonian regent. Let me know if you need to use that in any way."

He nodded and started for the door. "What do you plan to do while I visit this guy Breckinridge?"

"I'm goin' to start whacking the heads off some snakes."

Chapter Forty-Seven

Grant left the barbershop. He'd never liked going to a women's salon to have his hair cut. He preferred an old-fashioned barber's chair. Luckily, a few of those still remained, including one north of central DC that he preferred. It came with a striped pole out front and even offered a shave and shoeshine. His brown curly locks were gone, his hair now a pale brush cut. He'd also decided that one other precautionary measure needed to be taken, so he'd stopped at a Walgreens and bought some makeup.

As a child his birthmark had been a deep purple splotch, extending from the back of his neck to his left jawline. It wasn't a health issue, except if he cut the skin. Bleeding could be hard to stop. In grammar school he'd taken some ribbing for the discoloration. Once, his mother decided to put an end to it and applied makeup, which did hide the stain, but he just received even more abuse. So he learned to live with it, and anyone who had a problem with that received his fists. There'd been a few fights but, eventually, the bullies moved on.

Some makeup right now, though, seemed like a good idea. He'd been careful inside the museums, but the back of his neck may well have been noticed. The birthmark could provide anyone looking for him with a ready marker. As would his former hair. But that was gone and the stain was now hidden beneath a layer of foundation.

All in all an effective transformation.

Diane had listened wide-eyed as he told her only what he believed she needed to know, wondering the whole time if he'd done the right thing by being so open. He'd expected anger, accusation, even shock. Instead, his report had been met with silence, then approval. He doubted that her brother would be as generous. But he'd come to learn that Kenneth did what his sister told him.

The news that Vance was moving ahead to change Congress seemed exciting. He loved being a part of all this intrigue. Definitely beat his days as a paralegal. Thank goodness the gold coins he'd managed to secure from the cache they'd found in Kentucky were still paying his bills. He'd sold most of them to a collector who had paid top dollar. But he was anxious to find the mother lode.

The vault.

As a kid his father had been free with the

stories. Maybe he thought it a way for them to bond, or a fulfillment of the hope that the son would follow in the father's footsteps. But as it became apparent that he had no aptitude for academics, the information flow ended, and his father never made any secret of his disappointment. Any dream that he might work at the Smithsonian would never be. Instead he'd found a living elsewhere, and then happened to be in the right place, at the right time, to meet Diane.

Something to be said for luck.

Now he planned to make some of his own.

He'd dealt with Martin Thomas and the woman from the Justice Department. He'd found the Witch's and Trail Stones. They already had photographs of the Horse Stone, there for the taking in the Smithsonian archives.

Two stones remained.

Unfortunately, to find either he would need his father's assistance. He'd already decided this time not to fight the old man's dementia. Instead he would play into it. Online he'd found a site that sold Confederate uniforms to modern-day reenactors. It seemed a big business, so it was easy to buy officer's clothing, more than accurate enough to convince a sick mind. Some show-and-tell should help break through the fog. If that didn't work, he could always beat the information out of the old man.

And he would, if necessary.

He took a cab back to his house, found the uniform, and headed out to his car. He'd change at his father's house.

The objective now was to locate the Heart Stone.

Shaped as described, it was designed to fit into the indentation on the Trail Stone, one side etched with vital information.

His father had cleverly hidden the Trail Stone within the reef exhibit inside the natural history museum.

"I had to keep that fool Yankee, Davis Layne, from getting his hands on it. We have to protect our precious things. Northerners don't give a damn about what's important to us."

What a fight that must have been.

Two curators locked in a great battle.

But the fifth, the so-called Alpha Stone, remained a mystery. He knew little to nothing about it, and would have to coax his father into talking more on that subject. There'd been mentions here and there, but no specifics.

That stone was vital.

As it showed the starting point.

He dug his cars keys from his pocket, tossed them in the air, and caught them in triumph.

Things were finally going his way.

He climbed into the car and drove across town toward his father's residence. The new haircut should make him look more like a soldier, though not necessarily one from the 1860s. Long, shaggy hair had been the norm then. Hopefully his father's fading mind would not be thrown off by such details.

This quest was definitely winding down.

Time to retrieve the final pieces.

CHAPTER FORTY-EIGHT

Diane sat in the quiet of Alex's apartment and studied on her iPad the images of what Grant had managed to find. The Witch's Stone seemed easy. Its words were an introduction to the quest, a clear statement of intent.

This path is dangerous. I go to 18 places.
Seek the map. Seek the heart.

But the symbols?

Those were more complicated.

The lower torso and "legs" of the robed image seemed to represent more a stack of blocks, a foundation, or a pedestal, than a person, which might point the way to some pronounced, pointy landmark in a particular area. Her father had taught her that the Order loved to send mixed messages. Misdirection had been their forte. Playing a hunch, she'd Googled the Spanish word for "witch" and discovered it to be *bruja.* So if the robed figure was meant to portray a witch, perhaps it was a play on the word *brújula,* which meant "compass"?

A possibility.

She took another look at the Trail Stone.

The heart-shaped indentation had the same four numbers — *1847* — that appeared on the Witch's Stone, perhaps meant to link those, as did the Witch's Stone command.

Seek the heart.

Her father had managed to study the Trail Stone before Grant's father hid it away, and he'd told her all about it. Strangely, there were no surviving photos from its time within the Smithsonian, but she had pictures of the destroyed Horse Stone, which Martin Thomas had obtained.

The message on the left likely meant *the horse of faith*. A perplexing phrase, but her father had researched those four words in detail, eventually discovering that it might refer to an old Spanish expression taken to mean *I am a servant of the faith.*

Which fit the Order perfectly.

Their faith had been in a new southern empire, that inevitable golden circle that never came to be.

The Spanish wording to the right of the horse, *I graze to the north of the river,* had to be a reference point. What else could it be? So taken together, the phrases cast a double meaning. *The horse of faith, I graze to the north of the river,* or maybe, as her father concluded, *The servant of faith, I shepherd to the north of the river.*

The Horse Stone was somewhat of an anomaly. Its imagery had been part of the Smithsonian archives since World War I, which had lent it to study from time to time by those who'd understood its significance. Taken alone, though, it was meaningless. Which might explain why images of it had survived, since it led nowhere. The newly uncovered Trail Stone seemed more difficult. The 1973 feud between the two fathers had started over it. Both men had access but, in the end, Frank Breckinridge hid it away, stopping any further searching for the vault. Two years ago she'd gone to see the old man to get him to tell her where he'd hid it, hoping time might have softened him. But all she found was a fading mind with little hold on reality.

She studied the broad, undulating line that cut across the top of the Trail Stone, which could indicate a horizon, or maybe a river, since the letter *R* appeared on the right, perhaps indicating *rio,* as on the Horse Stone.

432

The large dagger seemed important. Its hilt formed an arrow that pointed straight at the recessed heart. Below that a curving dotted line seemed like a trail with evenly spaced markers. What had the Witch's Stone said?

I go to 18 locations.

But only four dots were visible.

The rest had to be revealed on the Heart Stone.

Surrounding the recessed heart were a series of wavy squiggles, which could be indicators of mountains, hills, canyons, or other terrain. But it could also be mere "white noise," added to make things appear more complex and confuse the searcher.

She knew what had to be done.

The Trail Stone had to be fitted with the Heart Stone, then both connected to the fifth and final piece of the puzzle.

The Alpha Stone.

That one could prove impossible to find since, as far as she knew, the Order no longer existed. She was hoping, as her father had hoped forty years before, that modern technology could breach the gap and reveal the missing starting point. The Trail and Heart Stones, when assembled, should form a reasonably complete map. But nothing about this had been made easy. Understandable, given the enormous prize. And the effort had become even more complicated thanks to the passions of men who'd taken it upon themselves to protect that lost wealth.

Like Frank Breckinridge.

In 1973 her father had wanted to find the gold, believing its time had come. Back then there'd been no Internet, no twenty-four-hour news, no social media. So it had been easy for two academics to battle it out with each other. Today their fight would have been fodder for too many websites to count. Nothing seemed private anymore. But it all ended when Frank Breckinridge secreted away both the Trail and Heart Stones.

One had finally resurfaced.

Now it was up to Grant to locate the other.

The apartment's lingering quiet had turned into an ominous, brooding silence, and she found herself listening to sounds she might normally ignore. The creak of a floor, a pipe groaning, the low murmur of a far-off television. This was Alex's space, and she felt like the walls were judging her. If so, then they'd just been party to a shocking scene between her and Grant. Taking him here, in Alex's bed, had been important to her. A statement of defiance she hadn't been able to express while he lived.

She felt caged and restless, so she paced, trying to squeeze the anticipation from her mind. She could still hear the bedsprings creaking from their lovemaking, and felt some shame and embarrassment, along with joy and release. Interesting how such polar opposites could coexist inside her.

"You were the hypocrite," she whispered to Alex.

She was still shocked by Grant's killing of Martin Thomas, but had kept her objections to herself. Kenneth might be right. Grant could be reckless. Thankfully, self-doubt was not part of Grant's makeup, so it probably had to be done. And he was right, too. If a way existed to link her to any of it, the calls would have already come her way.

But nothing had happened.

Things were moving along in the right direction and a weight seemed to be lifting from her shoulders. So she'd keep all of what Grant had told her to herself.

Neither her brother nor Vance would ever know.

Along with one other thing.

CHAPTER FORTY-NINE

Cassiopeia drove with Lea toward the mine.

"These knights are bad people," Lea said. "I never realized how bad. I'm ashamed that some of the local men are even part of it."

"Tell me about that."

"They meet every once in a while. I just considered it like some kind of club, a chance to get together, drink beer, tell stories to one another. Grandpa went a few times. Once was when I went up to the mine with that special friend I told you about."

"Your grandfather tell you anything about the local group?"

She shook her head. "He's real good at keeping secrets. You do know that he only talked to you and Mr. Malone because he didn't want me to go to jail for shootin' at you."

"I get that."

"He went with those men to keep them away from me. I should have shot 'em. But my rifle was here in the truck."

"What about your grandfather's rifle?"

"Those two men got it away from him."

She heard the deep regret in the girl's voice.

The time was approaching midday, the sun high and bright, so getting close to the mine without being seen could prove a problem.

"Is there another way besides the road we took last night?"

Lea nodded. "But it'll take a few extra minutes."

Which gave her more time to think. Earlier, she'd noticed something behind them, on the truck's rear bench.

A longbow and arrows.

"Do you use that bow in the back to hunt?" she asked Lea.

"I've been tryin'. But I'm not the best shot."

She, on the other hand, loved the bow and arrow. Her father had taught her how to use one as a child and she'd kept up her proficiency. At her estate she'd installed archery targets, and her bow collection was impressive.

Lea motioned and they left the highway, driving down an unfamiliar dirt road, deeper into the woods, finally parking in a small clearing.

"We're about half a mile north of the mine. Coming at it from opposite the road you took last night. We can hike up through that pass."

"This is as far as you go," she made clear.

"I'm coming," Lea said.

"No, you're not. This is no game, Lea. You saw that when we were here before. They wanted us both dead. We got lucky then. Your grandfather sacrificed himself to keep you out of harm's way. Don't make that for nothing. I have a better chance of doing this alone."

She still carried the gun, but retrieved the bow and arrows from the truck. "I'm going to borrow this."

"I should go with you," Lea said.

"Do you want me to get your grandfather out of there alive?"

"Of course I do."

"Then let me do my job. What you can do is this. It's nearly 4:00 P.M. If I'm not back in two hours, go to the sheriff's department for help and have them notify the U.S. Justice Department."

She pushed through the trees and underbrush, no real trail defining the way. The path ahead cut a swath between two forested mounds. Lea had told her that the mine sat on the opposite side of the outcropping to her left. She crossed a ridgeline and the familiar decaying buildings of the mine came into view below. Bending over, she moved along the slope, using the brush for cover, then eased between two boulders, which offered not only protection but also a clear line of sight.

A large paneled truck sat parked, the double doors to its cargo bed swung open. Two men were loading the gold bars inside. She counted three other men standing outside the collapsed structures, only one face she recognized. Proctor. Morse was nowhere to be seen. Discussion seemed to ensue, then something wrapped in towels was transferred from a nearby pickup to the inside of the paneled truck. Had to be the Witch's Stone. Then two of the men left, climbing into the pickup and driving away.

That left Proctor and the other two.

The bow she carried was a little over a meter long, a practical combination of wood, fiberglass, and magnesium. Light, not even two kilos. She'd tested its pressure: Tight, with solid resistance. At full draw, maybe thirty-five kilos of firing pressure. Enough to take down a bear. The arrows were likewise high quality, made of aluminum.

She unlimbered the bow, nocked one of the arrows, and drew back for a three-quarter pull. Anything more and the arrow would go straight through. Her aim was made trickier thanks to the boulders on either side. But she imagined herself inside her castle, high in the ramparts before one of the arrow perches. She lined up the peep sight on Proctor, the fletching just grazing her right cheek, and drew a long breath. Pursing her lips, she allowed the air in her lungs to sift slowly out.

439

One of the men closed the double doors on the paneled truck.

She relaxed the bow.

They were leaving?

Not good.

Proctor suddenly disappeared into the collapsed building, now out of the line of fire. The two men followed. She needed to know where that gold was headed, and one glance at her wrist gave her an idea about killing two birds with one stone.

She fled her perch and carefully bumped down the rocky slope, slinging the bow across her back. She found the ground and halted her approach beside the trunk of a thick tree.

All quiet.

A flock of pigeons appeared overhead, banked sharply, then flew away.

She made her way to the front of the truck.

None of the men were around. Ahead, through the ruin, was the same path she and Lea had taken into the mine.

The hum of a generator could be heard.

On her wrist was a Magellan Billet–issued watch, similar to the one Cotton wore. Both contained GPS trackers that worked off a special app that she'd used yesterday to track Cotton.

Now it would tag the truck.

She removed the watch and crept her way back to the double doors, which were closed, slightly ajar, not yet locked into place. Cracking one open she slid the watch inside, along the metal bed, toward the front, past the gold bars, which rested stacked beneath the black tarp.

Noise from behind signaled that someone was coming.

She found refuge behind a pile of rubble.

Two men appeared.

She watched as they closed and locked the double doors, then climbed into the cab and drove off.

She waited until the truck was out of sight, then laid the bow and arrow aside, found her gun, and headed into the mine.

CHAPTER FIFTY

Cotton found where Frank Breckinridge lived, a small cube of a house in a quiet Virginia neighborhood. The kind of place where people existed their whole lives. The house itself was wood-framed, painted white, with a big porch and square-paned windows. Rick Stamm had told him a little about Breckinridge, who defined the job of Castle curator. Before Breckinridge the responsibility for the building's preservation had been scattered across several people, a hit-or-miss proposition, and not all that efficient. Now one person ran the show.

He parked on the street.

Stamm had provided the keys to his personal vehicle. They'd talked about Stamm coming along, but Cotton thought he'd have better success alone. He followed a weather-stained brick walk to the front porch, rubbing his weary face. He'd caught a couple of hours of sleep on the flight east from Arkansas, but had rested poorly.

The front door was open, a screen door keeping out any creatures. He knocked three times on the jamb before he finally heard footsteps headed his way. The face that greeted him from behind the gauzy screen was creased and narrow, with a beak of a nose that overshadowed a thin, straight mouth. Silver hair hung shaggy and uncut, more than two days' worth of stubble on the chin.

"Who are you?" the man asked.

"My name is Cotton Malone. I've come to speak with you about the Smithsonian."

"Cotton Adams? Captain, is that really you?"

The connection caught him by surprise. But the tone and excitement he saw on the old man's face told him that there were reality problems. Dementia? Maybe. Or worse. So why not play along?

"Yes, sir. It's me. Captain Adams."

The door creaked open.

"Come in. You shouldn't be out there in the open. There are Federal eyes and ears everywhere here in the capital."

He stepped inside and Breckinridge poked his head out, listening, waiting for something.

"It seems okay," the old man said. "I think you made it without being followed."

He was unsure where the old man's mind had settled and was a little perturbed that no one had mentioned any impairment — maybe Weston had not known — which called into question whether he should waste any more time. But he decided to give it a few minutes.

"Come in," Breckinridge said, motioning with a bony hand and stepping across the squeaky floorboards.

He followed his host into a small den.

"Sit down, Captain. Please. Take a load off your feet. I'm sure you're tired from the journey."

"I did travel a long way."

"From Richmond?"

"That's right."

The old man eased himself into an upholstered recliner. Cotton chose another chair. He'd expected a musty, olden waft. But everything was surprisingly clean and tidy. So he asked, "Do you live here alone?"

"No, my wife's around here somewhere. Julie. Julie. We have a visitor. Make some coffee."

Stamm had told him that Breckinridge's wife died years ago, not long after he retired. There was one child. A boy. Grown by now, and Stamm knew nothing about him.

"Is your son around?" he asked.

"Gosh, no. He's off teaching somewhere. Left this house long before the war. Tell me, Captain. How is the fight going out there? We get told only what the Yankee newspapers want us to hear."

His dilemma rose. The answer to the question depended on timing. If Breckinridge was

444

living prior to early 1863, the South was doing okay. Winning battles, driving hard north and west. But all that changed with Gettysburg and Vicksburg. Those defeats doomed the Confederacy.

He decided on a middle ground. "We're making good progress. Things are working out."

"I want to know. Is it true about your name? Did you really hide in a mattress, beneath a sick man, to escape the Yankees?"

"I did. It seemed the only way, and it worked."

Breckinridge laughed. "Damn ingenious. Well done. We need more cleverness like that. So what brings you back to the capital. Are you on another assignment?"

He nodded. "We have a problem and need your help. Do you remember the Heart Stone?"

The narrow head nodded. "Oh, yes. Definitely. I saved it, you know."

"I do know. That's why I'm here. We need its location."

"Who's we?"

"President Davis sent me."

He was hoping that lie would add importance.

But Breckinridge spat on the floor.

"Damn fool. That's what he is. He's going to cost us everything. The man worries about stupid details and won't delegate a thing. The people loathe him and why he fights with the state governors I'll never know. That's just asking for trouble."

Interesting how the sick mind remained sharp for detail, since everything he'd just heard was historical fact. "You keep up with things."

"I hear stuff. There are spies, like you, all around us here. I want to know, did Joseph Henry send you my way?"

He nodded and said, "The secretary said you knew everything."

"Did you give him the key?"

The ceremonial key? He'd have to wing it. "I did."

"You were there when the Castle burned, weren't you? What was it like?"

The man's knowledge was impressive. "Quite a sight, and sad, too."

"I bet it was. But it worked to your advantage. You did good, Captain. And your journal is safe. I hid it away, too."

He recalled what he'd been told about Angus Adams' involvement in the 1854 southwest expedition and what Weston said about the journal.

Gone for a long time.

"Between you and me," Breckinridge said, "I don't trust the people over there in the Smithsonian Castle. I think the Federals are onto them."

He decided to push. "President Davis wants

my journal, too."

The oily eyes narrowed. "How do I know I can trust *you*?"

"You don't."

The old man chuckled. "You're a sly one, Captain." Then a gleam filled the eyes. "Are you up for a little test?"

Not really, but he had no choice. "Fire away."

"Name the stones."

That he could answer. "Witch's, Horse, Trail, Heart, and Alpha."

"Damn good, Captain. Will you be wanting to see the knights' commander while you're here?"

Something new. The commander? "Definitely."

"I can arrange a meeting. Good and private, not to worry."

"Where could that be arranged?"

"In that damn Temple of Justice of his. He rarely leaves it, anyway." The older man sat forward. "Between you and me, Captain, I don't trust the commander. He says he's one of us, but I'm not sure. That hair around his bald head makes him look too much like a priest to me. We have to be careful. Real careful. Let's face reality, the war is lost. We both know it. There was no need for the whole damn thing in the first place. We could have done this another way. Hell, the South had the Supreme Court. Look at *Dred Scott,* they ruled 100 percent for us. Slaves aren't people. They're property. Even Lincoln told us, when they swore him in the first time, that we could keep slavery. Just leave the Union intact. But no. Hotheads and fools wanted war."

"Was there another way?" he decided to ask.

Breckinridge pointed a finger. "You're damn right there was, and if that moron Jeff Davis had listened we could have done things within the law. But no one would listen. Jeff Davis shows too much favoritism toward his friends. He can't get along with people who disagree with him, and he doesn't know beans about leading an army. It pains me to say, but Lincoln is a much better war leader."

All facts, too.

"The fight is about over," Breckinridge said. "When that happens, it'll be up to us to keep things going, but I doubt the commander's dedication. Like I said, I don't trust him."

All of which was irrelevant, so he decided to stick with urgency. "Everything you've said is true, and it's why I'm here. The war is lost. But before it's too late, I have to locate the Heart Stone and my journal."

Grant made his way toward the back of his father's house. On approach he'd seen a car nestled at the curb. Nothing unusual. A lot of people in the neighborhood left cars on the street. What piqued his interest was the Smithsonian permit affixed to the windshield. So he'd rounded the block, parked, then hustled back, finding the narrow alley that ran between his father's house and a neighbor.

He crept up the stoop.

Cotton waited for Breckinridge to answer him.

"The Heart Stone is safe, and has been for a long time. So is your journal. I personally handled both. There were problems, you know. People wanted to use them to find the vault. Federals after our gold, but I stopped 'em. You can tell Jeff Davis he has nothing to worry about."

"I need details. That's why I'm here."

The old man sat ramrod-straight, elbows on the armrests, as if waiting for the executioner to switch on the electricity.

"Why does Jeff Davis care?"

"It's not for me to question my president."

"Why not? Davis had the five stones made, then ordered them hidden away. The whole crazy thing was his idea."

"Now he wants them back."

Another finger was pointed his way. "You lie, Captain."

He wondered how much this old man's sick brain knew about Angus Adams. Enough, apparently, to connect *Cotton* to the surname.

Warren Weston certainly knew a lot, too. Perhaps they'd both learned from the same source.

The Smithsonian archives.

He decided indignation, and a slightly thicker southern accent, might work. "Sir, I resent your implications. I am an officer in the Confederate army and I do not lie to a fellow gentleman. I've been sent by the president of the Confederate States to retrieve my journal and the Heart Stone. You are ordered to give me their location."

Breckinridge remained silent.

Then the old man reached for a pad and pen on a side table. Cotton watched as he scribbled, flipping back and forth between two pages, composing something. Finally he finished and tore off one of the sheets, handing it over.

"Prove yourself, Captain. Decipher that."

Grant listened to the odd exchange between his father and another man, the second voice familiar.

His pursuer from Fossil Hall.

He'd managed to slip into the kitchen and could hear the conversation. His father was back in the past and the visitor was playing along, actually making better progress than he'd ever been able to achieve. Why was the guy here? Most troubling was the fact that he knew about the Heart Stone.

And had come here for a reason.

Cotton studied the sheet the old man had handed over. On it was written five sets of letters.

TSIM ESEKA EVEL NEBN HTAE

He nearly smiled.

God bless his grandfather.

As a child of twelve he'd learned about Confederate codes, none of which were overly complicated since they were created at a time when most people remained illiterate. Simple substitution matrixes were a norm. Today those would be broken in a matter of minutes. He and his grandfather used to toy with them, his eidetic memory making them easy to unravel. This one was not even a code. More a jumble, designed only to confuse any snooping eyes.

"Can I borrow that pad?" he asked.

Breckinridge ripped off the other sheet upon which he'd written and handed it over.

First, he rewrote the letters, reversing the five groups.

HTAE NEBN EVEL ESEKA TSIM

A simple matter from there to combine the four sets into a single line.

HTAENEBNEVELESEKATSIM

Then reverse the line.

MISTAKESELEVENBENEATH

And he immediately noticed three words.
He was right. Just a jumble.
One more reverse and the message became clear.

BENEATH ELEVEN MISTAKES.

He wrote out his findings and handed the pad back.

Breckinridge read, then nodded. "Good work. That's where you'll find the Heart Stone."

"What about my journal?"

"One thing at a time, Captain. One thing at a time."

CHAPTER FIFTY-ONE

Danny had learned something interesting. After he'd rattled off the names of the people who'd been inside the Willard Room to his new chief of staff, she'd immediately seen a connection.

"They're all on the Rules Committee," she'd told him. *"Speaker of the House appointments."*

Why had Vance needed to have lunch with his own people? It wasn't necessary to kiss their asses. He recalled something Ian Fleming wrote in one of the Bond novels. *Once is happenstance. Twice is coincidence. Three times is enemy action.* Good advice from a novelist trained by British intelligence. That lunch happened for a purpose and every part of his mind screamed it was related to what Vance was planning. His visit to the Willard had certainly rattled the Speaker. There's no way it could not have. So one snake was probably already slithering out from the burning bush. Surely Vance had found Diane on the phone and they'd had a heart-to-heart chat, both of them wondering how in the world he could have known what they'd said. Diane had certainly, by now, discovered the notebook was gone. Once she heard what Vance had to say, the prime suspect would be clear. And the second snake would be on the move.

All in all not a bad start to his first day as a senator.

But he had to know more.

So he'd left his office in the Dirksen building and caught a cab toward the National Mall. It was a little odd puttering alone around DC, where before he could not even leave his office without a contingent of Secret Service agents following in his wake. His new second in command had proved her usefulness again by contacting the chief of staff for Texas congressman Paul Frizzell. He'd known Paul a long time, and though of different political parties, they'd always been close. He'd seen Paul in the Willard Room, perched at one of the tables, and caught the wink of one eye. Paul was a longtime veteran, on his fifth or sixth term. Seniority meant everything in the House, and Frizzell had managed to snag a plum assignment. Member of the Rules Committee. What had Ben Franklin said? *Diligence is the mother of good luck.* So true. And he'd caught a bit of good luck, too, with Frizzell being in the right place at the right time.

The cab sped down Independence Avenue and eased to the curb in front of the National Air and Space Museum. He paid the driver, who seemed especially thrilled to have a former president in his backseat, and added a $10 tip, which the guy seemed to like even better. The hour was approaching 4:00 P.M., the spring day warm and sunny. Inside was crowded, people everywhere, which was nothing unusual, as this was one of the world's most visited museums. If truth be told, it was his favorite among the Smithsonian's stable. Space had always been an interest. He'd followed the Mercury, Gemini, and Apollo missions closely and could still recall, as a teenager, sitting in front of the television the night Neil Armstrong set foot on the moon. During his time in the White House he'd been generous to NASA, funding the agency far better than any of his predecessors. He wondered how well it would fare with the Fox administration.

He turned right and headed for the *Space Race* exhibit, trying to ignore the stares from some of the visitors. He entered the hall, where full-scale rockets from Germany, America, and Russia stood at attention. He knew them by name. V-2, Viking, Minuteman, Jupiter-C. Most impressive was the massive Skylab space station. At the far end, just before the entrance to the food court,

455

stood a lunar module. Six of them had ferried astronauts to and from the moon. This one was a backup vehicle that, thanks to a lot of shortsightedness by politician at the time, never got the chance to fly. Frizzell stood off to one side, admiring the display. He knew Paul was a space freak, too, which was why he'd chosen this spot to meet.

He shook hands with his old friend.

"Congratulations, Senator," Paul said. "Good job snagging that appointment."

He decided to get right to the point. "Your lunch from a little while ago and my appointment are related to each other."

"I could see no love lost between you and the Speaker. But that's nothing new."

"No, it's not. But this is different. It involves Alex."

Paul and Alex Sherwood had been friends.

"I hate what happened," Paul said. "He was a good man and died far too early."

He led Paul into an adjacent gallery labeled MOVING BEYOND EARTH where more large-scale models and spacecraft replicas waited. Fewer people milled about in the dimly lit space, and they retreated to a far corner, near an exhibit of space suits.

"There's a lot about Alex's death that doesn't add up," he said. "He goes for a stroll and falls off a cliff? That man walked those mountains all his life. I can't go into details, but believe me there are real questions.

Enough that the governor of Tennessee sent me here to get answers."

He was being his old self, straight shooting, pulling no punches.

"What does this have to do with me?" his friend asked.

"Vance is involved. I know he's planning something big. What I don't know is what. But I'm bettin' you do."

He caught the immediate concern on Frizzell's face. "If I did, I couldn't tell you."

"That gathering back at the Willard. It had somethin' to do with what I'm talkin' about, didn't it?"

"Danny, you do realize the horrible position you're placing me in."

That he did. No one from the majority party made it to the coveted Rules Committee unless they possessed two things. Longevity and an unquestioned loyalty to the Speaker of the House. The former was simply a matter of record. But the latter had to be proved, day in and day out. For Paul Frizzell to even think about challenging that sacrosanct principle amounted to political treason.

"I get it, Paul," he said. "I'm asking a lot. But we've known each other a long time and you've yet to walk away from this talk. I see it in your eyes. There's somethin' goin' on."

Silence confirmed he was right.

And his old friend seemed to be struggling

with some painful but overwhelming conviction.

So he kept pressing.

"Let me tell you a story. A few years ago I went deer huntin' with the president of Bulgaria. We paired off in twos for the day. That night, one of the Bulgarian hunters came back alone, staggering under the weight of an eight-point buck. A really solid kill. He was asked about his partner and replied that the guy broke his foot and was a couple of miles back up the trail. The president asked why he left the hunter and carried back the deer. The guy didn't hesitate. He said no one would steal his partner. That's you, Paul. No one is gonna steal you. We can weather this."

"Okay, Danny," his friend whispered.

And he listened to what Lucius Vance was planning.

CHAPTER FIFTY-TWO

Diane sat in the great room and considered her options. Alex had just left on his afternoon walk, their confrontation finished. Her brother had definitely placed them all in a difficult place. Alex could end everything they'd worked for. How could Kenneth have possibly thought he could be an ally? He'd known Alex as long as she had, and should have known his brother-in-law's failings. Three years of work was about to be erased. There'd be no radical change in Congress, no lost gold found. But Alex would remain a senator. A respected gentleman of Tennessee. His political life would go on. He'd keep complaining about Washington, sympathize with others who voiced similar objections, then change nothing.

And that galled her.

She rose from the chair and headed out the glass doors. Down off the deck she pushed through the trees, finding the trail that led up into the foothills, its worn path bearing evidence of Alex's many trips. Only occasionally had she ever made the journey. She negotiated the incline, her mind finally certain and unhesitating, careful with her steps on the loose rock. Dense trees rose all around, forming a canopy that allowed only shards of sunlight to pierce the foliage. A bitter, spicy scent of leaves filled her nostrils, the woods alive with noisy birds. Spring was coming to the mountains, the air finally ridding itself of winter's chill. She liked this time of year, summer even more. Winter depressed her. A lot like her life, which seemed to be moving from cold to warm.

She rounded a corner and caught sight of Alex.

He saw her coming, gently rapping his pipe against the bark of a tree. "More, Diane? Did we not say enough back at the house?"

She wondered how a man competent in matters of state seemed so ill informed about how to deal with his wife. "A poll a few weeks ago showed that 75 percent of the American public is dissatisfied with how the country is being run. And I don't mean the people running it. The poll tested the institution of government itself. That's an overwhelming negative majority not happy with the way things are. What we plan will offer those dissatisfied people an alternative."

"What you plan is a revolution. One that will elevate one man, the Speaker of the House, to lord emperor of this country. That's something entirely different."

"Maybe it's time to see if another way might

work better?"

"Vance tried to be president and his own party rejected him. He never made it past the Iowa caucuses. His district has, maybe, 200,000 people in it. This country has over three hundred million people. It was never intended that one congressman, from one district, should hold the kind of power you want to give him."

"Senators do. They wield it every day. Jealous?"

He chuckled. "Hardly. I'm concerned. Yes, we have the filibuster and our precious procedural rules, which are misused all the time. But there's a check on that. Sixty senators can shut it down with a cloture vote. The leadership can also refuse to give the floor to that senator. There are ways to stop him or her. What you propose comes with almost no checks and balances. It is unrestrained and will cause more problems than it solves."

The pressures of the coming tasks had been mounting on her for some time. She'd already let go of the past. The future was all that mattered anymore. Part of that was a realization that their long marriage had battered itself to a bruising standstill. They did little more than share space, the once cursory use of the other's body fading to nothing. A lack of intimacy had led to a lack of respect. There was something to be said for lust. It had advantages. But it also made it easier to make poor choices.

Bleak thoughts chased one another through

her mind.

One in particular lingered like a stranger, at the edges of her thoughts, doubtful of its welcome, but nonetheless there.

They stood side by side on the rocky bluff.

Alex took a moment and primed his pipe with tobacco, then lit it. When it drew to his satisfaction, he waved the match to extinction, then tossed it over the side to the river fifty yards below.

"Warren Weston came to see me," he said through puffs.

That was news.

"He told me you've been abusing your position on the Smithsonian Libraries Advisory Board. You've had one of the employees researching in some restricted archives, violating policies. Is that true?"

She resented being questioned like a schoolgirl by the principal. "Every word."

"He wants you to resign."

"Too bad most of us never get what we want."

"He told me that if you don't resign, he'll act to remove you."

"And you agree with him?"

He shook his head with an odd mixture of pleasure and reluctance, then seemed to avoid any complicity or embarrassment by moving away from her, still sucking at the pipe. He smoked only in private and always outside, usually on the deck. Since she had no intention of vacating her seat on the advisory board, she asked what she really wanted to know. "Who is she, Alex?"

He turned to face her. "As long as we're being honest?" He paused. "She's a woman I met quite by chance, who turned out to be a wondrous thing."

"Do you love her?"

"I do."

"Do you plan to divorce me?"

"Not now. But when my time in Washington is over. Yes, our marriage should end."

Over the past two hours her cozy, ordered world had been upended by some ugly realities. First Kenneth's notebook and Alex's objections. Now another woman. The weight of those defeats settled onto her shoulders like a heavy cloak. Not to mention the personal rejection. Her thoughts and aspirations had been cast aside, as if his were somehow superior.

And that galled her.

That thought on the periphery took a step forward. She now hovered at the edge of a dark chasm, trying to decide whether to leap or stay.

A familiar place of late.

As when Kenneth had come and asked for her help. Or when two men offered themselves to her and she'd accepted both. Or when she'd maneuvered Alex to have her appointed to the advisory board. Each time she'd leaped.

But this time was different.

Everything was at stake.

And she would swallow her indignation at his

pretense no more. The solution here called for something far more radical than she was accustomed to delivering. Thankfully, on the walk up she'd wiped fear and doubt from her mind, ready to face him with a clear resolve. But first she wanted to know, "I assume I would have had no say in that divorce decision?"

"I imagine you will welcome the move. Especially considering your admission of sleeping with two men."

"Whom you have not asked about at all."

He puffed on the pipe. "Because I simply don't care anymore."

"I agree," she said. "Our marriage is over. So why not leave me in peace, and don't interfere with what we are doing."

"Because that's not possible. And you know it."

The hand holding the pipe stabbed the air for emphasis.

Every opportunity had been offered, so she eased closer to the edge and glanced down at the white-flecked rush of water, the river full from spring rains. Rocks peeked out along its course, smoothed and tamed by the constant flow. She thought of her father and all his lost opportunities. And of her life the past decade, empty and unfulfilled. She'd learned to make do, stay silent, and settle, to be the dutiful political wife. But for the past three years she'd worked her own agenda. She thought of failure and what that would mean, which allowed her to do the one thing she hadn't done in a long time.

Cry.

The last time was at her father's funeral.

So she added thoughts of his loss and began to sob, head down, a hand to her forehead.

Alex moved toward her, wrapping an arm and drawing her close. She allowed the gesture, sinking her head onto his shoulder.

"I'm sorry, Diane. I really am. I wish I could stay silent here. But I can't."

"I've messed everything up," she managed through her tears.

His free hand gave her shoulder a reassuring pat, trying to offer comfort, but the patronizing gesture only enraged her. She slowly pulled back and embraced the rash thought that had now moved front and center.

She lunged forward, slamming her shoulder into his chest, propelling his feet out from under him. His head snapped back and he staggered, trying to regain his balance. She stared into his eyes, the pupils darting like warning signals, the lips moving without words. He still held the pipe in one hand.

Surprise filled his face.

She'd shoved him over the cliff.

The body dropped for several seconds, not a sound coming from his mouth. Her eyes scanned all around. She saw and heard no one. The land for miles in every direction was owned by Alex. He hit the water hard, the current lift-

465

ing, then dumping him, dunk after dunk. The river seemed malevolent, like her, increasing in strength, dragging and lunging. Bones had to have broken in the fall and the water quickly claimed him, his body rushing away, helpless in the current, the roar constant with undiminished violence.

Her mind jolted back to the present, still sitting in Alex's apartment. She recalled walking back to the house that day, letting herself in through the garage, standing in the quiet for nearly an hour, hands trembling, swallowing the fear, wondering if anyone had seen her. She could still see Alex's arms flailing in the water, the mouth open, desperate for air. Her greatest fear had not been what she'd done, but rather that she would be caught. When the sheriff came hours later to inform her that the body had been found, she'd had to fight hard not to show relief. Nothing pointed to foul play and no one suspected her in any way.

No witnesses had come forth. To the world she was a woman who'd lost her husband in a tragic accident. The fact that he was a longtime member of the U.S. Senate had only added to the level of grief.

Which she'd milked at the funeral.

She took a few deep breaths and gathered herself, savoring again the great wave of relief that had swept over her the day Alex died.

That was all in the past. The future was now hers for the taking.

Her cell phone rang, its chime like an alarm.

The display indicated it was Lucius Vance. She answered.

"We need to talk, right now," he said to her. "In private."

She heard the urgency, which was troubling. "I'm in town, at Alex's apartment. This is as good a place as any."

"Tell me where. I'm on my way."

CHAPTER FIFTY-THREE

Grant waited until the visitor left. He'd heard it all. His father had offered some sort of code, which the guy from the Smithsonian, whom his father had been calling Captain Adams, had broken.

And fast, too.

The answer supposedly led to the Heart Stone.

The man had not stayed long after that, his father lapsing into more and more nonsense about the past. Finally the front screen door opened then banged closed. He waited in the kitchen until he heard a car engine rev, followed by his father's footsteps back to the den. He hadn't brought the uniform in with him and should probably go and get it. But what for? What he needed to know had just been told to a total stranger. He could simply beat the same information out of the old man.

He was beyond pissed. He'd had to put up with nonsense for two years, obtaining information in bits and pieces, never getting the whole story. Now to know that his father was lucid enough to craft a code, and pass on the location of the Heart Stone, only swelled the anger rising inside him. Further fueling him was the piece of new information he'd heard. Some sort of journal that seemed important.

He stormed from the kitchen and entered the den.

"Where'd you come from?" his father asked.

He wondered if his face had penetrated the fog. "Do you know who I am?"

"I do not, sir. Are you with the captain? He just left."

"No, old man. I'm your friggin' son. Could you for once remember?"

The eyes that stared back were blank and listless. His gazed searched the room, looking for the pad of paper that had been passed back and forth.

Which was nowhere to be seen.

"Where is the pad you were writing on?"

"That was between the captain and me. No strangers allowed."

Interesting how short-term memory seemed to be functioning today. So he tried, "Tell me about the code."

"Were you listening to us? Tell me, boy. Were you spying?"

"I'm not going to ask again. Where is the pad?"

No reply.

He grabbed his father by the shoulders, gripping each arm hard, and shook. "Do you want a fist in the gut? Is that what you want? Those bones of yours can take only so much. A trip to the hospital could be the end for you. Tell me what I want to know. Now."

His father's body went limp, the head tilted to one side, which made it hard to hold him up, so he released his grip and dumped the old man into a chair.

Then he saw the pad.

In a back pocket.

He slid it free, but there was no writing on any of the pages.

"Where is it?" he screamed. "Where is what you wrote?"

"The captain . . . took it . . . with him."

Dammit.

But if the old man remembered once, he could again. Especially with proper motivation. Which Grant intended on supplying.

He tossed the pad down to his father.

"Write what you wrote to him."

"You know how to solve the code?"

He nodded. "Yes. Yes. I know the code. Write it down."

He'd take whatever he could get. If he could not figure it out, Diane certainly could. At least they'd have the information.

"Did the captain teach you?"

He had to play along. "Of course. I work with him."

His father righted himself in the chair, found the pen, and wrote. When the pad was handed over, the top sheet seemed an unintelligible jumble.

FATAHW UOYLOO NOSERA

"This is nonsense," he roared. "Do you want me to beat the hell out of you? Is that what you want?"

His father shook his head, and he saw a familiar fear. Good. Finally. He might be getting through.

"Tell you what," the old man said. "I'll unlock it. Will that help?"

"Damn right. Do it."

His father did as instructed and he yanked the pad away, reading the single line of deciphered letters.

Whatafoolyouareson

"Break the line into words. Can you read it?"

He could.

WHAT A FOOL YOU ARE SON.

His father stood from the chair, holding a gun, aimed straight at him. "My little charade is over. You'll not lay a hand on me again."

The words came clear, concise, and with a

familiar harshness. In a firm voice he hadn't heard in years.

Then he realized. "You're as sane as the rest of us."

A smile came to the thin lips. "More so than you can say. Elder abuse seems not to bother you."

He was too shocked to speak. Finally, he managed, "Why would you pretend like that? And let me beat you?"

"Because I needed you to do things I could not do on my own. All war is deception, but I doubt you would appreciate such a truism. But savor what a French poet once said. *It is double pleasure to deceive the deceiver.*"

His father moved a few feet away, toward the front windows, and motioned with the gun that he should retreat a few steps, too.

"That gold has an amazing pull, doesn't it?" his father asked.

"Damn right."

The old man shook his head. "Without that Layne woman, or Sherwood as she calls herself now, you would have made no progress. Her father taught her well."

"You tricked her, too? When she came to see you?"

"Of course, but I also determined how much she knew. Then I watched as the two of you became acquainted. And when you kept coming back, wanting more information, I learned that you were together. So I

472

led you both where I wanted you to go."

Then he realized. "You want the stones. You can't get them on your own, so you had us do it for you."

"See, you're not always so stupid. Sadly for you, though, your usefulness is waning."

He began to acquire a more healthy respect for the gun aimed at him.

"Why does this matter?" he asked his father.

"I am a knight of the Golden Circle. I have been most of my adult life. I may, in fact, be the most important knight in the Order's history."

"Because you control the vault."

"There it is again. Those flashes of brilliance that peek through the idiocy you so easily display. What does that Layne woman see in you?"

"You know about our relationship?"

"I know a great deal, son. More than you may ever realize."

"You're also a sentinel?"

"I am *the* sentinel. Of the vault. I have protected it a long time. But I'm old, and there are tasks I must do before I die. The stones had to be acquired, and you offered the fastest route to accomplishing that goal."

His father pressed an empty hand to the front window.

"I could be a sentinel," he said.

"You have neither the brains nor the character for the job. You remind me of Davis

Layne. All he wanted was the gold for himself. Greed does not become a knight of the Golden Circle."

A thought suddenly occurred to him.

"Kenneth. Diane's brother. He's a knight?"

"Of course. He was sent to enlist his sister's help, as she had the knowledge."

"So why did you need me?"

The screen door opened and two men entered.

One of them pounced, wrapping an arm around his neck, the other pinning his hands behind his back. The second man jammed a fist into his right kidney.

Pain shot through him.

Bile rose in the back of his throat.

His father smiled. "These men are now going to provide what you so easily gave to me."

Another fist slammed his abdomen.

CHAPTER FIFTY-FOUR

Cassiopeia entered the mine, the same lights from before burning bright, the way ahead clear. She kept to one side of the tunnel, the gun tight in her right hand, finger on the trigger. She came to the gash in the side wall that led to the gold chamber. Back to there? Or keep going deeper into the main shaft?

She heard voices.

From beyond the gash.

So she headed toward the gold chamber.

The wooden door she'd shoved her way through before hung wide open. Shadows danced along the interior walls.

Voices continued.

"You're friggin' crazy," a man yelled.

She made her way to the doorway, careful with her own shadows. A quick peek inside revealed three men lying on the earthen floor, hands and feet bound with rope. The same three from the bee house at Morse's place. Proctor stood over them with a gun aimed downward. Where was the other man she'd seen loading, the one who hadn't left with the truck?

She stepped into the chamber.

Proctor saw her.

But before he could raise his weapon she fired a bullet at his feet.

"Let the gun drop," she said.

He smiled and did as ordered. "I've been waiting. I assumed Morse's granddaughter would find you after I took the old man, and that's exactly what she did. We left enough of a trail that anyone could follow."

"Where is Morse?"

"Gone. In the truck."

"I didn't see him."

"He was tied in the back, unconscious."

She did not like the sound of any of that. "What's the rule? No knight kills another. Except you?"

He turned his palms upward and shrugged. "I simply administer justice."

She motioned for Proctor to step toward the maw in the floor, the same one she and Lea had been imprisoned in. "Your turn to jump."

He stepped to the edge.

The three men still lay on the floor, one now close to where she stood. A quick glance down and she saw that the bindings on his wrists were not tied. The rope simply lay loosely across his skin. Before she could react to the new threat, his arms shot out and

476

clipped her legs out from under her.

She pounded to the ground.

Another of the three men from yesterday pounced and her gun was wrestled away.

"Excellent," Proctor said. "Good work." He reached down and relieved her of the gun. "These three offered to assist, and who am I to refuse such graciousness."

She felt like an idiot at being played.

"Get up," Proctor ordered.

She stood.

"We all had a little talk before you arrived," Proctor said. "It seems that a gentleman back in Washington, a man named Grant Breckinridge, hired them to impersonate knights of the Golden Circle. They were sent to find the Witch's Stone."

"Which you now have," she noted.

"That I do. I explained to these gentlemen that before and during the War Between the States, membership in the Order was deemed an honor. Men were carefully screened and vetted before being asked to join. The North was the enemy, and all who did not see it that way were regarded as the enemy, too. Even if those men be Southerners. I envy those times. Things were so much simpler."

"We did as you wanted," one of the three said. "Can we go now?"

Proctor held up his hand. "In a moment. First, indulge me."

The other man she'd seen earlier entered

the chamber and she caught a slight nod of his head toward Proctor.

A signal that something had been accomplished.

"The Order's induction ceremony back then was most impressive," Proctor said. "Men wore crimson robes with silver lace. They had turbans on their heads and sandals on their feet. Then there were the masks, painted to represent a human face. Not their own, of course, but another of their choosing. So perfect were the masks that, in the right light, they appeared real. Two oaths were required. Both taken solemnly before God. Once done, all of the knights would remove their masks, revealing their true selves, and clasp the new member with hugs and handshakes."

"Sounds like a big boys' club," she said.

"That it was, meant to build an army, and it did. Tens of thousands became knights. They went on and became soldiers, administrators, governors, legislators, infiltrating every aspect of the North and South. A network of eyes and ears that wreaked havoc. What an honor it must have been to be a part of all that."

Proctor fired three shots, one each into the skulls of the three other men. Their bodies collapsed to the ground.

"These imposters disgraced the memory of it all." He lowered the weapon. "I imagine death is no stranger to you."

"It seems to be your best friend."

"I do my job."

Proctor motioned and the remaining man scooped up some of the rope and bound her hands behind her back. He then shoved her to the floor and tied her ankles. The man then stepped back to the doorway and retrieved two rucksacks, which he laid down on the other side of the chamber. From inside each he removed some sort of electronic device with wires running from it.

"Those backpacks contain dynamite," Proctor said. "We've already left more in the tunnels. It's time for this place to disappear. With you inside. But, as I said when we first met, I am a gentleman, so I plan to give you a sporting chance."

He reached down, grabbed her bound ankles, and dragged her ten meters away from the floor chasm. He released his grip and she rolled over to see him step back to where the rotted wooden ladder jutted up from the opening's edge. He removed a knife from his pocket and flicked his wrist, exposing an impressive serrated blade, which snapped into place.

He crouched down and jammed the tip deep into the old wood.

"It might be helpful," he said. "Then again, maybe not."

He stood and headed for the doorway. The

other man pushed buttons on the top of each device and a LED display indicated three minutes.

"Goodbye, Ms. Vitt," Proctor said.

And they left.

CHAPTER FIFTY-FIVE

Diane opened the apartment door and invited Lucius Vance inside. The Speaker appeared flustered.

"We have an issue."

She closed the door and listened as he explained about Danny Daniels' visit to the Willard Hotel.

"You didn't know he'd been appointed to Alex's vacant seat?" Vance asked, reading her face.

She shook her head. "I haven't paid attention to the news today."

"No one called you?"

There'd been calls, but she'd ignored them. "I've been here, working on things in the quiet."

Vance knew zero about the gold hunt. Why should he? He knew only about Kenneth's initiative with the state legislatures and the call for a second constitutional convention. Amazingly, Kenneth had apparently kept the gold part of their endeavor close, not sharing it with either Alex or Vance, as neither of them had ever mentioned anything about lost treasure.

"He knew exactly what we said last night," Vance said. "Word for word."

Which was troubling.

"Your protective agent thought he heard something. Remember? You told him it was nothing. Apparently, you were wrong."

"I don't recall your being overly paranoid, either."

No, she had not been. "Which means if Daniels knows what we said, he also knows what we did."

The kiss.

And their talk of an affair.

"He's after us," Vance said. "My guess is he secured that Senate appointment to give himself a beachhead."

And Kenneth's missing notebook now made sense. It had to have been Daniels who took it. He had opportunity, and now she knew he had a motive. But she kept that conclusion to herself. "What are you going to do?"

"Not a damn thing. We're going ahead, as planned. I just met with my people on the Rules Committee. They're ready to adopt the change first thing tomorrow. They understand the risks and are ready to take them. There'll be a twenty-four-hour delay from the time they take their committee vote until the measure goes to the House floor for a full vote. I can't get around that. And even if I could, it wouldn't be smart. It would seem too much like a ramrod. So there's going to be some attention. But the House is sick and tired of the Senate's shenanigans. Everyone I talk with is ready to change things up."

"What about the White House?" she asked.

"Fox? That moron? Before he realizes what's happened, he'll be impotent. After that, he won't matter."

Vance seemed both sure and confident.

"Daniels was asking about Alex's death," Vance said. "He even threatened me on it, thinking I might have been involved. Is there anything to worry about there?"

"He asked me the same questions."

A curious look came to his face. "You never mentioned you and he spoke."

"After the funeral. He came to the house. I invited him."

"For what?"

"He and Alex were close friends. And he *was* the president of the United States. What did you want me to do? Brush him off? That would have been stupid. He and I do not get along, I never thought he would actually come. But he did."

And while there, he'd stolen Kenneth's notebook, which probably explained the visit.

"As I told him then, Alex died from a tragic fall. There is absolutely nothing to suggest

483

anything otherwise."

"That's the official conclusion?"

She nodded. "The sheriff told me so himself. And the FBI took a look, too, since a congressman was involved."

She forced her eyes to tear, knowing that would add to the veracity of what she was saying.

It worked.

"I didn't mean to upset you. It's just that this has escalated. We never figured Daniels to be in the picture. He should be long gone. But he could cause problems."

"With the Senate? Who cares? There's nothing they can do."

"With the people. He's popular and trusted. And he knows how to work a crowd. That's a deadly combination."

Her analytical mind clicked through the options. "But he's out of time. This will be done before Daniels can even figure it out and muster any support. And let's face it, I doubt the public is going to rise up and defend the U.S. Senate. Nobody is going to care. The sentiment will be, *Anything is better than what we have.*"

Which was exactly what they'd been hoping for all along. Polls, pundits, and the people all liked to complain about government. Candidates loved to get elected on being an "outsider," not part of the Washington establishment. Then, within ninety days of taking office, they all melded into the system, recognizing a fundamental truth. To be effective, you had to get along. That's why things never changed. It's why men like her dead husband would scream for a new agenda but never actually enact one. Far better to work within the system that already existed, as there were ways to manipulate, control, and even bypass it, if one were smart and careful. It took time to become really effective. The longer someone was around, the more favors they accumulated. Eventually, those favors paid dividends. Every single person elected to Congress quickly learned those truths. The ones who stayed around the longest were the people who never forgot them.

One fundamental truth never changed. Everyone wanted to be remembered. Presidents particularly. The first term was for work. The second for history. For congressmen the rules were different. Legacies took decades to mold. And Lucius Vance was about to fashion his by proffering more real change than anyone since the time of the Founding Fathers.

"You're going to win this fight," she said to him.

He seemed to steel himself. "Yes, I am. But I want to know something."

She waited.

"Before I take this plunge, I have to know, right here, right now. Is there anything I'm going to regret not knowing?"

She knew what he meant, but feigned hurt. "My husband is dead. Why can't all of you just let him rest in peace. He died from a tragic accident."

"Is there any possibility he killed himself?"

Now that was a thought. One she hadn't really considered.

"Since none of us were there, we have no way of knowing. All I can say is that I saw nothing in the days before that would lead me to think he did. But that may not mean a thing. Alex was quite adept at hiding his feelings."

As she now knew.

"I just want every base covered. Danny Daniels is an accomplished political warrior, and he'll be a formidable opponent."

"You sound afraid."

"Not in the least. But you have to know your enemy. He had a lot of inside information on you and me. We have to wonder what else he knows."

A thought suddenly occurred to her.

The cross-and-circle necklace.

Daniels had said Alex dropped it while visiting his house. Surely that was a lie. It must have been Kenneth who gave it to Alex, and it ended up with Daniels. Which could mean Alex had confided in his old friend.

That would explain all the questions and the stealing of the notebook.

Vance was right.

What else *did* Daniels know?

CHAPTER FIFTY-SIX

5:20 P.M.

Danny found Teddy Solomon on the first floor of the Russell Office Building in the Senate gym. He remembered the place fondly as a safe haven, an oasis, where senators could trickle in at all hours and work out, undisturbed, being themselves without fear. Strange how being in politics meant not being yourself. Most tried to be what others wanted, pandering for money and support. He'd never fallen into that trick bag, always staying true to himself, which had, on occasion, caused problems. He'd also never been much for physical exercise, but he liked the gym's loose atmosphere. A lot of deals had been made among the sweat and machines. A separate locker room and smaller workout space accommodated female senators, but many of them used the men's side more often than not, which no one seemed to mind. A keypad controlled access. He didn't know the code but the Secret Service man stationed outside offered him a quick entry.

Solomon jogged on one of the treadmills, swinging his arms, inhaling and exhaling in short, strenuous gasps. "I'm betting . . . you never once . . . used this place."

"Not for a workout. But I did use it. The question is, what are you doing here?"

The vice president slowed and shrugged. "I came here for a long time as a senator, so I saw no reason to stop now that I've been demoted."

He grinned.

No one else was around to hear the comment.

"We need to talk," he said.

Solomon stopped his workout and powered down the machine. "Hold on."

His old friend grabbed a towel, then walked to the door, breathing hard, telling the agent outside to make sure they were not disturbed.

"At least there's one perk to being VP. You can get the gym to yourself."

"I know what Vance is planning."

Solomon patted sweat from his face and hair.

"He's going to use Article I, Section 5, Clause 2 of the Constitution and change the procedural rules in the House of Representatives."

"That happens all the time. So what?"

"Not like this."

Earlier, as he'd listened to Paul Frizzell

489

explain what was happening, he'd thought back to Kenneth Layne's notebook. Finally its bullet points began to make perfect sense.

"We all know that the Constitution allows the Senate and the House to set their own internal rules," he said. "They can pretty much do whatever they want, and the courts have little to no say in the matter. Separation of powers, and all that crap, gives Congress free rein over its own procedural rules. Vance plans to use that freedom to the max. It's actually quite simple in execution, but massive in effect."

He saw that he had his old friend's undivided attention.

"He's adding a new rule that states that the House of Representatives will consider, and vote, only on legislation that originates in the House."

He waited for the words to sink in.

"Damn," Solomon muttered.

It had not taken long for the dots to connect.

"And it's totally constitutional," he said. "It's how the country was governed for the first twenty years. There wasn't a rule that said it, but the Senate was nothing back then. All legislation came from the House. The Senate would look at it, offer an amendment, maybe, then vote yes or no and send it back to the House. Simple and sweet. There was none of the shenanigans that we have today.

No filibusters. No senator gave a thought to offering his own version of the legislation. No one rewrote anything. The Senate was merely advisory to the House. That's it. So Vance is going to bring that concept into the modern world."

"And make himself king."

Precisely.

Teddy Solomon had grasped the true significance in such a simple change. By not considering any legislation except that which originated in the House, there would no longer be any worries about the U.S. Senate. A bill would start in the House, be approved, then be sent to the Senate for it "to propose or concur with Amendments," as the Constitution defined the Senate's advisory role. True, both houses of Congress would have to agree before anything could be passed and sent to the president for signature. But the House of Representatives would become the dominant legislative body. If a senator wanted to propose anything new he or she would have to convince a House member to introduce that measure in the House. And no longer could one senator shut down the entire legislative process. Instead 435 House members, elected by the people every two years, would call the shots.

All led by the Speaker.

Of course the Senate did not have to agree with any legislation sent to it by the House.

The Senate's only function would be to vote yea or nay on the entire bill. One hundred senators casting their votes, on the record, fifty-one needed to secure a majority to either approve or disapprove.

In the modern world floor votes rarely happened, as Senators were able to hide behind cleverly crafted rules that rarely forced anyone to take the blame for anything. Bills were routinely torpedoed with no fingerprints on the bomb at all. Under Vance's change, the entire Senate would now have to vote on each measure as forwarded by the House. True, it could offer amendments. But again, the entire body would have to vote on those, then the House would be given the chance to agree or disagree. No cherry-picking. No rewriting. No stalling. Just yea or nay. Even more difficult, if something was delayed because the Senate chose not to vote at all, then the entire Senate would be the one to take that blame.

Talk about a game changer.

Everything would be different.

"Senators are like bomber pilots," Solomon said, speaking from years of experience. "We're in the war. But we kill people anonymously from thirty thousand feet. It's fairly easy to do, and even easier to rationalize. Now senators would have to join the infantry and the fighting would be hand-to-hand, face-to-face, with casualties. They haven't been in that vulnerable position for a long time."

"The scary part," Danny said, "is that the public will support this. Everyone hates gridlock, and the Senate is, without question, the number one cause of it. Which is its job, by the way. It's the whole reason the Senate even exists."

The Founding Fathers had been familiar with the House of Lords and the House of Commons. One elected by the people, the other a hereditary right. No one at the first constitutional convention had wanted the people to have uncontrolled reign over government. The danger of rash thinking and impulse decisions frightened everyone. So they conceived a legislative body not directly responsible to the people. The Senate. Its members chosen by state lawmakers. The Senate's sole job was to make sure the more representative body, the House, did not do anything foolish, exactly as the House of Lords had done for centuries to the House of Commons. Originally, the Founders had wanted no salary paid to a senator — only men of wealth could serve — but that idea failed. Finally they settled on a minimum age of thirty, five more years than the House, a six-year term, with elections staggered so no more than one-third went up for election in each year. It was not a perfect system, but a workable one of checks and balances that had served reasonably well.

Sure, there were problems from time to time. But the alternatives were worse.

"This will affect everything," Danny said. "At a minimum it'll make every member of the Senate skittish. They'll go gun-shy, since the only way to get anything done will be to have a House member in your corner. They're not going to want to offend anyone over there. All the horse trading will simply shift from one side of the Capitol to the other."

"With the Speaker the gatekeeper for it all," Solomon noted.

"Which the White House won't be able to ignore. The president would have to cultivate a close relationship with not only the Speaker, but every ranking House member. A bicameral legislature would effectively become unicameral."

"And Vance will essentially become the federal government," Solomon said. "Everything will flow through him. Right now, nothing comes to a vote without the Speaker's okay. But with this change, that power is magnified a thousand times since the House will be the only place any legislation can start. The really crazy part is that it will be approved, since every House member, on both sides of the aisle, will acquire a crap load more influence. You strip the Senate and elevate yourself at the same time, all with the people saying, *Damn right, do it.* It's a no-brainer. The public will never grasp the significance of what's really happening until it's far too late."

"I'm told the Rules Committee will vote on this tomorrow morning. It will go to the House for a floor vote the next morning."

Solomon chuckled. "Amazing what can be done quickly when you want it done."

They stood in silence for a few moments. Combined, they possessed nearly a century of political experience. Danny had always grinned when candidates ran on being a "Washington outsider." To him it was like going to a brain surgeon and the office receptionist saying she was a "medical outsider" and could actually do a cheaper and better job of operating on you. The cheap part was definitely possible. But better? Hardly. To get things done you had to know the lay of the land. And the only way to acquire that knowledge was from experience. Sure, people can learn. But just like the receptionist performing brain surgery, there were going to be a lot of bad mistakes made along the way until the know-how was found.

Thank goodness he and Solomon were doctors.

"There is a way to stop this," he said. "In fact, it might actually be the only way."

He could see Solomon was interested.

So he said, "It'll take someone with the

Chapter Fifty-Seven

Cassiopeia rolled her body across the rocky floor toward the knife Proctor had left. The timer continued to silently count down, the red illuminated numbers indicating two minutes and twenty-three seconds left. She had to avoid one of the corpses that had been left behind, which slowed her progress.

As she rolled, her mind assessed the options. No way to remove the knife and cut her bindings. Her hands were behind her back, which affected coordination. Freeing her feet seemed the priority since that would allow her to run. But if Proctor had been telling the truth, the tunnels beyond were likewise rigged to explode, and she had no reason to doubt him. Sealing off the entire mine was the smart play. Nothing that happened here would ever be known.

But she wasn't dead yet.

"Sporting chance"?

More than that.

She stopped rolling and positioned herself

feetfirst in front of the knife, which projected from the ladder about a quarter meter off the floor. The sharp edge faced up and she centered it between her ankles, moving her legs back and forth, slicing through the rope. She had to apply pressure, but was careful not to press too hard and dislodge the blade.

She kept sawing, her gaze darting across the chamber to the timers.

1:50.

The rope split.

No time to cut the bindings on her wrists.

She had to go.

1:35.

She rolled and pivoted upward, fighting for balance, her bound hands making it difficult to stand and eating precious seconds. Finally she was up and ran toward the open door.

A final look.

1:27.

She'd been in tight spots but now this one would leap to the head of the list. Down the tunnel she spotted another rucksack and timer, this one a few seconds behind the two back in the chamber. She kept going, finding the gash in the tunnel wall that led to the way out.

She plunged forward and emerged in the main shaft.

Another set of explosives was right there, 0:59 showing on the timer.

She turned and started to run but her boot

caught on loose gravel and she fell forward, managing to twist her body and land on her shoulder.

Which hurt.

She shook off the pain and waddled up on her feet, beginning to realize just how important arms and hands were to balance. The exit loomed twenty meters ahead, but she could see another batch of explosives just inside, 0:32 on the timer. A deep breath calmed her nerves and she told her legs to keep moving, lowering her head and hunching forward to ensure her footing stayed sure. She could not afford any more stumbles. She could see light beyond the archway that had been dug through the rubble at the mine's entrance. If she could get beyond that point she might be able to survive the explosions. But four bundles of dynamite were going to pack a punch.

She kept running, not able to achieve full speed, but enough that she found the archway.

The last timer read 0:22.

The two back in the gold chamber were slightly ahead so the fireworks would start there and work its way out to here.

She emerged from the mine.

Her gaze raked the scene before her and she decided on a pile of rubble to her right, which she leaped behind.

A deep rumble signaled the gold chamber

was no more.

Then more explosions followed.

Finally the dynamite near the exit joined the medley, sending dust and rock and noise spewing outward.

She lay with her face to the ground.

A thick cloud of dust swept through the dilapidated building and out into the late afternoon. She coughed away the remnants in her lungs and spit out what had settled in her mouth. She stood with her hands still bound and calmed herself.

That had been close.

The mine entrance was gone, now once again packed tight with soil and rock.

The dust cloud thinned.

Someone started clapping. A slow, steady, almost mocking gesture. She walked out toward daylight and found the source.

Proctor.

Bastard.

"Well done," he said. "I gave you only about a 20 percent chance of making it in three minutes."

She shook her head to clear her face and hair of dust. "And what would have happened if I hadn't?"

He shrugged. "Problem over. But you did make it out. So now you and I are taking a trip."

She had little choice. "Can I ask to where?"

"You can, but I won't answer."

"And what if I refuse?"

"As you know, I have Terry Morse. If I don't arrive soon after that truck arrives, my associate will kill the old man."

She had no reason to doubt the statement. This man seemed to enjoy killing. So she simply asked, "Do I get my hands free?"

"If you're a good girl."

Which she intended to be since she needed them unbound. Once that happened, she'd deal with James Proctor.

And the truck?

Thank goodness it could be tracked.

CHAPTER FIFTY-EIGHT

Cotton returned to the Smithsonian, finding Rick Stamm in his office beneath the Castle. The entire encounter with Frank Breckinridge had been troubling. How much of that old man's mind was really gone? Hard to say. The man clearly lived in the past, yet retained a solid hold on history, which might explain the ability to so easily code the message he'd passed on.

BENEATH ELEVEN MISTAKES.

He told Stamm everything.

The curator shook his head. "Amazing. I know exactly where we have to look."

Grant roused himself.

He hadn't passed out from the beating, but it had been close. The two men had taken a play from his book and expertly administered the punishment with just enough force to make the point, but not enough to damage anything. Luckily he was in good shape, and his tight abs had absorbed most of the blows. He lay in his father's den on the floor, the old man talking on the front porch to his two thugs. He'd caught bits and pieces, but not enough to know what was going on. At least he now knew how his father had lived alone. There was nothing wrong with him. The whole thing had been a ploy, one used quite effectively he had to admit. And he'd done exactly what his father had wanted, without ever realizing he was being manipulated.

The screen door opened and closed.

His father stepped into the den and sat in a chair. "How'd that feel?"

"I get it, old man. I gave it to you. And you gave it back to me."

His father laughed. "I do like your bravado. You never were afraid of much. You had so much potential, but you never showed a shred of the discipline needed to channel it. Then, all at once, you focused on gold. Greed really is a powerful motivator, isn't it?"

He winced against the nausea building from the beating. "I wanted that treasure."

"But it's not yours."

He rubbed his sore stomach. "So who gets it?"

"That remains to be seen. Right now, I require your help."

Cotton settled into a chair and faced Stamm, who sat behind a cluttered desk.

"*Beneath eleven mistakes.* Breckinridge is talking about James Smithson, the man who left the initial gift of $500,000 that started the Smithsonian."

"How do you know that?"

"I can show you upstairs. How much do you know about Smithson?"

"Little to nothing."

"We try hard to make Smithson appear more than he was. Unfortunately, he wasn't Indiana Jones. He was just an ordinary, nondescript 19th-century scientist. He studied things like coffee making, human tears, and snake venom, and managed to discover a mineral that was eventually named for him after his death. Smithsonite. But it's a relatively useless ore. Nothing Smithson did was revolutionary or particularly enlightening. But he lived at the time when chemistry was emerging as its own science, drifting away from alchemy, becoming a respected discipline. In a small way he helped forge that distinction."

"And he's buried upstairs."

Stamm nodded. "In the crypt, just inside the north entrance. He's been there since 1905, just after his remains were brought over from Italy. He was originally buried in Genoa, but Alexander Graham Bell, one of our regents at the time, convinced everyone to bring the bones here. Bell traveled to Italy in 1903 and personally supervised their return."

Stamm told him how Smithson's coffin then went on public display inside the Regents' Room upstairs for over a year, while a crypt adjacent to the north entrance was prepared. It was originally intended as a temporary resting place until funds could be found for a more elaborate memorial. But those moneys never materialized. In 1973 it was decided to renovate the crypt to make it more welcome to visitors.

"That's when Breckinridge took it upon himself to open the grave," Stamm said. "The secretary at the time was out of the country, in India, which was surely no accident on Breckinridge's part. He chose the moment carefully. Afterward, there was a lot of debate about what he did."

"He had no authority to open the grave?"

"That's hard to say. He was Castle curator, and they were renovating the crypt. So he could do whatever was necessary to get that job done, but he did not have the regents', or the secretary's, specific okay to open the tomb. A lot of people were present, though, when it happened. The undersecretary, several assistant secretaries, curators, archivists. Then some staff member called the *Washington Star-News* and reported what was happening. They also turned us in to the DC authorities. It seems you need a permit to open a grave within the district, which Breckinridge did not have. To diffuse all that atten-

505

tion, a reporter was invited over and shown the bones. He eventually ran a sympathetic story that nobody cared about."

"So what was inside?"

Grant listened as his father explained, "They're going to reopen James Smithson's tomb."

He knew his father had done the same thing, years ago. "How can you be so sure?"

"Because the man who came here earlier is the same one investigating all of this for the Smithsonian. I pointed the way, provided he's smart enough to figure it out. I'm betting he is. They won't be able to resist taking a look. And they'll do it tonight."

"How did you know about him?"

"It's my job to know everything. I've been watching all of this closely for a long time. I have many eyes and ears."

"I don't get it. Why would you point the way?"

"You were able to find the Witch's and Trail Stones. I led you to both. But the Heart Stone is something different. I left it inside Smithson's tomb in 1974, after I opened it for a supposed historical inspection. I took that chance because I knew that tomb was the perfect hiding place. Davis Layne wanted the five stones to get to the gold. He wouldn't stop. I tried conventional methods, even a threat or two, but they all failed. So I hid away the one piece of the puzzle he could not do without."

He could hardly believe what he was hearing.

"You should know that I now have the Witch's Stone," his father said.

"How? My men took photos of it in Arkansas, but were not able to get it."

"And they failed. So I sent *my* men, who are far more competent. They now have the stone. Your men are dead."

He was shocked.

"I was forced to eliminate them, thanks to you," his father said.

Who cared? They were not his problem.

He had bigger ones.

"What did you manage to obtain on the Trail Stone?" his father asked.

"Only photos. I was interrupted."

"I heard about what happened in Fossil Hall. You're lucky not to have been arrested."

"The guy who was here. He's the one who tried to stop me. I recognized his voice."

"Then it's fortunate he did not know you were here. You do understand that you've made this a thousand times more difficult. I never dreamed you would kill a man, then shoot a federal agent."

"But it's okay for you to kill three men."

"Those deaths will never be discovered. But that federal agent you shot is still clinging to life in a hospital. You're lucky that they are keeping this close, for the moment."

"I got what you wanted, didn't I?"

"Oh, yes, that you did. But you've drawn a lot of unnecessary attention. Far more than we ever anticipated."

"Who's *we*?"

"That's not necessary for you to know. What's important is that I'm going to give you one more chance to redeem yourself."

"And do what?"

"Get the Heart Stone."

Cotton read from the two pages Stamm had printed off the computer.

A report from the Smithsonian archives.

Subject: Exhumation and
   Reinterment of the Remains
   of James Smithson
From: Frank Breckinridge,
   Curator of the Smithsonian
   Institution Building
Date: 5 October 1973

The coffin containing the remains of James Smithson, located in the crypt, Smithsonian Institution Building, was exhumed on Wednesday, 3 October 1973, and reinterred on Friday, 5 October 1973. This report is made for the record and will be placed in the archives. I cannot foresee any reason for any future exhumation of the Smithson remains since a careful and complete study was made at this time of the location and condition of the coffin and of the skeleton itself.

In mid-September 1973 I asked the Building Management Division to explore the floor area of the crypt to locate the coffin. Records relating to the installation of the tomb and coffin from 1904 gave conflicting reports. On 1 October 1973, we opened the lid of the sarcophagus-shaped vessel atop the tomb but found the interior chamber empty. On 2 October 1973, I had a hole drilled into the north side of the tomb base. That afternoon we were able to determine that the coffin was inside the base. The four marble sides of the base were permanently secured by iron pins, so I had the north side of the base broken with drills. An identical piece of the same Italian marble has been ordered to replace this section.

Upon removing the coffin lid, a copper box was found fitted inside a wooden coffin, sealed by means of solder. It was decided to open the copper box by using blowtorches to melt the seals. Workmen melted the solder, and the lid for the copper box was removed to reveal Smithson's skull at one end and the remaining bones scattered throughout the box, mixed with dirt and pieces of wood from the original 1829 coffin. The blowtorches melted the solder but, in so doing, set the silk lining on fire. The foreman sent the laborers into the hall to fill their mouths with water from a fountain so as to extinguish the small fire that developed, without disturbing the skeleton. A nearby fire extinguisher was not needed. The lid to the copper box was replaced, then covered with a tablecloth and carried across the Mall to a laboratory in the natural history museum. No manuscripts of any kind were found within the copper box.

The bones were measured, photographed, x-rayed, catalogued, cleaned, then placed in separate plastic bags. At 1:00 P.M. on Friday, 5 October 1973, a group of witnesses assembled in the machine shop of the natural history museum. Typed reports were placed inside the coffin before it was sealed stating why it was opened, when, and condition of the remains at the time. The lid for the copper box was sealed by soldering, then it was transported across the Mall by car. At 1:45 P.M., 5 October, the box was replaced within the ornately carved mahogany coffin with six sterling-silver handles and a silver plaque bearing Smithson's name. Then it was placed back in the base of the tomb with an iron plate until the marble arrived from Italy.

"That replacement panel did not arrive until February 1974," Stamm said. "So Breckenridge had four months to remove the iron plate and hide anything he wanted inside the base. He was curator, with free access anytime, day or night."

Cotton recalled what Weston told him about the feud. "Davis Layne wanted the gold. I'm assuming without the Heart Stone it's impossible to find. So Breckinridge concocted a reason to open Smithson's grave, then stashed the Heart Stone inside, where no one could ever look. He even says that right here in this report. *I cannot foresee any reason for any future exhumation of the Smithson remains.*"

"But he was wrong," Stamm said. "We're going to open it again, tonight, after closing time. I'm the curator, too, with unfettered access. But one thing bothers me. After all these years, why did Breckinridge point the way?"

"Because that old man wanted us to know."

And he'd been thinking about a plan of action.

But he'd need help.

So he called Magellan Billet headquarters.

CHAPTER FIFTY-NINE

Grant rode in the rear seat of his own car. His father and one of the men who'd pummeled him sat in the front. They were driving across DC. His gut still hurt, but he'd survive. His cell phone had been taken, along with his gun. He felt like a child being disciplined, helpless to do much of anything. Where before he'd enjoyed being empowered, now once again he was nothing. He'd misjudged his father. Even worse, he'd been used. He wondered if any of what he'd accomplished was real, or just all part of a plan that he would have ultimately played no part in.

"There are some things you need to know," his father said from the front passenger seat. "And this time I will provide them without your usual means of persuasion."

"You ever going to give it a rest? Your apes made your point."

His father chuckled. "You'll have to forgive me. I'm old and so little amuses me anymore.

You're about all I have left."

"I haven't missed the insults, either."

His father turned around and faced him. "How about I just put a bullet in your head and be done with it?"

Not a hint of amusement laced the threat.

"Get to the point. What do you want to tell me?"

Angus Adams was glad to see Joseph Henry. The last time they were together had been the day of the fire. January 24, 1865. Twelve years had passed. A lot had changed. They sat inside Henry's first-floor office. The Castle had been restored, the building once again a vibrant, working museum, the inside different from before.

Thank God the war was over. Those years had been difficult on everyone. Especially spies. Afterward, many went into hiding or took new names, new identities, trying to escape a career of lies. Feelings of ineptness, powerlessness, and depression were common. Suicides rose. Not surprising. Once spies lost their nerve, death was not far away. A few had been hunted by Federal troops, then killed. And not after being charged or tried, just shot and left to rot. The more successful the spy, the more determined the hunt. He'd been one of the best, and the Federals had sought him. But he'd escaped to a place where no one would have ever looked.

"I was thrilled when I received the telegram saying you were coming for a visit," Henry said. "I've always wondered what happened to you."

He chuckled. "I barely made it out of the city the day of the fire. Apparently my mission had been compromised."

Henry told him more of what happened that day.

"The Federals were looking for the Confederate government records. They knew they'd been evacuated from Richmond and were told that they were to be given to the Smithsonian. That captain you saved came to see me a few days later and wanted to know why I had that key and your journal on my desk. I told him that you had come and wanted to make a donation to the institution, but the fire interrupted our conversation, so I never learned the details and no donation was made. I told him you left the key and journal on my desk when we realized the building was burning. He then told me about your violent encounter in my office and I told him that I saw you carry him to safety. You may well have saved his life. In gratitude, he let the matter drop for all concerned."

"Generous of him, considering he had no key and no journal."

Henry grinned. "Thanks to your quick thinking."

"Thank heaven for Marianna McLoughlin being right there to spirit me away. Whatever happened to her?"

"She still lives here, in the same house. I can arrange a visit, if you'd like."

He shook his head. "I think it better to keep my appearances to a minimum."

"What did become of you, Angus?"

"I moved west, where I've lived since the war. In the New Mexico Territory."

"That's part of what you explored in 1854."

He nodded. "I was so taken by it all I decided that was where I should live. I have a ranch in the Sangre de Cristo Mountains, near the Rio Grande. A long, low adobe house that melds into the landscape. Many rooms, surrounded by a shady veranda. I wish you could see it."

And he told his old friend about the refuge. The chores of feeding the cattle, shutting up the pigs, and seeing to it the chickens remained out of the coyotes' reach. The evenings on the veranda, where a couple of hours of coolness refreshed from the summer heat. And the nights. So dark. The only spark an occasional match to light a cigar, the only discomfort the mosquitoes.

"They're the worst pests," he told Henry. "You either get used to their sting or get good at slappin 'em. The only thing that really keeps 'em away is a wheelbarrow full of manure, lighted, then placed windward so the breeze carries the stinky smoke your way."

"Sounds lovely."

He caught the sarcasm. "It actually is, Joseph. It's a paradise. They have these beans, refried

516

in hot fat. *Frijoles refritos.* Refried beans. You just mop 'em up with bread. My kids love 'em."

"I'm glad things worked out for you. Are you still painting?"

His former boss looked tired, the years catching up. He had to be near eighty, but he was still in charge of America's greatest scientific institution.

"From time to time I have been known to favor a canvas. It still brings some pleasure."

"You were one of our best illustrators. I loved your drawings."

He appreciated the compliment. "I'm glad the war did not cost you."

"Those were tough years. We had so little money. We barely kept the doors open. But we've rebounded and now we're flourishing."

That was good to hear.

"The fire turned out to be a blessing," Henry said.

An odd statement. "What was the cause?"

"Stupidity. Workers in the picture gallery were cold, so they brought in a stove and inserted the exhaust pipe into what they thought was a flue. Instead, it was just an air space in the outer brick lining. For a week hot embers collected under the roof, until they exploded."

"I always thought it was the Yankees' doing. Just too damn coincidental that it happened that day."

"Sometimes fate is on your side. It was for

us. There were questions, but it all ended quickly."

"Were many paintings lost?"

"Most of Charles King's and John Stanley's work was destroyed. All of their Indian portraits are gone. Cherokee statesmen. Potawatomi warriors. Osage chieftains. Probably the most valuable collection in the country. A tremendous loss."

He remembered them all, having spent many hours in the picture gallery.

"We also lost all of Smithson's personal effects," Henry said. "His personal trunks, an umbrella, walking cane, sword, and a small traveling chemical laboratory. Thankfully, his library was stored elsewhere and survived."

Which brought him to the purpose of his visit. He reached for a leather satchel that he'd brought with him on the train and removed two objects. "I thought it was time to finally redeliver this."

He handed over the skeleton key.

The same one from the day of the fire.

Henry accepted the offer. "Good thing I did not have it after the fire. We would have never been able to go near those records back then. Do the archives still exist?"

He nodded. "They do. But they've been moved. And I'm afraid they must stay hidden, at least for a while longer. Know that they're safe and, eventually, I want the Smithsonian to have them, just as Jeff Davis wanted."

"What's *'a while longer'*?"

"Seventy-five years."

Henry seemed surprised. "Will they last that long?"

"I think so. I made sure."

"Are the knights still out there?"

"They are. But things are changing."

Henry examined the key. "So what do I do with this?"

"Hold on to it."

He removed one other object from the satchel. A beautiful, leather-bound journal adorned with shiny gold edges, and handed it over.

Henry immediately seemed to know what it was. "Your field journal."

He nodded. "It's a little different from the original. I created a new copy free of the trail dust and grime. I thought I'd leave it here on loan for a little while. My observations of the first Smithsonian expedition to the Southwest, dated 1854."

Henry thumbed through the handwritten pages. "It's lovely. I see the artist in you has not waned."

He smiled. "I'm just an imperfect man who was fortunate to witness some important history. That journal should make a great addition to the collections. I thought seventy-five years would be more than enough time for a loan."

He saw Henry caught the connection to the key.

"After that, have it returned to my family in

Georgia."

"For you, old friend, anything. I'm sure our geologists, naturalists, and geographers will appreciate studying your observations. They were the first ever made of the region. Tell me, have things changed much out there?"

"Not in the least. It's another reason I so love living there."

"How do you know any of that?" Grant asked his father.

"Those of us in positions of leadership within the Order know exactly what Angus Adams did that day in 1877. He documented the completion of his original mission, with one change. Instead of retrieving his field journal, he returned it to the Smithsonian."

"And the key?"

"It's still important, which is why you have to retrieve it."

He'd left it with Diane at Alex Sherwood's apartment.

"You do realize, son, that we don't need the Sherwood woman. We can find the gold without her. But we need the key."

"I thought my usefulness was over."

"You can redeem yourself."

He knew what to say. "I can get the key."

His father smiled. "I thought you might be able to. Tell us where and we'll go there now. We have time."

■ ■ ■ ■

Grant climbed the stairs to the Sherwood apartment, the building quiet in the late afternoon, most of its tenants not home from work. He was trying to think of what to say to Diane in order to obtain the key. He could just take it, but he decided not to burn that bridge completely.

Not yet, anyway.

He found the apartment door and lightly knocked.

No answer.

He tried again, this time sharper.

Still no answer.

He tested the knob.

Locked.

Where the hell was she?

He could call her on the phone, but that would only raise questions. He stood frozen and listened, hearing nothing. Hopefully, none of the neighbors on this floor were home. He raised his right leg and slammed the heel of his shoe into the door.

It gave, but did not yield.

Another kick and the bolt broke free from the jamb, the door buckling inward.

He entered and saw the skeleton key lying on the desk.

The apartment was empty.

Diane must have gone out.

Perfect.

He grabbed what he'd come for and left.

Danny's cell phone vibrated in his pocket.

He was still inside the gym with the vice president, discussing what to do, formulating a plan.

He checked the display.

UNKNOWN.

But he answered anyway.

"Mr. President, it's Taisley Forsberg. That man who took the notebook, he just smashed in the door to Alex's apartment."

CHAPTER SIXTY

Cotton checked his watch: 7:00 P.M.

The Castle had closed ninety minutes ago, but a few employees still lingered inside. The administrative offices on the upper floors were empty. Here, on the ground floor, in the main hall, the snack bar was being cleaned and the gift shop wound down for the day. Stamm had told him that in another hour the building should be empty.

He made his way toward the north exit doors and into a vestibule that led to Smithson's crypt. He'd read a little downstairs, from Stamm's book on the Castle, about the tomb's symbolism. A massive urn sat atop four carved lions' feet, the vessel capped with a pinecone finial, which supposedly symbolized regeneration. A large central medallion, a moth inside a laurel wreath, represented new life after death. The wreath itself signified achievement, victory, and eternity. The entire sarcophagus rested atop a red marble base, inside of which at floor level lay Smithson's remains.

He stepped closer and admired the inscription etched into the stone.

SACRED TO THE MEMORY OF JAMES SMITHSON ESQUIRE, FELLOW OF THE ROYAL SOCIETY, LONDON, WHO DIED AT GENOA THE 26TH JUNE 1829, AGED 75 YEARS.

"It's wrong," Stamm said.

He hadn't heard the curator approach from behind.

"Smithson was sixty-four when he died. Not seventy-five."

Now he understood Breckinridge's message.

BENEATH ELEVEN MISTAKES.

"That error is noticed by almost no one," Stamm said. "But Breckinridge would know about it."

The tomb was flanked on either side by flags, one of the United States, the other Great Britain, as Smithson had been English. A display case housed documents, memorabilia, and a copy of the famous will.

"Breckinridge did a good job opening this room up," Stamm said. "Before his remodel, it was closed off and dark with an iron gate that prevented entrance. You looked in as if you were in jail, through bars. After, it

524

became a place people could enter and explore."

Cotton pointed at the marble base. "How do we get inside that?"

"It should be really easy."

He was still bothered. "That was one subtle message Breckinridge sent. Eleven mistakes. Pretty damn good for a guy with his mind in another era."

Stamm threw him a curious look. "What are you saying?"

"We have some time before this place is vacant. Nothing here is going anywhere, so let's you and I pay that old man another visit."

Diane returned to Alex's apartment. She'd gone out for a bite to eat, taking a cab to one of her favorite DC restaurants. Vance had not stayed long, and she was still troubled by his visit. But he'd assured her that things would be handled tomorrow as planned. She also hadn't heard from Grant, and wondered what he was doing that did not include her.

She climbed the stairs and turned down the hall. At the apartment she stopped. The door hung half open, the jamb splintered.

She heard movement inside.

A burglar?

Impossible.

She shoved the door all the way open.

And saw Danny Daniels.

"What in God's name are you doing here?" she asked, still standing outside. "Did you break in?"

He shook his head. "That's the way I found it. Someone else did, though."

Her gaze darted around the room but immediately settled on the desk. Her iPad was still there, but not the key.

"Come back to steal more from me?"

"I see you figured out who has your brother's notebook."

"I'm calling the police," she said.

"That's a good idea. I think it's time they got involved."

He stood across the room, dressed in a suit and tie, tall and smug, staring her down.

"What are you talking about?" she asked.

"The Knights of the Golden Circle."

She stepped past the broken door into the apartment, ignoring his attempt to rattle her. "Why did you take that notebook?"

"To finish what Alex started."

"He talked to you?"

"I know exactly what you, Vance, and your brother are planning."

Rage rose inside her. Her husband was dead, yet here was another man, one she'd resented for a long time, trying to keep her down. "What we're doing is perfectly legal."

"But murder isn't."

Was he bluffing? Hard to tell. "What are you insinuating?"

He did not answer her.

"I asked you a question. Answer me, dammit." Now she was yelling.

"You should be concerned," he said.

"That's not an answer."

"No, it's not. But whatever the person who broke in here took should concern you."

"And how did you just happen to be around?"

"The guy who broke in here killed a man last night. He may also have shot a federal agent. I want him. He has a port wine stain on his neck and used to have brown curly hair. Now it's cut short."

What had Grant said?

"I need a haircut."

"I have no idea who that is."

"Really? Because the guy you sent in here a few days ago to take that notebook and Alex's books, which I saw in your study, had brown curly hair and a port wine stain."

How in the world did he know any of that?

Her rage boiled over. "Get out. Get out. Now."

She had to be careful. Her anger and the despairing rhetoric was betraying a grinding anxiety.

One she did not want him to see.

"That necklace I returned to you is the symbol for the Knights of the Golden Circle," he said. "You have one, by your own admission. Alex threw his away. He rejected what you, your brother, and Vance are planning. And now he's dead. What an incredible co-incidence."

"You're a pompous, arrogant ass. That's what you've always been. Finally Pauline saw you for what you are and got out. Good for her. Too bad your daughter never got that chance."

Danny's eyes flashed hot. She'd crossed the line. But he'd pushed her hard, hoping for an admission. Instead she'd gone on the offensive, hitting him at the one spot where he remained vulnerable. Yet he'd be damned if he was going to allow her to use his dead daughter as a weapon.

"Mary, God rest her soul, is gone because of my carelessness. That's a fact. And the pain will never leave me. You, on the other hand, seem to have no pain at the loss of your husband. I watched you at the funeral. Yes, you played the part of the grieving widow. But then it all seemed forgotten later, out on the deck, with Lucius Vance."

He watched her as carefully as he had Vance, noting she was not near as good as he was at concealing surprise.

"I saw the kiss. I heard what you said to each other. You're a cheating, lying adulteress. And I suspect a murderess, too. I can't prove it. Not yet. But I will. You can count on it."

He headed for the door.

"I have only two words left for you," she muttered.

Which he could easily imagine. But she needed to understand the severity of the situation. So he turned to face her and pointed an accusing finger. "A woman I care deeply about is fighting for her life in a hospital, thanks to your partner, whoever he is. I'll get him, along with you."

He left.

Outside, in the hall, he caught the cracked-open door across the hall and saw Taisley's face. Surely she'd heard everything that had been said thanks to the busted door. It had been her, on the phone, who'd told him about the killer's changed appearance. Their eyes met, and he shook his head, motioning for her to go back inside and close the door.

As yet, she hadn't become a part of this.

And he intended on keeping it that way.

He descended the stairs and exited the building. He should head back to the hospital and be with Stephanie. The Magellan Billet agent on guard had called earlier and said there'd been no change. She was still in a coma. The doctors were allowing her to rest, which they said was the best medicine at the moment. The surgery seemed to have been successful. No more bleeding or trauma.

All of which sounded good.

But she was still listed as critical.

He needed a cab, but realized one would not be found on this quiet side street, so he turned and walked down the sidewalk toward the far corner and a busier boulevard. He heard the thrum of an approaching vehicle from behind him and, ever alert, caught its profile out of the corner of his eye. A change in the engine's throaty pitch signaled that the vehicle was slowing.

Then it stopped.

As did he, turning to see a black sedan, not unlike a thousand others that roamed the DC streets. The rear door opened and Congressman Paul Frizzell stepped out.

"Someone would like to talk with you," his old friend said, the eyes holding neither welcome nor hostility.

"Do I want to talk to them?"

Paul nodded. "I think you should."

Icy fingers of apprehension clutched his gut. "There's more to this than you told me, isn't there?"

"A lot more, Danny."

CHAPTER SIXTY-ONE

Cotton and Rick Stamm climbed steps to the front porch of Frank Breckinridge's house. Evening had passed into night, the time nearly 8:00. No lights burned inside, the front door still swung open. He knocked on the jamb and stared past the screen into the foyer. Last time it had taken several tries before the old man had responded.

So he knocked again.

Still nothing.

"Mr. Breckinridge," he called out. "It's Captain Adams. From earlier."

Still no reply.

So he opened the door.

"Is that wise?" Stamm asked.

"In my line of work it's vital."

They stepped inside.

Everything was quiet, like a church on Monday.

"Let's make a quick search to see if the old man is here," he said.

And they did, finding nothing except a

531

house in good order.

"Maybe he went to see a neighbor?" Stamm said.

But something wasn't right about any of this. He still had doubts about whether he'd been played during his first visit. Now an empty house with the front and back doors wide open? Had the old man wandered away? Or did someone with dementia really live here?

He started to pay closer attention to things he'd overlooked during his first visit. The threadbare carpet, scarred wall desk, worn sofa, sagging armchairs. And the decorations. Some porcelain. Lamps. Vases. A mirror. Nothing, though, that stood out. One note-worthy point was the absence of technology, except for a flat-screen television. Framed prints adorned the faded wallpaper. Not many. All historical. Battle scenes. Yellowed and old.

He surveyed them.

One was of Fredericksburg, 1862, the South's most lopsided win. Union losses were two-to-one versus Confederate. Another showed the Battle of Chickamauga, which stopped the 1863 Federal advance into Tennessee. A maritime print depicted nine Union ironclads being repelled during the First Battle of Charleston Harbor. One more illustrated the end of the *Housatonic*, when the Confederate *Hunley* became the first submarine to ever sink a ship in combat.

It was like the South's greatest hits.

And where before the rooms seemed sterile, now they began to fill with the presence of Breckinridge's passion.

"Cotton."

Stamm stood in the dining room, pointing at another frame.

He stepped over.

"He got this the day he retired."

The certificate, embossed and headlined with SMITHSONIAN INSTITUTION, thanked Breckinridge for thirty-six years of service and awarded him the Legion of Merit, signed by Robert Adams, as secretary, and Chief Justice William Rehnquist, chancellor. Dated October 6, 1992. Two color photographs were also matted inside the frame. One showed Breckenridge shaking hands with Rehnquist, a woman standing beside him whom Cotton assumed was Mrs. Breckinridge. The other was a family picture in front of Joseph Henry's statue that stood outside the Castle. Breckinridge, the same woman, and a young boy, maybe eleven or twelve.

"Do you notice something?" he asked Stamm.

The curator studied the images. "That boy's neck is discolored."

"Like a port wine stain."

He knew what he had to do. "Keep watch out front and tell me if anyone comes. I've got some searching to do."

He'd already noticed the lack of any family pictures. Usually a seasoned homestead like this would be littered with memories. So he decided to see if he could find any stored away.

He started checking the closets and hit pay dirt in the upstairs hallway, where he found a cardboard box filled with framed images tossed inside with no particular care. Most were of Breckinridge and his wife, but there were several that showed a boy, then a teenager, and finally a young man. Where visible, the neck was definitely discolored. Also in the closet he discovered another cardboard box that contained photo albums. He paged through, checking for anything on the son. Then he saw three high school annuals. He grabbed the most recent one, dated 1999, which would have placed the son at or near eighteen, considering his age in the Smithsonian picture downstairs. He found the senior class and went to the B's.

And saw Grant Breckinridge.

Short hair, neck discolored, the same face — though younger — that he'd seen inside Fossil Hall.

He ripped out the page and headed downstairs.

"The son's our killer," he told Stamm, showing him what he'd found. "And that old man isn't crazy."

He saw the concern in Stamm's eyes.

His gaze raked the parlor, his radar now on high alert. The same rolltop desk from earlier sat open, full of empty pigeonholes. An old-fashioned gramophone stood in one corner. He'd noticed it during his first visit. A plugless lead trailed from the bottom, its turntable long rusted to immobility. It seemed not worth keeping. So why had Breckinridge? He walked over, crouched down to the cabinet door, and tested it. Locked. He tried to pry it, but a steel bolt had been added for reinforcement.

Which was odd.

His cell phone vibrated.

He hoped to God it was Cassiopeia. He hadn't heard from her, and his two calls had gone unanswered. But the display indicated it was Danny Daniels.

"Get me a knife from the kitchen," he said to Stamm.

He answered the call.

"Your killer has changed his looks," Daniels said.

And he listened to a new description.

"We also know his identity," he told Daniels, explaining what he knew.

"Let's get the no-good bastard."

"I'm on it," he said. "I'll keep you posted."

And he clicked off the phone.

Stamm returned with a butcher blade. Cotton attacked the old wood, digging out chunks and splinters until the lock fell away and the door swung open. A pile of obsolete records in torn paper sleeves lay inside, which certainly did not need the protection of a steel bolt. He slid them out, then noticed a size disparity between the inside and out. The inner shelf did not extend as far as it should. He tested the rear wall, tapping lightly, then tracing his fingers until he found metal.

Which he pushed.

"You're observant," Stamm said.

"Comes from years of people trying to kill you."

A panel released, revealing a concealed compartment.

He saw a book.

Stamm reached in and removed it, cradling it in his open palms as if it were a piece of glass. Cotton understood the affection. This one seemed in excellent condition, its blue leather bindings nearly perfect, the edges gilded.

"Open it," he said.

Stamm carefully hinged up the front cover to reveal a beautifully handwritten title page in an Edwardian script.

Notes & Observations From An Expedition to the Newly Acquired American Southwest May 1854 to March 1856 As Authorized By The Board of Regents of the Smithsonian Institution

"It's Adams' journal," Stamm said.

His spine tingled as he realized that his namesake ancestor had both created and held the book.

"Our records indicated that it should have been returned to your family in 1952. Now we know what happened. Breckinridge took it."

Your journal is safe. I hid it away.

"He told me when I was here that he hid it, but I didn't pay the comment much attention. I just thought it was more of his delusions. Why is this journal so important?"

"I truly don't know."

"But Weston might?"

Stamm did not reply. He pointed to the last four words on the page. "*The Servant of Faith.* That's straight from the Horse Stone. And did you notice the front cover?"

Embossed into the leather at the top and bottom right were a *4* and an *8*. He checked. On the back cover, at the top and bottom left were *N* and *P.* "Those numbers and letters are from the Witch's Stone."

"That's more than a coincidence," Stamm said.

"You think? We passed coincidence a long time ago. Everything happening here is deliberate."

"So how do we handle this?" Stamm asked.

"We don't. Not now. First we have to get inside that tomb."

CHAPTER SIXTY-TWO

Grant was back inside the Castle, this time with his father. They'd slipped in a little before five thirty with the final few visitors of the day drifting around the ground-floor exhibits, easing their way into Schermer Hall, the same place from which he'd made his earlier escape.

"It's different," his father had said. *"They've painted and remodeled."*

"You haven't been back since the day you retired?"

"Never saw the need."

The presence of cameras was different, too. And Schermer Hall had its share.

He still carried Martin Thomas' swipe card, but using it again would not be smart. The experience in Fossil Hall had taught him that people were watching. Which made him question why he and his father were even here, but his father had said they had no choice.

Inside Schermer Hall, twenty-five years ago, was where his father's retirement ceremony had been held. That day it had been packed with well-wishers. Today the crowd was all tourists. Along the north wall, in a corner, stood the same arched doorway that had been there then. A sign affixed to its exterior warned DO NOT ENTER STAFF ONLY. Only a doorknob with a simple lock protected it. And he'd been surprised to see that his father held a key.

"That lock has been there since World War II," his father had said. *"Things like that don't change often in this place. The Smithsonian is both a student of and a slave to history."*

"Why did you keep the key?"

"In case I had to return one day."

Cameras watched the hall, but were all focused toward the center and the public display areas. None watched the corners. So they'd waited for the right moment, as people were streaming out toward the exits, then casually opened the door and entered. Which put them back at the spiral staircase that rose from the basement to the upper floors, the staircase he'd used last night to gain access to the rotunda. They climbed past the second floor and found refuge in one of the north tower rooms, where boarders had lived for free in the early days, young men who worked in the Castle cataloging exhibits and assisting the scientists.

There they'd settled down and waited for

540

the building to clear.

"During the Civil War, Joseph Henry was arrested and taken to face Lincoln," his father said. "The most learned man in the government's employ, head of the Smithsonian Institution, accused as a spy."

He hadn't known that.

"The officer who made the arrest had been warning his superiors for months that Henry was a rebel. Now he had proof, having personally witnessed signals being flashed to the Confederate army from right here, in the north tower, the night before. So the officer brought Henry before Lincoln. The president pointed a finger and said, 'Now you're caught. What have you to say, Professor Henry? Why should a sentence of death not be immediately pronounced on you.' But all Henry did was smile. Lincoln then turned to the officer and explained that he, Henry, and two others had climbed the north tower the night before and flashed signals toward the hills around the city as an experiment. Case closed."

He'd wondered about the story.

"That officer was wrong in more ways than one," his father said. "Joseph Henry was not one of us."

"You keep saying *us.* How many knights are there?"

"Enough to get the job done."

The time was approaching 9:20 P.M. Little

541

sound filtered up to the tower room, so it was hard to know if the downstairs had emptied. At some point he'd have to descend and check. Through a window, outside, he saw that the Mall still buzzed with people enjoying a pleasant spring night.

"You fancy yourself bold," his father said. "All right. Listen carefully, Grant. Sometime tonight they are going to open Smithson's tomb. When they do you'll be there, and it's imperative you do exactly as I say."

Cotton reentered Smithson's crypt.

They'd returned from Breckinridge's house and found the tools needed in the basement workshops. The Castle was empty, the ground-floor cameras switched off for a couple of hours, per Stamm's order, with no security guards anywhere around. Some sensitive renovations had been the excuse given, a task the curator himself would be overseeing.

He and Stamm knelt down at one side of the tomb.

"The red marble panel here at the bottom was spot-glued into place," Stamm said. "Enough to keep it there, but not enough to make it hard to remove, if the need ever arose. I've read all of Breckinridge's notes and reports on what happened."

The red marble that measured about twenty-four inches high and a little less than

542

a yard long. Two joints ran vertically down the side. Cotton assumed it was all façade to a plain concrete base. Stamm nestled a chisel to one of the joints, tapping the end with a rubber mallet, then repeating the process downward until the mortar cracked. He then mimicked the process along the other joint. A lip separated the lower base from another level of red marble, revealing the gray marble of the decorative upper tomb. Stamm freed a narrow strip of red marble near the lip, making it easy to work the chisel into the gap between the panel and the base. Cotton kept his hands to the outside, ready to catch the panel once all of the adhesive loosened.

And it did.

He allowed the panel to hinge downward, settling on the floor. It had come away clean, an easy matter to reattach later. Beyond was an inner niche that extended the length of the concrete base. Narrow, maybe eighteen inches wide and the same tall. He also saw the end of a small mahogany coffin adorned with silver handles.

"It's only bones inside," Stamm said. "So it didn't have to be large."

"And if you were going to hide something, you wouldn't put it on this end," he said.

Which meant the coffin had to be removed.

He reached in and gripped the silver handle. The heavy box slid out with some resistance. He recalled Breckinridge's report, which noted that Smithson's remains had first been placed inside a copper box, which had then been sealed within the wooden container. As the coffin emerged, more silver handles became exposed. Stamm positioned himself on one side. Cotton squirmed over to the other and together they freed the coffin and laid it on the floor.

"Seems Smithson can't rest in peace," Stamm said. "This is the fourth time his bones have been moved."

Cotton bent down on his knees and stared into the empty niche. At the far end he saw an object. He reached in and carefully slid it toward him, revealing a heart-shaped stone, about a foot long and an inch or so thick.

He carefully brought it out.

The side facing him contained a series of squiggly lines, but the one in the center, with five evenly spaced dots, jumped out.

Like the line on the Trail Stone.

Only this time there was an end point, with

an arrow and an inverted *U* that symbolized a mine. He carefully turned the stone over and saw that its backside showed a diagonal column of six small rectangles. He assumed that when the stone was inserted, front side on top, into the heart-shaped recess on the Trail Stone, which waited over in the American history museum, most of a coded map would be revealed.

Stamm followed the plan they'd discussed earlier and quickly snapped a series of images with a 35mm camera he'd brought up from his office, then a few with his phone.

"Let's get this tomb sealed back —"

The lights extinguished.

And the building plunged into darkness.

Chapter Sixty-Three

Danny rode in the rear seat of the Town Car, Frizzell sitting beside him. A driver and another man, neither of whom had said a word, sat in the front. He knew their type. Acolytes. Doing what they were told. But he wondered who they were here to watch over. He also took note that whoever had wanted to speak with him had been smart enough to send Frizzell, as he would not have climbed into the car with just anyone.

"What have you gotten yourself into?" he asked his friend in a low voice.

"It's more what you've gotten yourself into."

They sat in silence as the car found I-66, then sped west into Virginia. Traffic was done for the day, the going clear.

"Good thing I don't have Secret Service protection," he said, trying to loosen things up. "This little trip would have been a lot more difficult."

"Not necessarily," Paul said.

He saw that his old friend was serious, more so than he'd ever seen him before.

"This reaches that deep?"

No reply.

"You're in this with Vance? You agree with what he wants to do?"

"I agree with his aims, but not with either him or his method."

A strange reply. Then he recalled what Cotton had told him about the Knights of the Golden Circle.

He extended his hand. "Are you on it?"

Frizzell appraised him with a hard stare, then accepted the offer and said, "I am on it."

And two of their fingers locked in an odd feeling.

Paul released his grip. "I know you're not of the Order. But it's good to know that you appreciate what's involved here."

"Maybe not. Are we talking treason?"

"Never."

Past Fairfax, the car left the interstate at a darkened exit with no rest or gas facilities. Danny wanted to know what this was all about, but he also was concerned about Stephanie. This trip was delaying his return to the hospital. Still, he knew what she'd say.

Forget me and do your job.

They drove for a mile down a black highway before turning into an empty parking lot at a closed diner. They stopped and the two men in front quickly exited and opened the doors for both him and Paul.

"I haven't had that courtesy in a while," he said, stepping from the car into the warm night.

"In here," Paul said, motioning toward the building.

They approached the front door, which was unlocked, and stepped inside. Immediately, he caught the waft of old grease and bleach. Not a light was on, everything sheathed in darkness.

"Come in, Mr. President," a voice said from across the room.

Electronic. Modified.

His hackles rose. "Is that necessary?"

"I wish none of it were," the disguised voice said. "And I apologize for the precautions, but it was time we spoke face-to-face."

"Which we're not doing."

"Unfortunately, this is the best I can offer."

He'd already figured some of it out. "How long have you been watching Alex Sherwood's apartment?"

"For a time. Starting shortly before his death. When we learned of his involvement."

He ran the possibilities through his mind and only one conclusion made sense. "Diane Sherwood is a problem for you."

"An understatement, but accurate."

"You always so paranoid?" he asked.

"I'm cautious, as Lucius Vance and Diane Sherwood should have been."

Clearly, neither one of them was connected with this man, but another link made more sense. His new chief of staff had provided him with more information on Diane's brother, Kenneth Layne. He headed the Committee to Save America, headquartered near the Capitol in an area of town not noted for cheap rent. She'd also obtained a photograph of Layne, which he'd immediately recognized as the third man at the Sherwood home gathering last night.

"So Vance or Diane told Kenneth Layne about how much I know. Layne told you. Then, when I made contact with Paul, for a *cautious* guy like yourself, you had lots of questions."

"Not exactly. But reasonably close," the voice said.

This guy was beginning to grate on his nerves, so he decided to cut to the chase. "My guess is you're financing Kenneth Layne's Committee to Save America. Somebody has to be. God knows Layne doesn't have a pot to piss in."

"Which is our right, as citizens of this nation, with freedom of speech and assembly."

"I never said it wasn't." He faced Paul. "You're involved with this nonsense?"

"Danny, we're real close to the thirty-four states needed to force Congress to call a second constitutional convention."

That was news to him. "Careful what you wish for." He turned back to the voice across the room. "Layne gave Alex Sherwood a notebook to read, which detailed what he was up to with both his committee and Lucius Vance. I'm betting that was against Order policy, which is what sparked your interest. Am I getting *reasonably closer*?"

No reply.

"And when Alex Sherwood wanted no part of any of it, the next thing you know he falls off a cliff." He was reaching, but why not? These guys definitely had a motive for murder.

"That's the thing, Danny," Paul said. "We had nothing to do with involving Alex, his death, or what Vance is planning. Nothing at all. Which is why we're talking to you right now."

Diane had fled the apartment just after Daniels departed. She no longer wanted to be anywhere near the place. Too many ghosts, too many visitors. She still hadn't heard from Grant, which was bothering her, and she decided that a hotel would be better.

Everything seemed to be unraveling. Where just a few hours ago things had been progressing, now the situation dangled perilously. Vance was panicked, but not to the point of being paralyzed. That was the thing about strong men. Adversity acted more as stimulant than impediment. He'd assured her that all would happen in the morning when the Rules Committee voted, then the full House would vote the next day. Regarding the treasure, they now had three of the five stones. Hopefully Grant was securing the Heart Stone so they could start the final search for the vault. But who'd broken into the apartment and stolen the key? She'd tried twice to call Grant, but both attempts had gone straight to voice mail.

She sat in her hotel room in the quiet and tried to force her mind onto new thoughts. But worry, anger, and despair had settled in.

Depressing her.

Her phone chiming startled her. She grabbed the unit, hoping it was Grant. Instead, she saw it was her brother.

"What is it, Kenneth?" she said, answering.

"Mrs. Sherwood, it's important we speak."

An unknown voice.

Male.

"Where is Kenneth?"

"He's here, with us."

Not a threat, but fear still prickled her spine.

"Who are you?"

"What you pretend to be."

It took her a moment to grasp the significance.

"What do you want?"

CHAPTER SIXTY-FOUR

Grant watched as Richard Stamm and the man from Fossil Hall opened Smithson's tomb. He'd worked his way, unnoticed, down from the north tower and into a gallery on the opposite side of the north vestibule that faced the crypt's entrance.

While he'd maneuvered himself into position, his father had used the spiral staircase to descend to the basement, the idea being to shut off the lights and provide them with a few moments of surprise. A text between them, from his phone, which had been returned, served as their communications link. He'd also noticed two calls from Diane, but ignored them. He'd been surprised to learn that his father owned a cell phone, but a lot about the past few hours had been shocking. His father certainly knew every inch of the Castle, including its wiring, so once he signaled that the Heart Stone had been found the building had gone dark.

He used the moment to rush ahead through

the vestibule and into the crypt. The Heart Stone lay on the floor. His father had told him that there would be only a few seconds before emergency lights switched on, which would glow a dull red, but would offer more than enough illumination to betray his presence.

So he moved fast.

He knocked both men, who'd been crouched down, aside, and grabbed the Heart Stone.

Cotton tumbled to the floor as if blocked by a lineman. He was having trouble seeing, as everything was out of focus from the jarring switch from light to dark. But somebody had definitely appeared. Now that someone seemed to be heading away.

He rolled over and hopped to his feet.

"You okay?" he asked Stamm.

"I'm fine."

Red lights switched on in the vestibule, near the exit doors.

"The emergency lighting," Stamm said.

He ran from the crypt just in time to see a shadow turn into the Great Hall, cradling something.

The Heart Stone.

He found his gun.

Aimed.

And fired.

■ ■ ■ ■

Grant felt exhilarated. He'd managed to steal the stone, which was small and light, and was now making his escape. He was back in the Great Hall where he'd eluded the Justice Department woman. A few more feet and he'd be away.

A loud bang echoed off the walls.

A bullet pinged past him, ricocheting off one of the stone columns.

He found safety behind another column.

"You're not getting out of here," a voice called out.

Cotton had the guy trapped.

Even in the dim reddish light, he could see that there was nowhere to run where he could not take him down. He had no idea if his target was armed, but he had to assume so.

Stamm came up close from behind.

"Everything locked tight?" he asked Stamm.

"Absolutely. No fire escapes this time."

They were standing against a partial wall, the Great Hall exposed through archways.

The double doors that led to Schermer Hall suddenly swung open.

"Captain Adams," a voice yelled. "So good of you to join us."

Frank Breckinridge.

Still playing the part.

555

And the old man aimed a gun and fired three rounds. They were exposed in that direction and Cotton reacted by taking Stamm and himself down to the floor, a half wall above them now offering protection.

Bullets zinged by overhead.

Grant used the moment of his father's entrance to rush from his hiding place, through the double doors, his father following and closing the doors behind them.

"We have to hurry," his father said.

They hustled ahead.

Cotton sprang to his feet and saw that the two intruders had fled the Great Hall. Stamm should stay here, but he needed the curator's local knowledge. So Stamm led the way, down a narrow, closed corridor, then into the vaulted exhibition space of Schermer Hall. He stepped over to the doorway that led to the fire escape and tested it.

Still locked.

And no alarm had sounded.

That meant they'd used the concealed spiral staircase.

Stamm pointed at a wooden arched doorway, marked for employees only, and produced a key from a thick ring.

"The old man had a key?" he asked.

Stamm nodded. "Apparently."

They descended the spiral staircase since

Stamm had already told him that, unless they could fly, there was no other escape from the upper reaches.

Back in the basement they entered Stamm's office.

And heard movement.

Grant saw that his father was not nearly as spry as the old man wanted others to think. Their descent of the staircase had been slower than they could afford, their escape into the Castle's basement corridors slowed even more by the old man's lack of breath. Unfortunately, this mission was definitely a two-man operation.

He knew they were headed toward the Ripley Center, which lay beneath the quadrangle and gardens above, even lower than the basement where they now stood. It had been dug into the ground and built in the 1980s to house art galleries, offices, and conference space. The public accessed it from ground level through a copper-domed kiosk just outside the Castle, but there were also several emergency exits leading up.

They followed a long hall, through a set of double doors, to an elevator and staircase that led down into the center. He'd always found it odd how the top floor was labeled 1 and the bottom 3.

Nobody had, as yet, come in pursuit.

His father remained winded.

They rode the elevator down to the conference level and exited. Towering ceilings and backlit glass cast the appearance of a building high above ground.

"This way," his father said.

Cotton stood at the door that led from Rick Stamm's office into the Castle basement. They hadn't pursued the intruders any farther.

"You were right," Stamm said.

Once he realized that Breckinridge had wanted them to open the tomb, and then discovered that their killer was the old man's son, they'd called the security office and arranged a review of television surveillance of the two Castle entrances. It had not taken long for father and son to be spotted, having entered separately but then meeting in Schermer Hall, gaining access to the spiral staircase. Stamm had surmised that they might hide in the north tower's upper reaches, and that was exactly what had happened. The plan involved sacrificing the Heart Stone, but the critical element had been to secure plenty of digital images.

And they had.

He'd called Magellan Billet headquarters from the Breckinridge house. Two more agents had already been dispatched to DC to investigate Stephanie's shooting. He asked that they be diverted to his control. Though he was no longer on the payroll, just occasional contract help, the staff in Atlanta were eager for his input, so his request had been granted and he'd told the two agents what he wanted them to do.

"The cameras are back on," Stamm said.

He walked over to the desk and watched as the two Breckinridges made their way through, then up and out of the Ripley Center into the gardens above.

"Good call on your part," he said to Stamm. "You were right on how they'd leave."

"I know my buildings. Just like Breckinridge."

But the escape had to be convincing.

So he'd arranged for a little show.

Grant followed his father out of the pavilion at ground level into the gardens between the Castle and Independence Avenue. People milled about, enjoying the illuminated spring flowers, the Renwick Gates to his right still swung open for the night.

"My man," his father said, "should be beyond the gate, waiting for us in the car."

He still carried the Heart Stone, being careful since, unlike the more substantial one from Fossil Hall, this felt fragile. They slowed their pace and tried not to look rushed, conscious of people and cameras. But no one paid them any attention.

They kept moving toward the gate.

Independence Avenue loomed on the other side, the busy boulevard paralleling the Mall all the way up toward Capitol Hill.

His father passed through the gate.

"Stop," a voice yelled from behind.

A quick glance back showed a uniformed security guard. He knew none of them carried weapons but this one did hold a portable radio. He had a hundred-foot lead and used it to his advantage by darting through the Renwick Gates.

"Stop. Now," the voice said.

Their car from earlier was waiting at the curb, illegally parked, flashers on.

Thank God.

His father was already climbing into the rear seat.

He ran and jumped in behind him, yanking the door shut.

The car sped away.

Cotton watched what was happening out on Independence Avenue. Stamm's computer feed to the exterior garden cameras showed it all, including one of the Magellan Billet agents dressed as Smithsonian security trying to stop the two Breckinridges. This was his first good look at the younger man, whom he assumed was the son, and he noted two things. The son matched the new description Danny Daniels had provided, and the face was indeed the same from Fossil Hall.

"They're gone" came the word over Stamm's portable radio.

"Good job," Cotton said into the unit.

The idea had not been to stop them, rather to spur them on.

"What now?" Stamm asked.

"We watch."

CHAPTER SIXTY-FIVE

Danny wasn't sure what to make of any of this. He knew nothing about the modulated voice across the dark diner and had no reason to either trust or believe him. But Frizzell was a different matter. He'd known this man for years and had never doubted his word.

"Paul," he said, his voice low and calm. "You're going to have to make yourself clear. This is all a bit out there, if you know what I mean."

"I do, Danny. But you were correct in the car. I'm a knight of the Golden Circle. The gentleman across the room is the current commander of our Order."

"Who has to remain hidden?"

"We've stayed in the shadows a long time," the voice said. "We find it safer. This is an extraordinary gesture coming here tonight, speaking with you."

"Ain't I the honored one. You'll have to forgive me if I'm not impressed."

"Danny," Paul said. "After we spoke earlier,

I made a call. I was asked by my colleagues if you were a man that could be trusted. I said, absolutely."

He got it. His friend was vouching for him, so lay off the sarcasm.

"The Order was important during the Civil War," Paul said. "And yes, it advocated slavery and used violence. Both horrible. But that was the belief and way of that time. After the war, it went underground. The radicals faded. A new set of men took control with more moderate ideas and practical thinking."

He recalled Kenneth Layne's notebook. "Like Alexander Stephens?"

His friend nodded.

"He was a member until he died in 1883," the modulated voice across the room said. "Stephens was brilliant. If people had listened to him in the 1850s, I doubt the Civil War would ever have occurred. The change the South sought would have come through legal ways. Unfortunately, his brand of revolution was rejected."

"Like calling a second constitutional convention?"

"Exactly," Paul said.

"And the idea, before 1860, had been to move for a new convention," the voice said. "Where the Constitution would have been clarified. Disputes settled. And if those changes had been accepted by the states, 500,000 dead Americans would not have happened. Unfortunately, more brash thinking prevailed."

Which brought to mind what Rhett Butler had said about the South in *Gone with the Wind*. A line Danny had always liked. *All we've got is cotton and slaves and arrogance.*

"After the war, during Reconstruction," the voice said, "any type of constitutional change advantageous to the South would have been impossible. The southern states did not govern themselves. Instead, the North ran roughshod over them with the military in charge. But in the 1870s, when Reconstruction ended and the South regained control over itself, it decided that states' rights were more important than changing the Constitution. Of course, the North was no bastion of progressivism, either. It had its Black Codes and segregation. Ultimately, the Supreme Court made things easy when it ruled that 'separate but equal' was constitutional. A stupid decision, but it nonetheless became the law of the land. So the South was satisfied."

"You know what happened next," Paul said. "During the 20th century millions of people migrated from north to south, shifting the balance of power in Congress and the electoral votes for president. The South literally rose again. Today winning that region is absolutely critical in every presidential election. And while that happened, the Order sat back and watched. Our membership dwindled from tens of thousands in the 1850s, to thousands after the war, to now about 550. We are not fanatics, Danny, or terrorists, or radicals. We abhor slavery and segregation. We're also not romantics wanting a return to some antebellum past. We are simple patriots who disagree with some of this nation's fundamental points, intent on changing them through legal means."

And he got it. "Not the way Lucius Vance intends."

"Exactly," the voice said. "Diane Sherwood taught him things only those within the Order knew. Her father taught her. He was not of us, but he knew a lot about us. That was partly our fault, as we cultivated him as a resource to gain access to the Smithsonian's archives. Sadly, we realized too late that Davis Layne was only after our wealth."

He recalled all that Malone had told him. "Are you involved with what's happening at the Smithsonian right now?"

"We are aware of the situation," the voice said. "It's another reason we're having this talk."

"Danny," Paul said, "what Vance plans is madness. Having the House vote only on bills that originate in the House is an idea whose day has passed. That would concentrate too much power in the Speaker of the House.

But that change is going to be recommended. The Rules Committee will endorse the concept tomorrow. And I've already heard the talk in the House. They're willing to try anything. And they're not blind to the fact that Vance will wield enormous power, but he's one of them and they're more than willing to trust him rather than the Senate or the president."

"Vance will be emperor of the hill. You won't be able to take a crap in the bathroom without his okay."

"Which is the last thing any of us want," the voice said.

"Not a fan?"

"Hardly."

His eyes were now fully adjusted to the dark. Only threads of ambient light sneaked past the front window blinds. The man behind the voice sat about twenty feet away in one of the booths among deep shadows, nothing at all discernible about him. He'd casually surveyed the diner's interior and found light switches near the front door, only a few feet away. He really wanted to get a look at the current commander of the Knights of the Golden Circle. Nothing in the accent, timbre, diction, or syntax of the synthetic voice shed any light on identity.

"Tell me, Mr. President," the voice said. "Are you familiar with the Confederate constitution?"

He needed to buy some time, so he lied and said, "Can't say that I am."

"Interesting, coming from a man who served as governor of Tennessee."

"It's not something that really comes up much anymore."

His tone conveyed, *Except from nuts like you.*

"You really should study it. It's an amazing piece of work. All the more remarkable given it was drafted in just a matter of weeks. Right in the preamble it invokes in no uncertain terms *the favor and guidance of Almighty God.* Quite a powerful statement. No doubt about where its drafters stood. And there are many other significant differences between it and the original. May I point out a few?"

"By all means."

"There's a line item veto, which allowed the president to accept some and reject some of each piece of legislation. As you well know, no such power exists in our current Constitution. Wouldn't it have been nice to have that power?"

That it would have been.

"Protective tariffs were forbidden, so no industry was given an unfair advantage. Congress had no power to forgive a debt. Think about that one. Nor could it pay for any internal improvements within a state. That was all left to the states, individually, to handle. So no pork barrel legislation. The postal service was expressly required to financially sustain itself. Can you imagine? There were even specific provisions designed to prevent corruption in the spending of public money.

"Most important, states, not the central government, were regarded as supreme. And yes, that constitution still sanctioned slavery and demeaned the human rights of all the people in bondage. That is its one central flaw, a gross mistake of the time. But know this, no one who has served in the Order during the last seventy-five years believes that anyone should be denied their civil rights. It's contrary to everything we stand for."

"All minorities? Gays and lesbians?"

"Absolutely."

"Okay," Danny said. "I get your point. There were aspects of the Confederacy that made sense. Things that could go a long way to fixing what's currently wrong with the federal government. But come on, that document has the stink of slavery. No one would ever cite it as authority. Look what happened with the Confederate battle flag. That image is now totally repugnant."

"As it should be," the voice said. "It was used to fight for the continuation of slavery. But the modifications we need today reach far across racial lines. Black and white both want governmental change."

"Just a different kind."

"Not necessarily," Paul said. "Vance has

strong support from the Black Caucus in Congress for what he's about to do. They're going to promote it."

"Because they smell a power grab. They realize that as Vance moves up, so do they. There's somethin' there for everyone, and plenty enough to go around."

"The difference," the voice said, "between us and Vance is that we want our changes legally adopted at a constitutional convention after open debate and discussion, then submitted to the states for ratification."

"And you'll do your damndest to sway your way."

"Which is our right. I'm prepared to trust this country's fate to the will of the people. Are you?"

Unfortunately, it wasn't that simple. Every pundit and scholar agreed that once a constitutional convention was called there were few to no rules on what happened next. Some argued that a convention could be expressly limited to a specific subject matter. Others asserted that such a restriction would be illegal. After all, the 1787 constitutional convention had been called only to revise the existing Articles of Confederation. Instead, the convention abolished the Articles and created an entirely new constitutional government. So if a runaway convention was good enough for the Founders, it was good enough for everyone else.

"There's no way to control what would happen," Danny said. "It could be a free-for-all. Which probably explains why a convention has never actually been called. Not even by those *wise men* from the 1850s. They didn't fight their battles from the safety of the dark."

"No," the voice said. "They did not. But this is a different time, with different ways. And come now, Mr. President, don't you think the American people could handle a convention? After all, it is their country. And by the way, the Confederates were far more progressive on this point, too. Their version of Article V allowed as few as three states to call for a gathering to propose changes. Our constitution requires an unwieldy two-thirds. Even so, we're nearly there."

"The immediate concern," Paul said, "is stopping Vance. But I can't do it. I'm one of his picks on the Rules Committee. For me to openly buck him would be suicide, and we'd lose our eyes and ears on Rules. You have to stop him."

"I was planning on doing just that."

"I came here," the voice said, "so you could hear, firsthand, where we stand. We know of your connection with Alex Sherwood. We also know that Kenneth Layne tried to recruit the senator into what he, his sister, and Vance are doing. Needless to say, Kenneth Layne was playing both sides. When we became aware of his duplicity, we began to carefully watch all concerned. Layne should have never involved the senator. We know that Alex Sherwood confronted his wife and told her he planned to openly protest what Vance was doing. Less than two hours later, the senator was dead."

They monitored the Sherwood home? "What are you saying?"

"Show him," the voice said.

Paul stepped close and produced a cell phone with a video on the screen. Taken in a pine forest, through a column of trees, it showed a rocky bluff and two people. Alex and Diane. Talking. Alex smoking a pipe. More talk. Diane appeared to cry. Alex comforted her. Then she shoved him off the cliff.

He could hardly believe his eyes.

He looked up at Frizzell, whose strained face was visible in the ambient glow.

"She killed him? You've known this, yet done nothing?" he asked both men.

The figure across the room kept a stolid silence.

So Danny made clear, "I asked a question."

"We've been debating what to do," the voice said. "All of the choices come with an assortment of risks and rewards. We heard your conversation with Mrs. Sherwood, in her study, after the funeral. We also know about Taisley Forsberg. And when you challenged Vance today at the Willard Hotel, we realized why you were appointed to the Senate. You want the truth, Mr. President. So do we."

"What about Vance?" he asked.

"To our knowledge he knows nothing of the murder. He confronted Mrs. Sherwood earlier, in the senator's apartment, but she denied any wrongdoing."

"You people have bugs everywhere?"

"Only where we need them."

"That's when we knew we had to speak to you," Paul said to him.

"Stop Lucius Vance," the voice said through the darkness. "Do what you have to do. If you need help, we're here to assist where we can."

He'd had enough of the games. "What about Diane?"

"We *are* dealing with her. Which is something you cannot take the lead in. Let us —"

He lunged for the light switch and flicked it upward. Fluorescent fixtures flickered on, their ballast catching, warming, then flooding the bulbs with current, which threw out bursts of white light. He squinted against the glare, trying to see, but the man was gone.

He ran across the diner and saw a door leading back to the kitchen. He pushed through and found a rear exit.

He yanked it open and stepped out into the night.

Only to see a pair of taillights turning left, rounding the building, then vanishing.

CHAPTER SIXTY-SIX

Diane stepped from the cab in front of the Lincoln Memorial. The caller on the phone had told her to come here with all the information she possessed. Everything she had was on her iPad and in files stored in Dropbox, so she'd brought the device with her, tucked into her purse.

The memorial stood at the west end of the National Mall. A broad flight of steps led up. Off to the east, past the Reflecting Pool, the floodlit Washington Monument pierced the night like a warning sword. It was approaching 11:00 P.M. and though no massive streams of chattering tourists milled about, the place was not deserted.

Above her, at the top of the steps, the immense statue of Lincoln sat inside its shaded colonnade. Thirty-six columns held the roof aloft, each, she knew, representing a state in the union during Lincoln's time. She climbed the steps and caught sight of the sad, brooding face of the dead president, which had a quieting effect and added to the atmosphere of a shrine.

Standing near the foot of the seated giant was a squat, brown-haired man with ball-bearing eyes, small ears, and thin lips. She was drawn to him though they hadn't yet exchanged a single word.

"What is this all about?" she asked in a quiet but annoyed voice, when close. "And where is my brother?"

"You can start by losing the attitude. You're not in charge here."

"And what makes you think that I haven't already called the police?"

He shrugged. "If you have, then I'm going to have to show them this."

He held out a cell phone.

A video started.

Showing her killing Alex.

A cold cloud rushed through her.

"Still want the police involved?" he asked.

She said nothing.

"Let's you and I take a walk."

They left the memorial, descending the stairs and crossing the street toward the Reflecting Pool. He led her down a paved walk that paralleled one side of the shallow pond.

Her nerves were frayed from the video, her body cold.

"Your brother has done a bad thing," he said. "He was working in conjunction with us, furthering our agenda. You being brought into the picture was our idea, but involving Lucius Vance was another thing entirely. And finally, there is the issue of your late husband."

"Are you with the Knights of the Golden Circle?"

"Why do you seem surprised? Your father studied us for years. You've studied us, too."

"In the abstract. He never told me that the organization still existed."

"Because he never knew. His battle was with Frank Breckinridge, not with us, though Breckinridge is a knight. Your father wanted the vault. As apparently do you and the younger Breckinridge."

"Where is Grant?"

"On that I have more bad news. It seems that he's found a new benefactor and does not require your assistance any longer."

Now it made sense. "He broke into Alex's apartment and stole the key."

"He needed it back."

"He's going after the vault?"

He nodded. "Without you."

"So you're not really interested in having me arrested for murder."

"Not at the moment. We need your assistance. I showed you the video so that you would understand how seriously our requests should be taken."

She stopped walking and faced him.

"Where is Kenneth?"

He turned his phone around, tapped the screen, then showed her. On it she saw her brother, being held upright by two men, a third pummeling his abdomen with swift blows. Kenneth reeled from the punches, seemingly struggling to breathe.

Then he vomited all over himself.

The two men holding him upright released their grip and he collapsed to his knees, gasping for air, swiping his arm across his mouth.

"He's being taught a valuable lesson," the man said to her. "We created the Committee to Save America. We funded it. We staffed it. We gave it a mission and purpose. It was originally run by someone else, but when you and Grant Breckinridge started your quest, we hired Kenneth. He was offered membership in our organization and told what was at stake. Eventually we had him make contact with you. He was to be our conduit for information from you and Grant Breckinridge. But then he started creating his own agenda. Connecting you to Lucius Vance was not in our plan. And when he involved your late husband, that altered everything."

"So why didn't you stop him?"

"By the time we knew it was happening, things were too far gone, and we've been cleaning up ever since."

On the phone screen a pail of water was thrown over her brother, reviving him. Then the two men lifted him back to his feet. She saw the look of fear on his face and the helplessness in his eyes.

More fists pummeled the chest and kidneys.

"Why not just kill him?" she asked.

"A bullet to your brother's stupid brain would be simpler. Fortunately for him, he has a job to do." He motioned at the screen. "He just requires some policy instruction and proper motivation."

The two men again let Kenneth go and he dropped to the floor. She knew she should feel something for her twin brother, but nothing flowed through her except the image of her shoving Alex over the cliff.

"You expect him to keep working with you?" she asked.

"Of course. He has no choice. He has some terrific relationships across the country with many key state legislators. I think after tonight he'll be more than anxious to please. Of course, he won't be participating in your venture, nor will Grant Breckinridge. Which means you're on your own."

Now she understood. They were isolating her. Rendering her impotent, with no allies, no support.

Insignificant.

Just as Alex had wanted to make her.

"Your treasure hunt is over," he said, sounding proud. "Did you bring what I asked?"

She nodded. "It's all on e-files stored on my iPad and an off-site server."

He handed her a slip of paper. "Email everything to that address. Then erase all the files and never think of the vault again. I assure you, if you make any attempt to locate it after tonight, we will know and you will be arrested for murder. If you stay silent, we stay silent."

She had no choice.

"We're doing you a favor. Grant Breckinridge has already killed one man at the Smithsonian and shot a federal agent."

Exactly what Daniels had told her, too.

"The agent's name is Stephanie Nelle. She heads an intelligence division of the Justice Department. She's in a coma at Sibley Memorial Hospital. Please know, Grant Breckinridge is about to be a seriously wanted man."

"That's his problem."

"True. I just wanted to make sure it didn't become yours."

They'd walked about half the length of the Reflecting Pool.

Few others were around in the darkness.

The man faced her. "I believe that concludes our business. Hopefully, this will be the last time we ever speak."

And he walked off.

But there was one point he hadn't mentioned.

"You don't care that he's dead?" she asked.

He stopped and turned back to her.

She'd intentionally not used Alex's name.

"You saved us the trouble."

CHAPTER SIXTY-SEVEN

Cotton's phone rang.

He was back across the Mall in the American history museum, inside the secured archive where they'd left the Trail Stone. They were still monitoring the Breckinridges. One of the two Magellan Billet agents on the scene was overhead, watching the car used for the escape from a safe distance. The skies over DC were regularly patrolled by military helicopters, so the presence of one more would arouse no suspicion. And besides, it was nearly 11:30 P.M., with darkness providing perfect cover. The second agent was following the car at a discreet distance, being guided by the chopper, no need to get close. They were all headed outside DC, west into Virginia. So he and Stamm had taken a few moments and transferred their base of operations from the Castle.

He checked the phone's display.

Magellan Billet headquarters.

He excused himself, drifted to the far side

of the archive, and answered among the shelves.

The report was disturbing.

Cassiopeia had disappeared several hours ago. Lea Morse had been there. She'd been told to stay back, out of the way, but disobeyed Cassiopeia and watched as an explosion rocked an old mine, then Cassiopeia was led away at gunpoint by a man Lea identified as James Proctor, someone who'd tried a few hours earlier to kill them both. Her description of the vehicle was not much help. Even more disturbing was that Terry Morse was also missing. Cassiopeia had gone to find him. Lea had found the sheriff, but the locals had waited a long time before informing the Justice Department. Finally they made contact and were eventually routed to the Billet.

"They think Morse might be trapped inside the mine," came the report. "So they're digging. We initially tried Cassiopeia's GPS tracker and got nothing. But a few minutes ago it came back on the grid."

Like himself, Cassiopeia wore a Billet-issued watch that provided GPS locating. She'd used his to find him inside that incinerator, and now he learned that her watch was near Amarillo, Texas, heading west, along Interstate 40.

"That's a long way from Arkansas. Give the tracking info to the Texas Highway Patrol and find it."

"Already being done. We just wanted you to know."

He ended the call, worried about Cassiopeia. Nothing he'd heard sounded encouraging. He walked back to where Stamm sat at the monitor, a greenish night-vision video feed still coming from the helicopter following the Breckinridges.

"They're headed toward Manassas," Stamm said. "There's a regional airport there."

He got the message. They could be leaving. "We can follow, but we need to know the destination."

He grabbed the radio they'd brought with them and told the agent in the chopper and the one in the car about the nearby airport.

Grant wondered where they were headed. His father had provided the driver with specific directions. So far no one had pursued them.

Which was good.

"There are some things you need to know," his father said.

They sat together in the rear seat.

"The current Order numbers around 550 members. At present there's a schism among the knights. One group, led by our commander, wants to move forward with legal changes to the Constitution. You're familiar with that through Kenneth Layne. What you don't know is that the Order funds his organization. The other faction, led by me, prefers that we stay dormant."

Why wasn't he surprised.

"A few hundred people do not make a revolution," his father said. "Whether any significant constitutional changes could ever be implemented is a huge question. There would be conventions, debates, then any amendments would have to be ratified by three-fourths of the states. That takes time and an enormous amount of resources. The Order's wealth was hidden away for a second civil war. A revival that, hopefully, this time we'd get right. We would dishonor the legacy of all the men who made that possible by squandering it."

Now he understood. "That's why you want the stones. So no one can find the vault."

"They must be secured. The Heart Stone, there in your lap, is the most vital."

He was puzzled. "Why not just leave it where it was? Nobody knew."

"Because eventually that tomb might have been reopened and the stone discovered by people with enough information to find the vault. Better we take advantage of the current opportunity and destroy it. That way there's no risk at all."

"But how would anyone ever find the vault?"

"They won't."

He was shocked. "You mean all that gold will just stay buried?"

"It's not mine or yours to have. It belongs to posterity."

"And how will the future know it even exists?"

"I'll make sure there's a path. And I understand, you were in this for a payout. I can provide one. I have one of our larger caches outside the vault secured in Arkansas. I have a substantial amount of gold, some of which can be yours. More than enough for you to live comfortably."

But it wasn't the vault.

They rode in silence for a few minutes, and he considered his options.

"You do realize I did you a favor," his father said.

No, he did not.

"Our commander has made a move on both Diane and Kenneth Layne. You would have been next, if I had not intervened." His father paused. "Did you know Diane Sherwood murdered her husband?"

He was shocked and it must have shown.

"I didn't think so."

"What are they doing to her?"

"Simple blackmail to quell her interest in looking for the vault. Her brother, on the other hand, did the unthinkable and violated our secrecy by involving Senator Sherwood in the first place. I would imagine his punishment will be more painful."

"Like what you did to my men in Arkansas."

"Violence is no stranger to me, or to those who work with me. There were two federal agents in Arkansas, whom the men you hired encountered. I knew all about Terry Morse and what he guarded. So I dispatched knights to handle the situation, and they did. While there, they also retrieved that gold cache. It's much larger than the one you located in Kentucky. The Sherwood woman pointed the way, but I made sure there were no impediments to your search. I assumed you needed the money, and I needed you to keep doing what I wanted."

"Surely you didn't retrieve the cache in Arkansas just for me."

"I was hoping it would be a peace offering, one that would satisfy our commander. I'm not unsympathetic to his goals, I just don't see the need to violate the vault to accomplish them. Thankfully I have both the Witch's and Heart Stones, so all is secure."

He decided to poke a stick in the spokes of his father's wheel. "You do realize that the other side doesn't actually have to have the stones. This isn't the 1800s. Computer imagery can put them together. The two men in Smithson's crypt took pictures of this Heart Stone before the lights went off."

But his father seemed unconcerned. "They have a bigger problem."

He waited.

"The starting point. They have no clue. And

this is a big country."

"And you know it?"

"I told you about Angus Adams and his visit to the Smithsonian in 1877, when he returned the key and his field journal. Adams was the knight who created both the vault and the stones."

Now he understood. "His journal? It has the starting point?"

His father nodded.

"I have it hidden away."

Cotton was concerned about Cassiopeia.

Hopefully the GPS tracker would lead them to her. He hadn't heard anything back from Billet headquarters, but he was sure things were being handled. His problem was still on the computer screen.

A car traveling on a dark highway.

He made a decision and told Stamm, "They're definitely leaving."

The car was off the main highway, headed south on a two-lane state road. He grabbed the radio and ordered the agent on the ground to head for the Manassas Regional Airport. He also told the helicopter to fall back but not lose the car.

Angus Adams's field journal lay on the table beside the Trail Stone. He grabbed the book and examined its handwritten pages. Frank Breckinridge had kept it close for a reason. He faced Stamm. "I'm assuming we can merge the Heart and Trail Stones by computer?"

"We have some of the best digital imagery on the planet here. I've already sent the images downstairs to our lab. They're working on it, sizing everything, getting it ready. The question is, where does the trail start?"

He pointed at the computer. "I'm hoping they're going to supply that answer."

He still held the journal.

And wondered.

What was so important about it?

Grant saw they were turning into a small regional airport outside Manassas labeled HARRY P. DAVIS FIELD. Only a few lights burned in the small terminal building.

"One of the knights owns a Gulfstream that we'll be using," his father said.

He was still stinging from his father's insults. He'd done well tonight and did not deserve to be put down. But he wanted to know, "What happened to the two federal agents in Arkansas?"

"One left. The other I have in custody."

"For what?"

"We might need some insurance."

The car stopped and his father stepped out into the night. He followed. Beyond the terminal he heard the rev of jet engines.

"Our plane is ready to go," his father said.

"You don't think taking a federal agent

587

hostage could be a problem?"

"As far as we know she was alone, with no opportunity to report in. My man was able to capture her neatly. And people left on the ground report that the local authorities have no idea where she went. So no, it's not a problem."

He could not believe what he was hearing.

"And you call me reckless."

CHAPTER SIXTY-EIGHT

Danny stepped back into the diner, the lights once again off.

"You should not have done that," Frizzell said. "He came in good faith."

But his mind was racing, that video still replaying over and over. "This is bullshit, Paul. You should go to the police and have Diane Sherwood arrested for murder."

"It's more complicated than that, Danny. She's after something, and we have to make sure we have it before she's taken down."

"The vault?"

"That's right. The knights are in a state of chaos at the moment, busted into two factions. It's a mess. I stand with our commander who wants to work for peaceful, legal, constitutional change. We also want the vault. It was hidden away for just this use."

"So what does the other side want?"

"They advocate doing nothing. Holding our resources for another day."

"And Lucius Vance is about to throw a

monkey wrench into both sides of the fight."

"That's an understatement. If he succeeds, we're afraid public opinion might sour on more meaningful constitutional change. We actually like the Senate just as it is — a check and balance on the House. What we don't like is Congress as a whole and, as the commander noted earlier, there are things from the Confederate constitution that would fit quite nicely with our own. Ideas that would improve things, ones we think the people will embrace. But they may not after a taste of Emperor Lucius Vance."

He got it. "Nothing sours a revolution more than a greedy revolutionary."

"Something like that."

"Paul, this is more complicated than you know."

He told his friend what Cotton had reported, adding, "Malone's working an angle right now at the Smithsonian. We think the guy who shot Stephanie Nelle is a man named Grant Breckinridge."

"It was him."

"You people were watching that, too?"

"We weren't there for the shooting of Ms. Nelle, but it wasn't hard to surmise who did it."

"I want that SOB."

"So do we, Danny. But as you've seen, the elder Breckinridge and his son have teamed together, which is a problem for us all."

He wondered why that was the case for them. Only one explanation made sense. "You have no idea where the vault is, do you?"

"Unfortunately, no. Commanders once knew some of the clues, but that information was lost to time. Frank Breckinridge, though, is its self-appointed sentinel. He assumed that job back in the 1970s when he sparred with Davis Layne. The Order was much weaker then, so a zealot like Breckinridge could easily dominate. But a new commander assumed power in the late 1970s and reorganized everything. You just spoke with him. To his credit, Breckinridge kept the vault away from treasure hunters, but he also refused to share anything he knew with the Order. That's been a sore spot ever since."

"So much for all-for-one-and-one-for-all."

"Actually, Breckinridge would say he is being loyal to the Order. He disagrees that now is the time for us to act. Especially if that revolution is led by the man you just spoke with. He and Breckenridge do not get along. Unfortunately, it's going to take a lot of money to influence not only that second constitutional convention, but the thirty-eight states needed to ratify whatever is adopted. So we have to allow Breckinridge to lead us to the vault, or at least to the stones. Thankfully, at the moment he seems to be doing that."

"Am I to assume that your knights in Congress are few and far between?"

"Just me and two others, all in the House. I have ranking seniority. But there's nothing we can do. If I raise one iota of objection, even privately, Vance will remove me from Rules. The Order doesn't want that to occur."

"What happens with Kenneth Layne?"

"We still need him. He has a lot of contacts and influence with state legislators around the country. I don't know the details, nor do I want to know, but he's currently learning the price to be paid for disloyalty."

"And what about Diane Sherwood?"

"We've already dealt with her. She's been shown the video, so she knows that we know. She's also lost Grant Breckinridge and, if we're successful, Vance too. Once all that happens, and we learn about the stones or the vault, we turn her in to the police. I agree with you, she's a murderess who must be punished."

He was glad to hear that.

"You came back to the Senate because of what Vance is planning," Paul said. "I know you, Danny. Tell me what you have in mind for him."

Earlier, he'd explained to Teddy Solomon how he thought Vance might be stopped. But the video had added a new dimension.

So he told his friend what he now had in

mind.

Diane stood outside the World War II Memorial and considered everything that had just happened. She cleared the east end of the Reflecting Pool and entered the solemn site, its plaza and fountain lit to the night.

Her entire world had crumbled.

The messenger was gone, the final few minutes of another Wednesday ebbing away as midnight approached.

Everything was over.

Her marriage. The relationship with Vance. Grant. The gold. All of it. Gone. Where before she was at least the wife of a U.S. senator, now she was nothing but his widow. Even worse, somebody knew she'd killed Alex. They'd simply watched, filmed, and waited. They could not care less about Alex's life.

But she got the message.

Back off or go to jail.

She strolled among the granite pillars, standing at attention like sentries. She knew she should feel some sort of emotion being here, but nothing registered. She was numb. And afraid. Even if she backed off, at any moment people could destroy her life. And that cloud would never blow over.

They'd own her.

Forever.

And Grant?

He'd abandoned her, taking the key, saying

nothing, just disappearing.

With *"a new benefactor,"* the messenger had said.

With all these horrific turns of events she'd have been better off staying married to Alex, existing in a passionless relationship with a man she'd neither respected nor liked.

What would she do with the rest of her life?

She could no longer fulfill her father's dream and find the vault. She had some money and could sell the house to acquire more. There'd be a pension from Congress and dependent's Social Security payments. Income, for sure. Together, more than 99% of what the average American made. But nothing like billions of dollars in lost gold.

She stopped before words etched into the granite above her.

A quote from Eisenhower made on June 6, 1944.

D-Day.

YOU ARE ABOUT TO EMBARK UPON THE GREAT CRUSADE TOWARD WHICH WE HAVE STRIVEN THESE MANY MONTHS. THE EYES OF THE WORLD ARE UPON YOU. I HAVE FULL CONFIDENCE IN YOUR COUR- AGE, DEVOTION TO DUTY AND SKILL IN BATTLE

She'd also been on a great crusade that was

now over.

Yet one last thread remained.

Danny Daniels.

The bastard had come into her home, stolen the notebook, somehow managed to spy on her and Vance, then interjected himself into her business. The thought of his succeeding turned her stomach. And he was still standing, going strong, a sitting U.S. senator. He had stature, respectability, and a future.

All thanks to her.

That bastard she could do something about.

CHAPTER SIXTY-NINE

Cassiopeia sat in the passenger seat of the car being driven by James Proctor. Six hours had elapsed since they left Arkansas. They'd traversed the entire state of Oklahoma, staying on a four-laned superhighway, and were now in Texas, about thirty kilometers from a town called Amarillo. Her hands remained bound behind her back, Proctor not making good on his pledge to free them. They'd caught up with the panel truck, staying a couple of miles behind it, both vehicles maintaining a steady course due west.

"Do you plan to tell me where we're going?" she asked for the third time.

He hadn't been talkative, which was why she'd dozed off to sleep for a little while. Strange, but she did not feel threatened. At least not until they reached their destination. Proctor had brought her along for a reason. If he'd wanted her dead, he would have shot her back at the mine. Instead he seemed to enjoy toying with her. She assumed her status as a federal agent played into his decision. Was she insurance?

For what?

"We're headed to the great state of New Mexico," he said.

Another place she'd never visited.

"You kill people with great ease," she said.

"Only those who need to die."

"Spoken like a true sociopath."

He laughed. "I'm just a guy who does his job."

"For money? Or something else?"

"Mainly for money. The Order is generous. Ten bars of that gold ahead of us is mine."

"And the men who came with you?"

"They'll all be well paid, too."

"Except the dead one."

"Whom Morse killed. You think he's a sociopath, too?"

"No. Just an old man holding on to something that connects him to his past. But your man threatened his granddaughter and he reacted as any grandfather would."

"I underestimated him."

"You're going to kill him, aren't you?"

"That's not my decision to make."

"Back in the mine you talked about the Golden Circle as though it were a religion. You don't really buy into all that, do you?"

He kept his attention on the dark highway, sparse with cars but heavy with truckers pushing their rigs hard.

"My father thought it was all nonsense," he said. "But my grandfather — he was a believer. He hated the way this country was run. He served in Congress back in the 1940s and was never a fan of FDR. He loved Truman, though. My grandfather told me about the Order, and introduced me to men who, later in life, allowed me to become part of it. I've made a good living doing what they need done."

"Aren't you the good little soldier."

"Every army needs them. The knights once numbered in the tens of thousands. They were everywhere, but history books never mention them. Which is a travesty. They were a clever bunch."

"How proud you must be."

"Actually, I am proud. The South had no chance of winning that war, but it fought hard with what it had."

"How about untying me. My arms hurt. I already promised to be a good girl."

"But you and I know that won't happen."

"Are we going to stop at any point? Some food and water would be great. Not to mention a bathroom."

"Do I look that stupid?"

Her gun and cell phone were gone. Proctor had both. And she had no idea of the surrounding geography.

Lights began to strobe inside the car.

She turned her head and saw police cars

approaching from the rear.

In both lanes.

Proctor saw them, too, and she caught a moment of indecision as he assessed the situation. He reached beneath his jacket and laid his pistol in his lap. She wondered how messy this might get. So she told herself to be ready to act. Luckily, her legs were not bound.

Sirens now blared.

Close.

They were driving in the right-hand lane. She looked back again and saw the lights directly behind them shift to the left lane, then four police cars, labeled TEXAS HIGH-WAY PATROL, roared by. Brake lights glowed as traffic began to slow.

Proctor was forced to slow down, too.

Both lanes congealed as one police car stayed behind the panel truck, another in front, with two at its left side.

She glanced at the dashboard.

45 MPH.

More brake lights glared in the dark.

The police cars finally forced the truck onto the shoulder, officers emerging with guns in hand.

"I guess you won't be getting those ten bars of gold," she said.

"Shut up."

In order to attract the officers' attention, she'd have to bend her knees, then flex her body down and up, swinging around to use her legs and feet as weapons. A swept kick to Proctor's head should do the trick, sending the car reeling. But she'd have to be fast to avoid the gun in his lap.

Traffic had slowed to less than 20 MPH.

The police forced the driver from the truck.

She readied herself to move but before she could do a thing, something hard slammed into her left ear.

Everything spun.

Then hope vanished.

CHAPTER SEVENTY

Thursday
May 27, 1:30 A.M.

Cotton glanced out the window and watched the lights of Washington, DC, recede. He'd just taken off in a Department of Justice Gulfstream, the same one that had ferried him to and from Arkansas. Another day had ended, a new one beginning with him again flying west. Luckily, he'd thought ahead and had transportation on standby and, as he received reports from the agent at the Manassas Regional Airport, he'd heard that he'd been right.

The Breckinridges were leaving town.

Their flight plan called for a trip to another regional airport, just outside Taos, New Mexico, an artsy community about seventy miles north of Santa Fe in the Sangre de Cristo Mountains. They had a nearly two-hour head start, but the DOJ pilots thought they might be able to make good time. The Breckinridges were aboard a slower Learjet

601

registered to a Richard Choi, who lived just outside DC. The Billet was busy gathering what they could on Choi, who surely had something to do with the Knights of the Golden Circle.

Rick Stamm had stayed behind, working on digitally assembling the Heart and Trail Stones so they could have some idea of what they were facing. But he had brought Angus Adams' journal along with him. He'd examined every handwritten page, though nothing had jumped out at him. The book seemed far too elegant, the pages clean, the handwriting containing no mistakes, for it to be an original field journal. More likely some sort of reproduction. He assumed Adams himself had penned it, since both the title and last page were signed in a stout, Edwardian-like script.

Angus "Cotton" Adams

His grandfather had told him that, after the war, Adams was never seen again in middle Georgia. Around 1900 Adams' eldest son returned with his own family to work the family farm. His grandfather's father. And brought with him a trunk of his father's prewar letters, some personal papers, a few illustrations and paintings, and a book.

A laptop lay on a small work desk before him. Stamm had provided it, and he quickly secured an Internet connection. The video link established and he saw Stamm's smiling face inside the archive at the American History museum.

"We did it," the curator said. "Look at this. The two stones joined."

And the screen filled with an image.

"At least we know the end point," he said.

The dotted line on the Heart Stone now connected to a similar one on the Trail Stone to define a clear path with nine markers. The inverted *U* symbolized that a mine waited at the end. But he knew from what his grandfather had taught him that the arrow from the dagger to the mine signified danger.

A clear warning.

"We still have no starting point," Stamm said.

No, they didn't. And he assumed that the remaining Alpha Stone would show the other

603

nine markers, so as to fulfill the inscription from the Witch's Stone.

I go to 18 places.

Along with the starting point.

Something told him that Frank Breckinridge was not working under the same disability. He replayed again every word uttered during his visit with Breckinridge. Plenty of Civil War history. Jefferson Davis. Lincoln. The knights. Then —

"Son of a bitch," he muttered.

"What is it?" Stamm asked through the computer.

"Breckinridge tested me on the stones, which I passed. He tested me on the code and I passed that, too. Then he asked me if I wanted to meet with the commander while I was in town. I took *'the commander'* to mean the head of the knights. He wanted to set up a meeting and I asked where. He told me, *'In that damn Temple of Justice of his.'* "

"You know what that refers to, don't you?" Stamm asked.

He did. "The Supreme Court building. I read a book on its history. When they moved into it, most of the justices weren't happy. The whole place was made of marble with columns and looked like something from ancient Greece. They called it pretentious and inappropriate. One of them said they ought to enter the courtroom riding elephants. Another equated the justices to *nine black beetles in the Temple of Karnak.* The analogy stuck and it became the Temple of Justice. I've been so focused on other things, I didn't notice the discrepancy."

Stamm looked puzzled.

"While talking to me, Breckinridge seemed back around 1865, toward the end of the war. The Supreme Court then met in the Old Senate Chamber inside the Capitol. The new building didn't come until 1939. So in his so-called delusion, why did he refer to it as the Temple of Justice?"

"Could be just his mind traveling back and forth."

"It could, but it's not. We know that old man isn't crazy. He was sending me a message. He told me he didn't trust the commander. He said, *'That hair around his bald head makes him look too much like a priest.'* Who does that sound like?"

"Chief Justice Weston."

"You got it."

"That can't be," Stamm said, a little incredulous. "Weston is the commander of the Order?"

"Why not? He certainly knows a lot about all of this. And I don't think Breckinridge threw in the Supreme Court clue by accident. Everything else he did was calculated. He sent us to Smithson's tomb and he sent us to Weston."

"We'd have to be damn sure before treading into those waters," Stamm said.

He agreed, staring again at Adams' journal. "It would explain how he knew so much about my family and Angus Adams. Along with his huge interest in all of this. Have you heard from him?"

"Not in several hours."

Everything was beginning to make sense.

He checked his watch.

"I should be on the ground around 5:00 A.M., New Mexico time," he said to Stamm. "Keep working on the graphics. We'll need the best images possible."

"You want me to talk to Chief Justice Weston?"

He'd been thinking about just that.

"No. I have someone better in mind."

CHAPTER SEVENTY-ONE

Washington, DC
2:30 A.M.

Danny was back on the move.

Paul Frizzell had dropped him at the hospital after their encounter, and he'd spent a couple of hours beside Stephanie's bed. Her condition had remained unchanged, though the doctors were sounding more hopeful. He'd finally dozed off, awakened by his cell phone. He'd listened to Malone then told him he'd handle it immediately.

So he'd taken a cab to the residence of Warren Weston. His new chief of staff had provided him the address, after he'd woken her from a sound sleep. He was liking her more and more, as she hadn't uttered a word of protest, only a resolute *"I'll be back to you shortly."* She reminded him of Edwin Davis, who'd been equally resourceful during his time in the White House.

Everything he'd heard from Malone about Warren Weston had sent daggers through his

607

gut. But he agreed. Frank Breckinridge had tossed them the scent for a trail that had to be followed.

He was a little surprised to learn that the chief justice lived in the heart of Georgetown. He'd never known Weston to be a man of money. His Supreme Court job knocked down barely $250,000 a year. A solid salary, for sure, but barely enough to pay what Georgetown real estate commanded.

He realized he may have to deal with the Supreme Court police, who were charged with protecting all the high court's justices. An agent was on duty near Weston's front door. Surprisingly, a light burned in one of the house's ground-floor street-side windows. He stepped down a short brick walk and approached the sentry.

"Good evening, Mr. President," the man said to him.

"Bet you're wondering what I'm doing here at this hour?"

"Actually, no sir, I'm not. The chief justice said you might be coming by."

He nearly smiled.

Warren Weston was a lot of things, but he wasn't stupid.

"He said if you did, to just go inside."

He opened the door and entered. The light he'd seen from outside burned in a front parlor, not unlike his own back in Tennessee. Weston sat in a high-backed leather chair, nursing a drink.

"Come in, Danny. If you want a whiskey, there's some on the table."

"Where's your little gadget for the voice?"

"I told my colleagues that precaution was a waste of time, but they insisted. I would have much preferred the talk we're about to have."

The room was wood-paneled with a warm, cozy décor.

He sat on a small settee.

"I meant what I said earlier," Weston said. "The Order is not some fanatical organization. We are committed to working within the law."

"But let's get real, Warren. The Knights of the Golden Circle was a terrorist organization. It may well have been the largest, most successful terrorist organization in American history. They wreaked a lot of havoc and spawned the KKK."

"That's all true. From 1854 to 1865. But we moved past that. And for over a hundred years we've been quietly waiting for a time when we might do what Alexander Stephens envisioned."

"Change the Constitution?"

Weston nodded. "The people are ready."

He shrugged. "You might be right. The problem comes when deciding what that change will be. On that the people may not agree with you. But as you said back in that diner, it's your right to try."

"The more immediate problem is twofold. One is Vance. The other is what's happening within the Order. We have our own version of the Civil War happening as we speak."

"Is that why Breckinridge ratted you out?"

"I thought that might be how you found me."

"A lot's been happening at the Smithsonian tonight."

"I've been out of touch, dealing with you. Can you tell me about it?"

So as a courtesy he told Weston what he knew.

"Breckinridge pointed Malone toward me," Weston said, "because he wants me preoccupied, so he can do what he plans."

"Which is?"

"Destroy the five stones and prevent anyone from finding the vault. He thinks that wealth should be left alone, until he says it's okay to use it. Interesting how all this seems to be not about gold, but power. Both Breckinridge and Vance want an unchecked version."

"Malone's on his way after the old man. The son is with him. And that bastard shot someone near and dear to me."

"I'm sorry about what happened to Ms. Nelle. I never realized you were that close to her."

"More than you think. I want Grant Breckinridge. We know they're headed to New Mexico. Where exactly?"

Weston did not answer him, which was irritating.

"Warren, maybe you don't get it. The game's over. If you want Vance stopped, I'm all you got. If you want Breckinridge stopped, Malone is your only bet. He's on their tail, but I need to get him ahead of the game. Where are they going?"

"Pasto al Norte."

"My Spanish is lousy."

"Shepherd of the North."

Cotton stared at the computer screen.

He'd added the images of the Horse and Witch's Stone to those of the now merged Heart and Trail Stones.

The phone on the desk beside the laptop buzzed.

He answered on speaker.

"Cotton," Danny Daniels said. "I'm here with the Chief Justice. And you were right. He is the Order's head honcho. The two you're after are headed to a tract of land once owned by your relative Angus Adams. When he died, he left that land to the federal government and it's now part of the Carson National Forest in the Sangre de Cristo Mountains. The vault is there."

Cotton stared harder at the stones on the screen.

"There's an old mission, which was part of Adams' land. And a church called *Pasto al*

Norte. Shepherd of the North."

"That's on the Horse Stone. But I read the Spanish as *The horse of faith, I graze to the north of the river.*"

"The Spanish is ambiguous," Weston said. "We've long thought it to mean *the servant of faith, I shepherd to the north of the river.*"

That made sense.

Then another dot connected.

He reached for the journal and found its title page. "Adams's field journal contains the words *the servant of faith.* He seems to call himself that."

"You found the journal?" Weston asked.

Apparently Daniels had not passed on that piece of information.

So he told the chief justice how and where.

"We need to talk," he heard Weston say.

And not to him.

"We'll call you back," Daniels said.

Danny ended the call to Malone and stared at Weston.

"Angus Adams is the key," Weston said. "After the war, he personally supervised the consolidation of the Order's wealth. By 1890 most of it had been gathered and moved west to his land in New Mexico, inside a repository he secretly created."

"The vault."

"That's what he called it. Previous to that,

612

he oversaw the creation of the stones, which were hidden with sentinels around the country. But secrets being what they are, they don't stay secret forever, and people started looking for the stones. In the early part of the 20th century, some Smithsonian curators found three. The Horse, Trail, and Heart. But in 1909 one of our historians was killed looking into this."

"The Smithsonian wanted the gold?"

"Definitely. Billions of dollars in wealth just sitting out there. For an institution that lives off donations, that would have been the mother lode. But they found nothing, and everything went quiet until the 1970s, when Davis Layne started looking again. That's when Breckinridge stepped in and shut things down."

"And when did you assume the role of the knights' commander?"

"I've been a member since I was twenty-seven. But in 1980 our commander died and I was chosen to replace him. I was two years into my Supreme Court appointment. As chancellor of the Smithsonian I had access to a vast archive, and I've spent the past three decades learning what I could. I tried to get Breckinridge to open up and tell me what he knew, but the old fool refused. He and I never saw eye-to-eye." Weston paused. "I do know the starting point, though. It was created and preserved by Angus Adams. That information

Chapter Seventy-Two

Cotton kept staring at his great-great-grandfather's journal, remembering the gold cross and circle he'd seen in his mother's jewelry box. She'd never told him much about it, but now he knew its likely origin.

Her ancestor.

Angus Adams.

A knight of the Golden Circle.

No wonder she thought the tradition of passing the necklace down through the generations should stop with her. He shook his head. He was so much like her. So easy for them both to keep things to themselves. But she had shared one thing.

A book.

From the old trunk in the attic.

"Where did it come from?" he asked his mother.

He'd never seen one like it before. The library at his elementary school contained many books, but none like this.

"It belonged to a relative of mine. A spy during the Civil War. But he was also an artist. He painted for the Smithsonian and made this book."

He read the title.

The Servant of Faith.

He'd first noticed the words on the Horse Stone but had dismissed any connection since, at the time, he'd known little of Angus Adams' involvement. But when he found the journal in Breckinridge's gramophone and saw what Adams had written at the bottom of the title page, he'd made the connection.

"Is this book old?" he asked his mother.

"The date inside says 1889. It was a gift from my great-grandfather to my grandfather, who lived here on the farm. But it's not an ordinary book."

Which he'd seen after opening the cover. Past the title page there was writing on only two of the hundred or so pages. The rest were blank, though they were all elegantly gilded on three sides.

"It has only a poem inside," his mother said. "I assume it was written by my great grand-father. His name was Angus. He titled the poem 'The Servant of Faith.' "

His eidetic memory recalled every word.

Ye aging knights of silver grey,
We ask you not to fade away.

616

Though your hair has turned to white,
Your weary bones no more to fight.

While at last the time has come,
You ride into the setting sun.
Then again you ride once more,
On honored fields just like before.

When at last you need your rest,
The South will face its greatest test.
O Elder Knights all clad in grey,
Lead the charge into the fray.

Our Confederate Nation ask of thee,
Ride once more and set us free.
Silver Knights have walked this land,
In golden years they make a stand.

Almighty God we plead with thee,
Give them strength that we might see.
Stand with them we pray this day,
Our aging warriors all clad in grey.

He'd always admired the lyric prose, ornate and elegant, replete with clever figures of speech. Its meaning now much clearer.

"There's something else special about the book."

He saw the twinkle in his mother's eye and was intrigued. Usually the stories about the family's past came from his grandfather.

But not today.

He watched as she parted the covers and grasped all of the pages with her thumbs and forefingers. Applying pressure, she fanned out the long edge. The gold gilt slowly dissolved into the image of a pueblo-like building, in a desert, with mountains in the distance.

He was amazed and said, "That's like magic."

His mother smiled. "It's called fore-edge painting, an old art form. The artist would force the pages into this position and use a vice to hold them fanned. He would then paint what he wanted on the edge. Once dry, he released the fan, then gilded the edges to hide the color. It can be revealed only by refanning the pages. The technique was quite popular after the Civil War."

"What's the building?"

"We think it was where he was living out west, but I really don't know for sure."

He'd waited until now, wanting to be alone, to see for himself.

The embossing at the corners of the front and back covers of the *4, 8, N,* and *P* seemed a sign. Like the odd trees in the woods. There, but not there. Meaningful only if you were able to make a connection. Angus Adams had placed them on both the Witch's Stone and here on the journal for a reason.

Warren Weston may have been right when he intentionally involved him in all of this.

He did know things.

Time to find a secret.

Danny was growing impatient.

Malone was waiting for answers, as was he.

"It's the book Malone has," Weston said. "Frank Breckinridge apparently stole it from Smithsonian collections and hid it away. I never was able to actually see or touch the book. I know only that Angus Adams handed it over to Joseph Henry in 1877, not long before Henry died. It was to be returned to Adams' family seventy-five years later. I was hoping that might have happened, and that Malone knew about it. I never knew, until now, that Breckinridge had the book. When I learned about Adams' connection to Malone, I decided to see where it would lead. Maybe the book had been returned in 1952. The Smithsonian is conscientious in honoring gift conditions."

"You should have been up front with Malone. That's a hard man to corral. He doesn't take to a saddle lightly."

"Which I've learned."

"What about the book? Why is it important?"

"Adams had a great affection for both the Smithsonian and Joseph Henry. He also was the only man alive who knew everything about the vault. But the Order chose well with Adams. He was a man of honor and protected that wealth as if it were his own. By the 1890s the vault had faded to obscurity. Henry was dead, Adams was an old man, and the Order had deteriorated. We know that Adams made a point to deliver both the key and his journal back to the Smithsonian in 1877. Perhaps he thought that the safest place for both to rest, unnoticed among countless other artifacts. Beyond that, I don't know how the book points the way to the vault. I only know that it does."

Cotton grasped the pages in Adams' journal, just as his mother had with Adams' book all those years ago, using the two numbers and two letters on the covers to position his hold on the pages. He was careful, making sure not to clamp the old paper too firmly. Slowly, he fanned the edges out, the gilt dissolving, as he remembered with his mother, into a defined picture.

He brought the book close and examined the image. A river dominated, beside which stood what looked like a church and three other buildings. His gaze shot to the laptop and the images of the Witch's and Horse Stones.

Together they said, *The servant of faith, I shepherd to the north of the river. This path is dangerous. I go to 18 places. Seek the map. Seek the heart.*

On the Horse Stone, extending from the head, he followed the squiggly line with a cross beside it. In the upper left corner he studied the other squiggly line marked *RIO*. Spanish for "river." Three dots surrounded what looked like a *5*, but it had been intentionally angled. Like an *L* attached to an inverted *U*. Classic Golden Circle misdirection. You thought you saw one thing, but it was actually quite another. He glanced at the fore-edge painting again and noticed that there were three buildings before the church, arranged in a triangular shape.

Just as on the stone.

Adobe houses with heavy tiled roofs, sash windows, and chimneys, among grass and trees.

He released his grip on the pages and smiled.

Now he knew.

Danny listened as Malone explained through the phone what he'd found.

"The stones are not meant to be read in any particular sequence. Instead, they're random instructions, scattered over the four that we have. Part of the puzzle is learning how to assimilate that varied information. The Witch's Stone is like an introduction. It tells us that the path is dangerous, that there are eighteen markers, and to seek the map and the heart. I suspect the hooded figure and other symbols on there are going to be relevant at some point. The Horse Stone narrows things to a specific location. *North of the river.* So we need to know more about Adams' landholdings."

"It was over ten thousand acres," Weston said. "In northern New Mexico, which have remained public lands since the turn of the 20th century."

"The vault is on that land, and the starting point is the church north of the river. We need some satellite mapping. Have Rick Stamm wake somebody up and let's pinpoint exactly where we're headed. I've got two hours until I'm on the ground. I need an answer by then."

"You're assuming," Danny said, "that Breckinridge found the fore-edge painting."

"He did. You can count on it. The good thing is, he doesn't know we have, too."

"He'll destroy all the stones," Weston said. "Including the Heart Stone you allowed him to take."

"That shouldn't be a problem," Malone said. "I'm sitting here looking at the Trail and Heart Stones combined elctronically. There's still the Alpha Stone, the one that actually gets you going in the right direction. Only nine markers are visible on the merged map we now have. There are nine more on the Alpha. My guess is that stone is waiting at the shepherd north of the river."

"So you have to beat him to it," Danny said.

"That's the idea."
He ended the call.
And faced Weston.
"We're not done here."

CHAPTER SEVENTY-THREE

Grant woke from his sleep.

The drone of the jet engines had lulled him into rest, which he'd needed. Yesterday had been a long day. He checked his watch and noted he'd been out for over two hours. They had to be halfway across the country by now. His father sat across the cabin, spread out on a white leather sofa, looking entirely comfortable in the lap of luxury.

"Sleep some more," his father said.

There'd been food waiting for them in the galley, and he'd eaten before dozing off. He felt refreshed, ready to go. But some of the wind had gone from his sails. He was no longer on a hunt for gold. Instead he was a prisoner of his father. Sure, he'd been promised a consolation prize. But he wondered if he might be able to get back on course.

"I can be useful," he said.

His father did not seem impressed. "You have no idea what it means to be a knight."

"Tell me."

His father sat up. "They took an oath to freely sacrifice life and everything dear for the perpetuity of the Order's principles. They pledged death and destruction to abolitionists, leaving no means untried to circumvent their schemes."

"That was 150 years ago."

"Honor is timeless."

"Slavery is gone."

"As it should be. But the Order stood for much more than that. Things many Americans today might find attractive."

"Name three."

"Representative government. Political accountability. Voter responsibility."

He decided to stop being antagonistic and asked, "Have you been part of the Order all of your life?"

"Your grandfather was a member and he encouraged me. But my true calling came during the fight with Davis Layne."

"How did you find the key?"

His father reached into his pocket and removed it. "A total accident. I was barely on the job in the late 1950s. I was in the Castle attic working on repairs — and there it was beneath some insulation. One of the workers found it and had no idea of its significance."

"Why did you?"

His father tossed him the key. "Look at the end of the stem."

He did and saw that the rounded brass was

notched, forming a cross in a circle.

"That cross is needed for the lock it fits. But it also sets that key apart. There's only one like it in the world. I knew the moment I saw it that it was the same one Angus Adams left with Joseph Henry. Remember, I told you that it originally would have opened the Confederate archives. But those were moved to the vault, along with the wealth. That's when the key took on a greater significance."

"How could this key possibly have any relevance now? It's been such a long time."

His father pointed a finger at him. "And that's why you could never be a knight. You lack faith."

"I'm just being realistic. Maybe an inattention to reality is why the knights faded away."

His father went silent for a moment and the drone of the engines dominated.

"Some of what you say is true," his father said. "We did become indifferent to a changing world. Which makes what we're about to do all the more meaningful."

His confusion still ran rampant. "What are we doing?"

"Settling a dispute."

Danny was trying to decide if his opinion of Warren Weston had changed, and he concluded that it had. He now thought even less of him.

"We still have an agent missing," he told

626

Weston. "I know her. She's also Malone's girlfriend."

"That gold found in the truck in Texas," Weston said, "was Breckinridge's way of appeasing my side of this fight. He sent word that he had it and that it would fund whatever fight we had in mind. But he obviously has no idea what it costs to sway public opinion."

"Needless to say, the Order won't be getting that gold. The Yankees have it now."

Weston chuckled. "I suppose that's true. But that cache pales in comparison with the vault. In addition, the Confederate archives are most likely there. Those documents could rewrite history."

"And maybe not in a good way. Those could be secrets that are better off staying secret."

"I'm willing to take that chance. A long time has passed and here we are, still waiting for change. You heard what I said about the Confederate constitution. Things are there people today would embrace. A line item veto. No pork barrel legislation. States fending for themselves. No debt forgiveness. Those make sense, Danny."

"Yet there's disagreement even within your precious Order as to whether they should even be debated."

"Some do prefer to wait for another time."

"And you both want the vault."

Weston nodded. "I want to spend it. Use it

for what it had been intended for. That's why I decided to use Diane Sherwood, Grant Breckinridge, and Cotton Malone to see if I could obtain it."

His anger arose again. "You led Stephanie Nelle into a dangerous mess, without telling her what she was facing."

"Believe me, I had no idea Breckinridge would kill Martin Thomas or try to kill her. None at all. Things had been happening for nearly two years without even a hint of violence. The older Breckinridge seemed to be using his son in an odd way, just as I was using Diane Sherwood. We each were after the same thing, but neither one of us could get it on our own. I simply wanted Ms. Nelle's assistance, and the president offered."

But something else was bothering him.

"This can't all be about just finding some lost gold and a difference of opinion, maybe changing history. Tell me, Warren. What more is at stake?"

Grant listened as his father explained the dispute.

"In 1861 the South decided that violence was the only way to end its arguments with the North. The Order was not part of that decision. Instead it was made by ill-prepared men who lost that fight. We have to learn from those mistakes. The next war cannot be fought from a position of weakness. Quite

628

the contrary, in fact. Unfortunately, there are those among us who have not learned that lesson."

"So you disagree with what Kenneth Layne is doing, trying to call a constitutional convention?"

"I see the wisdom, but I told the commander in no uncertain terms that I would oppose it. His desire to move forward with constitutional change, to my way of thinking, involves far too much compromise. If we're smart and patient, which the Order has always been, we can grab it all instead of achieving it piecemeal."

Grant didn't see the importance, or value, in any of it.

His father *was* nuts.

Cotton was waiting for Rick Stamm to access satellite maps of northern New Mexico. The Smithsonian possessed digital imagery of every square inch of the planet. Librarians inside both the American and natural history museums were up and working, despite it being the middle of the night in DC.

He'd also been both disturbed and encouraged by a call from Magellan Billet headquarters. Cassiopeia's watch had been located inside the back of a paneled truck that contained a huge cache of gold bars. Terry Morse had been found tied up in the back of that truck and was now safe. Morse told them that some man named James Proctor had knocked him unconscious at the mine, but not before he'd seen the three men who'd assaulted them in the bee house. As to what happened to them, Morse had no idea. Likewise, Morse had not seen Cassiopeia and knew nothing about her whereabouts. But Cotton knew from Lea, who'd been there, that Cassiopeia had been taken away at gunpoint by Proctor. He'd been hoping that her GPS watch would lead them to her.

But that had not happened.

Where was she?

He wanted to be on the ground, looking for her, but he was hurtling through the dark sky, gaining time somewhere over Texas. Another hour and a half and he'd be in New Mexico.

Not knowing if she was okay tortured him. This was not her fight. She'd come along only because of him.

He gently pounded his fist on the tabletop.

Maybe they took too many chances? Perhaps it was time, in light of how they felt about each other, to be more cautious. Both of them were middle-aged, seasoned, and should know better. What gave him hope was that she'd intentionally planted that watch. Which meant she'd been on the move. Hopefully, both she and the man named Proctor would turn up.

He unbuckled himself, stood, and paced

the empty cabin.

Billet headquarters had determined that the plane with the two Breckinridges remained about an hour ahead of him. The flight plan seemed unchanged, as they were still headed for Taos Regional Airport. So he'd told his pilots to head there, too, since they would arrive after their targets had left. They'd secured the assistance of the local sheriff, who would post someone at the airport to keep an eye on things. He assumed the Breckinridges would be heading for the land once owned by Angus Adams, and he needed to give them a wide berth so they'd lead the way.

The laptop signaled an incoming communication.

He clicked open Skype to see Stamm's smiling face.

"I think we have it."

CHAPTER SEVENTY-FOUR

Cassiopeia had been awake for over an hour, the taste of sleep still sticky in her mouth. She'd been knocked unconscious by Proctor, out for a couple of hours at least, maybe more. She'd lain still and not let him know she was back among the living. Twice his cell phone had vibrated and she'd listened to the call. The first time he'd reported what happened with the gold. The second call had been shorter, Proctor doing more listening than talking, as if being given instructions. He'd seemed unconcerned with her. While still groggy, she vaguely recalled their stopping, probably to gas up. Water bottles rolled on the floorboards among packs of peanut butter crackers. Apparently, Proctor had been thirsty and hungry.

Road signs indicated they were in New Mexico, but not on the same westbound four-laned highway. The road was two lanes now, and they were headed north. Her arms were still bound behind her back, and her shoulders ached. Just one opportunity. That's all she'd need.

And he'd pay.

"I know you're awake," he said.

She'd been slouching with her head angled toward the door.

She sat up straight.

"Your breathing changed once you came around," he said.

They must have been on the road ten hours. Dawn at least two more hours away. The terrain had changed from flat and treeless to high, rugged forest. She could also tell they were climbing in elevation.

"We're headed to a special place," he told her. "Land that was long ago utilized by the Order. I never thought I'd get to see it."

He sounded proud.

"Is there a point to this trip?" she asked.

"Of course."

"Do you get to kill some more people?"

He seemed not to appreciate her sarcasm. "I hardly think those three pieces of scum I shot back at the mine qualify as people."

"What about me and Lea Morse?"

"You left me no choice. But what does it matter? You both survived. No harm, no foul."

She did not reply.

Nor did she agree.

Danny wanted an answer.

What else is going on here?

633

"The Knights of the Golden Circle respect history," Weston said. "And though we may be divided at the moment, both sides are interested in the vault. And not just for its wealth. There's a legend."

He remained enraged. "Legend? Stephanie Nelle is fighting for her life because of this nonsense."

"It's not nonsense," Weston said. "This country was founded by men who stood together, bound by common desires and beliefs. Ideas were important to them. They meant something. And look what they created. The greatest nation on earth, one that has endured going on three centuries. The men who started the Golden Circle were honorable. At least at first. Eventually, though, as what happens with untempered movements, their actions evolved into unrestrained, irrational violence. They got caught up in a war that was unwinnable. The knights who came after the Civil War were more thoughtful, more lawful, more patient. They saw things differently. As the Order faded in the late 19th century, while the vault was being prepared and stocked, it's said those men left instructions on what they wanted us to do."

"Marching orders?"

Weston shook his head.

"More a lost order."

Cotton stepped out of the Gulfstream to a dark tarmac where deputies from the Taos County Sheriff's Department informed him that the Breckinridges had landed a little over an hour ago. His watch read 4:50 A.M. The Learjet was in a nearby hanger, the pilots in custody. The Breckinridges themselves had left in another car that had been waiting at the terminal.

"We managed to GPS-tag it," one of the deputies told him. "We thought you might want to know where it was headed."

"That is the question of the day."

"Right now it's going north, into the Carson National Forest."

"I need to get ahead of it. Or better yet, above it."

Which he'd already communicated to Magellan Billet headquarters, as it had been working with the local authorities.

"They told us you were a navy fighter pilot."

He nodded. "I can fly most anything with wings."

The deputy smiled. "That's good, 'cause what we have is definitely unique."

Following his father's instructions, Grant drove the two-laned highway up into the Sangre de Cristo Mountains, entering the Carson National Forest. Twice his father had made a call from the plane. The first had been to obtain information, the second to provide instructions to the person on the other end. Apparently, someone else was headed for the same place.

"Unfortunately, the police have intervened and seized the gold I was shipping out here," his father said.

"What about my payout?"

"It's gone."

"How would the police have known about that gold?"

"My guess is we have you to thank for that. Far too much shooting and killing that drew too much attention."

"A chip off the old block."

His father smirked. "Far from it. When we use violence, it's always with caution. You, on the other hand, don't know the meaning of the word."

"I'm not sure what you're going to do when you don't have me to blame for your mistakes anymore. How could what I did in DC lead to that gold in a truck on its way here? Seems like you're the culprit there."

No reply, and he could almost hear the old man's mind churning through the possibilities.

"It's impossible that anyone knows we're here," his father said, as if trying to convince himself.

"And why are we here?"

"To retrieve the fifth stone."

Good. That was just what he needed.

"We will find and destroy it," his father said.

Or maybe not.

Cassiopeia was becoming concerned. Her watch had led the police to the gold, but not to her. She was out in the middle of nowhere with a man who had little to no conscience, his intentions regarding her all too clear.

He planned to kill her.

Her hands remained bound behind her back, her arms sore. She was tired, hungry, and thirsty. But she'd been in worse predicaments.

"How about some of that water and crackers," she said. "On the floorboards."

"When we stop I'll feed you," Proctor said. "It's close now."

Dawn seemed not far away.

She'd been brought along as insurance, which apparently Proctor and his allies had thought a good idea, an easy matter to dispose of her in this wilderness. The seizing of the gold truck had surely given them pause. But only she knew that was from her efforts, which meant Cotton, or someone at the Magellan Billet, was on her trail.

Just be patient, she told herself.

And wait for the right opportunity.

■ ■ ■ ■

Danny had heard enough.

He was tired, the night weighing on him, and he needed to get back to the hospital.

"What the hell are you talking about? What lost order?"

"You must understand," Weston said. "We're talking about the deep passions of dedicated men. For them history was not something in a book. It was alive, part of them. It mattered. For them, to be a knight was to be something of importance. They saw themselves as the means for reshaping the country in a fundamental way. Those passions remain today in the current members. Maybe even more. So for us, it's important to know what those who came before us have to say."

He'd had enough. He was done. "Warren, a man is dead at the Smithsonian and Stephanie Nelle is in a coma —"

"Which was all done by a man outside the Order."

"You brought that dead librarian and Stephanie into a firestorm, without telling either one of them the danger they were facing. You sent Malone into it blind, too." His voice had risen. "This is not some intellectual exercise. People are dying because of it."

638

The room passed into an uncomfortable silence.

"Frank Breckinridge has gone to find the Alpha Stone," Weston said. "He surely knows about the fore-edge painting, so we have to assume he knows the starting point for finding the vault. Once he obtains that stone, he'll destroy it and this will all be over. He'll have exactly what he wants. We won't have the vault, which means you'll have what you want. It remains to be seen if Lucius Vance will get what he wants."

"He won't."

He'd heard the surrender in Weston's voice. Time to leave.

He stood. "I'll be in touch."

"I appreciate all that you're doing here," Weston said.

One more thing.

"When I was president, you refused to resign, though you should have left the bench a long time ago. I knew that was because you didn't like me, so why give me the plum appointment of your successor. Okay, I can respect that. It's your call. You're the one with the lifetime job. But now I learn you're the head of a covert organization that wants to change this country. I'll say this for you, I can't recall a single decision you've made as a justice that reflected your private bias. I'm sure it crept in here and there, but not enough for me, or anyone else, to notice.

Again, that's your call. All judges have biases, some more than others. Now that I know yours, though, I'll give you thirty days to resign. On the thirty-first day, if you're still there, I go public. Sure, I might sound crazy, but that's not unusual for me. I assure you, it'll be enough noise that you'll be asked a lot of uncomfortable questions. So do yourself a favor and leave gracefully."

He headed for the door.

"What are you going to do right now?" Weston asked.

"End this."

CHAPTER SEVENTY-FIVE

Washington, DC
7:25 A.M.

Diane reentered Alex's apartment building. She'd stewed over everything that had happened and decided few options remained. Yesterday, she and Grant had searched the place, finding nothing that related to them or to what Vance was planning. But none of that mattered any longer. Exposure was no longer a problem.

Instead, revenge had taken hold.

She climbed the stairs, defeated.

Always before she'd been ready with her next move, calculating every angle before acting. She prided herself on deliberateness. Never had she pursued an uncalculated route. Even when she killed Alex, she'd sat in the quiet of their home and debated the pros and cons, deciding that she had no choice. Interesting how murder had become so easy an option. She supposed that desperation accounted for most of its attractiveness, along

641

with a nothing-to-lose mentality.

And that was exactly where she found herself now.

She came to the right floor and walked down the corridor. The door to Alex's apartment hung half open and she could hear someone inside.

Like yesterday, with Danny Daniels.

She burst in and saw a woman. About her age. Curvy. Dark hair. Glasses. Attractive.

A stranger.

Then she knew. "You were my husband's mistress."

The woman had been tidying up, but stopped and faced her. "Mrs. Sherwood. I apologize for —"

She moved farther into the room and took advantage of the other woman's shock. "I assume that since you did not deny my allegation, that you were Alex's lover."

The other woman seemed to steel herself. "That, I was not. But we were in love."

"Do you have a name?"

No reply came.

"Come now, don't I at least deserve to know who you are?"

"Taisley Forsberg."

"You live nearby?"

"Across the hall."

"How convenient. I don't recall ever seeing you."

"I made sure that did not happen."

She appraised the opposition with the gaze of a scorned wife. Easy, since this woman knew nothing of her own hypocrisy with Grant Breckinridge or Lucius Vance.

"Alex also told me you never slept together," she said. "Interesting how you both say the exact same thing."

"Your husband was an honorable man. I respected that, and I loved him enough to wait until he was free."

How magnanimous. "What are you doing here?"

"I always kept the place in order for him. Apparently, someone broke in yesterday. The doorjamb was splintered. So I called the building superintendent to have it repaired."

"No police?"

"I saw no need. I also didn't see any clothes or a suitcase, so I assumed you'd left. I didn't realize you were coming back."

Neither had she. But the presence of this woman seemed a sacrilege. She was not Mrs. Alex Sherwood. And though this apartment meant nothing to her, she was not about to cede it over to a woman who'd been in love with her husband.

"You do know that you were not the only one," she said. "Alex had many women."

And she immediately saw her lie had no effect.

"It's not necessary for you to disparage him," Taisley Forsberg said. "He's gone and can't defend himself."

The rebuke only enraged her more. Her competition stood across the den, near the kitchen, quite comfortable with her surroundings.

"And please don't play holier-than-thou," Forsberg said. "I saw you yesterday, kissing that other man."

Interesting. Apparently she'd been observed with Grant. Which raised a question, so she decided to try a bluff. "Danny Daniels said you were observant."

"He told you about me?"

"Oh, yes. He was here, yesterday, too. I'm sure you saw that also. He told me you knew all about my retrieval of books and a notebook."

No reply.

Which was confirmation.

She walked toward Alex's desk. She'd returned here for a specific purpose, one related to Danny Daniels, and now fate had tossed her another prize. The mistress herself. From right across the hall.

Forsberg watched her with a wary look, one that confirmed the upper hand was here on this side of the room.

"Not to worry," she said to her competition. "Our marriage was over and, as you've probably already concluded, I was not the most faithful partner, either."

"I came to that conclusion only yesterday. I

went to President Daniels since he was the only one I thought might be able to help. When I did that, I thought you would want to know what happened to Alex, too."

"I know exactly what happened. I killed him."

Shock filled Taisley Forsberg's face and Diane used the moment to slide open the middle right drawer in Alex's desk. As always, the gun lay ready. Alex had been a solid Second Amendment advocate, an NRA favorite and gun-rights proponent, one of the few political stances he'd taken without equivocation.

She gripped the weapon and pointed it across the room.

Forsberg froze. "Oh, my God. What are you doing?"

She shrugged. "What? You have the nerve to seduce another woman's husband, but not the nerve to face her down."

She stepped around the desk, the gun aimed. "How many nights were you here in this apartment? On this sofa? Sitting here with him. Sharing the day. Each other. How many?"

"Please don't hurt me."

"Hurt *you*? What do you think you did to me? It's a little late to be worrying about each other's feelings."

Forsberg had backed herself against the wall, nowhere to go. She loved the feeling of power a gun provided. And strange how the fear that coursed through her adversary produced not a hint of sympathy within herself. Instead, it seemed only to amplify her anger. Which she would need for what lay ahead. But she'd never shrunk from a challenge.

Never.

So why not.

She pulled the trigger.

Once.

Twice.

Both shots to the woman's midsection.

Forsberg slumped to the floor, blood pouring from her in thick rivulets. Gurgling spurted from her throat as she tried to breathe.

More blood spewed from her mouth.

Then, silence.

She did not linger, moving quickly out the door, into the hall, and to the stairs. Behind her she heard doors opening. The shots had attracted attention. But she would be away before anyone spotted her. Surely there were cameras in the building, and her exit would not go unnoticed. She'd be identified and hunted, but not in the next couple of hours.

Which was all she'd need.

To finish what she started.

CHAPTER SEVENTY-SIX

7:50 A.M.

Danny slouched in the recliner, his eyes closed, next to Stephanie's hospital bed where he'd slept the remainder of the night. He'd left Warren Weston's house more confused than angry, traveling by cab back to the hospital. A different Magellan Billet agent was on guard outside the door, and he'd slipped in quietly to keep watch over his girl.

He opened his eyes.

Stephanie was staring at him.

He blinked, focused, and saw that it wasn't a dream.

"How long have you been awake?" he asked.

"Just a few minutes. I decided to let you sleep."

He pushed himself up from the chair and approached the bed, taking her hand. "You okay?"

She nodded. "I'll live. But I don't recommend getting shot. It hurts."

"I'll remember that advice."

It was good to see her eyes alive again. And the smile. He'd missed that. Though she was tough as nails with her people, he'd seen the softer side, as she'd witnessed from him.

"What's happening?" she asked.

"A lot. Seems this was nothing but a nasty hive, full of mad hornets."

A curious look came to her face. "I don't recall your being involved at all."

"I wasn't. Until I was."

And he told her all he knew, ending with, "And I'm now a U.S. senator."

She appraised him with a look he'd seen before. "I knew you couldn't just fade away. I was wondering how you'd get back in. And by damn, you found an imaginative way."

"Doesn't change a thing for us. The divorce will still happen. In fact, I don't really give a crap what anybody has to say on the subject. Seeing you in this bed has changed things all around."

She smiled. "Why Danny Daniels, you really are in love, aren't you?"

He nodded. "Yes, ma'am, I am."

She tightened her grip on his hand, which he liked. "I'm worried about Cassiopeia, though. No word on her is not good."

"Malone's on it. As soon as he deals with the two Breckinridges, he's going to find her."

"I should have been more careful. But it all happened so fast." She paused. "I'm so sorry about Alex Sherwood."

"He was a good man who didn't deserve to die that way."

"What do you plan to do?"

"I have to stop Vance. Today. Preferably before the Rules Committee does anything public. The less attention on this, the better." He looked around the room. "How do you call a nurse? I think they should know you're awake."

Stephanie lifted the bedside control with her right hand.

"As should somebody else be notified," he said.

And he released his grip on her hand and stepped out into the hall, speaking to the Billet agent. "Let Atlanta know that the boss is awake. I think she's going to be fine."

The man nodded, seemingly relieved.

"And take a break. Get some breakfast. I'll stand guard till you get back."

"Is that a good idea?"

"The danger is long gone, on the other side of the country. We'll be fine."

The man headed off down the hall.

He couldn't see anyone from the nurses' station headed their way, so he allowed the door to close and walked back to the bed.

"I'll call a nurse in a minute," she said to him. "Hold my hand again."

Diane entered the elevator, recalling what Danny Daniels had told her. *A woman I care deeply about is fighting for her life in a hospital, thanks to your partner, whoever he is. I will get him. Along with you."* The man at the National Mall had told her the same thing, only he'd added a specific hospital.

Sibley Memorial.

And a name.

Stephanie Nelle.

The information desk had supplied the room number after she lied and said she was the patient's sister.

She'd fled Alex's apartment building without encountering anyone. Surely Taisley Forsberg's body had been found by now and the police alerted.

But she still had time.

The elevator climbed to the fifth floor.

Something about hospital elevators was always different. They seemed to move so quickly and smoothly. The doors opened and she stepped out into a corridor crowded with gowned nurses and attendants. She followed the signs toward the room number she sought, Alex's gun heavy inside her purse.

"A woman I care deeply about."

That's what Daniels had said. Why should he be allowed to care about anyone? All he'd done was destroy everything she'd worked for. And though she could do nothing about the interference of the Knights of the Golden Circle, Senator Danny Daniels could be dealt with.

A sign indicated that Stephanie's Nelle's room was around the next corner. She approached, turned left, then stopped, retreating out of sight. Ahead, Daniels stood in the hall talking to another man.

Good.

He was here.

She risked a peek and watched.

After a few moments the man left Daniels and headed her way. She drifted back, spotted an open doorway for one of the patients' rooms, and slipped inside. The space was dark and unoccupied. The man she'd seen walked by and headed on. She watched as he disappeared around a corner.

Back at her original position the corridor was clear.

Daniels was nowhere to be seen.

But she knew where he'd gone.

Danny approached the bed. "I'm having your man let Atlanta know that you're going to be fine. I'll tell Cotton when he checks in. We've all been concerned."

"Nice to know you care."

"It's more than that, and you know it. I love you."

She seemed surprised to hear the words. And maybe she should be. They'd been tough for him to say.

But not anymore.

"It's time we be clear with each other," he

said. "I always thought it would be me in that hospital bed. Not you. That's not a sight I want to see again."

Her eyes warmed. "I love you, too, Danny."

The door opened.

He turned, expecting to see a nurse or doctor.

Instead Diane Sherwood entered.

And he did not like the look in her eyes.

Especially when she locked the door.

"Who are you?" Stephanie asked.

Diane removed a gun from her purse and aimed it across the room.

"This ain't good," he muttered.

CHAPTER SEVENTY-SEVEN

New Mexico

Cotton examined the ultralight's square-tipped gray wings, delicate angular tail fins, and rear stabilizers, all connected by a thin skeleton of metal tubing that supported a single seat and controls. The whole thing resembled an enormous aluminum moth. An air-cooled engine, not much more power than a go-cart, and a single propeller provided thrust. He'd flown ultralights before, enjoying more than one Sunday afternoon cruising low over the Øresund. They were available for rental at a local airfield and he'd made it a point to take some lessons and learn. This one was a bit different from the Danish version. A little heavier, equipped for search and rescue.

The Taos County deputies had driven him to a grassy field just outside the Carson National Forest, where they kept a fleet of the flying lawn chairs. He was told that they were the fastest and easiest way to keep tabs

653

on a huge rural county, capable of long range and low altitude, with the ability to land and take off from almost anywhere.

He strapped himself into the seat and started the engine, which fired to life. He lifted his foot from the brake and maneuvered the craft toward the meadow. More throttle revved the propellers to full strength and he picked up speed, then quickly went airborne, scudding off the hard ground.

Rick Stamm had taken what they knew from the available stones and compared it with satellite imagery of the Carson National Forest. Since the park stretched across four counties and encompassed nearly 1.5 million acres, the target had to be narrowed. That information came from Danny Daniels, who'd learned that land once owned by Angus Adams was key. Luckily, the Taos County land records were digitized and available online, which allowed Stamm to isolate the correct 1500 acres of land. Northern New Mexico had once been inhabited by the Anasazi, who'd left behind a slew of adobe ruins. Eventually Europeans claimed everything, the titles all tracing back to land grants by both Spain and Mexico. In 1908 a national forest had been established, named for Kit Carson, with Angus Adams' initial gift forming its central nexus.

Inside his helmet he wore a headset, connected to a radio. He'd reported to Stamm what he'd discovered on the edges of Adams' journal. Amazingly, the church depicted still existed, more a ruin than a functioning building, the other three structures wasted away to their foundations, but still there in the satellite imagery, situated in a triangle as on the Horse Stone.

A river ran beside the four buildings, an offshoot of the nearby Rio Grande, one of many that crisscrossed the Carson forest, and the topography suggested that the church occupied a rise, just as the fore-edge painting had indicated. The folks back at the Smithsonian in DC had even provided GPS coordinates, which he'd entered on the cockpit's compass.

One of the deputies informed him over the radio that the vehicle with the Breckinridges was closing in on the same coordinates. Apparently the older Breckinridge either found the fore-edge painting or already knew where to look. He asked about the old church, but none of the deputies knew much about it. One of the park rangers was an expert on the local history, and the deputies were making contact with him.

He climbed to five hundred feet and admired the rugged mass of terrain. All around him were dark-brown contours of mountains, fissured sweeps of plateaus, green valleys, and endless stands of spruce, aspen, fir, and pine. The sun began to creep above the eastern horizon, casting crisp-edged shadows, slowly lighting the Sangre de Cristo Mountains with their namesake reddish hue.

The blood of Christ.

He suddenly felt a connection with Angus Adams, who'd lived amid this raw, undisturbed beauty. A landscape devoid of people. Not a speck of civilization in sight as far as he could see. Back then it would have been even more isolated.

The cyclic control stick moved between his legs, his feet resting on rudder pedals. He worked them both in unison, keeping the craft steady. He loved flying, particularly this kind — which was about as close to being a bird as a person could get. But it was a noisy experience, the engine whining loud behind him.

"We have some more information," a voice said in his ear. "The church has been there since the 18th century, but it suffered a lot of damage during an earthquake in the 1920s. It's been a partial ruin ever since. Hikers use it as a reference point since it sits high. It's fairly isolated and no one gives it much thought. There are a few hundred more just like it scattered all across New Mexico."

He hadn't heard what he really needed.

"What was it called?"

"It's had a few names, no one knows which one is right. We call it *Pasto al Norte*."

Which he immediately recognized from the

Horse Stone.
   Shepherd of the North.
   Good enough for him.

Cassiopeia stood outside the car, her hands still bound, but at least she was in brisk morning air. They were high in forested mountains, parked among the trees about fifty meters off the highway. Proctor was out, too, stretching his legs, clearly waiting for something. A cigarette dangled at a raffish angle from his mouth. Silence reigned around them. They'd been waiting for nearly half an hour, dawn steadily arriving in the eastern sky.

   She heard the growl of a car engine that drew closer, headlights cutting a jagged path through the trees.

   Another vehicle appeared and pulled to a stop.

   Two men emerged.

   One older, the other young. Proctor shook hands with the older man, who introduced the younger as his son, Grant.

   She made the connection. Grant Breckinridge. Who'd hired and sent the three men to Morse's bee house.

   "Is this our federal agent?" the older Breckinridge asked.

   "Cassiopeia Vitt," Proctor said.

   The older man pointed a finger at her. "I suspect she may be the reason we lost that gold in the truck."

"We can only hope." She was pushing her luck with the sarcasm and wondered how long her usefulness would last. They would kill her the moment she was no longer needed, which might not be all that far away.

Proctor finished his smoke. Then he and Grant opened the trunk of the car that had brought her from Arkansas.

"It's good to be back," the old man said, studying the ever-brightening sky and sucking deep breaths of the clean air.

The trunk slammed shut.

Proctor returned, shouldering an automatic rifle. Grant carried a pick and shovel, along with a backpack.

"Let's go find that stone," Breckinridge said.

She'd already surmised that there was nowhere for her to run. So she had no choice but to cooperate. Some feeling in her arms and legs had returned, though her tied wrists and shoulders hurt. The old man led the way into the trees, followed by Grant, then her, with Proctor at the rear.

A new sound disturbed the silence.

Like a high-pitched whine.

Constant.

Far away.

But drawing closer.

CHAPTER SEVENTY-EIGHT

Diane surveyed the scene before her. A woman, about her age, lying in a hospital bed, tubes and wires in and out of her. The former president of the United States stood beside the bed, glaring at her with a look she did not appreciate.

"Is this why your marriage failed?" she asked Daniels. "You chastised me? Judged me? But you're no better."

"I never said I was."

She aimed the gun straight at him. The woman in the bed reached out with her hand and grasped Danny's arm in a loving gesture, one that signaled a silent desire to stand with him. She had no such comforts. No one stood with her.

"I never realized how sick you really are," Daniels said.

"I would have been fine if you'd stayed out of my business. But you couldn't do that. You're such a damn hypocrite. Just like Alex. Both of you are no better than me. I met his mistress, too."

"And where did that happen?"

"In Alex's apartment. I found her there, cleaning up, as though she owned the place. I shot her. Twice."

She enjoyed the shock she saw on Daniels's face.

"Did you kill her?"

She shrugged. "I hope so."

Danny had a healthy respect for the gun aimed at him, since its holder was clearly disturbed. No telling what she might do. Hearing that Taisley had been shot ripped his gut. A lot of people were paying a heavy price for all that was happening. He needed to see about her. But he felt Stephanie's hand clasped to his right wrist, the alternating pressure in her grip telling him, *Be careful, don't be foolish.*

He dare not risk a look down at the bed.

Instead he kept his gaze locked on the crazy woman.

With a gun.

Diane said, "My father was a great man. He was smart and highly respected. He headed one of the finest museums of the world. On his deathbed he asked me to finish what he started."

"Looking for the vault?"

"The knights talk like that gold belongs to

them. It doesn't. They were common thieves. That treasure belongs to whoever finds it."

"A man is dead because of that treasure. Stephanie is lying here, in this bed, thanks to that treasure. Another woman may be dead in Alex's apartment. Hasn't enough blood been spilled?"

She resented his moralizing. "This is about you and me."

Daniels nodded. "I get that. You murdered Alex."

"And what makes you say that?"

"I watched the video. I suspect you have, too."

She wondered about the comment. "The knights contacted you?"

"Oh, yes. I talked to the commander himself, who told me all about you and Alex. They've been watching you both. Then he showed me the video. There was no need to kill him."

"You and Alex are just alike," she said, voice rising. "Both so smug in your positions of power, accustomed to people jumping when you speak. Alex was a fool. Just like you. Neither one of you ever took a tough stand in your life."

He seemed to resent the insult. "I was twice president."

"And what did you accomplish? What will history record of Danny Daniels' time in the White House? How many compromises did you make to get what you wanted? How many interests did you appease?"

"Enough to get the job done."

His lack of fear infuriated her.

"And enough to find my friend's killer."

Danny had no intention of backing down. If this nut shot him, then so be it. But he had not forgotten Stephanie's warning of just a few minutes ago about it hurting. So avoiding that would be better. "Diane, this is all over. Don't make it worse."

"Screw you, Danny. And screw those damn knights. My father hated them, and so do I."

"Then why wear a cross and circle?"

"That was my brother's idea. He wanted us all to feel part of the great movement. Of course, women were never allowed as knights. We were too stupid. Too delicate. Too precious to be involved. I'm sure it's the same even today. An all-boys club. But it was me who taught Vance what to do."

Stephanie's grip on his arm tightened and he agreed with her. Diane was rapidly losing control of what few faculties remained.

"What are you going to do about Vance?" Diane asked.

"He'll be stopped. This morning."

"Not if you're dead."

And his respect for the gun multiplied. This woman had killed once. Maybe twice. Why not again? He'd never cared for her. She'd always been distant and sullen. The one time she did approach him for a favor — to have Alex elevated to the Supreme Court — he'd refused. But through all of that he'd never suspected the depth of her instability, the breadth of her resentment, and the height of her ambition. She was clearly willing to do anything to accomplish her goal. She chastised him for compromise. But her version of "standing your ground" was to murder her opponent. Unfortunately, that option had never been available to him.

"I hate you," she spit out. "I hate you with every fiber in my being."

But he saw something in the eyes, something that contradicted her words. "No, you don't hate us."

Her pupils flashed hot.

"You hate yourself."

CHAPTER SEVENTY-NINE

Cassiopeia was led across a rope bridge that spanned a swiftly moving shallow river about twenty meters wide. The sun had risen enough to brighten the other bank, where she could see a stone tower rising above the treetops. It sat on a rise, three other sets of ruins below and off to the left. Once back on solid land, they climbed the rise to the tower and she saw the ruin of what had once been a large adobe church. The whine in the distance persisted, and she wondered about its source. Her three captors seemed to ignore it, the older Breckinridge focused on the ruins. The walls still stood, the windows devoid of glass, the front door gone. Some of a wooden roof remained, and she spotted more recent attempts at shoring up from lumber formed into braces.

"Pasto al Norte," the older man said.

Her Spanish was excellent. Shepherd of the North.

"This church has been here a long time,"

Breckinridge said. "But it once had another name. *La Capilla del Psalms.* The Chapel of the Psalms."

She checked its orientation and saw that it did indeed sit on the north side of the river. "Does this connect with the stones?"

"You know about those?" he asked.

"I saw the Witch's Stone and was told there are four more."

"Grant, if you please."

The younger man removed his backpack. Inside, wrapped in a towel, was a heart-shaped stone with etchings similar to what she'd seen in Arkansas. The older man studied the carvings, which she saw were on both sides.

"This is the Heart Stone, one of the five. It's vital to finding the vault since, without it, you'd wander these mountains for decades looking for the end point."

The old man slammed the stone down hard to the ground, atop a scab of exposed rock that poked from the dry earth.

It shattered into dust and pieces.

With the sole of his shoe he pummeled the larger bits into gravel.

Grant was in shock. He'd been hoping his father would have a change of mind. "You just said without that stone, no one can find the vault. How do you ever plan to do that?"

"I don't. Not right now, anyway. But I'll

665

make arrangements for others to be able to find it."

"You know where it is?"

His father nodded. "Of course. I'm its sentinel. And as I said, son, your greed is why you can never be one of us. We're caretakers. Nothing more. That gold is not ours to take."

He'd had enough. "That gold is for whoever gets it first."

"That's where you're wrong," his father said. "The knights have always, and will always, protect it from people like you."

"You had no intention of paying me anything."

"Not at all."

Now he knew why he'd been brought along, and he was in a quandary. No weapon. Out in the middle of nowhere with another man toting an automatic rifle. The woman could be an ally, since she probably had no idea who he was or what he'd done. Which he might be able to use to his advantage long enough to secure his freedom.

Of one thing he was sure.

She was not the only one whose life was in danger.

Cassiopeia sensed a clear division between father and son. The whine of the distant engine had waned, as if it had headed off in another direction.

"Follow me," Breckinridge said.

They entered the old church. The fieldstone was in bits and pieces. The walls that still stood were all bare brick. A raised dais at the far end suggested where an altar had once stood. Thanks to most of the east wall being gone, sunlight illuminated the interior.

"In the late 19th century, a man named Angus Adams owned this church and all the land around it," Breckinridge said.

Cotton's ancestor.

"Adams was a clever soul. He created the vault and devised the entire map of the stones. He served the Order with great distinction and here, on this site, he hid the Alpha Stone."

"How do you know all this?" she asked. "I thought it was a secret."

"I spent a lifetime learning the details, but I had access to information no one else possessed. The Smithsonian has been looking into the stones for a long, long time. I suspect it wanted the gold for itself. And Adams might have wanted to have it. Why else would he have given the key and his journal back to Joseph Henry?"

She had no idea what he was referring to, but the son seemed to understand.

"I managed to purge the Smithsonian records," the old man said. "Though I will say, my dear son here and his girlfriend gave going behind me their best shot. I understand you saw the Witch's Stone. Do you remember the images?"

She recalled the progression of symbols that ran in a defined line, emanating from the robed figure, starting with a rectangle with a cross.

"This church is the first symbol. The cross in a rectangle," she said.

"Correct."

Then there was a *4* inside a heart followed by an *8, N,* and *P.*

"The letters and numbers refer to a journal that Adams created and left with the Smithsonian. If you had that journal, then the Horse Stone becomes the key. Show her."

Grant brought his cell phone close and displayed an image of another stone, one with a large horse.

"The three dots in the upper left are the three ruins below. Take a look out that window."

She stepped over and peered out. From their vantage, down through the trees, she saw a cairn amid the triangle formed by the three aged structures.

"It's an old horse trough," the old man said. "Hence the horse on the stone. The numbers *1847* were once engraved on the trough, as they were once engraved here in the church. It's significant to the former name of this place. The Chapel of the Psalms. The only psalm with a 47th verse is Psalm 18. Do you happen to know what it says?"

She shook her head.

"*He is the God who avenges me, who subdues nations under me.* Quite fitting, wouldn't you say?"

She said nothing.

"Angus Adams built the trough," Breckinridge said, "and incorporated the Alpha Stone into its construction. A conical cap once sat atop it, resembling the robed figure on the Witch's Stone. I removed it when I found the Alpha Stone in 1972. I then decided to move the stone up here, which I did alone one night. Back then, this area was far more remote and much less visited."

"Why not just destroy it?" she asked, "as you just did with the other one?"

"Because back then I still thought it might be useful. Now I realize I was wrong."

Breckinridge walked to one corner of the church and knelt on the fractured floor. An assortment of rectangular-shaped tiles, in varying sizes, were bound by dirt joints from which weeds and grass sprang. The old man motioned for the pick and had his son work the joints around one piece until he was able to work it free. Proctor kept an eye on both her and outside. Grant bent down and turned the slab over, exposing etchings on the back side.

The old man brushed away the dry soil.

He pointed to a squiggly line running from one side to the other. "That's the river below. And here" — he motioned to a cross just beneath the river, beside what looked like a toaster — "that's this church. The arrow points to the first marker. Cross the river and follow the next seventeen and you come to the vault."

Cotton flew over a low ridge. The brisk air rushing past him was an effective cooling system, clearing his mind. He'd passed several other ridges, each with a saddle of rock where the ground would rise, then drop, then rise again like a roller coaster. He was following the GPS and, atop the next ridge, he spotted the ruins.

Below, off to the west, he saw two cars parked beneath drooping trees in a narrow glen, then a river and a rope bridge. He worked the control stick and aimed the ultralight toward the high ground and the church, seeing for himself the triangle formed by three ruins below the church and another small structure at their center.

He decided a close pass would be best.

So he dropped to barely three hundred feet.

Cassiopeia heard the engine approaching and realized it was a small aircraft of some sort. She was hoping that the pilot was someone she knew — and something told her that it was. Proctor's interest was likewise piqued and he rushed outside, his head up searching the morning sky. The two other men followed, the son motioning for her to lead the way.

Approaching from the south was a small ultralight, barely a hundred meters in the air, bearing down on the church.

"Take him down," Breckinridge ordered.

Proctor unshouldered his automatic rifle and moved to a position where he'd have a clear shot with heavy rounds.

That would do some damage.

CHAPTER EIGHTY

Diane resented Daniels' psychoanalyzing. The last thing she needed, or wanted, was his opinion. "Shut up. I hate you."

"And I believe her," Stephanie Nelle muttered.

"Do you really care for this idiot?" she asked the woman in the bed. "You couldn't possibly. He's a fake. A phony. A nothing. What has he ever actually accomplished, besides getting himself elected?"

A timid knock came to the door.

Then another.

"Ask them what they want," she said to Daniels.

"Go screw yourself."

She cocked the gun, its distinctive click telling him that she did not appreciate his refusal. Then she readjusted her aim toward Stephanie Nelle. Daniels moved into her line of fire.

"I can shoot you, then her. It's not a problem."

Another knock, this time more decisive.

"What is it?" Daniels called out.

"You must open this door," a female voice said. "We have to see about Ms. Nelle."

"She's fine. We need a few moments alone."

"I insist that you open the door."

Her gaze told Daniels what he had to do.

"And I'm telling you to back off. I'll open it in a moment."

"I can get a key," the voice said.

She shook her head.

"Please don't do that," he said. "It will only be a few more moments."

Time was running out.

She had to finish this.

Stephanie lay in bed watching Danny's response to the threat. Diane Sherwood had taken a serious chance coming here, but this woman had reached the end of her rope. She'd murdered her husband and God knew who else. Now she was threatening to kill her and a former president of the United States. Consequences were no longer a factor in her decision making.

Her left hand had been gripping Danny's right arm, but he'd broken free when the gun had been aimed her way. Now he stood directly in the line of fire, a shield between her and a bullet.

He had guts, she'd give him that.

Her right hand, though, still held the

control panel that allowed anyone in the bed to call for a nurse or switch the room's lights on and off. The problem was knowing which button to push without looking. It lay away from where Diane Sherwood stood, so it was not visible. She could push all of the buttons until the lights extinguished, but she was afraid that it would be as much of a surprise to Danny.

Which might get him shot.

She was proud of herself for thinking so clearly, especially having been out of it for so long.

But the adrenaline was flowing.

Danny kept himself between Diane and Stephanie.

"Okay, I got rid of 'em," he said. "What now?"

Unfortunately, more than enough air distance existed between him and the gun for Diane to react to anything he might do. If he dove out of the way the bullet could find Stephanie. So he stood still, just as he would when a nine-point buck approached through the trees on a cold winter's day.

Good things usually came to those who waited.

Diane's mind reeled with so many troubling thoughts. Like that final day when she confronted Alex, and the knight at the National

Mall. Now another man stood in her way.

Why must that always be?

Another knock came.

"We insist you open the door."

This time a male voice.

Another man interfering.

Enough.

She fired a shot into the ceiling.

"Go away," she screamed. "Now."

Danny froze.

He'd considered rushing her, but Diane had quickly brought the gun back, aimed at him. At least everyone outside was now alerted to the actual problem. Whatever good that would do. Stephanie's hand returned to his right wrist and squeezed twice.

A signal?

What was she up to?

Stephanie gripped the bedside controls. If she could plunge the room into darkness it might give Danny the moment of advantage needed to wrestle away the gun. The problem came with her not being able to tell him the plan. She hoped her touch on his wrist was enough to let him know that she was about to do something.

Diane Sherwood remained enraged. But her eyes seemed more sad than angry, and really confused.

"Get on your knees," she told Daniels.

Danny did not move.

"I won't say it again."

The command had been deliberately uttered in a low voice, as if challenging him to decline.

"Do it," Stephanie told him, releasing her grip on his arm.

He glanced down at her and she motioned with her eyes to the right. His gaze followed her lead and he saw the control in her hand. He didn't know exactly what she intended. But at least he knew she was going to act.

He slowly dropped to his knees.

She was about to kill the lights when she noticed something behind where Diane Sherwood stood.

The latch knob for the door's lock was slowly turning.

Someone was using a key to gain access.

Diane finally had Danny Daniels exactly where she wanted him. She stepped close and nestled the gun to his forehead. He stared up at her with not a hint of fear. She'd forced him to his knees, but he was telling her with his eyes that he was not submitting.

Which only enraged her more.

And gave her the courage to pull the trigger.

CHAPTER EIGHTY-ONE

Cotton flew close to the forlorn ruins. The church at the crown of the crest commanded rolling acres in every direction that his family had once owned. More had survived of it and the other three ruins than he expected, mostly partial walls supporting sections of clay roofs. Great old trees stood watch close to the foundations. The scene was definitely not as pastoral and complete as the fore-edge painting had depicted, but this was the same place. He was coming in low and close when he saw four people emerge from the church.

Three men.

And a woman.

Cassiopeia.

Thank goodness.

But he immediately noticed that her arms were stretched behind her back, as if her wrists were bound. One of the men disappeared into the trees, while the other two stood near Cassiopeia. He noticed that one was old, the other younger.

The two Breckinridges.

He'd make a pass then find a place to land.

He could do little from up here.

Cassiopeia assessed the situation and made her choices. Proctor was readying his rifle, his focus on the ultralight that was fast approaching. The old man had removed a pistol, keeping it trained on her, but she noticed that he could not keep his gaze from drifting skyward. Grant stood to her right, unarmed, also studying both Proctor and the aircraft.

Proctor had assumed a position behind one of the thick tree trunks, most likely planning on revealing himself when the ultralight was too close to veer away. That wasn't a fighter jet up there. Its maneuverability was severely limited, and its speed was a snail's pace. If that was Cotton, and she believed it to be, she had to do something.

"Stay real still," the old man said to her, the gun aimed her way.

Right.

Keep dreaming.

The ultralight was a few hundred meters away, coming in low. Proctor dashed from his hiding place to the center of the clearing, knelt, and aimed his rifle. Her right leg swung up and her boot caught the old man square in the chest. He slumped forward and she kicked the gun from his grasp. Not waiting a second, she pivoted and slammed the heel of her right boot into the son's crotch, doubling him over.

Proctor faced away, which gave her a few moments of freedom.

He started firing.

Rounds spit from the short barrel and headed skyward.

Cotton saw a fleeting shape, set apart from the landscape. There, then gone. Then back. Among the trees.

A man with a rifle.

He watched as Cassiopeia took out the two men standing beside her.

The rifleman had knelt and aimed skyward.

He heard shots.

Rounds whined by him.

He yanked the control stick and tried to make a quick turn, but he heard something snap as more rounds rocketed past.

Cassiopeia raced forward and slammed into Proctor.

His firing stopped.

He rolled on the ground and was preparing to pounce, but she was one step ahead of him, hammering her boot into his jaw, sending him back down. She had no time to hang around since it would be impossible to contain these three with her hands behind her back.

So she ran.

And heard overhead the sickening choke of the ultralight's engine.

Cotton had zero feel or pressure in the joystick, and moving it in any direction accomplished nothing. The craft's nose dipped and everything shook from turbulence.

Then, suddenly, control returned.

The engine kept sputtering and he assumed one or more of the rounds had found its mark, so he shut the motor down and used the rudder and aileron to fly on the wind. Apparently the horizontal stabilizer was gone, its cable perhaps snapped. He was flopping in the morning air, trying to find some measure of flight control. Pressing the right rudder pedal yielded no response. Luckily, the left one seemed to be working and he used it to draw the craft closer to the ground. Panic started in his toes and worked its way up his legs, and it took effort to fight it off.

Treetops were fast approaching.

He decided to use them to break his fall. If he was lucky he might be able to skip across a few, then settle down into one.

If not, the end of this flight was definitely going to leave a mark.

Grant fought the rise of nausea in his throat, vertigo turning his legs to rubber. The bitch had slammed her foot into his crotch and it hurt like hell. He fought the pain and brought himself to his knees. Proctor was recovering, too, beginning to stand, looking around for his rifle.

"Go get her," his father yelled from the ground. "Kill her."

Proctor found the weapon and ran off.

His father seemed woozy.

Then Grant remembered the gun.

Which Vitt had kicked away.

He searched the dry earth and found it, crawling over and quickly taking hold. He had the Alpha Stone, and though the Heart Stone was gone, images of it had been taken and somehow he'd get his hands on them. And now he knew the starting point. Right here. Diane could figure out the rest. She was plenty smart, and would do anything for him. Sure, he'd broken into the apartment and stolen the key, but that could be explained by using his father as an excuse. Which was actually the truth. What had his father said to him?

"I'm not you. I actually use my brain."

Not this time, old man.

He aimed the gun.

Comprehension dawned in his father's eyes. But there was nothing left to be said between them.

So he shot him in the head.

Chapter Eighty-Two

Danny wondered why Stephanie had delayed acting. He was in a precarious position, one he did not particularly like. The hard end of the gun's barrel boring into his forehead.

Then he saw the answer past Diane.

The latch for the door lock was turning.

Diane could not see what was happening, but he had a clear view as the door eased open and he saw the face of the Magellan Billet agent from outside.

"Not such a big man now, are you?" Diane said.

The gun barrel nudged his head back.

This was going to be close.

Stephanie spied the face of her agent and immediately lifted the control above her legs so he could see what she was about to do. Diane Sherwood had no idea that someone had gained access to the room. There was no telling what she might do, and that gun to Danny's head gave both her and her agent pause.

She sent a message with her eyes.

Finesse this. No power play.

And her agent nodded, signaling that he understood.

A moment of unexpectedness should work.

So she hit the switch.

Diane could not believe her good fortune. She'd managed to force Danny Daniels right where she wanted him.

Time to kill him.

Should she kill the woman, too?

Why not?

The lights in the room extinguished.

Stephanie heard a shot and quickly repressed the button on the control box.

The lights sprang back on.

She had no idea what to expect, as the last thing she'd seen was the gun at Danny's forehead. But it was Diane Sherwood who lay sprawled on the carpet, a bleeding wound in her chest. Her agent was in the room, gun drawn. But the threat had ended.

Danny reached down, checked for a pulse, and shook his head. "A lot of demons crawled around in that woman's head."

He stood.

"Seal this room off," she told her agent. "And call the police."

The man nodded and left, closing the door.

"I can't say that I have any sympathy for

her," Danny said. "She killed my friend and got what she deserved."

She did not disagree.

"I have to see about Taisley. The police have to be notified. She may need help."

"And you still have another problem," she reminded him, thinking like the head of an intelligence agency.

He glanced at his watch.

"It's a little before 9:00 A.M. I agree. I'll deal with Lucius Vance, too."

Cassiopeia raced headlong through the trees, down the incline past the horse trough. She heard a gunshot, but no round came her way. Her options were limited. She had only a minor head start on the three men back at the church. The whine from the ultralight had stopped and she wondered if Proctor had shot it down. Unfortunately, she could not worry about that at the moment.

Getting gone was her priority.

She spied the rope bridge back toward the cars, but those would be of no help with her hands bound behind her back. The bridge itself was far too exposed given Proctor and his rifle.

But the heaving river.

That might be her best bet.

She'd noticed earlier that it seemed shallow and carried a current fast enough to whisk her downstream and out of rifle range. She could work with her feet and stay as close to shore as possible to avoid drowning. Risky, for sure. But no less dangerous than her current situation.

She approached the riverbank and spied a drop of ten meters to the water, the pebbly slope eroded and dotted with man-sized boulders, stacked one atop the other with passages here and there. A thick growth of reeds and cottonwoods sprouted everywhere, providing cover but also making the way down more treacherous.

She turned back and spotted Proctor as he emerged from the trees.

He saw her and aimed the rifle.

No choice now.

She dropped over the side and rolled down. Bullets skipped behind her like flung stones. Dust caught in her mouth, nose, and eyes, making her cough. Gravity carried her downward until she hit a boulder. She glanced back up, head spinning. The sky wheeled. The river rushed by a few meters away, past more boulders that towered upward, forming small canyons among the stunted bushes.

Proctor would be on her in a moment.

She eased herself upright, feet scrambling heels-first, and blundered toward the nearest cover. Everything seemed desiccated, almost otherwordly in appearance. More dust filled her throat and she spat it away. Enough rocks now surrounded her that Proctor would have to come down to find her. She scrambled toward the river.

Shots rained down.

Bullets skipped off stone, rock slivers grazing her cheeks.

She stopped her advance.

Sweat bathed her face.

Then she heard it.

A low steady growl.

Looking up, she found its source.

A mountain lion.

Danny left Stephanie's room just as the DC Police and the FBI arrived. Both had been called, the FBI because a U.S. senator was involved. He did not mind the attention. In fact he welcomed it, since Diane's death had played right into his hands.

He'd reported a shooting in Alex's building, which the police were already aware of. A second call back to his cell phone told him that Taisley Forsberg was dead.

Which ripped at his heart.

He'd tried hard to keep her out of it, but failed.

He took a moment and gathered himself, using the composure that decades in public office had taught him.

Stay with the plan.

Get the job done.

The House Rules Committee was scheduled to convene at ten. That gave him forty-five minutes to act. He'd learned a long time ago that politicians were a lot like penguins entering the ocean. A whole horde would go right to the edge, but none would leap into the water until one went first. Then everyone followed. If one hesitated, they all hesitated, and the process started all over. Vance had taken them to the edge and leaped. Now the rest had to decide to follow. Was it clear and inviting, full of fish to eat? Or was there a shark or killer whale waiting to gobble them up? Vance had assured them of a safe ride.

But Danny was about to change that.

He found a quiet corner and dialed his cell phone. His chief of staff had provided him the Speaker's cell phone number just after his visit to the Willard.

The phone rang in his ear.

Once.

Twice.

Then it was answered.

"Who is this?" Vance asked.

"Danny Daniels."

"I guess I shouldn't be surprised you found me again. What could we possibly have to discuss this time?"

"Diane Sherwood is dead."

Silence.

"I'm listening," Vance finally said.

Cassiopeia stood paralyzed.

The big cat weighed at least fifty kilos, lying three meters up on top of a boulder beneath the shade of another. A smug certainty filled the animal's face, maybe a lordly indifference, its impressive paws extended like a harmless house cat's. She forced herself not to move, trying to breathe slow. She knew that wildcats were mainly night hunters and it would not be here now, amid noise and gunfire, if its belly was full. Most likely it had assumed an early-morning perch waiting for something tasty to come along for a drink of water. She'd been told once that moving prey evoked curiosity.

Stillness urged caution.

So never, ever run.

She swallowed drily, too unnerved to even twitch, trying to become accustomed to the predator's proximity. The pounding of her pulse thumped in her ears. Past the rocks, back from where she came, she heard Proctor sliding down the bank, heading her way.

The lion's ear flicked, not against an insect, more as a sign of catching the sound, too. She wondered. Now that the animal was fully alert, would the scent of her own fear distract it from the approaching possibility?

Or would it focus on something easier?

Within sight and reach.

CHAPTER EIGHTY-THREE

Grant headed for where the ultralight had crashed. He needed to deal with its pilot while Proctor killed the woman. Then he'd take care of Proctor. All the bodies could be tossed into the river where they'd head downstream, making it next to impossible to determine where they'd died. The small aircraft had skirted the treetops under no engine and he'd heard the final crashing impact.

He was again in command and on top. Good riddance to his father. He had enough pieces of the puzzle that he was sure Diane could connect the dots. And he had the ceremonial key back in his possession, retrieving it from his dead father. As soon as this was done, he'd get Diane out here. Together they could solve the puzzle and find the vault. The only rub would be the rest of the Order, since he now knew they were out there, watching.

He'd just have to be careful.

Shafts of light stabbed through the lacy canopy overhead. He spotted the wreckage dangling high above in a stately pine. Incredibly, the pilot had managed to avoid crashing to the ground. He approached close and studied the open cockpit. The seat was empty, the harness hanging free, as was a headset that stretched downward, a good twenty feet up in the air.

A helmet lay on the ground.

He came alert.

Where was the pilot?

Cotton had maneuvered the wounded ultralight to a stop, using branches to cushion his descent. It had not been as smooth as he'd wanted and he'd ended upside down, but the ultralight had lived up to its name, finally settling into the treetops. He then managed to ditch his helmet, slip from his harness, and climb down to the ground.

He was armed with a Beretta.

He assumed someone would come his way, so he'd taken a position behind one of the stately pines and watched as a short-haired, younger man approached.

The same guy from Fossil Hall.

Grant Breckinridge.

Just the guy he came to see.

Grant could feel he was being watched. Tall, old-growth trees rose all around him like a

691

natural cathedral, blocking the morning sun, casting long deep shadows. It was similar to the feeling he'd had in Kentucky months ago when he followed the signs in the woods, searching for one of the gold caches. He'd thought then that a sentinel had been stalking, but no one appeared when he found the end of the trail and dug the coins from the ground.

A shot rang out in the distance.

Most likely the woman dying from Proctor's rifle.

He needed to end this.

Cotton watched his prey.

This man had gunned down Stephanie Nelle without remorse. He was concerned about Cassiopeia and the rifle shot he'd just heard.

Not good.

But he kept his position behind the tree and angled himself so that as Breckinridge kept advancing, the trunk stayed between them. He waited until his adversary passed, then stepped out, aimed his weapon, and cocked the hammer.

The click said it all.

Breckinridge stopped but did not turn. "I knew you were here somewhere."

He wasn't impressed. "Drop the gun."

"I recognize the order. You're the same guy from the museum."

"For someone who hears so good, you're not doing as I asked."

"You with the feds?"

"Who else?"

"I thought maybe the Knights of the Golden Circle."

"They're the least of your worries."

He kept the gun aimed. This idiot actually thought he could one-up him. Apparently his spate of good luck had been so good, and so long, that he thought himself invincible. The killing of Martin Thomas, finding the Trail Stone, shooting Stephanie, stealing the Heart Stone. Quite a run, though some of the cards had been stacked in his favor.

He tried one more time.

"Drop. The. Gun."

Grant kept his finger tight on the trigger. He'd have only an instant once he turned. His hope was that this man, though equipped with a weapon, did not have the nerve to pull the trigger. Sure, in the heat of a moment, in reaction to a direct threat, to save their own hides, anybody would shoot. But if he was slow and careful he might be able to tick off a round before this guy knew what hit him. Then Proctor was next. And if he dawdled long enough perhaps Proctor would come looking for him and take care of this problem for him.

He heard the man order him for a second

time to drop the gun.

But he ignored the command.

And slowly started to turn.

Cotton could tell that this guy intended to see how much nerve he possessed. That was the trouble with wise guys. They never knew when to quit.

Breckinridge slowly swung his body around, as if he intended to drop the gun and raise his hands in surrender. The right hand still held the weapon, the left empty and heading upward.

A diversion.

And a poor one at that.

He decided to give him every opportunity, hoping not to be disappointed.

And he wasn't.

Breckinridge swung his right arm up, but never made it level.

One round left Cotton's gun.

The bullet bore a neat hole in Breckinridge's skull, passing right through, exploding a spray of brains and blood outward. Death came in an instant, the body collapsing in a lifeless heap.

He lowered the gun.

"That's for Stephanie."

But he immediately thought of Cassiopeia.

And ran back toward the ruins.

Cassiopeia lay on the rocky soil, the mountain

lion's staring eyes never leaving her, not even as the sound of Proctor approaching through the rock maze grew louder. The big cat heard it, too, tensing with a slight alteration of its shape and readiness, which it released, then built again, slowly rising to its feet.

She did not move a muscle, barely breathing.

"Be a good kitty," she muttered, swallowing, trying to control the tremor in her voice.

She could see no escape from either danger.

All she could do was watch.

Proctor rounded a corner and spotted her, the rifle held ready as by a hunter on safari.

"You saved me the trouble of carrying your body down to the river," he said.

The mountain lion growled.

Proctor heard it, too, and sent a bullet to the rock near the animal's head.

Which sent the cat scurrying away.

"It would be a shame to kill something so beautiful," he said to her. "Unfortunately, the same doesn't apply to you."

Cotton found Frank Breckinridge's body, the old man shot dead. That meant only the one other man and Cassiopeia remained.

But where?

A gunshot cracked.

And not all that far away. Toward the river.

He headed that way, following an uneven gravel path strewn with dead limbs. Overhead a vulture circled, riding the day's first thermals.

An omen?

He hoped not.

Cassiopeia had always wondered when the end would come. She'd tempted death many times, taking risks that most people went out of their way to avoid. Now she'd maneuvered herself into an untenable position, trapped on a riverbank, among a cluster of boulders, a man with a rifle staring her down.

"You do understand," Proctor said. "This is not personal."

"It is to me."

He chuckled. "I suppose it might be."

"My usefulness has waned?"

"I'm afraid so. The pilot of that plane is probably dead and you're about to join him. Then we knights disappear back into the shadows."

If that pilot was Cotton, she had to believe he was okay. And why wouldn't he be? He was Harold Earl "Cotton" Malone. The best man she'd ever known.

So she decided to do something radical.

Something she hadn't done since she was a child.

Cotton heard a scream.

Loud. Piercing.

Nearby.

At the river.

Since Cassiopeia was the only woman he'd seen for miles, it had to be her.

He ran toward it.

Cassiopeia kept up the ruse, feigning fear, buying time.

"I expected a little more courage from you," Proctor said.

"Nobody wants to die."

"No, I suppose not. But your time is here."

"Any way to talk you out of it? Like you said in the diner, women have been known to offer things when cornered."

He shook his head. "Not this time."

He aimed the rifle.

She had regrets, but not all that many. She'd lived life her way, on her terms, and could not complain. There'd been ups, downs, mistakes, misfortunes, and great successes. The one major regret was Cotton. They wouldn't get to finish what they'd started.

Which she hated.

But this fight was over. She could dive in the river, but Proctor would only shoot her. Without arms and hands she'd be little more than a floating duck. Apparently, there was no one around to hear her scream. It had been a calculated move that had not paid off. So in her final moments she dropped the pretense of fear, rose to her feet, and stared the gun down.

"Go ahead. Pull the damn trigger."

"Killing is never easy," he said. "But sometimes it's necessary."

She closed her eyes.

A shot exploded.

But no bullet pierced her body.

Instead Proctor lunged forward as something slammed into him from behind. Then another shot echoed and his head exploded from a high-powered impact. The body pitched from side to side before folding to the rocky ground.

She ran ahead, past the rocks blocking her view, and saw Cotton at the top of the bank. Relief swept through her.

God, she loved that man.

"You okay?" he asked.

"I am now."

She climbed up, kissed him hard, and said, "I thought it was all over."

"Never."

She liked the sound of that. "I was hoping you'd hear that scream."

"Good thing I came along to save your hide."

He was right. Lately, it had been more the other way around. "About time you start repaying the favor."

"I can't argue with that."

He found a pocketknife and freed her bindings. Her arms ached from being in one position for so long, her fingers numb and slow to flex. She stretched them toward the sky.

"What about the Breckinridges?" she asked.

"Both dead."

"Your work?"

"Only for the one that mattered."

"So that about wraps it up?"

"Not exactly," he said.

She knew what he meant.

CHAPTER EIGHTY-FOUR

Carson National Forest
Sunday, May 30

Cotton stood beside the old horse trough, built — he now knew — by Angus Adams. Two days had passed since the carnage. They'd spent yesterday connected by the Internet to the Castle and Rick Stamm, where they'd combined all five stones into a single digital mosaic.

Cassiopeia had shown him the Alpha Stone that Frank Breckinridge uncovered in the church. The five images had all been similarly sized and scaled, just as if the actual stones had been lying side by side. When the Trail and Alpha Stones were placed alongside each other, with the Heart Stone inserted, the line with eighteen markers formed a clear path leading to the center of the heart.

And the vault.

The stones had presented a substantial challenge, one that Angus Adams had surely meant to be difficult. Deliberately misspelled words. Odd phrases. Hidden meanings. Garbled, ungrammatical Spanish. Nothing in any particular sequence. All meant to be interpreted in conjunction with one another. A little bit here and there that collectively added up to the answer.

And the concept had worked.

Where the effects of weathering, erosion, and vandalism had obliterated other maps or signposts, the stones had endured.

With the help of the Smithsonian's natural and American history museums, satellite images were prepared of the topography extending from the church toward the north, across the river, just as the Alpha Stone indicated. Incredibly, the squiggly lines depicted the right canyons, in the right places, the line with eighteen markers carving a path up into the Sangre de Cristo Mountains. Determining distance had been the tricky part, but the dots along the curvy line that ended at the center of the Heart Stone seemed evenly spaced apart, which they'd taken as a clue. In

Adams' time the *varna* was the common unit of measure. About a yard. If that were correct, then comparing the stones with the satellite imagery, the dots on the path lay around five hundred yards apart. Adams had probably tagged that trail with eighteen defined markers, but Cotton doubted many of those still existed — and if they did, finding them could be tricky. Nothing about this quest had been easy, so why would Adams, at its end, have made anything different?

In the end, three possible locations, in differing directions, were identified and GPS coordinates acquired for each.

Danny Daniels and Warren Weston arrived yesterday. The chief justice had been relieved to know that the Breckinridges were both dead, along with Jim Proctor, who had long been one of the knights' bad apples. Both Weston and Daniels wanted to be a part of what was about to happen.

Four horses waited by the trough.

"I haven't ridden in a long time," Daniels said. "But I haven't forgotten how, either."

"I've never ridden a horse," Weston said.

Daniels chuckled. "This ought to be fun to watch."

"My predicaments amuse you, don't they?"

"Actually, they do. Quite a bit."

Daniels had told them what happened with Vance. He'd called the Speaker, started with Diane's death and ended with all he knew.

Then he'd offered a choice. Withdraw the rule change and never bring it up again, or the junior senator from Tennessee, who once was the president of the United States, would hold a news conference where he'd lay it all out again, this time in public, and then they would see how many on the Rules Committee would keep following Vance. Loyalty was one thing, suicide quite another. Nothing ended a revolution quicker than scandal, especially when it involved conspiracy, theft, and multiple deaths.

Not surprisingly, Vance called a halt.

Cotton squatted on his heels and traced a route in the dirt with his finger, showing them the path and what to look for.

"Let's keep our eyes peeled," he said. "What we want will be in plain sight, but difficult to see."

They saddled up and rode toward the first set of coordinates, crossing the river at a low point, downstream from the rope bridge. He'd learned that Adams' ranch house was gone, nothing remaining of the buildings. Rangers were not even sure where they'd been located. Little was known of Adams, as he'd kept to himself, which seemed characteristic. A painter, who became an illustrator, who became a spy, who became a knight of the Golden Circle.

Quite an evolution.

Sunlight blazed on the naked soil, reddish

brown against a cloudless sky. He breathed in the warm waft of dry earth and was glad to be here. They followed the GPS and rode for nearly an hour, the quivering horizon floating like a mirage. A dark sickle-shaped shadow raced across the ground. A few seconds later it returned, sweeping like a pendulum. He stared overhead and saw a hawk, with its spade tail, gliding along the warm currents of the midday air. They'd already spotted several good-sized bucks, running away from them.

The first site they encountered offered nothing in the way of promise. The cliff faces were too high and too sharp.

The same was true of the second site.

But to Cotton's eye, the third dangled possibilities.

It was the farthest from the trough, and a lot of erosion had occurred since Adams' day. Earthquakes had happened here, too. As had flash floods. This land was in motion, but there was also a continuity, which Adams had surely been banking on.

He stared at the sloping face of a steady incline, the weathered, rust-colored soil stretching up several hundred feet. Banks of shale were clear, where the sun, wind, and winter rains had washed the hillside bare. Large boulders littered the way, protruding from the ground like monuments. Clumps of scrub oaks and brush tried to stay alive in the parched soil.

"You see it?" he asked the others.

None of them did.

But he was getting good at this.

Probably those family genes.

"About fifty feet up the incline, that rounded stone."

All of the rocks were sculpted smooth from the wind and weather. But one had caught his eye. He spurred the horse toward a clump of trees and the others followed, swinging around to a different angle. Visible now was a second part of the stone, it too rounded, most of it embedded, but enough was visible to catch the shape

Like a heart.

"*Seek the heart.* That's what the Witch's Stone commanded," he said.

"You think this is the place?" Weston asked.

He dismounted.

"We're about to find out."

Cassiopeia felt better after a couple of nights' sleep, some good food, and seeing Cotton. Learning about his family's connection to the church and the trough had fascinated her. And he'd clearly been intrigued. More so than she'd seen in him for a long time. She liked that his family was important to him.

Cotton looked over at the chief justice. "What do you think? Is it a killer monument?"

She was curious. "You going to explain that one?"

"The Witch's Stone said that the path is dangerous. My grandfather told me about killer monuments."

"Was he a knight?" Weston asked.

Cotton shook his head. "I'm not really sure. I will say, he knew a lot about them."

She watched as Cotton unbuckled his saddlebags and removed two sticks of dynamite and a collapsible shovel. The park service had assured them that this area was restricted and that they would not be disturbed. Having an ex-president and the chief justice of the United States along helped with avoiding the inevitable questions, but a call from the secretary of the interior quelled all debate. Stephanie had briefed President Fox from her hospital bed on everything that had happened, which had brought immediate, high-level cooperation. Especially when the new president learned what the Speaker of the House had been planning.

Weston and Daniels climbed off their horses.

"The heart was a Spanish symbol for gold," Cotton said. "Broken hearts were another matter. Check out that one up there. It's cracked in three places."

"That could simply be from time," Daniels noted.

"It could. But it could also be something

else. Like, *Your heart will be broken, if this warning is not heeded.* Lightning bolts and zigzagged lines were all symbols for a death trap. The Alpha, Heart, and Trail Stones are loaded with those. Get the horses back while Cassiopeia and I set the charges."

She followed him up the incline, feet scrabbling among the loose soil, dust billowing around them. Closer now, the scale of the heart-shaped rock was impressive. It rose over two meters from the ground and had to weigh several tons.

"This rock is pretty obvious," Cotton said, "if you know what you're looking for. Adams had to assume that whoever came looking would be knowledgeable. So it's safe to say he'd plant a trap to hedge his bets."

He dug out an area at the base and nestled two sticks of explosives close to the stone, about halfway down its length.

"And they may not have come with dynamite," he said, examining his work. "This stone is lying at a really odd angle in relation to the slope."

She understood what he meant. "If it were free, the thing would slide down."

He grinned. "That was the whole idea. Hence, a killer monument."

He extended the fuse out about half a meter and found a lighter.

"Get ready to run."

■ ■ ■ ■

Danny watched from fifty yards away as Cotton and Cassiopeia worked on the slope.

"It is a killer monument," Weston muttered. "Do we need to tell him?"

Weston's eyes stayed on the slope. "You were right about him. He knows exactly what he's doing."

Danny was thrilled to be here. Stephanie was recovering and the doctors had said she would be fine. She'd insisted he go, but was standing by for a video report if anything were found. The press had been besieging his Senate office about Diane Sherwood, but he'd stayed silent, saying he had no comment for the moment. Martin Thomas' remains had been returned to his family with the explanation that he'd been the victim of some sort of foul play, his body not found in the tunnel for a couple of days. Everything was being investigated, they were told.

He saw Cotton bend down and light the fuses, then scurry with Cassiopeia down the slope. They arrived just as the explosion filled his eyes, spewing a pall of red dust outward, rock and scree rattling down the hillside like an avalanche.

But the heart-shaped stone had not moved.

CHAPTER EIGHTY-FIVE

Cotton examined the crater left by the explosion. Just as he suspected, beneath the heart-shaped stone lay a mass of gravel. He saw that Weston understood its significance, too.

He reached down and gathered a handful of the loose rock, his ears ringing with excitement. "You dig a pit down into the bedrock about four or five feet, then up, at a forty-five-degree angle under the boulder, making a pivot point. Gravel gets filled in the pit and under the boulder. As you can see, most of the boulder extends over the gravel pit. The whole thing is a giant lure."

"That it is," Weston said. "Someone not fully aware would start digging, thinking the stone marked the entrance. I'm guessing that once they dug down just a little ways, on the underside of the rock, they'd see carvings or symbols. They mean nothing, put there simply to entice them to keep digging. And they would."

"Until they dug enough to release the gravel

under the rock, which acts like ball bearings, with gravity providing a big assist," Cotton said. "Then over the killer monument comes, sliding down, doing its damage. A perfect trap that doesn't get worn out with time. And look at this."

He pointed at a roughly hewn cross, cut deeply into the face of the boulder's underside. And the letter *N*. Neither was a freak of nature, the chisel marks clear. "Adams wanted people to dig on this side. But it's a death trap."

"So where's the entrance?' Cassiopeia asked.

He recalled the Horse Stone and what was below the tail. A double bump. The square *U* meant an entrance.

But two *U*'s had been placed together.

Which meant a double entrance.

Another random piece of the puzzle that meant nothing until it meant everything.

"Simple," he said. "On the other side."

Cotton lit the fuse and ran away for the third time. The second explosion had cracked the massive heart. This one should turn the thing to rubble.

And it did.

He retrieved two more shovels and they all headed back up the slope. He, Cassiopeia, and Daniels dug. Three feet down his blade scraped hard metal. They kept digging, sweeping away the cloying dust, exposing a rectangular iron door, fitted into the slope like the entrance to a house cellar.

"There are no hinges," Daniels said.

Together he and Daniels lifted the cover to reveal a dark niche that stretched deep into the slope. Timber supports stood along the walls and ceiling at the opening, along with the telltale signs of miners' picks. From their packs, each removed a flashlight. Cotton led the way, followed by Cassiopeia.

"You two wait here," he said to Daniels and Weston. "Let's make sure it's clear. There could be more traps, and I don't need two dead or maimed public officials."

"We'll give you five minutes," Daniels said.

He slipped his backpack onto his shoulders and entered, allowing the beam of his flashlight to lead the way. Each step he took was like being in a minefield. Explosions, water traps, landslides, and cave-ins were all possibilities. Gunpowder could also be a problem, and it could still be potent even after a hundred-plus years.

A total cloaking darkness enveloped them, their combined lights only illuminating a few feet. He could walk fairly upright, only his shoulders brushing the sides. Tight, enclosed spaces were not his favorite, but he could see the entrance behind them and still feel the warm air. He rotated the flashlight from wall, to ceiling, to floor. Anticipation clawed at his gut. It was unlikely that this path would be unprotected.

Then he saw it.

And stopped.

Dug into the floor, spanning the narrow corridor from side to side, was a dark chasm. He approached and shone the light down into a pit. A sheet of thin leather had once sheathed the top, probably covered by a thin layer of earth. Something glittered like a coronet of diamonds from the bottom and, after a moment, he realized what it was.

"They tossed glass shards down there," he said. "Lots of it, too. You come by, fall in, get shredded. A dead-fall pit."

Not unlike another trap he recalled from southern France a few years before.

"These people were serious," she whispered.

That they were.

They jumped across.

Two more pits lay ahead, one with the leather still in place, which they collapsed onto itself.

At the end stood an iron grate with a locked gate.

"The route's clear. Let's get them down here," he said.

Cassiopeia headed back to the entrance while he examined the gate. The ceremonial key had been found on Grant Breckinridge's body. He fished the key from his pocket and examined it in the light. The lock on the gate seemed to accept a skeleton key, but its inner workings would surely be corroded. Then again, the climate here was dry, the air in the tunnel free of moisture. He could not blow the gate for fear of destroying the tunnel, and it remained sturdy enough to present a barrier.

So why not.

He inserted the key and turned.

Resistance fought back.

He worked it left and right.

The bolt started to move.

Not much, but he could feel some give. Luckily, he'd thought ahead and, from his backpack, he removed a can of lubricant. The key itself had suggested there might be a lock to deal with at some point, so any help he could give the inner workings would not be a bad thing.

He removed the key and doused the keyhole full of spray.

From behind, he heard the others approaching.

With the key back in, he worked the lock.

More spray.

Finally, the bolt freed.

The others arrived as he was swinging the gate open.

"The ceremonial key worked?" Weston asked.

He nodded. "That and some WD-40 did

the job."

The tunnel extended only for another ten feet, draining into what appeared to be a large room.

"Let's take this slow," he said. "As you saw, there's danger here."

He led the way, finding no more traps.

The others followed.

Combined, their four flashlights illuminated a chamber about thirty feet square and ten feet high. It seemed a natural cave, its size perhaps artificially enlarged, the floor covered in loose soil. Wooden containers of all shapes and sizes and large burlap sacks lay everywhere. Too many to count. All iced with a thick layer of dust and dirt and arranged in a circle around a single table at the chamber's center.

Upon which sat a wooden box.

"Welcome to the vault," he muttered.

"This is amazing," Weston said. "The Order was always comfortable underground, figuratively and literally."

"If all those containers are filled with gold and silver, there's billions of dollars' worth here," Daniels said.

Cotton examined the ground between where they stood and the nearest container. It seemed solid. He stepped ahead, one foot before the other, slow and easy. He approached one of the rawhide sacks and brushed away the dust. He found his pocketknife and cut loose the leather thong tied around the top. The contents spilled to the ground.

Gold pieces, coins, and small bars.

"Quite a sight," Daniels said.

He'd brought a small crowbar, hoping he might get to use it. He found the tool, pried open one of the crates, and saw a bright mass of more gold bars. He lifted one out. Solid and heavy.

"Look there," Cassiopeia said.

He followed her beam and saw a small forge and smelter. He approached and worked the bellows arm. The stiff leather cracked from the unaccustomed pressure. "It seems Adams thought of everything. He did his own smelting, right here."

"What are those?" Daniels asked.

Cotton had not noticed the steamer trunks. But it was hard to take it all in, like on Christmas morning when you rushed downstairs to see what Santa had left, toys everywhere filling your eyes. There were twenty or more of the old trunks. He led the way over to them and opened one.

Inside were stacked with paper, ledgers, and books.

"It's the Confederate archive," Weston said. "The Order was charged with its safekeeping. Hopefully the Order's records are here, too. They haven't been seen since 1865."

"You should see this," Cassiopeia said.

They all walked toward her where the light revealed a dark, leathery thing, vague in color and shaped like an old ball. Then Cotton saw the skull, some of the flesh still there, a chocolate veneer sunk tight against the forehead and down over the nose and chin, the corpse mummified and preserved.

"Any idea who it is?" Daniels asked.

"No telling," he said. "This was a tough business. There were surely casualties."

"Is it Adams?" Danny asked.

"Not likely," Cotton said. "He was the custodian of this place. The one who sealed it tight. So he would have been the last guy out. From what I recall from my grandfather, Adams died around 1900."

"Where is he buried?" Cassiopeia asked.

He had no answer, so he looked at Weston, who said, "I'm sorry. No one knows."

They were all drawn to the table at the center, which they approached with caution as anything so inviting might be bait.

But no traps lay in wait.

On it sat a carved wooden box about a foot long and that much high, the top engraved with words.

A La Muerte del Finado Angus Adams.

On the death of the late Angus Adams.

He tried to hinge open the top, but it was locked shut.

Another keyhole in the front.

"Try it," Weston said.

He found the ceremonial key.

"I've always wondered why the cross and circle was etched into the stem," Weston said. "Perhaps it's for just this lock."

Maybe so.

He inserted the key and felt the cross on the stem connect to something. Surprisingly, the lock turned with minimal resistance. Inside he saw two pieces of parchment with writing.

He lifted them out.

They read.

Life has taught me that the past is irremediable but the future is limitless. The best hope for a restoration to the pristine purity and fraternity of national Union rests on the opinions and character of the men who are to succeed this generation. It is my hope that they may be suited to that blessed work, one that compels them to draw their creed from the fountains of our great political history, rather than the lower stream, polluted as it was by self-seeking place hunters and sectional strife. In my old age I have come to learn that in any quest for a more perfect Union, the Founders intended for us to resolve our differences with words, not bullets. Such a shame that so many died to remind us of that point.

I have proudly served as a knight of the

Golden Circle. My individual charge was to protect the records and wealth that now surround you. Nearly all of the men who fought in the late great war between the states are gone, the remainder to fade away in the few short years to come, myself included. No new revolution looms, nor is one likely to ever come. The Union is restored and, by the grace of God, it will never be challenged again.

My hope is that the reader of these words has come from that hallowed institution of knowledge on the Mall, that Castle as it came to be known. I spent some of my happiest years painting there. How ironic that it took an Englishman to seed its creation, as nothing seems more American than the Smithsonian Institution. I have watched and marveled at its accomplishments. The advancements it has led in astronomy, geography, meteorology, geology, botany, zoology, anatomy, and natural history. Its faithfulness to the charge to promote all knowledge, not just the popular or practical, without pride or prejudice, learning for the simple sake of learning. I would have so loved to serve as one of its regents, but such an exalted position is not meant for a spy. Long ago I left what clues I could with Secretary Henry, hoping that one day either he or his successor would find this secret place. If the reader of these words is from the Castle then it seems only appropriate that both the records of the Confederate States of America, created through the honest work of good men, and all of this wealth, ill begotten and tainted as it is, be taken by the Smithsonian Institution for the benefit of all. In the event that this cache has been found by knights, I order you to likewise bestow all that you see herein to the Smithsonian and, as the last of the generation that created your cause, to abandon any fight, support a unified United States, and obey your oath of allegiance by doing as I have commanded.

Cotton Adams
October 6, 1897

"Seems your ancestor had many regrets," Daniels said to him. "And, Warren, it seems the legend was right. There is a lost order, a final command, but probably not what you imagined."

"Not even close."

"Did Adams really think that whoever found this would do as he says?" Cassiopeia asked.

"If it was knights," Weston said, "absolutely. That's what the whole fight has been about, internally. A fundamental disagreement on what those original knights wanted us to do."

"Now you know," Daniels said. "What will your members think?"

"Our disagreements just ended."

"Adams hit the nail on the head," Daniels said. "All this should go to the Smithsonian."

"That might be harder than you think,"

Weston noted. "We're on federal land. This gold belongs to the United States of America."

"I don't think that's goin' to be a problem," Daniels said. "Thankfully, the Speaker and I are like this." He held up two fingers nestled tight together. "I'm sure he's figured out by now that I own him. Lucky for him I'm a benign dictator, but I'll make sure he gets a bill through the House, which I'll get through the Senate. You'll definitely get the records. And you might not get all the gold, but you'll get a good chunk. Lucky for us, two Smithsonian operatives found it."

Cotton surveyed the room one more time. "There are billions of dollars here."

"Which the Smithsonian can put to good use," Weston said.

"And the Knights of the Golden Circle?" Cassiopeia asked. "What becomes of them?"

"We'll do what Alexander Stephens, Adams, and many others suggested a long time ago. Work within the law, and try to convince a majority of the people we're right." But a shadow of annoyance darkened Weston's eyes. "And we'll finance it ourselves, without this hoard."

The chief justice touched the parchment. So did Daniels and Cassiopeia. A moment of unspoken communion passed among them.

Sealing the deal.

Cotton asked, "Mind if I keep the document?"

A pride of ownership laced his inquiry. He felt a deep connection with the man who'd written it. A spy who fought against the Union but who, in the end, saw the error of his way.

"It rightly belongs to you," Daniels said.

Cotton caught the warmth in Cassiopeia's brown eyes, clear and innocent as a child's. She grasped his arm in a soft embrace.

"I'm heading outside to call Stephanie," Daniels said.

"I'll go with you," Weston said. "I have some calls to make, too."

They left.

He stood and kept soaking in the chamber. A few years before, he'd finally made peace with his dead father, settling issues that had lingered since he was ten years old. Now he'd dealt with another ancestor. One he'd never before known how much he resembled. Not only did they look alike, but they had the same nickname. Even the same profession.

"You okay?" she asked.

His mind roiled in turmoil, stunned by the magnitude of the find. But there was a force about this place, a pull that seemed alive and animate.

One he liked.

Tension bled from him.

His job was done.

"You ready to go home?" he asked.
She nodded. "Your place or mine?"
That meant either France or Denmark.
He smiled.
"Surprise me."

WRITER'S NOTE

The travel associated with this book happened over time. A few years ago Elizabeth and I made a trip to rural Arkansas, where we discovered its hidden beauty. We've also visited western North Carolina and eastern Tennessee on several occasions. The additional trips taken especially for this novel were all to Washington, DC, where we were shown all of the nooks and crannies of the Smithsonian's many museums. It's a fascinating behind-the-scenes world, one that has been heavily incorporated into this story.

Time to separate fact from fiction.

The great Smithsonian fire of 1865, described in the prologue, happened. A mistake repairing a flue, as described in chapter 59, remains the official explanation for its cause. Everything relative to the fire outlined in the prologue happened. We know these details thanks to several internal Smithsonian reports. My addition to the chaos was the presence of Angus Adams, the key, a field journal, and the Union captain. But the double-action revolver that makes an appearance was a cutting-edge weapon for the time, and the gathering at Navy Secretary Gideon Welles' home did happen during the Civil War.

The Knights of the Golden Circle (chapters 12, 14) existed, starting sometime in the 1850s and finally fading near the turn of the 20th century (chapter 26). It was the largest, most successful subversive organization in American history (chapters 12, 28, 40). Tens of thousands were members. Interestingly, historians tend to ignore it, though the Order's plans for a southern empire, a golden circle, were real (chapters 12, 25). The meeting at the Greenbrier resort in 1859 happened, and the rules booklet exists (chapter 12). The knights' motto was simple: *To maintain the Constitution as it is, and to restore the Union as it was.* Their odd handshake and secret words of greeting are factual (chapter 12), but connecting the cross and circle to the knights is purely my invention (prologue, chapter 8).

Most of the official records from the Confederacy did, in fact, disappear in the days before Richmond fell, and to this day they have never been found (chapter 85). Those vanished documents included most of the records on the Knights of the Golden Circle, so we will never know the full extent of its reach.

The treasure hunt Malone engages in (chapter 1) is based on an actual search that utilized similar physical clues. The Knights of the Golden Circle did in fact bury large hoards of gold throughout the South and left natural markers in the woods as described in chapters 1, 14, and 22. Most of that wealth was acquired from theft and looting, some even by Jesse James, whom many believe was a knight (chapter 22). James' and others' countless robberies may actually have been part of an organized, postwar terror campaign the knights waged on Reconstructionists. An excellent book on the subject is *Shadow of the Sentinel*, by Warren Getler and Bob Brewer.

The danger that Malone experiences in chapter 1 is likewise real. The warning Martin Thomas received while in Arkansas with a hanging effigy and spent shell casings happened in 1993 (chapter 16), and the term *huntin' cows*, as used in chapter 22 for killing potential treasure seekers, is from the accounts of men who would know. Do sentinels still exist? No one knows for sure. But, when they did, they were compensated from paycheck holes as detailed in chapter 24. Many say that a fortune in gold, hidden long ago by the knights, is still out there waiting to be found. To this day, only a tiny fraction of the Order's wealth has been located.

The five stones that are referenced throughout (including their images) are the Peralta Stones, which are shrouded in controversy. No one knows when they were discovered or where. The originals don't even exist, only copies. Legend says they point the way to the Lost Dutchman's Mine in Arizona. But who knows? Currently, they can be seen at the Arizona Museum of Natural History in Mesa, Arizona. All of the symbolic interpretations regarding the stones are part mine and part based on what others believe the lines and letters and numbers represent. Since nothing definitive is known about these stones, and no one has ever deciphered them, they seemed tailor-made for fiction.

This novel is loaded with real places: The Ouachita National Forest (chapters 1, 3, 5, 6), Carson National Forest (chapter 77), and Blount County, Tennessee (chapters 2, 7) are faithfully recounted. The abandoned mine in chapter 30 is based on real ones that still exist in Arkansas. The Vice President's Room in the Capitol is there (chapter 39). The Dirksen Office Building (chapter 41), the gym in the Russell Office Building (chapter 56), and the Willard Hotel, along with its famed Willard Room, exist. All that happened at the Willard Hotel throughout its history, including the supposed invention of the term *lobbying,* is true (chapter 44). The disparaging comments justices made about the Supreme Court building quoted in chapter 70 are factual. The National Air and Space Museum (chapter 51) and the geography and layout of all the Smithsonian buildings was kept as close to reality as possible, with only a few minor variations. Fossil Hall (chapter 35) is currently undergoing a total renovation. The Permian reef exhibit was inside for over two decades, but has now been dismantled (chapter 35). The Lincoln Memorial (chapter 66) and World War II Memorial, including Eisenhower's engraved quote, are there for all to see (chapter 68).

The feud between Jefferson Davis and Alexander Stephens happened (prologue, chapter 13). Stephens wanted to avoid war and eventually make peace with the North. Davis preferred armed conflict. Stephens' political career was long and storied (chapter 13, 38), and he was a great proponent of working within the Constitution. His involvement, though, with the Knights of the Golden Circle, and any plan to alter Congress, are wholly my inventions. All of the disparaging comments Frank Breckinridge makes about Jefferson Davis in chapter 50 are historical fact. The provisions of the Confederate constitution quoted in chapters 65 and 73 are from the original document. There are indeed elements of that constitution (dealing with Congress) that the modern world could easily embrace. The poetry quoted in chapters 11 and 72 is from "Silver Knights," which I found online with no author attribution. It's unclear if this poem is modern or from the 19th century, but its lyrical prose fit this story perfectly.

As related in chapter 25, President James Polk decided that the fastest way to increase the size of the United States was to have a war with Mexico, which was won after two years of fighting. The Treaty of Guadalupe Hidalgo (1848) ceded to the United States what would later become Arizona, New Mexico, Utah, Nevada, and California.

Angus Adams is based on Captain Thomas Hines, a famous Confederate spy. Hines' exploits are legendary, including hiding inside a mattress, beneath a sick man, to avoid Union soldiers (chapter 33). When I heard that story a few years ago I knew it would become part of Cotton Malone's legacy. A good book on Hines is *Confederate Agent,* by James Horan. All of what is described in chapter 33 about Adams was actually accomplished by Hines. Even the note left by Angus Adams after his escape was actually written by Hines. The spiking of cottage cheese with cotton (chapter 40) is taken from someone I know who actually did that, as a child, to a babysitter.

Alex Sherwood's office is based on Senator Lamar Alexander's offices in the Dirksen building, including the framed shirt on display in the reception area (chapter 41).

The jumble in chapter 50 is based on codes used during the Civil War. The 18th Psalm is indeed the only one with a 42nd verse, its words apropos (chapter 79). The newspaper excerpt in chapter 27 about lost gold, F. Lee Bailey, and John Dean comes nearly word for word from an actual news article printed in 1973. It was, indeed, illegal, from 1934 to 1974 for Americans to privately own gold (chapter 27). Fore-edge painting is a lost art (chapter 72), but it is amazing to see. I've wanted to include it in a novel for a long time.

The proposed 28th Amendment noted in chapter 4 has been suggested several times, but Congress has never considered it. Amending the Constitution by a national convention called by the states is one means of changing the document. It is true that there are few to no rules that would apply to an Article V convention (chapter 65). Similar to the first constitutional convention in 1787, which ignored its limited charge of only amending the existing Articles of Confederation, any new convention might likewise be unrestrained. There is literally no applicable law. At present a movement exists for a second constitutional convention, with a number of states already making the call. *Brinksmanship: Amending the Constitution by National Convention,* by Russell Caplan (cited in chapter 7), is an excellent read.

The early days of the House and Senate as

recounted in chapter 13 are historical fact, as is the rise of the infamous filibuster. That single achievement, more than anything else, elevated the U.S. Senate into one of the most powerful legislative bodies ever created. If sixty senators do not invoke cloture and vote to silence (chapter 13), a single senator can literally shut down the entire legislative process. In fact, it happens all the time. Most times today in private.

As related in the story, nothing comes to a floor vote in the House of Representatives unless the Rules Committee first approves (chapter 20), and that committee is under the total control of the Speaker. Congressional procedural rules (chapter 13) are vital to an orderly legislative process. They are created by each house of Congress (per the Constitution) with nearly no judicial oversight (chapter 13). In the early days of the country the Senate did little to nothing, other than advise the House (chapter 13). But all that changed in the 19th century. Altering the House of Representatives' rules so that it would only consider legislation that originates in the House is not only possible (chapter 56), it's perfectly legal. The idea is not mine. It came from *Ending Congressional Gridlock,* by Gary Larsen. And such a change would effectively elevate the Speaker of the House into the most powerful person in the country.

Congress is a mess. It may be the one thing

all Americans agree on, but it is equally true that Congress has kept this country going for 200-plus years (chapter 9). So we take the good with the bad. Gridlock is now a word in our vernacular with an unflattering meaning. But most people do not know that the U.S. Senate was specifically created to act as a legislative impediment. Its whole purpose was to create gridlock. Contrary to what many pundits think today, the Founding Fathers simply did not trust popular rule (chapter 56). That mistrust was reflected in both the electoral college (where the people do not actually elect the president) and a bicameral legislature (with a Senate chosen not by the people, but by state legislators). There is a famous story: Thomas Jefferson had just returned from France and was having breakfast with George Washington. Jefferson asked Washington why he'd agreed at the constitutional convention to have a Senate in the first place. It really wasn't needed. The House represented the people and could handle everything. Washington posed a question back, *Why did you just now pour that coffee into your saucer before drinking it?* To cool it, Jefferson said, noting that his throat was not made of brass. Washington smiled and explained, *We pour our legislation into the Senatorial saucer to cool it too.*

Speakers of the House do have a security

detail (chapters 2, 21, 44). Ex-presidents have the same, but they have the option of refusing Secret Service protection. The oath of office quoted at the end of chapter 39 is one every senator repeats. Danny Daniels moving from the presidency to the Senate not only is possible, but actually happened in 1875 when Andrew Johnson was the first to do it (chapter 21).

This novel is centered on the Smithsonian Institution (not the Smithsonian Institute as it's sometimes called). It was created after an unknown British chemist, James Smithson, left $500,000 in his will for that purpose. His bequest is even stranger given that Smithson never once visited the United States. It would be seventeen years after Smithson died before Congress finally created the institution. All of the political doubts detailed in the prologue about whether to honor Smithson's request are real.

The Smithsonian is governed by a seventeen-member board of regents, appointed as outlined in chapter 10. The chief justice of the United States acts as chancellor (chapter 23). Each museum has its own citizens advisory board that works closely with that museum's administration. Presently, I serve on the one for the Smithsonian Libraries. The Cullman Library inside the National Museum of Natural History (chapter 15) and the library inside the National

Museum of American History, where Martin Thomas worked, are two of those.

The tunnel beneath the National Mall between the Castle and the natural history museum exists (chapter 16). The only difference is I added a bend in the path. In reality, it's a straight line for 730 feet. The spiral staircase winding through the north tower of the Smithsonian Castle is there (chapter 19) and its provenance, as detailed, is accurate. I made one change, adding an exit on the second floor, which no longer exists. Owls did in fact once occupy the northwest tower (chapter 19). The Castle's rotunda is as described (chapter 19), including the enormous gilded case that holds the institution's ceremonial objects (chapter 23). The key is real (chapter 11), found in the Castle attic in the late 1950s, and subsequently incorporated into the induction ceremony for all incoming secretaries (chapters 19, 23, 25). The original stays on display in the rotunda's gilded case, with a copy presented to each successive secretary (chapter 25). All of the intrigue surrounding the key was my invention.

A few other Smithsonian notes: The quote by James Smithson in chapter 13 is from one of his letters. Smithsonite is named for Smithson (chapter 23, 58), and is a relatively useless mineral compound. A small chunk of it, though, adorns my desk. Jefferson Davis served as a Smithsonian regent and later as secretary of war (chapter 25). But there was no 1854 Smithsonian expedition to the American Southwest (chapter 25). The post of Castle curator is real (chapter 11), currently occupied by Richard Stamm, who became a character in the novel.

Joseph Henry acted as the first Smithsonian secretary from 1846 to 1878. During the Civil War he worked with the navy to evaluate inventions and proposals (prologue) acting, in essence, as Lincoln's science adviser. His lack of enthusiasm for the Union cause (prologue) is fact, as is his insistence that the Smithsonian remain neutral.

But he was never disloyal.

The story about him being arrested and charged as a spy, as told in chapter 62, is probably just that, a story. The account was published in Carl Sandburg's biography of Abraham Lincoln, about sixty years after Lincoln's death. Most agree that Sandburg probably embellished the tale, as he provided no source for his version. Lincoln did participate in the experiment as an observer, but he was not with Joseph Henry on the roof of the Castle, as Sandburg related. Instead, he was on the roof of the Soldiers' Home about four miles northeast of the Castle, while Henry stood on the roof of the Castle's tower. We know this because two other accounts of the event exist, which are much less colorful and neither as well known nor as oft repeated as

Sandburg's.

The mistake about Smithson's age, engraved on his tomb inside the Castle, is real (chapter 60). How Smithson's bones eventually made it to Washington, DC, is accurately told (chapter 58). The report quoted in chapter 58 on the 1973 opening of Smithson's tomb is taken nearly verbatim from an actual Smithsonian document. The silk lining did catch on fire and workers extinguished it by filling their mouths with water from a nearby fountain. The opening of the tomb was not without controversy. To this day no one knows exactly why it was done and the explanations given at the time were weak. How Cotton and Rick Stamm reopen the tomb (chapter 62) is exactly how it would be done.

Today the Smithsonian Institution consists of nineteen world-class museums, a zoo, and nine research centers. At the heart of most of these facilities is a library. By and large, those libraries do not sit out on an exhibit floor. No signage points the way to them. Instead, they are tucked off to the side, out of the way, but working hard every day.

Like a heart.

The human heart beats sixty to eighty times a minute. You don't feel it, or notice it, or really even pay it much attention — until it stops.

The same is true for the Smithsonian Libraries.

Its collections are amazing. Over two million books, manuscripts, maps, prints, paintings, research data, and physical artifacts. Anything and everything you could possibly imagine. The subjects are likewise all-encompassing, including aerospace, anthropology, astronomy, astrophysics, art, biology, botany, history, sociology, zoology, and much more. For 2016, nearly $17 million will be spent keeping the doors open, ensuring all of that information remains readily available to researchers, scholars, and the public at large. Nearly 10 percent of that budget has to be raised from individual and corporate contributions. And unlike in the novel, there is no vault of gold waiting to be found.

Instead, it takes all of us to keep it running.

For over 170 years the Smithsonian Libraries have proudly supported the mission of the Smithsonian Institution. Once that happened solely from physically visiting one of the libraries. Now the Internet provides constant access. In 2016 there were over than 1 million Web visitors and nearly 17 million Web content downloads.

That's a lot of use.

Right now, as you read these words, amazing things are happening at a Smithsonian library. Each one is truly a world-class place of learning — where people come to both test and expand their ideas — where we can all turn for answers. So the next time you wander through Air and Space, or the American history museum, one of the portrait galleries, the National Zoo, or any of the other museums or research centers, remember —

At the heart of every one of those is a Smithsonian library.

To make a contribution or learn more about the Smithsonian Libraries, visit www.library.si.edu.

ABOUT THE AUTHOR

Steve Berry is the *New York Times* and #1 internationally bestselling author of a dozen Cotton Malone novels and several stand-alones. He has 21 million books in print, translated into 40 languages. With his wife, Elizabeth, he is the founder of History Matters, which is dedicated to historical preservation. He serves on the Smithsonian Libraries Advisory Board and was a founding member of International Thriller Writers, formerly serving as its co-president.

The employees of Thorndike Press hope you have enjoyed this Large Print book. All our Thorndike, Wheeler, and Kennebec Large Print titles are designed for easy reading, and all our books are made to last. Other Thorndike Press Large Print books are available at your library, through selected bookstores, or directly from us.

For information about titles, please call:
  (800) 223-1244

or visit our website at:
  gale.com/thorndike

To share your comments, please write:
  Publisher
  Thorndike Press
  10 Water St., Suite 310
  Waterville, ME 04901